Hold My Hand

Also by Serena Mackesy

The Temp
Virtue
Simply Heaven

HOLD MY HAND

Serena Mackesy

Constable • London

Constable & Robinson Ltd
3 The Lanchesters
162 Fulham Palace Road
London W6 9ER
www.constablerobinson.com

First published in the UK by Constable,
an imprint of Constable & Robinson, 2008

First US edition published by SohoConstable,
an imprint of Soho Press, 2008

Soho Press, Inc.
853 Broadway
New York, NY 10003
www.sohopress.com

A copy of the British Library Cataloguing in Publication
Data is available from the British Library

UK ISBN: 978-1-84529-639-1

US ISBN: 978-1-56947-533-1
US Library of Congress number: 2008018861

Printed and bound in the EU

1 3 5 7 9 10 8 6 4 2

For Ant and Honor

Whoooooooo! Scary!

Prologue

I won't go back. I won't. I hate them . . . hate them. She can look all she likes, bloody bitch. Bloody bitch Blakemore . . . I won't go back. Won't go, never . . .

For a while, rage and fright drive back the cold, warm her from within. But she's barefoot and the evening gown stolen from the attic trunk is made of moth-scarred chiffon. Now she's no longer holding it up, it drags in the snow, tripping her with its increasing weight and deepening the chill as meltings creep up her legs.

Bugger her. Buggery bitch Blakemore. Bugger Rospetroc and bugger all of them. I hate them. Hate them all. They'll not see me again, I'd sooner die . . .

And now, for the first time, she is aware enough of her surroundings that she sees the snow isn't only lying on the ground: it's all around her, drifting deadsoft through frozen air, spirals in the wind.

Lily is not a child who has been raised in the romantic tradition, but she sees that it is beautiful. Deadly beautiful, like a cobra. She looks up at the clouded sky, closes her eyes and feels the fall, knows herself tiny. She isn't conscious of it, but her core body temperature has already dropped to 95 degrees. All she experiences right now is an increasing shiver, the ache in her hands and feet: but she *would* feel discomfort, barefoot in the snow.

I shan't go back. Bugger them. I shan't go back.

Perhaps you should. It's cold out here.

She glances back across the yard, through the stone gate-arch, and what she sees causes a tiny qualm in her cooling stomach. The front door is closed. It's closed, and the house lights, obscured by blackout curtains, shed no illumination on black night.

Lily hesitates. No. They're like that. They think they can scare me. They think they can break me. Make me come back and beg. I won't go back. I'll leave, tonight. No one will ask about me if I go. I'll go back to Portsmouth. I'll find it somehow. I can live there, even if I don't find my mum. I don't care. I can steal food . . .

But she knows she'll not even get as far as Bodmin dressed as she is. She needs to find a coat. Coat and boots. Maybe take some food to eat on the long walk. It was hours on the train when they brought her down here, she remembers that, and the few trips she has taken beyond the village have involved long treks through bleak moorland. She's not even sure which station is the nearest: just that they are a long, long way from it.

I'll go back in, she thinks. She won't hear me. Deaf old bitch.

Lily pads across the courtyard garden, dress swishing a trail like a broom through sand. The bushes – rosemary, privet, lavender – which line the path are white lumps in the snow, dark at their roots. They crouch in camouflage, ready to pounce. She's not given to flights of imagination. A life full of conflict, of snatching and clawing for survival, doesn't leave much space for make-believe. But her route zigzags along the path as she skirts the borders of their capacity to leap.

She is not the sort of child who cries, nor apologizes. But she is wondering, now. Though hate drives her forward.

In the dark porch, she listens for signs of life, hears nothing but the swoosh and flump as a branch of the yew, overloaded, lets go its burden on to the ground. *She could be inside. Just inside the door, waiting.*

Yes, but what can I do? It's cold. So cold.

My hands are shaking.

She fails to steady them as she reaches out to the pendulous iron door handle, turns it.

The door doesn't move. It is bolted from the inside.

She has partly expected this. Mrs Blakemore is a punisher. She locks things. Children are routinely locked in bedrooms, in the cupboard in the four-poster room, in dark places where spiders lurk, in this household. Blakemore takes pride in it. 'No child is spanked in my house,' she proclaims to admiring villagers. 'I won't hear of it.' But there are worse things, for a child dragged up in the Portsmouth docks, than a clout round the arse. Those dark places: Lily has seen a lot of them since she came here. Dark places and gnawing hunger.

She won't have done it with *all* the doors. She's just done it to teach me a lesson.

They don't lock doors in the country. Are boastful about it. A few people in the village have taken to locking up since the Italian prisoners of war arrived on the farms, but no one really locks up.

Trudging through the drifts at the side of the west wing, she rubs briskly at her upper arms, is surprised to find herself dislodging a shower of snow as she does so. Where did that come from? I've not been out here that long, have I?

It's been twenty minutes since she ran out. But she doesn't know it. As her body temperature drops – it is 93 now – she has started to experience minor fugues, *petits mals*. Emerging from the shelter of the porch into the vicious bite of the wind, she seized up altogether for a full minute, simply stood, statue-still, by the white-cloaked sundial, as though touched by the gaze of the Medusa. Her legs emanate so little heat that the folds of the dress are beginning, quietly, to freeze against them.

Lily doesn't know she is in such danger. Thinks that all the cold will give is discomfort. She is only nine years old, after all.

She reaches the west kitchen door, lifts the latch. Again, no give. Again, no light shows around it, or through the window beside it. Even if the lights were on, the blackout would block any trace of their warmth from leaking into the night. The windows are up high in the wall, way out of her reach. And besides, her fingers are now so numb, so stiff, that she would be unable to grip to climb. Everywhere is silence: cloaked, muffled, but also a self-conscious silence, the silence of obedience.

Bugger her. Bitch Blakemore. Bugger them all. They can hear me out here, tucked up out of the cold, listening to what happens to bad little girls who won't do what they're told. Yes, Mrs Blakemore. Thank you, Mrs Blakemore. Please don't punish me, Mrs Blakemore. All right for them. All right for the others. Their mummies and daddies came back for them. Nobody even knows who my daddy was . . .

She sets off for the eastern scullery. In the walled garden, facing north, the wind cuts through the air like a scimitar. Snow has piled up against the house so deep she has no alternative but to take herself away from the lee of the wall, foray out into the middle of the lawn, where it feels as though an animal is tearing at her clothes with icy claws. Feet numb now, she stumbles, once, twice, then falls altogether, lies still in white comfort, allows the crystals around her to leach the heat from her back.

Stars. There are stars.

The snow drifts down.

Lily is beginning to get sleepy. Forgetful. She struggles to remember what it is she's intent on doing. After two minutes, three, memory returns, and she rolls on to her knees, pushes herself up. The effort makes her, briefly, dizzy. Her breathing has become shallow as her blood has thickened and her brain is already failing from lack of oxygen.

I really, really need to wee, she thinks. Maybe I should just do it here, on bitch Blakemore's precious lawn.

Supercilious windows gaze blank on her struggling form. Somewhere in there, Mrs Blakemore sits shrouded by blackout curtains, feet up on the fender. Though rationing bites through the rest of the house, there is always a fire in Blakemore's study. Lily can see it now, glowing warm through the panels of the east kitchen door. I'll say sorry, she thinks. I don't care. I'll say sorry and she'll let me sit by it. No good going tonight. Tomorrow I'll leave.

The door is locked.

She huddles against it, holds herself up with a wrist draped through the handle. Raises the other hand to knock. The rap sounds feebly through the scullery beyond, doesn't penetrate the main body of the house at all.

'Let me in!' she calls. Her voice sounds small, far away. 'I'm sorry! Let me in!'

Rospetroc turns its shoulder, turns away.

'I'm sorry!' she cries again, scratches the faded turquoise paint. 'I'll be good! Let me in!'

And finally it dawns on her: she is not to be allowed back. She is shut out, for good. She can no longer feel her hands or feet, but someone is stabbing her, over and over, with a skewer.

I must get under cover.

She casts around. The sheds are locked. They never unlock them, except when they're punishing people. Pearl was put in the old laundry for two hours once; came out screaming.

I must. I must. I must get under cover.

Across the lawn, on the edge of the pond, the boathouse. She went in there once. It's cold and rotten, and hasn't been used in decades, but it has a roof, and walls.

Better than nothing. Better than out here, in the wind.

The going is heavy across the lawn, new snow lying on old. Her feet break through the crust below the surface, jar to knee-depth. Each laboured step is harder than the last. When she gets there, the door, heavy and loose on its hinges, needs a lift and a hard shoulder before it gives. But she's in, and it's black. Around her, nameless forms, hard and crouching; the soft drip of water on water. Above her, a low ceiling. Yes, she thinks, logic slipping away with body heat, a hay-loft. There will be hay up there. I can wrap myself in the hay and get warm.

At least I'm not shivering any more.

One hand on the ladder, no grip. She winds a forearm around the upright, puts a foot on a rung. It feels like standing on burning glass. Lily almost screams, but hasn't the energy. Up. Up. I must go up. Her progress is slow, excruciating. She has to stop after each lift of her body, lean her head against the cross-struts and breathe, five, ten, fifteen times as she waits for her heart to slow. Come on, come *on*.

The top. Arm, then arm, flat against rough planks, then body, thighs, burning feet. A sluggish tear slides from one eye, drops on to the floor.

The loft is empty. The fantasy of pile on pile of caressing hay bursts, like bubbles. There is nothing here: just a couple of old jute sacks and a length of rope.

She would cry now: even loveless Lily would cry, but there is nothing left to come. She crawls – drags dead limbs – across the floor, struggles to get beneath the sacks. Doesn't even really remember how she got here, just that she is tired, so, so tired, that she wants to sleep. Curls up, a bundle of skin and hair, beneath the sacks, notices that the floor seems warm to her body.

Lies.

Lies.

Lies.

There. I'm warming up.

The floor beneath her seems to be heated. How lucky. There's heat coming from the floor. So strong it's almost uncomfortable.

Let it work. Let it warm me.

Oh my God. It's burning. It's boiling.

Eighty-four degrees. She sits, suddenly, bolt upright. *I'm burning.* Holds her hand out in front of her and sees it, clear as daylight. It's burning. Burning green. And there's something – *something* – on her clothes. *They've come while I've been sleeping and they've poured boiling water on me. Where are they? Why can't I see them? Oh my God, it hurts! It hurts! It's burning my skin!*

And she claws. At herself, at her sodden clothing. At the very skin that has turned upon her. *What is it? Get it off me! Get it off!*

A small gutter child in a deserted loft on Bodmin moor. In the dark, pulling: tearing away her feeble coverings, throwing them across the room to land in corners, she screams, and screams, and no noise comes out. *Get it off! Get it off!*

And then she knows. She knows clearly, no fog, no escape. There is no heat. There are no people. There is only me. There has always been only me. And I am dying.

Lily crawls with the last of her strength back into the corner, curls up on her side like an unborn child. Face slack, she lies and stares at unbroken darkness.

I hate them. I hate them. All of them. I won't leave. I won't leave, now. I will stay here and I will make her every day a living hell. I will have my revenge. On all of them. All of them . . . hate them . . . all of them . . .

Chapter One

She was eating beans on toast just before she disappeared. The state of the kitchen would give the impression that she had simply got up from the table and gone into another room to answer the telephone, were it not for the fact that the remains of the meal have been sitting on the table, the pan unwashed in the sink, bread spilling green from its plastic wrapper on the work surface, for two weeks.

The room smells of rot and sugar.

At least, he thinks, she did it late in the year so there aren't any flies. But for someone who doesn't turn a hair at the slaughter of livestock, he is surprisingly squeamish, and the thought of cleaning the plate and pan is enough to set off a queasy lurch in his stomach.

Tom Gordhavo doesn't enjoy Rospetroc. It feels perpetually dusty, despite the fact that he knows how much work goes into keeping the dust at bay. And it always feels, somehow, when he's there, that the house is watching him, that just behind the door, whichever room he's in, someone is standing, and biding their time.

He pulls on his rubber gloves, tears a new black bag off the roll he's brought with him. Mouth downturned with distaste, he picks up the plate, the knife and fork stuck firmly to it by the thick layer of fungus that has grown there, and drops the whole lot into the bag. He doesn't have long, and has no intention of wasting more time here than he strictly has to.

Chapter Two

She's twenty minutes early, but an old blue Fiesta is already here, parked on the sweep of mossy cobbles outside the garden gate. Bridget pulls in beside it, tucking the car in neatly as though lines were painted on the ground. The gate, heavy painted metal let into a gothic stone arch, stands slightly ajar, and the front door beyond lies wide open to the wind.

'Well, they're obviously not worried about the heating,' she says out loud. Bridget spends so much time alone these days that she's taken, like many solitary creatures, to talking to herself. If she didn't, nothing but child-talk would pass her lips from one day's end to the next. Yasmin is lovely, but she's at the age where she tends to greet conversation about grown-up stuff with rolling eyes and heavy sighs.

Now she's close up, she sees that the garden is badly in need of its winter overhaul, is overgrown like a Victorian secret within the enclosing arms of the house's horseshoe wings. Tumbles of straggly lavender stray on to the flagstone path leading to the front door. Lumps of dark laurel loiter beneath thick stone window sills. High stone walls, knotted with winter-naked vines, keep the edge of Bodmin moor at bay. An old swing, one rope rotted and snapped, dangles from a yew branch.

Bridget thinks it's beautiful.

She feels suddenly nervous, now that she's here at last. The long drive through unfamiliar country kept her distracted, but now that she's minutes from her first interview in years, she feels trembly, slightly sick. Back in the day, she didn't worry about anything much; used to pitch her services to the powerful without a moment's doubt. But she's lost a lot of her courage since she married Kieran, still feels like a swimmer caught in a rip-tide, swept along by circumstance with no power over her outcomes. That's why she keeps up this one-way dialogue with herself. To admit that no one can hear her would be to admit that she is alone.

'Come on,' she says out loud, because right now she is considering slamming the car into reverse and going straight back to London without ever facing this Gordhavo man, whoever he is. It's been ten years since she last put herself up for work in a formal manner and the prospect makes her slightly sweaty. Who's going to entrust a house like this to a tired, beaten single mum who hasn't worked since she fell pregnant? What's the point? It's just another wasted day, wasted petrol, wasted courage . . .

'Come *on*, Bridget,' she tells herself again, more sharply this time. Forces her hand on to the car door handle.

The path is showing early signs of slipperiness. I'll have to do something about that, she thinks. It's the sort of thing Yasmin will turn turtle on, crack open her head. And that swing. And the sills on the upper storey look dangerously close to the floor. And that pond: my God, why didn't I take her for those swimming lessons when I had the chance? I'm such a bad mother. The worst. It's impossible. I can't bring a child here. It's a death-trap.

She steps over the threshold into the hall. The same flags inside, patinated grey with centuries of mud and scrubbing. Buttermilk walls lead to a black-studded garden door, their plaster so lumped and loosened by age that much of it is only held on by the layers of paint on top. A bunch of keys that could double as an offensive weapon sits on a console table. Rows of heavy-duty iron coat-hooks trail down the walls, fixed to boards, Shaker-style. Each one is empty.

Low, wide doors – doors designed for short people in

wide dresses – lead off the hall, to the right into a dining room where a naked, scrubbed oak table crouches between – she counts them – eighteen upholstered modern chairs which she recognizes from the Ikea catalogue. The nearest Ikea is in Bristol, she thinks: I suppose it would be worth the trip if you were buying eighteen chairs at once.

To the left, a drawing room: white walls, tapestry curtains, three sofas, each big enough to host an orgy, surrounding a coffee table that would roof an entire house in parts of other countries. A fireplace fit for tree-trunks yawns dark and cold beneath monstrous beams. A pair of large and gloomy ancestors fill the alcoves either side of the fire. Somewhere in the distance, the rhythmic tick-tick-tick of a clock.

Bridget has never been in private rooms this size without paying for a ticket before. She understands, now, why whoever it is has left the door open; it is, if anything, letting warm air into the house from the outside, even though it's November.

She checks her watch. Still ten minutes early.

'Hello?' she calls, tentatively.

A clitter of nails on black-stained floorboards, and a smiling cocker spaniel appears at the far end of the dining room, wags its way towards her. Pleased – oddly relieved – to see another living creature, she drops to her haunches, chucks him behind the ears and is rewarded with a squirm of elegant backside and an onslaught of enthusiastic pink tongue.

'Hello, boy,' she says, laughing and holding the grinning head away from her mouth. 'Where's your master, then? Eh? Where is everyone?'

The dog glances over her shoulder into the drawing room, pulls back from her clasp and heads suddenly, decisively, back the way it has come. Bridget follows. The curtains here are thick blue velvet, hanging down from ceiling height to cover window seats let into walls three feet thick. The windows themselves start some six feet up in the air: too high to afford a view to a standing person, let alone one sitting. This must have been some sort of business room, she guesses: a place where smock-clad tenants waited to be summoned into the smaller reception room – panelled, carpeted, cosy, less imposing than the ones she's seen so far – that she glimpses through the door to her right, in the wing of the U. The dog trots on through the door ahead of her and she follows. A kitchen, industrial-style. Stainless steel oven and eight-ring burner built into the old fireplace; warmer-cupboard, double butler's sink, American fridge-freezer: all incongruous with old pine cupboards and drainers, the tiny, stone-framed window that looks out over a waterlogged lawn. More flags on the floor: she can feel the winter seep up through the soles of her shoes.

There is another door on the far side of the kitchen, closed.

'Hello?' she calls again.

Still no response. The dog sits – crouches to keep his rump from the flags – by the door, looks at her over his shoulder with big, sad eyes. Raises a forepaw and strokes the panel with it. She notices, as she lifts the latch, that it has a lock. Puts her head into a cobbled lobby where more industrial equipment squats: washing machine and tumble-dryer, vacuum cleaner and sheet press; tangles of retractable washing lines above her head. To her right, another room – once, she guesses from its panelling, an ante-room to the receiving room. A chaos of broken furniture, high-piled lampshades, cardboard boxes and paper. A dead room; the sort of room you would only find in the ungenerous confines of an urban house when the occupants had been carted away by Social Services. Old magazines. Photograph albums. Legless chairs. Chairless legs. Things that are sharp and things that are heavy and things that are coated with the dust of decades.

Yasmin flashes through her mind. I'll have to keep this locked, she thinks. And if there isn't a lock, I'll have to fit a bolt, out of her reach. There are things in here that could kill her.

There are things everywhere that could kill her. The world is full of deadly situations for six-year-olds. She could go under an SUV on Brixton Hill, for God's sake. Her school could catch fire. She could get her hands on any number of chemicals under the sink in that cramped little kitchen, fall head-first from a climbing frame, get snatched from the street. She's so precious and so vulnerable. Did I used to be like this before Kieran? Did I worry, every second of the day, like this? Was that why I made such a mistake? That I thought he was strong, that he'd protect me?

The dog slips past her, shows her a path between tables and cupboards and plinths that leads to a narrow door which stands ajar. She can see an equally narrow staircase beyond; steep steps between the damp-stained walls of a lean-to. And, at last, the sound of movement above: bumping, the sound of something heavy being dragged. A dead body? she wonders. It could be . . . this could all be a front to get women alone in a –

Kicks herself. 'Hello?' she calls again.

The movement stops, as though someone is listening. She hears, once again, the clock in the distance. But it's not a clock: the rhythm isn't quite right, isn't quite regular enough. It's more like something flicking, flicking, flicking against a floor somewhere.

'Hello?'

Footsteps. A man's voice: reedy, open-vowelled, indisputably posh.

'Hello?'

'Hello?' she calls again.

He's on the stairs, now, coming down. She sees the hammer in his hand before she sees his face.

'Who's that?'

'Bridget Sweeny.' She's started calling herself by her mother's maiden name recently: the one on her birth certificate, though few people know that. Her feelings towards her married name have changed with experience, but more importantly, if she's going to pull this off, she needs to distance herself from the stuff Kieran will remember.

'Ah.'

He is framed in the doorway. Spare, like the voice; a jutting Adam's apple and dark hair that has receded into double-V peaks from his forehead. He's in his late thirties, she guesses – half a decade older than she is – and favouring the older end of his age-group, his skin not helped by clumps of rosacea scarring that pit his cheeks.

'You're early,' he says, an edge of reproof to his voice.

'Sorry,' she replies. 'It's hard to get the timing bang on, coming down from London.'

He misses the nuance. 'Never mind. Better than being late, I suppose. I'd been hoping to get the flat a bit more sorted out before you got here. The last incumbent left it in a bit of a . . . Tom Gordhavo.'

She momentarily thinks that this must be some local idiom before she remembers that this is his name. 'Nice to meet you,' she says, shaking his hand.

'How do you do,' he says.

Chapter Three

Well, she seems respectable, he thinks. Though of course you can never tell at first sight. But in Tom Gordhavo's experience, dishonesty is usually accompanied by overfriendliness, and this woman is, if anything, a bit stand-offish. He likes that, though. He doesn't have time for staff who want to share every detail of their history and health issues. She merely asks if it would be possible to put a gate in the hedge which divides the garden off from the old pond, to prevent her six-year-old from wandering down there by herself, which seems a reasonable request to him. He's been meaning to do it anyway, as a couple of the renters have complained about the risk over the last year and an accident would very likely be a bit of a dampener on his inclusion in the brochures, so he agrees readily enough. He deliberately keeps a bit of a Frances Hodgson Burnett vibe about the grounds as a USP for the house, but there is stuff renters see as colourful and other stuff that is simply dangerous. He stores the suggestion away as evidence that she shows signs of having some sense about her. Proactive, she would probably call it, being infected, no doubt, by the buzzword vocabulary of London business. He decides to try the word out, to see.

'I need someone,' he says as he walks her through the dining room, 'who can be a bit proactive.'

There's the tiniest of pauses behind his back as she takes the word in, suppresses a grin. 'Well,' she says evenly, 'I ran my own business for several years before I had my daughter. So I think I'm reasonably used to making decisions.'

'Oh yes?'

Own business, he thinks. Could be anything. Public relations. Envelope stuffing. Could have gone bankrupt, for all you know. Why else would someone be applying for a housekeeper's job, if they'd had any other options?

'What sort of business?' he asks, trying to keep the suspicion from his voice.

'I was a florist.'

They come to a halt at the front door end of the room, in front of a table which carries a giant display of immortelles and thistle heads in an old ginger pot. They've seen better days, he thinks. It must be ten years since they were put there.

'Oh yes?'

'Yes. I had a shop on Lavender Hill. In London,' she continues, as though worried that he won't know she's been trading in the capital. 'Though I did business right across most of the south-west of the city. Flowers for boardrooms and reception areas, that sort of thing. Parties. Weddings. Weekly deliveries to . . .' She pauses as she considers whether it's the right phrase to use to a rich man as he obviously must be, decides he's not the type to approve of princessish manners. '. . . save the Ladies Who Lunch from having to actually *do* anything . . . you know. I had three employees at one point, and a delivery driver. It was a pretty successful outfit, I guess. For a small business.'

'I see. So why, if you don't mind me asking, don't you go back to that?'

'Lots of reasons.'

She runs a finger over the table, leaves a long stripe in the dust.

'The last housekeeper left a month ago,' he says hurriedly, 'in a bit of a rush. And I don't think she'd been doing her job very well for a while before that.'

She rubs index finger and thumb together, studies the ingrained grey in the pads non-committally.

'My husband died eighteen months ago,' she tells him. Glances in his direction to see if he's picked up on the lie.

She needs to be convincing, if this is going to work. 'So it's just me and Yasmin now. And running a shop doesn't really go with single motherhood. Especially not that sort of shop. The five o'clock in the morning New Covent Garden run isn't really compatible with normal nursery hours.'

It always amazes Tom, the way people can talk about bereavement with such seeming equanimity. She can't be more than thirty-five, he guesses, yet she talks about her widowhood with none of the rage that he knows would assail him if he were in the same position. He noticed it with his mother, as well: she seemed to accept his father's death with a calm that, three years on, he still hasn't achieved. And yet, he thinks, there probably isn't a person on the earth who guesses about his moments, those times when he sees a view his father would have enjoyed, when he longs for his father's counsel, when he is driving up the drive to Penwithiel for the Sunday lunch he has eaten there throughout his adulthood and remembers once again that he comes from a family of three, not four, and a wave of sadness breaks over him so strong that he feels it will suck him under. Does she, he wonders, lie awake at night and weep for this dead husband? Or is her life so hard, now, so full of coping, that she has no time for emotions? Certainly, she looks as though life is toughening her up. It's easy to see that she used to be pretty under that mop of home-cut mousy hair, that she probably could be again; just hard to see how it would be achieved.

'I'm sorry,' he says lamely. 'It must be hard for you.'

Bridget shrugs. 'These things happen,' she says. 'I don't suppose many of us have the lives we thought we'd have when we were fifteen.'

'I should think not. I was definitely going to be a pop star when I was fifteen.'

She laughs. 'And I was going to be a model.'

It hangs in the air between them: *Only one of us has ended up with the money, though.*

Ironic, she thinks. Having money was definitely part of

the game-plan for Kieran and me. We encapsulated the yuppie dream. He was going to go up in the City, get on to the trading floors, not be a backroom boy forever, and I was going to open Branches. Be the Oliver Bonas of flower arranging. It was part of the attraction, part of the reason I picked him, out of all the choices I had: that he was going places. That we were going to go places together. And instead, look at it: I marry a man who was going to help me to be rich, I put my ambitions in someone else's hands, and now he's got money and I've ended up hostage to poverty, and bailiffs, and the curse of the CSA.

She stamps on the train of thought. Can't afford self-pity. Have to be an optimist. It's the only thing I've got left.

'So . . .' she sweeps a hand through the air, gesturing round the room, 'aren't you worried, leaving all this stuff here for holiday tenants? They're never exactly careful, and you never know who they might be . . . they could turn up with a removal van, for all you know.'

'Well, yes, that's one of the reasons we need a house-keeper,' he says. 'Keep an eye on things. But don't worry. You're not actually looking at a houseful of priceless antiques. They're repro. We bought most of it as a job lot in Indonesia and brought it back in a container.'

'But the pictures?'

'Good, aren't they? All family stuff, of course. Just not the originals. You'd be surprised how convincing a finish you can get nowadays, with computerization. It's only if you look closely that you can see that the brush strokes aren't related to any actual images.'

She steps close to a huge portrait of an eighteenth-century squire, gun over his shoulder, square felt hat on his head and boxy dog at his feet. He is standing, she notices, in the fields through which she has just driven; Rospetroc, tiny in the background, is surrounded by a whole clump of yews where the solitary one still stands. 'Gosh,' she says.

'We find people like having portraits. Even more than landscapes and stuff. Gives them more of a sense of authenticity.'

'Yes, but I can see why you wouldn't want to trust the originals to them.'

'Absolutely. It would be like having someone smash your family gravestones, if anything happened to them. This chap's in my parents' –' he corrects himself, as he still has to after three years – 'mother's house.'

'Who is he?'

'Another Tom Gordhavo. My . . . I'd have to work it out how many great-greats he is to me.'

'Did he live here, then?'

'No. This house came from my mother's family. The Gordhavos owned the big house.'

Bridget wonders how big the big house can be if this isn't it.

'So if you don't mind my asking, why doesn't one of the family live here now? How can you bear to be letting a place like this out to strangers?'

He has no intention of telling her the full story. Knows through the generations that servants are prone to superstition and will immediately start seeing things if told about them. They've not managed to recruit a housekeeper from the local vicinity since the war, despite the constant laments about lack of local employment and incomers driving people from the land.

'The family isn't as big as it used to be,' he explains, 'And this is the most isolated of the houses we've got. It made sense not to have one of us flung miles away from all the others.'

She accepts this without murmur.

'You'd be all right, would you,' he asks, 'with the isolation? You can't really walk to any of the neighbours, and the village is a good couple of miles away.'

'To be honest, it sounds like heaven, after London,' she tells him wholeheartedly, thinking of the grease-caked whores who work the pavements of her small patch of Streatham.

'Because,' he says, 'we've had a few disasters with housekeepers down from the city. They all think they can handle the isolation, but I don't think many people take in what it actually means. The winter's a long, dark thing, even down here. Nobody to bump into on the streets even if you do get down to the village; they do everything by car in the winter. And we don't have many renters out of season . . .'

'I understand what you're saying,' she says. 'There's a school in the village, though, isn't there? What's it like?'

'Not bad, as far as I know.' He's a governor, of course, but knows it's unlikely any child of his would pass through the doors for anything other than the Christmas bring-and-buy.

'Can't be any worse than where she is at the moment.'

'Granted. Let me show you the rest.'

She follows him through the drawing room with its bungalow-sized fireplace. 'TV, video, DVD in here. You'd be amazed. They think they've come down for a communal week in the country, but they can't do without *EastEnders*. And pornography, probably, for all I know. Fireplaces are all working, of course. You'll need to clean them out daily when visitors are here. Each room needs a weekly hoovering, dusting and polishing. Bathrooms, top to bottom between visitors and a quick daily wipe-down when they're here. Kitchen seems to need a total revamp every time it's used. You'll be surprised how long it takes.'

No I won't, she thinks. It's *huge.* The drawing room alone would fit her and Yasmin's flat twice over beneath its blackened beams.

'You need to make up all the beds and strip them and do the laundry, of course. Between groups, and weekly if they're staying longer. There are two full sets for each bed, plus the odd spares against wear-and-tear. The turnaround in the summer can be quite hellish. Checkout's at ten and the new ones start arriving around three. There are a couple of women in the village on standby to come in and help out with the fast turnarounds, but you'll have to do it all yourself most of the time. You must keep me updated on what needs replacing, of course, and there'll be a petty cash fund for cleaning stuff . . .'

'How many bedrooms?'

'Twelve. Six doubles, four twins and a couple of attic rooms that are sort-of-dormitories. Three beds each and a couple of camp beds. They usually park the older children up there. A couple of cots in the shed, as well. Their mattresses are in the ghastly jumble you just found me in.'

She nods, but as his back is turned he doesn't see. 'Fine,' she says.

'Of course,' he continues, 'I was sort of hoping for a couple.'

'Oh. Well, I'm sorry about that. Only one of me.'

'They stay longer. Company for each other. And of course the day-to-day maintenance . . . we deliberately keep the garden looking a bit wildernessy, but there's a limit, obviously. It's going to need a good going-over before spring.'

'Oh.'

He has no idea how desperate she is for this job. How much she is prepared to cede, simply to get away from where she is, from the whole situation, from Kieran and fear and the urban poverty which is far, far worse than the rural kind. I could grow vegetables, she is thinking, and perhaps I can pick up some home work to fill the evenings. This would be a new start, a new chance. Imagine my little girl growing up in a place like this, all that space to run in, a school where she won't learn to respond to everything with 'fuck off'. Being able to sleep through the night without fear of what might come through the door. Please don't let me blow this, please.

'I'm pretty handy,' she assures him, following him past another panelled room – book-lined, presumably with the stuff the family hasn't wanted to read again – and up a dark oak stair to the first floor. 'I can do most of the basic stuff. Washers and plugs and fuses and things. Basic carpentry: you know, shelves and mending things, hinges . . .'

And this, at least, is true. I've had to. There's been no

one else to do it for me, even when I did have a man about the place. I learned pretty early on that asking for that sort of help was nagging, and leaving stuff was neglect. And that both were corporal offences.

'Are there many other applicants?' she asks, and is unsurprised when he hedges about the answer.

'Well, I suppose . . .' he says, 'there are people, after all . . . plumbers and the like . . .'

'I'm very good with a telephone.' She attempts to lighten the atmosphere.

They are standing in a narrow lath-and-plaster corridor: doorways on either side and a Persian runner, the longest she's ever seen, vanishing into the distance. 'Perhaps you could supplement your income a bit by doing the flowers,' he says, suddenly, 'for the weddings and stuff. Dances.'

'Weddings?' She can't keep the shock from her voice.

Tom Gordhavo laughs. 'Don't worry. There are only a couple a year, and a couple of dances. We get contract gardeners in, and you won't be expected to clean up after them. Well, not much. Obviously, you'd have to do the final sweep as you'd be the only one who knows where everything goes. You can never expect contractors to do the job you'd do yourself.'

'Okay,' she says. They are walking down the corridor, pausing to glance into quiet bedrooms. Iron bedsteads, painted boards, heavy chests-of-drawers with bowl-and-ewer sets on top. 'Very *Homes and Gardens,*' she remarks. 'I was expecting it to be a bit more four-poster.'

'Well, there's one in the master bedroom,' he says, 'but they're terrible dust magnets. This is far more practical.'

'How many bathrooms?'

'Six. None en-suite. You don't get many complaints about it, except from the Yanks. I think most people understand they didn't build for bathrooms in the Tudor era. Mind you, the Yanks complain about the floorboards being uneven. They don't quite get the idea of a house that's more than fifty years old. So what do you think?'

'It's . . .' She struggles to keep the enthusiasm from her voice. 'Well, it'll certainly be a full-time job.'

'Certainly will,' he says cheerfully. 'Think you're up to it?'

He stands in the doorway of the master bedroom, above the dining room, arms folded, and looks her up and down. Not exactly strapping, he thinks, but she's got the air of a coper. And besides, a single mother can't be anything but a good thing. Someone with ties is what I need, someone who can't just up and take off again.

'How soon can you start?' he asks.

Chapter Four

The bailiffs have been again. At least the trip and the early start have spared her from having to hover indoors all day with the curtains shut. Spared her, also, from coming out to find that the car, the only thing of any value that she still owns, has been towed away. She's been parking it in the roads off Brixton Water Lane for a while now, in the hope that it won't be spotted and swiped against the water rates.

We'll need it, she thinks, to live in once the flat gets repossessed. The worst thing I ever did, taking myself off the council list and throwing myself into home ownership. But then again, how was I to know that mortgage payments aren't covered by social security, whatever your circumstances? That the DSS would rather have you living in a B&B than give your child some prospect of a permanent home?

The *Mail* reader in her understands the argument about the mortgage, that it isn't up to the taxpayer to provide scroungers like her with a bricks-and-mortar nest-egg, but it doesn't seem fair, either, the way the system waits until families are on the street before anything is done to help. I'm a statistic, that's what I am, she thinks. Something to be trotted out at party conferences to cop the blame for the state of the nation's youth.

Nearly twelve hours on the road altogether today, and her fingers and knees are cramped from holding their positions for so long. She should be grateful, she knows, simply to have a car at all in her circumstances, even if it is ten years old and the seals round the doors have perished, but she misses her little Merc, long since traded down to cover the mortgage for a few more months, with its cruise control and its easy gearbox. She can feel the beginnings of a headache clamping down on the back of her neck. She is unused to long stints of motorway driving, and the combination of her terror of SUVs and worry that the car might not last the distance has turned the muscles between her shoulder blades to concrete. She's pulling herself up the stairs by the banister like an eighty-year-old. She hates these stairs, after years of bump-bump-bumping up and down them, juggling child and pushchair and shopping bags and handbags and change bags.

Thudding jungle comes from behind the closed door of the ground-floor flat. It will carry on that way until the small hours, unless the occupants go out clubbing and give their neighbours a few hours' respite until four, five in the morning. The worst thing about jungle, she thinks, is the whole stop-start thing. That and the fact that it obviously renders those who listen to it deaf. Or selfish. Can music change your personality? She thinks it probably can. The occupants respond to neither knocking on the door nor rings on their doorbell. And she's never seen them in the flesh, in the year they've been in residence. Traffic noise, even the boom of the television, can be incorporated into one's existence, but jungle . . . those few seconds where it all goes quiet, where you can feel the whole house hold its breath in anticipation that the cessation might be permanent, the palpable sigh of despair when the beat starts up again.

She sometimes wonders if the music hasn't been planted on a timer switch by a crafty property developer intent on driving the sitting tenants like Carol out. Only the large number of black bags that appear outside on bin day persuade her that anyone lives there at all.

She's had the heating off all day – every penny, after all, counts – and the flat is cold, with the dankness of neglect. It feels more like a basement than a second floor. Bridget drops her keys on to the cloth-covered cardboard box that suffices for a hall table since she sold the real one to pay the gas last year, scans the handful of letters she collected from the mat along with the bailiff's card. The usual bundle of worries. Water rates, overdue. Council tax – she feels particularly resentful that she is paying money she doesn't have to receive social workers' homilies and bugger-all help. TV licence. She pulls a wry face. At least, she thinks, I won't have to pay *that* once the bailiffs have taken the telly away. There's another one, too: an unfamiliar type. Heavy watermarked cream envelope, longer and narrower than the usual, the address typed on to the paper rather than showing, as they usually do, through a plastic window.

Looks like a lawyer's letter, she thinks.

Her heart jumps.

Someone's died.

She turns it over, scans the back as though this will give her some clue as to the contents.

Maybe, she thinks, it's someone I don't know; one of those distant cousins in Canada you read about, the one who never married but played their children-money successfully on the stock exchange and had no one to leave it to.

Jesus, she thinks. Has it come to this, that I'm hoping someone somewhere has died because it might get me out of this mess?

Maybe someone's won the lottery and made an anonymous donation. One of my friends. One of the people I used to know, before, who's heard about what's happened to us, who wants to help . . .

She can't face opening it right now. Knows deep in her core that it will be more bad news, that salvation doesn't just appear out of the blue. She feels like she's been running all her life, just to stand still. It seems so random. Time and again the papers report multi-million-pound settlements for trophy wives, and here she is, stuffing envelopes and assembling inserts all night to try to cover the child support her husband won't pay out of protest at being denied the right to scare the crap out of his daughter.

We live in a two-tier world, she thinks. The rich and the rest of us.

Clunk. She is plunged in darkness as the electricity key runs out.

'Shit,' says Bridget. 'Shit, shit, shit.'

Why does this only ever happen at night, when the only place to get a top-up is the garage on Streatham Hill, where you're as likely to get mugged as buy a Mars Bar?

Because, obviously, she tells herself, you use the electricity at night. And it happens often because you never have more than a fiver spare to put into it when you go. It's not the world conspiring against you, however much it feels like it.

She keeps candles and matches in every room against the electricity, on high shelves to keep them out of little hands. The nearest is in the kitchen, on top of the cupboard. Bridget feels her way along the corridor, stubs her toe on something – probably one of Yasmin's discarded toys – knocks something with a crash on to the stupid slate-tiled kitchen floor she and Kieran installed back in the days before pregnancy, in the days when he seemed like a dream come true, when she thought he was moving in and letting his flat out as a first step up the property ladder. We were going to be out of here and into a house in Clapham in two years, she thinks. I never in my wildest dreams thought that the starter flat I bought twelve years ago would be my prison now. I'm worse off than I was in my early twenties. At least in my early twenties the only way to go was up.

She feels along the edge of the cupboard door and finds the junkshop saucer on which the candle stands.

In the flare of the match, she glimpses a figure in the corner. Jumps, heart thudding, nearly drops the match. It's Kieran, of course. Always Kieran. Always there, watching over her, making himself seen from the corner of her eye, waiting to jump.

And she's blinking back tears again, eighth time today, twelve thousandth since the day she met him. And then she blows out the match, drops the letter down on the kitchen top and, ignoring the apron which hangs from the hook where it has always hung, goes to fetch her daughter.

Chapter Five

Yasmin hasn't forgotten her father. Sometimes he comes to her at bedtime, when she feels sleep begin to take her limbs. It's then that she hears him speak as well, the way he used to, the way he used to be before. She feels him close to her, feels the quilt tuck in around her, block the draught from the window above her bed, feels his lips brush her forehead, on the temple, at the hairline, his voice whisper, 'Night night, precious angel.' And half-asleep, she will turn on to her side and mutter, 'Night, Daddy,' and if she's more awake, she will jump, and shriek, and shout for her mum because he shouldn't be there: he shouldn't be anywhere near them. When she's awake, she doesn't remember the Nice Dad, the one who cuddled her, the one who gave her baths and took her to the swings in Brockwell Park. All that's been blotted out by twisted lips and fists like concrete. It's only in her dreams that he comes back: makes her warm and safe and fills her head with disturbing confusion.

Now, sleeping in Carol's big soft bed, she hears her mother's voice but registers it more as a dream than an intrusion. It's only recently that she has understood about dreams, though she has many of them. And she vaguely understands, from the other side of the bedroom door, that her mum is crying, but she cries so much lately that, for Yasmin, the sound is simply an extension of a normal day. She rolls over under Carol's Brixton Market bedclothes, drifts deeper into the dark.

In Carol's living-room-kitchenette – she lives in the

converted attic of the building, in what used to be the servants' sleeping quarters, all sloping ceilings and eaves cupboards – Bridget hunches on the sofa with a wad of kitchen paper clutched in her hand. 'It wasn't meant to be like this,' she sobs. 'It wasn't meant to *be* like this.'

'Course it wasn't,' says Carol from the depths of the fridge. 'I don't suppose there's a single person on this road who thought it was going to be like this when they were kids. I certainly didn't. I was going to be rich like everyone on the telly. And married. Big house in Esher. Couple of kids. Gym membership . . .'

'I could see you like that,' says Bridget.

'Couldn't we all? Isn't that what's supposed to happen to air hostesses before they get pensioned off? I always thought so. So did my mum. Definitely. It was a good career move when I started out. Best access in the world to the Frequent Flyers. Nobody said anything about pensions and mortgages in those days. My pension was meant to come with a wedding certificate attached.'

'Christ, you're not pensionable yet,' says Bridget.

'Honey,' says Carol, 'if you're forty and pushing a trolley you might as well be sixty-five. Doesn't go with most airlines' images, the prospect of varicose veins and night-time cocoa.'

She finds what she is looking for, emerges brandishing it. 'There we go,' she says. 'Adult cocoa. Don't know why I buy spinach. Takes up so much space I can never find the wine, and it's not like I ever eat it before it goes off.'

'What am I going to do?'

'Same with broccoli,' says Carol, making with the corkscrew. 'I only buy it so it can make my fridge smell like old bathing towels.'

She fetches the bottle and two tumblers – her sink, with its arching mixer tap, is so small she's long since given up buying wine glasses with their fragile stems – over to the sofa, pours out and waits while Bridget blows her nose and mops the traces of mascara back up her cheeks. 'There you go.' She hands her a glass. 'Jacob's Creek. Mother's little helper.'

Bridget takes the glass, takes a big slug, says: 'Thanks. It should have been me giving you wine, really.'

'Don't worry, darling,' says Carol. 'She's a pleasure, you know that.'

'Yes, but –' Bridget starts to tear up again.

'Stop it, Bridget,' says Carol firmly. 'There's no point. Crying's a waste of energy. It won't make a smidge of difference to how things turn out.'

Bridget sniffs. 'I'm sorry. I'm tired.'

'Right,' says Carol. There is an unspoken agreement between them that all of Bridget's emotional collapses – and Carol's – should be written off as tiredness and healed with white wine.

'What happened to me?' she asks, for the millionth time.

'Kieran happened,' says Carol. 'You know that, I know that. The only person who doesn't seem to know it is Kieran. You were a proper doll when you first got here. I remember. I remember thinking I'd never get to be friends with you 'cause you were so . . . well, it was obvious you were going places. I never thought you'd stay. You could tell you were one of those girls on the way up. He's sucked the life out of you.'

'It's been years, Carol.'

'Mmm,' she says. 'But you had years of fear before that. People like Kieran, they confuse you as much as anything. All those flowers and apologies and you-made-me-do-its: you didn't know what you were thinking for donkey's years, he'd turned you upside-down so much. You can't expect to get over something like that overnight. Especially when he's still hanging around, giving you grief.'

'But I should have worked it out. I'm so stupid. *Stupid*.'

'Yes,' she says, 'that's right. You're stupid like every other woman who's ever had it done to them. You should have seen through it, even though nobody else did. It took me ages to realize he was a wrong 'un myself, and I wasn't the one he was Jekyll-and-Hydeing at.'

'I should have . . . I don't see how I managed to be so stupid. Have I got "victim" written on my forehead in Magic Marker or something?'

They drink, contemplate.

'You know,' says Carol, 'a lot of the people in the concentration camps felt the same way. Like it was their fault in some way. Like they'd done something to bring it on themselves. But that doesn't make it true. It just means that, if you're told something about yourself over and over again, you begin to believe it. There are nasty people in the world, Bridget, it's as simple as that. Some people are just plain nasty, and their lives are dedicated to doing nasty things. You got involved with one of those. End of story.'

'But why didn't I spot it?'

Carol snorts. Lights a cigarette. 'Well, they'd hardly get away with it long-term if it was tattooed on them, would it?'

Bridget sighs. Carol changes the subject.

'So tell me about it,' she says, 'apart from the amazing news that Cornwall's a million miles away. What do you reckon?'

Bridget sighs, stretches her back. 'It was – oh, what's the point? It's not like I'm going to get the job . . .'

'Mmm,' agrees Carol. 'That'll be how come he asked you when you could start, then. Tell me about it. What was the house like?'

'God, Carol, it was amazing. Amazing. The sort of place you usually only get to go into if you pay.'

'Big?'

'Yuh-*huh*. Huge. Twelve bedrooms and all the lounges are big enough to fit yours and my flats into with room over. God, you could fit them into one of the *settees*.'

'Crikey,' says Carol. 'And that's a *spare* house?'

Bridget sips: a more controlled sip, this time, now that the edge has come off her hysteria. 'I know.'

'How on giddy earth big are the others, if that one's going spare?'

'I'm not sure. I have a feeling this one's the biggest, actually. The boss lives about ten miles away and most of the family are round about there. All within walking distance.'

'Now, there's incestuous.'

'It is a bit, isn't it?' says Bridget.

'Especially if you've got a twelve-bed house ten miles away.'

'Well, I don't know. Maybe they like the view better where they are. Or maybe they just can't afford to live in it when they can get holiday income off it. Even small cottages go for four hundred a week down there in the high season.'

'I bet it's got ghosts or something,' says Carol.

'Don't be stupid,' says Bridget.

'Could be.' Carol, eyes wide and staring, plays an imaginary harp in the air by her ears. 'Whoooooo!' she says. '*Whoooooo!*'

'Stop it, Carol.' Bridget's surprised to find that she really means it. 'I don't need putting off, okay?'

'Ghosties and ghoulies and long-legged beasties,' says Carol.

'Don't talk like that in front of Yasmin. Please.' Bridget, like many parents, uses her child as camouflage for her own feelings. 'It's going to be difficult enough without you putting things like that into her head.'

Carol stops, but she's smiling, now. 'Right. So you *are* going, then?'

'I don't know. I don't. It would be – God, I can't even really think about what it would mean if I got it.'

Carol pours more wine. 'It would be the solution to everything, the way I see it,' she says. 'Kieran, your debts. Yas growing up to be one of those mini-slags hanging about outside the offy. A new start. What's your accommodation like?'

'Gorgeous. Well, a lot better than here, anyway. The top floor of one wing.'

'Wing?'

'Yes. It has wings. The flat's got two bedrooms. Like proper, full-sized ones. There are two beds in Yasmin's.'

She doesn't notice that she's already started talking about the rooms as belonging to them. Carol does, though. 'And there's a living room twice the size of mine. It's all panelled out – tongue and groove, bare wood, like the inside of a log cabin. Smells piney and clean. And the kitchen! My God, Carol, you can *eat* in the kitchen!'

'Don't know what's so special about that.' Carol jerks her head behind her at the Baby Belling, the tea-towel hanging from the cup-hook over the sink. 'I do it every day. So go on, then: what's the catch?'

'Well . . . it *is* in the middle of nowhere.'

'Wonderful.'

'The village is two miles away.'

A car alarm begins to howl in the street outside.

'I can see,' says Carol wryly, 'how you would miss Streatham.'

'And it's only tiny.'

'So where's the nearest town?'

'Wadebridge.'

'Wadebridge is nice. I used to go there with my nan and gramps. Not exactly Nightclub Central, but it's nice.'

Bridget heaves an exaggerated sigh, clamps her palms to the small of her back. 'My clubbing days are long behind me.'

'Oh, I'm sure we can find you a nice *knitting* circle.'

'Yeah,' says Bridget, 'you think you're joking.'

'I'm sure there'll be discos in the village hall. Maybe you'll meet a nice farmer.'

Bridget laughs.

A window downstairs goes up. 'Shut that bloody thing up!' a voice bellows into the empty street. 'Shut it the fuck up!'

The women roll their eyes at each other.

'I don't know how you can even be contemplating leaving.'

'I know.' She laughs again, though tears are filling her eyes. 'The glamour. The fun. The wild social life. By the way. Can you shout me a tenner till Friday? Only my leccy's gone and I've spent all my cash on petrol.'

Carol does a good Margaret Thatcher. 'The trouble with these people,' she says, 'is they have no idea of budgeting. Baked beans only cost 13p at the cash and carry. You should have laid in stocks against the winter like the squirrels.'

'Jesus,' says Bridget. 'Like living on beans is going to sort my problems.'

They drink again.

'I don't know what I'm going to do,' she says, 'if I don't get it.'

'I know,' says Carol. 'I know.'

Chapter Six

The figurines won't stay still.

There are only three of them now, since the house was let out to holidaymakers; the family were doubtful about leaving anything at all that could fit so easily in a pocket, but Landmark let it be known that the sort of tenants who take Cornish manor houses rather than marina flats or villas on the Costas tend to be disappointed if those houses come free of embellishment, in the same way they would always rather an old brass bedstead than a modern, germ-free divan. Even Americans will put up with antique plumbing if they find enough chipped Meissen and oils of the surrounding countryside scattered about the place.

'Gen-yew-whine,' he mutters as he passes through the dining room and sees that they've turned again: Charles II, Prince Albert and Disraeli, facing in toward the dresser mirror, gazing sternly out, downturned mouths and steely porcelain eyes reflected into the room.

He's used to it now. It's been happening since his childhood – he remembers his grandmother muttering much as he is doing himself as he turns them back out again – and the fixed and disapproving faces in the glass no longer have the power to make the back of his neck prickle as they did when he was an imaginative teenager. They've tried everything over the years – Blu-tack, even superglue – but nothing seems to hold them in place. It's just another feature of the house. Another reason why not one member of the family wanted to take it over when Granny died her lonely alcoholic's death at the bottom of the back stairs in 1975.

He has the last of Frances Tyler's belongings in a bin-liner, is taking them out to the shed. The bag contains clothes and shoes and other stuff that won't be well suited by the damp out there, but he feels that it's no more than she deserves for leaving him in the lurch like this. It's been a bloody long day, thanks to her, what with having to wait for the two no-shows and the sole interviewee who did bother to turn up, and he'll be glad to be gone. It gets no better after dark, this place. When they were children his sister and he used to refuse to come after sunset; became hysterical, even though they were allowed to share a room, if his parents tried to leave them for the night. Not that they often did: even at the age of five, he sort of knew that there was something wrong with Granny. He remembers why, now: it's not just that Rospetroc is full of dark corners and inexplicable moving shadows; it's the noises. Scutterings and murmurs; odd clatters in other rooms and whispers as of silk on silk.

Old houses are full of sounds. He knows this only too well, having lived in them all his life. But his own home makes sounds of adjustment: groans and thumps as it expands and contracts with heat and cold; the creak of a loose floorboard, the judder of window-frames in the wind. Not these anticipation-filled silences that suggest someone is hiding round the corner, holding their breath, waiting to jump out. Not the feeling that someone is peeping out from behind the curtains, stifling their laughter.

Will she stay the course? he wonders. I can't go through this every couple of months. She seemed . . . there's something she's not saying, that's for sure. Is she going to take off with the contents of the house? Or is she just one of those people who's running away from something? It attracts odd-bods, this job. Normal people won't put up with it: the isolation, the unremitting slog of keeping the dust down and being discreet and tolerating the sort of people we get down here, sometimes. Doesn't pay enough for people with ambition.

They've had the lot under this roof, and none has lasted: not even the couples. Writers, artists, dispossessed Zimbabwean farmers, hippies, people with ambitions in the tourist trade, downsizing city folk, history freaks, retired school caretakers, Eastern Europeans to whom five-hundred-a-month-plus-accommodation-and-bills must have looked like a fortune: each, in turn, has handed in notice (or, in the case of Frances Tyler, not), packed bags and headed for civilization. Leaving, more often than not, some sort of chaos behind them – breakages and daubings, beds unmade and doors unlocked – and spreading tales in the village that make it practically impossible to get back-up labour even for crowd events like weddings.

Why do the working class have to be so bloody superstitious? he thinks. It's all very well selling the Daphne du Maurier line to the tourists, but when the locals start buying into it, it leads to nothing but chaos. He turns the figurines back to face the room again, picks up the bin-liner and heads out of the back door.

In the courtyard, no longer surrounded by six-foot-thick walls, his phone picks up a signal, beeps twice. It's annoying, the way the phone signal comes and goes down here, but it's the same across much of the county: as though the phone companies are part of some great conspiracy against the Celtic Fringes. He checks it, sees the message icon, dials through to voicemail. There's a light Bodmin drizzle in the air, but he stays in the open because he will lose the signal if he gets under cover.

Two messages. One from his three o'clock: his wife doesn't want to uproot herself from Sheffield, sorry, hopes he understands, no point in coming all the way down there and wasting both their time. Tom stabs at the 3 button, deletes it. Don't worry about wasting *your* time, he thinks. *I've* just been hanging around here all day waiting for you.

'Yes, well,' he says out loud, 'at least he had the manners to ring, I suppose. Which is more than the other one did.'

The second is from Bridget Sweeny, at four o'clock. He

notes the time because she can't possibly have got back to London by then. Keen, he thinks. Imagines her in the car park at the Exeter services, pacing up and down by that run-down little banger as she speaks. She looks run-down herself, he thinks. Tired, but perhaps that's not so surprising with a six-year-old and no husband. Perhaps I'm being too suspicious. She looks like someone who needs a break.

And possibly, a smaller voice tells him, *like someone who doesn't have too many options to leave once she gets here, either.*

'Hello, Mr Gordhavo,' she says. 'It's Bridget Sweeny here. Your one o'clock interview. I just wanted to say that I enjoyed looking round the house, and meeting you, and . . .' He hears her pause to think, hears her consider her words so she doesn't sound too eager, too desperate. Notes it with a tingle of hope. She wouldn't be uprooting a six-year-old just before Christmas unless there were pressing reasons, after all. '. . . and I'd just like to say that I'd be happy to come and work for you if you thought I was suitable. I checked out the village, and the school, and I think that . . . anyway . . . that's beside the point . . . Anyway, I wanted really to give you my number, just in case . . . you know . . .' She reels off a list of figures: a mobile phone number, not a landline; one of the signs of economic change, the pay-as-you-go world being as much a sign of a bad credit rating as of anything else. '. . . and I'll look forward to hearing from you. Thanks. Goodb— Oh, actually: one other thing. We can come fairly much whenever. Whatever suited you. Okay. Well, bye.'

Tom finishes his walk across the yard, unlocks the shed door. The single light bulb fizzes slightly as it comes to life, illuminates an interior where spiders have run unchecked for a hundred years. This is the old smithy, beams hung with chains, a platform for animal fodder less than a foot above him which trickles woodworm dust on to his head as the breeze enters with him. It's used as storage only for the stuff that's too far gone, too ugly, too worthless even for the attic. Stuff that people have occasionally thought might come in useful as timber, or lumber, or kindling at least, which has been forgotten over the decades as new loads of stately logs more suited to a tourist's idea of fuel for Rospetroc's great fireplaces have been stacked on either side of the porch. It smells of rot and beetles.

The trouble with families like ours, he thinks, is we can never throw anything away. Once something has meant something to someone in the family – even something as little as their simply having bought it – we are constitutionally incapable of letting it go, however inconvenient. History (at least the stuff that reflects well on us), property – even clothes stay in trunks and wardrobes until the moth has eaten them away to nothing but a pile of brownish fluff. This house, for instance: there wasn't a single Gordhavo – or Blakemore, for that matter – who wanted to live in it after Granny died, but selling was out of the question. We could have bought up half of Rock, before it got trendy with the Fulham set, for what this place would have fetched, and each of those Cornish fishermen's bedrooms would have brought in twice as much in rent as they do here, and would have been far more likely to be occupied, to boot.

Yes, but if we sold it we'd have to clear it out. Far better to leave that to the next generation, he thinks. Shudders. God knows what's up there on that platform, or in any of the other outhouses. The ladder must have given way decades ago and no one has had any reason to poke their head up there to see. There are so many places like that about this property. No one's been into the coal shed since the heating was turned over to oil – he doesn't even know where the key's gone – and the upper floor could have gone out of the boathouse altogether, for all he knows. Certainly, no one's been near the place, apart from to change the padlock and put a DANGER NO ENTRY sign up, during his lifetime. The pond's a nasty, weed-choked thing, its source spring too feeble to keep it clear, and he can't imagine that the boathouse can have been very appealing, even in the house's heyday.

Gosh, we live differently, he thinks. Other people would

think we were so spoiled, letting entire buildings fall to rack and ruin, but we have too many. The simple truth is, we have too many.

He half-drops, half-throws the bag on to a shard of empty space to his right. Hears something break and feels a small twinge of satisfaction at the sound. That'll teach her to bugger off without a word.

Bridget Sweeny. Doesn't look like she's going to run off with the first surfer she comes across in the summer. Didn't seem too appalled by the workload. Didn't ask a single stupid question about the house's history or make any silly remarks about atmosphere. Didn't come across as one of those people who have hysterics at the first problem. Seemed pretty sensible.

He throws the light switch as he turns to leave the outhouse and the circuit in the main house trips.

She'll need to be, he thinks, as he feels his way back across the courtyard under a starless sky.

Chapter Seven

Crash.

Oh God, did I lock it? Did I lock it? Did I remember all the locks?

Terror throws her rigid in bed, straight as a plank, sweat starting out on her forehead as though she has just walked into a Turkish bath. And yet she is cold, she is freezing under the thick covers because she knows that Kieran is outside, knows what he will do if he gets in.

Crash.

Now Yasmin is awake too: eyes like soup-plates in the light creeping in round the curtains, she lies flat against the mattress as though some unseen force is crushing her downward.

Crash. He's using his foot. If I forgot to put the bolts on, forgot the mortise, the Yale won't hold for more than a few of those kicks.

Instinct tells her to hide, to get as far away from the noise as they can, to crouch somewhere in the dark, hands over faces, hope he'll go away. But he won't go. Not if he gets inside, and in this cramped flat there is nowhere to run to.

I've got to go and check.

No-no-no-he'll-kill-you.

Crash.

Oh, Jesus, help me now.

She sits up. Feels naked, vulnerable, once the covers are off and all that's between him and her skin is a pair of flimsy pyjama trousers and a cotton camisole, and maybe a flimsy lock. Swings her feet toward the carpet.

Yasmin realizes what she is about to do, that she will leave her, that she will be alone, starts up a wail. 'Mummy! Mummmeeee!'

'Hush, darling.' She tries to keep the tremble from her voice. Need to stay calm. Need to stay brave for Yasmin. My baby. *Don't let him get my baby.* 'Shhh. You need to be quiet now, baby.'

Her voice sounds like a stranger's heard underwater. She feels the rush of blood in her ears, feels her tongue struggle to unstick from the roof of her mouth. 'I'll be back,' she assures her. 'I promise.'

'Don'tleaveme don'tleaveme don't *leave* me.'

I don't have time. I don't have time for this. I have to go, don't you see? I have to go. It's unbearable. To protect you I have to leave you, oh, baby, don't you see?

Crash.

She reaches for the bedside lamp, remembers the electricity is still out. Well, that's one strike in our favour. He doesn't know his way around the way we do, in the dark. It's two years since he was last inside, and everything's moved about since then. Won't be able to see us, straight off. Maybe we can make a run for it.

Run where? This bloody city. No one moves themselves for a scream in the street. The yuppies on the first floor, the same ones, no doubt, that couldn't be arsed to double-lock the front door when they came in tonight, never registered anything that happened up here while he was still in residence: never called for help, came to investigate. Used to pass her on the stairs and turn their gaze away from the bruises, embarrassed. They'll shout out of the window about a car alarm, but they'll let a man beat his family half to death on the floor above and not raise a bloody finger . . .

Come on. Come *on*, Bridget. You have to go. You have to go and check.

'Get under the bed,' she tells her daughter. 'Come on, quickly. Just hide under the bed and don't come out till I tell you. Don't come out for anything. Go on. Quickly.'

Yasmin moves quickly now, understands that speed is the only defence, that hiding is the only way. Rolls out of bed and slips beneath, wriggles in behind suitcases and storage boxes, curls herself up as small as she can go.

The hall: pitch black because all the doors are shut. The noise much louder here, crammed down into the tiny space. She can hear him swearing, muttering on the other side of the door. Can see him in her mind's eye, tendons like hawsers on his neck, formal shirt half-buttoned in the post-drink City-boy fashion, his mouth twisted with venom and rage. Why can't they see? Why can't they see what he's like, these people he works with, the ones who stood as moral references to keep him out of court?

Of course they don't care. He brings in results, after all, negotiates the snakepit with grit and skill, and so what if a guy's a bit aggressive if that's what it takes to bring in a bonus?

She stubs a toe on her travelling bag, barely notices the pain as she creeps toward the door, into the lion's jaws, feeling each inch along the wall. Did I lock it? Did I? Is he just using soft blows right now, so he knows I'll be right there when he finally goes for force, brings it crashing through on to me?

She's there. Can feel him now, face suffused with drink, leaning against the wood and listening for her, sweat from his exertions slicking down that dealer's quiff. 'Fucking fucking fucking,' he mutters, 'you're fucking in there, I know you are.'

She can't bear to look through the spyhole, to see his face. Pressed back against the wall, she feels out in the dark for the mortise key, permanently in the lock as protection against picking. Twists it to the right. It turns, takes with a tiny click. Not so tiny he can't hear it.

'I fucking hear you, you fucking bitch!' he shouts. 'Let me in! Come on! Let me into my fucking flat!'

It's not your flat. It never was. It's mine, though thanks to you that won't go on for much longer.

And now he's kicking with full sincerity, throwing his

whole body against the panels, thundering with his fists, boots raging on the timber. Bridget jumps back, instinctively, has to force herself closer again to take hold of the bolts and shoot them home. Has to struggle with the bottom one because the door is jumping in its frame, fourteen stone of estranged husband ramming himself against it in an effort to get to them. Oh, Yasmin, oh, my baby, he won't get you, I promise. I'll do anything. Anything.

It shoots home and the rasp produces a renewed battering from the other side. 'I'll fucking get you, Bridget! You can't keep me out! You can't fucking shut me out of my own home!'

Come on, come *on*. Where are you? Someone! Carol! Someone!

She can't remember where she put her bag. Now the door is secured she has bought some time until the police arrive, but she has to call them first. Crawls along the floor, feeling, blind with hands outstretched, for the familiar touch of leather bought in better times. Finds discarded toys, cardboard boxes in place of chests, shoes, books, hears his rage pump through the house.

And then she hears Carol, at the top of the stairs. No hint of the fear she must be feeling: just her booming voice, commanding. 'Kieran! I've called the police! They'll be here in a minute. You'd better go.'

Chapter Eight

Carol's hands are shaking. She realizes this as she grips the banister to support watery legs. The timer switch, which allows only the athletic to get from floor to floor while still in light, goes off, plunges them both into darkness. She thumps a fist against the wall where she knows the knob to be and now she is looking down into his eyes, his pupils big and dark from the change of illumination and the fact that he has obviously been drinking. Of course he has. He never does this when he's sober. He's too smart. Knows the meaning of 'exclusion zone'. Knows how far he can push it. Before he gets on to the lager.

Yet again she is struck, as everybody is, by what a handsome creature he is. You'd never think, she ponders, that such a sensitive face could mask such a brutish interior. No one ever does. That was one of the problems. God knows, if I'd been Bridget, I'd've fallen for it myself. He could sell burgers to Hindus, that one. That bone structure, those innocent blue eyes, the strong-but-gentle mouth: everyone reads the outer package, whatever they say. The good-looking have an easier ride through life than the rest of us, however rotten their core, because people just assume goodness in them.

He's like a turd in Christmas wrapping, she thinks. That poor woman, black and blue under her clothes and everyone telling her what a lucky girl she was. She keeps the heel of her hand on the light switch, a talisman against him.

Kieran's pupils contract. There's a faint sheen of exertion

on his forehead; kicking doors in is harder than they make it look on the TV. 'Fuck off, Carol,' he says.

'You know I can't do that, Kieran,' she replies. 'But you'd better, if you've got any sense. You know you're not meant to be here.'

'I just want to see my kid,' he says.

No you don't, she thinks. You want to kick eight bells out of her mother.

'Not now,' she says, 'and not without a social worker. You know the rules. It's the middle of the night.'

Kieran gives her a look. White light courses through her veins. My God, he is evil, she thinks. I'd almost managed to forget.

'You'd better go, now,' she repeats. 'They'll be here any minute.'

Please, she prays, please let him believe me. He doesn't know I've run out of minutes. That I couldn't call if I wanted to. If I sound confident enough he will believe me.

He does. Begins to retreat. Disappears from her field of vision as he begins to descend the stairs.

She thinks, decides. She would rather see him go than keep her hand on the light. I'll be able to see his shadow in the streetlight better than I will him, once he's down at the bottom, she thinks: be able to tell that he's actually left rather than dodged back inside to hide until I've gone down there and got her to open up. She crosses the landing and leans out over the stairs.

He walks slowly, looking upward. Their eyes meet again. Carol forces her features into a deliberately neutral expression. Don't let him see what you think of him, she thinks. Don't give him excuses.

He drops his head, continues on his way.

The light goes out. She hears him pause. Which do I do? Do I go back and switch it on, cover the sound of his movements with my own, not know where he is? Or do I stay here, trust my hearing, believe that if he doesn't break into a run he must be going down?

There's a light coming from under downstairs's door.

She can see the shadows of a pair of feet pressed up against it. God, I hate them, she thinks. Bet *they* haven't called the plod, even though they could. Just waiting to make sure no damage is done to their property, then they'll go to bed and complain at work all day tomorrow about their noisy neighbours. One of us could get killed up here, and all they'd do would be to get mouthy about the blood spoiling the paintwork on their ceiling.

She hears his footsteps: deliberate, careful. He wouldn't be so careful if he were coming up. I'm sure he wouldn't. He's feeling his way.

Relief floods her as the sound of his shoes changes. He's on a hard surface now: on the Victorian tiles on the ground floor. She's never liked them much: they're cold, too ornate for the use the building's been turned to. She loves them now.

Inside the front door, Kieran pauses. She can hear him thinking.

'Go on,' she calls. 'I'm still here.'

She is surprised to hear how steady her voice sounds. That look on his face a minute ago – drunk, yes, but suffused with the Neanderthal rage she'd managed to forget over the months since she last saw him – gave her a bigger fright than the initial sound of his foot smashing against the door.

'A hundred metres,' she calls, forcing herself to sound confident, sure of herself; gripping the stair-rail hard with both hands to try to steady her body and keep the tremble from her voice. 'You need to be at least a hundred metres away by the time they get here. You know that.'

The latch clicks below, and his large shadow is cast across the old tiled floor. 'Doesn't matter,' he says, and his voice, though quiet, echoes up the stairs. 'I can come back. You can't be here all the time.'

The door swings to. Carol waits, holds her breath, on the step, listens for signs that he might still be inside.

Nothing. No shifting, no rustles.

He could be like a cat, she thinks. He could be able to

keep so still that even tiny prey animals are lulled into a false sense of security, come out because they think the coast is clear.

She steps back across the landing, turns the light on again. Cranes out over the banister in an effort to see into the shadows below the stairs.

The hall is empty.

She thinks.

Carol thumps the light again, races down, switch to switch, past Bridget's, past the yuppies'. Takes a breath and runs into the hall. Skids across the tiles in her bare feet, races to the front door. Throws the latch on the Chubb lock and, strength washing from her limbs, collapses against the heavy painted panels and breathes again.

Chapter Nine

She always feels nervous coming home, even when she's only been away a few minutes. All it would take is a few minutes: he could be in and out and no one any the wiser without her there. It's no way to live, this single life, she thinks. I'm going to be one of those old ladies whose body has mummified by the time anyone notices I'm missing.

I'm getting too old for this, thinks Carol as she mounts the front steps. It's all very well, but I'm nearly forty-five, a middle-aged lady, and middle-aged ladies weren't meant to be up all night, even in crises. She feels washed out, grainy. Yas was clingy at the school gates, the way she always is when Kieran's made a visit. I need a nap. A nap and a bath and several cups of coffee.

The house is silent, the front door double-locked. She pauses in the hall, listens. Nothing. Just the hum of traffic on the High Road. She climbs the stairs. Taps on Bridget's front door, finds that it swings back off the latch.

'Hello?' she calls. Peers inside, with trepidation. All looks normal. No signs of struggle, no bloodstains.

'Bridge? Hello?'

'In here.'

She follows the voice to the kitchen. Bridget is sitting on the lino, coffee mug cooling beside her, a letter lying loosely in her lap. Tears stream down her face.

'Oh, honey,' says Carol. Gets down on her knees and wraps her arms round her head.

'Well, it's a good thing, really,' says Bridget.

'What is?'

'This.'

She hands her the letter. It bears the address of a large Central London lawyer's but it's from the building society, as Bridget had suspected last night. She reads it, slowly, takes in its stiff and formal language, lays it down.

'A month? That's all they're giving you?'

Bridget sighs. Shrugs. 'They've given me more than a year. You can't expect them to hang on forever. They're not a charity.'

'Yeah, but you've got a kid.'

Bridget shakes her head. Drops it forward and allows the tears to flow.

'It's time we went, anyway,' she says eventually. 'It can't go on like this. He'll just be back. You know that.'

'You're knackered,' says Carol.

'I'm right, too,' says Bridget. 'Oh, God, but I'm so tired as well.'

Carol sits down, rests her back against the kitchen cabinet. Takes Bridget's hand in hers and squeezes it.

'Did she get to school all right?'

Carol nods. 'Of course. I'll go and get her later.'

'I'm sorry,' says Bridget. 'I'm really sorry, Carol. This is so unfair on you.'

'Oh, honey,' says Carol. 'Look. We'll work something out. We will. It'll all be all right, you'll see.'

'Oh, come *on*. How's it going to be all right? *How?*'

'I don't know,' says Carol. 'We'll . . .'

She stops, because she can't think how. Can't see beyond this morning, to be honest. It's always darkest before dawn, she reminds herself. It's always when you give up hope that something turns up.

'I'm tired,' says Bridget. 'Tired of all of it. Tired of struggling, tired of trying to put a brave face on, tired of telling Yasmin it'll be okay. Tired of walking down the street looking over my shoulder in case he comes out of nowhere. Tired of having to choose between shoes for my daughter and food for myself. Tired of waiting to be repossessed. Carol, I really can't do this any more.'

'Oh, don't. Oh, honey, don't.'

'Maybe I should just . . .'

Carol waits. Bridget doesn't continue.

'Babe,' she says eventually, 'you know you're going to carry on. It's what we do, isn't it? What alternative is there?'

Another tear slides down Bridget's cheek. She feels all cried out, salted inside like a kipper. Finds it hard to believe that she has any tears left.

'You never know,' says Carol. 'That bloke might ring.'

'Oh, *please.*'

She bundles the letter into a ball, throws it at the wall.

'As if,' she says. 'Jesus, what a waste of time that was. And petrol. He's not going to call. Why would he call? My luck never changes. Never. It never has. It'll just go on and on like this, spiralling downwards, forever. You know it, Carol, and I know it, and there's no point in pretending otherwise. I might as well –'

In the bedroom, in the interior of her handbag, the phone starts to ring.

Chapter Ten

Eight hundred pounds. I've got eight hundred pounds in my pocket. That's more money than I've had at one time in . . . how long? Feels like forever. God, I used to take that much down to New Covent Garden in cash every other day, back in the old days. Before Yasmin, we used to think a hundred quid was a reasonable amount to spend on an ordinary night out, and now it feels like a fortune.

Yes, she thinks, but it's not a lot to show for a lifetime, is it? Two hundred of it's Carol's and two-fifty is the flight fund, scraped together out of Child Benefit against emergencies. And fifty for my engagement ring.

She glances down at her newly naked finger. Selling the ring was as much a gesture to the end of her relationship as a financial necessity, the fact that the diamonds turned out to be cubic zirconia almost perfect in its irony. Really, she should be surprised that the gold was real gold. After all these years, she has finally let go of the last vestiges of Kieran, and received a final proof of his duplicity, of the value he put on her. When he gave the ring to her, top of the Eiffel Tower, champagne weekend, jacuzzi suite and all the luxuries, she felt like a princess. Now – she's ashamed of what that hotel room cost. She could have squeezed two more months out of the mortgage for the price of that weekend.

Three hundred pounds: everything that's not, or not in, this crumbling car – furniture, kitchen appliances, all those decorative fripperies that dripped away the thousands over the years, when we weren't saving, when I thought that incomes only ever went up when you were in your twenties – was worth three hundred pounds, and that only because the house clearance man took pity on my crestfallen face when he offered me two-fifty. Christ: he wouldn't even take the telly. Said it was so old a burglar would have left it.

Yasmin stirs in the back. Tranquillized with chips and hot chocolate, she has slept since the services two hours back, almost buried among bedclothes and cushions. If we crashed, thinks Bridget, checking the wing mirror because the rear-view is blocked with boxes of pans and books, shoes and toys, crockery and chemicals, all bundled together with the haphazardness of haste, she'd undoubtedly survive. Though whether she'd be found in the wreckage before she suffocated is anybody's guess.

One thing Bridget has already discovered: there is no good radio west of Reading. By Bristol, apart from a couple of piratey drum 'n' bass outfits, the world has become a cosy one of two-mile ring-road tailbacks and Christmas fairs. It's as though London didn't exist, she thinks, apart from the odd suspicious comment about edicts from Westminster. It might as well be on another planet, or at least in another country: as relevant to these people as Rome or New York. By Exeter, on her third feature on decorative chutney-making, she concedes defeat, fiddles with the buttons until she finds Radio 2. They're playing Duran Duran: 'Girls on Film'. The final tune at her first school disco, when they put the lights back up after the slow dances. Back then. In another life. When she thought the future held nothing but adventure.

Bridget smiles for the first time today, beyond the false rictus of reassurance she's carried about for her daughter's sake. Sings along – with the chorus, anyway – as she turns on the headlights. As always in house moves, they got on the road later than she had intended, boxes and bags so much heavier to carry and harder to stow, even with Carol's help, than she had anticipated, and it's already almost four o'clock. It'll be pitch black by the time we get there, she thinks. I'll have to leave most of the stuff in the car until morning, just bring up the bedclothes and the cooking things. We're going to the country. We can leave a car full of valuables, such as they are, overnight, and I can still expect them to be there in the morning.

My God, I'm tired, she thinks. I must be getting old. And then she laughs out loud because she has realized that she's just tuned a car radio to Radio 2 for the first time in her life. You may not be old yet, she tells herself, but you've sure as sherbet passed one of the milestones of middle age.

'What's so funny?'

She glances in the rear-view. Yasmin is sitting up, craning, like a meerkat. She's strapped on to the booster seat, her legs sticking out in front of her, too short to bend fully at the knees, her dark hair crushed down on one side of her head from sleep. Bridget feels one of those hourly surges of love. My baby. Not a baby any more, but not big enough to kick the back of the seat, either.

'Nothing, baby,' she says. 'Just something I heard on the radio. Are you thirsty?'

Yasmin considers the question, stretches to see out at the gloomy road. 'Yes,' she says, absently, imperiously. 'When did it get dark? It must be awfully late.'

'It's winter, darling. It gets dark early in winter.'

Children are so odd. The things they notice and the things they don't. Six winters Yasmin's gone through now, and she's only just discovered about the darkness thing. 'Why?'

Good God, thinks Bridget, I don't actually know the answer to that. Is it because the course of our orbit is different at different times of year? Or does the earth tilt on its axis? Or is it something to do with the Wobble they go on about on the science programmes?

'It's just one of those things.' She settles for the it-just-is route. 'It's why it gets colder in winter, you see. There's less sun.'

'Why?'

'Why what?'

'Why is there less sun?'

'Because it's winter –' she begins. Realizes that she's painting herself into a corner, changes tack. 'We need the winter so all the plants can have a rest. It's like you needing to go to sleep.'

'But plants don't need to go to sleep,' says Yasmin the logician. 'It's people who need to go to sleep.'

'Mmm,' says Bridget non-committally.

'And cats. Cats sleep. A lot. Sometimes you can't wake them up.'

'Yes, they do.'

'Can we have a kitten?'

'We'll see,' she says. A phrase she hears passing her lips thirty, forty times a day.

'I shall call him Fluffy,' says Yasmin with finality.

Please don't, thinks Bridget. It's tough enough being a child's cat without being called Fluffy.

'Are we nearly there yet?'

'Another couple of hours, I'm afraid.' Bridget fishes a mini-carton of Five Alive from the door pocket, unwraps the straw with her teeth and passes it back.

'Another couple of *hours*?'

'Yes. I told you it was a long way.'

'Practically,' says Yasmin, in that strange, suddenly grown-up way she has, 'America.'

Not far off, thinks Bridget. After all, it only takes seven hours to fly to Florida.

'Mummy, I'm bored.'

Oh God. Don't let her start. We've got such a long way. 'Do you want to play a game? How about I Spy?'

'Okay. I spy with my little eye something beginning with H.'

'Um . . .' Bridget casts about her. 'Headrest?'

'No.'

'Hair?'

'No.'

'Um . . .'

A car passes on the other side of the road. 'Headlights!'

'Yup,' says Yasmin. 'I spy with my little eye something beginning with H.'

'Headlights,' says Bridget.

'Yup. I spy with my little eye something beginning with H.'

'Okay. I get it. Drink your drink.'

A rattly slurp from the back seat. 'How much longer?'

'One hour and fifty-nine minutes.'

'I'm *booored.*'

'Look!' cries Bridget. 'A camel!'

'Where?' She sits up again, boredom forgotten.

'Oop, missed it.'

'What's a camel doing here?'

'They get everywhere, camels.' Especially when small children need distracting. They're very useful for that. And elephants.

'Well, how come *I* never see one?'

'You're just not quick enough, that's all. I'm sure we'll see another one. I should think there'll be quite a few along this road. We'll be going through a place called Camelford, after all.'

'Tchuh,' says Yasmin. 'Sometimes I think you're just making them up, Mum.'

Oh, damn. I knew it was too good to last.

'We need to think,' she says, 'what colour to paint your bedroom. It's cool, isn't it, having a bedroom of your own at last?'

'S'pose so,' says Yasmin. Bridget feels a touch of disappointment. She'd expected more enthusiasm, but she guesses that it's hard for a child Yasmin's age to get too excited about something she's never had. Except a kitten. Perhaps she should think about the kitten. It's a tricky one. Even harder to move on if it doesn't work out, if you've got a pet to leave behind.

'You've got a spare bed, as well,' she says cheerfully. 'You can have your friends to stay.'

Yasmin picks up her monkey from the seat beside her, starts pulling at its ears. 'All my friends are in London.'

'You'll make new friends,' she promises.
'How?'
'Well, you'll be going to a new school –'
'I don't *want* to go to a new school . . .'
She can hear her daughter's voice well up. Oh, no, please, she thinks. I can't do any more tears today. I've just handed the keys to my home in to the building society. I've just become homeless. I've left everything familiar and run away to a place full of strangers . . .
And she carries on, like mothers do: forces her voice light and finds a joke the way she always has. My daughter won't grow up knowing about unhappiness. She won't grow up thinking the world is a threatening, dangerous place. I won't let her. I won't let Kieran poison her future.
'How about lime green,' she asks, 'with purple spots?'
'Eeeuugh!'
Yasmin is easy to distract. Storms turn to sunshine rapidly in her world. She giggles. 'No!'
'Well, how about orange with electric blue stripes?'
'Noo!'
'Um . . .'
'Pink,' declares Yasmin. 'I like pink.'
Of course you do. You're six years old.
'With stars on the ceiling. Those stars that light up in the dark.'
'Okay. I'm sure we can find some of those.'
'And a special cushion for Fluffy. Because he'll need his own bed, won't he?'
'Um . . .' She endeavours to find a creative way of being non-committal, fails, leaves it.
'And I want one of those lights.'
'Which lights, dwarfy?'
'The ones that go round and round. With the pictures. So I get stars and fairies on my walls.'
Jesus. Stars and fairies? What have they been teaching her at that school? Still, I suppose it's better than drive-bys and crack pipes.

'Fluffy's black and white,' says Yasmin. 'With a pink nose. I love him *sooo* much.'

They fall silent. Think their thoughts as they pass the sign for Okehampton. Maybe she'll forget about the cat thing in a while. Once she's at school, and she's got friends, once she sees lambs gambolling in the fields and . . . I don't know . . . maybe she can start an earthworm farm or something . . . or maybe . . . as long as she doesn't start wanting a pony . . .

Yasmin shifts again, struggles against her seat-belt. 'Are we nearly there yet?'

Chapter Eleven

'Hello?'

'Hi, it's me.'

'There you are! I was beginning to worry.'

'Sorry. Sorry.' She checks her watch. It's gone ten. 'Sorry,' she says again. 'It just . . . time's got away from us.'

'No problem,' says Carol, and Bridget hears her light a cigarette. 'I just worry, that's all. You know what I'm like.'

'Yes, I know. And I'm grateful.'

'So: what's it like, then? Are you all settled in? Little one asleep?'

'Only just. And I think it's more passed out from exhaustion than actual sleep. It's taken forever.'

'Well . . . new place and everything . . .'

'Yes. That and . . .' Bridget giggles, partly from amusement and partly from the sheer tiredness. 'Oh, God, Carol: it just hadn't occurred to me.'

'What?'

'Well . . . she's never slept by herself before. Not in a room she doesn't know.'

Carol is drinking something with ice in it. Bridget hears the chink as she raises it to her mouth. 'Oh my God. So what did you do? Surely she's used to going to *sleep* by herself?'

'Well, yes . . . but not in a strange bed in a strange house. She's always just tucked up in my bed in our room, since Kieran left. You've never heard such shrieking.'

'I still live in Streatham, remember?' says Carol. 'I hear it every night.'

'It doesn't help that it's colder than a witch's tit. He's obviously had the heating off since the day I came down for the interview. We're going to have to go and buy some new bedclothes first thing tomorrow. As it is, I've got her sleeping under a couple of coats, and I've taken down the living-room curtains to put on my own bed. Bloody lucky the pipes haven't frozen, to be honest.'

'Surely it's warming up now?'

'I'm sure it would be if I could only find the boiler. It's obviously not on the same system as the house, but I'm damned if I can work out where it is. I'm too tired, to be honest. The lights were out when we got here and it took me half an hour of fumbling around in the dark with a cigarette lighter before I found the trip switch.'

'Oh, honey, how horrible. Were you scared?'

Bridget laughs. 'Naah. What would I be scared for, wandering about a huge strange house in the dark? And Yasmin was hanging on to my trousers every step of the way, howling. Actually, I had too much on my hands to think about being scared. It's pissing it down, here. Started raining on Dartmoor and didn't stop, and I wouldn't be surprised if the wind wasn't gale force. It practically took me off the road a couple of times when we were crossing Bodmin. I was more worried that we were going to get hit by a flying roof slate than anything else.'

'Have you eaten?'

'Heinz Tomato Soup and cheese on toast. Neither of us was very hungry. And she'd been eating crisps fairly solidly since Junction 5.'

'And she's asleep now?'

Bridget sighs. 'Yes. Though I've had to leave her bedroom door open and all the lights on. I don't suppose I'm going to be much longer myself.'

'Get yourself a drink and get in the bath,' Carol advises.

A lovely idea, thinks Bridget. A long hot bath is just what I need. And I'd have one if we had any hot water. And if the bath wasn't an inch deep in spiders. 'Yeah, you're right. That *is* what I need.'

'By the way, I tucked a present for you into Madam's left wellington. Half a bottle of vodka. Thought you might need it.'

'Oh, Carol. You shouldn't have.'

'It's only Asda,' says Carol, 'nothing posh or anything. I just thought . . . well, I knew you wouldn't have thought of anything like that yourself and I know what it's like trying to get to sleep somewhere new. Even if you aren't six years old.'

'You're a true friend. You know that?'

'Sure am. Still, I'll get my reward now I've got free summer hols for the rest of my life.'

'You know you can come, any time.'

Bridget suddenly feels lonely. The summer holidays are six months away. 'You know you're welcome,' she continues in a small voice. 'Can't you come sooner?'

'No,' says Carol, and Bridget's stomach lurches. 'You're not to get maudlin on me,' she continues. 'I'll be down as soon as we can both manage. You know I will.'

'Yes.' Bridget holds back a sniff, swipes the back of her hand across her eyes.

'It'll be fine. In the morning. Once you've got everything unpacked and started finding your way around. You're doing the right thing, you know you are.'

'Has he been round?' she asks, suddenly unable to stop herself from thinking of Kieran.

'You've only been gone half a day. He's hardly had time. And anyway, the pub's not let out, has it?'

'He's going to be so –'

'Yeah, well,' Carol cuts her off, 'it's nothing more than he deserves. And nothing I can't handle, either. Just stop it with that. That's *tired* thinking. Go and run that bath.'

'Of course I will.' No point in telling her just how grim things are looking right now. It'll be better in a couple of days.

'Pour yourself a nice big drink and take it in there with you. I guarantee you'll get off to sleep in no time, however cold it is.'

'Okay,' she says.
'I'll call you tomorrow. At least we know your phone works down there, eh?'
'It's not Siberia,' says Bridget. 'It's only Cornwall.'
A buffet of wind slaps into the side of the building, rattles the casements. There's no way she's going back out across that yard tonight to find Yasmin's wellies buried somewhere in the boot of the car.
'Sleep well,' says Carol.
'Thanks. You too.'
'That bloody car alarm's going off again,' she says. 'I doubt it. Just be grateful you're where you are. Honestly, Bridge. It won't be long before I'm envying you.'
In the middle of nowhere. With a wind that sounds like someone's scrabbling to get in through the roof. Oh, God, have I made a terrible mistake?
'Night night,' says Carol.
'Night,' she replies. Hangs up and sits, elbows on the tiny kitchen table and face in hands, while she allows a couple of fat self-pitying tears to roll over her fingers. She can't cry in front of Yasmin: has made a pact with herself that she will try not to. But that doesn't mean she doesn't want to, most minutes of most days. How did I end up so lonely? I was pretty, once, and popular, and now I'm the kind of person nobody notices when I walk by in the street. I don't even get noticed by builders any more: they fall quiet as I pass.
Not surprising, she thinks. The self-pity emanating from you would be enough to put anyone in their right mind off. Amazing, though. How short a time it takes. Ten years ago I would have dreaded passing building sites because of the attention I attracted. Now I feel the same way for exactly the opposite reason. Life with Kieran was like the drip drip drip of water on stone: you never notice the effects by watching them, but a decade of it was enough to wear my confident veneer through to the dull grey clay beneath. He was like a vampire: sucking my self-esteem to replenish his own.

She feels, in the cabin-like kitchen, like a sailor lost at sea. It's warm enough in here, for she's turned the oven on full whack and left the door open, but she knows that going out into the corridor will be a different matter. The wind, stepping up a gear, howls against the walls like a wild animal. She's always been a city child: lived with her mum and dad in Peckham until she was grown up, would probably have gone back there with Yasmin if she'd had the option. She's never been alone somewhere where the orange glow of streetlights and the occasional sound of passing footsteps couldn't give at least the illusion that someone was at hand. Out here, miles from anywhere . . . anything could happen and no one would know.

Abruptly, she pushes her chair back. It's the tiredness talking, like Carol said. This has to be better than Streatham. There's nothing worse than being surrounded by people and knowing that no one will help you. You're not to go down this road. You're still healthy, your daughter is beautiful and bright and loving and life is going to get better. It has to. Tomorrow we'll buy double-thick duvets and a couple of fan heaters and hot water bottles, and I'll get the kettle and the clothes and the TV from the car and we can start to make a little home here, at last. But tonight you must sleep.

Something clatters out in the yard, makes her jump. Don't be silly, she thinks. There's a wind. It's probably a branch or something, blown loose and bowling down the hill. And now there's rain rattling off the window like gravel thrown by a teenage lover. It doesn't mean anything. He's not followed you. He will have been at the office when you left. It's just nature, and you're in the middle of it.

She considers, for a moment, leaving the oven on overnight; turns it, reluctantly, off. No point in testing the fuse box; it obviously doesn't take much to make it trip.

Entering her bedroom is like stepping into a fridge: a month standing empty in early winter has left the whole house shivering with neglect. Pulling the curtains, she feels a blast of cold air from the window, creeping round the ancient casement. She remembers her father, one winter of her childhood before they could afford vinyl replacements, going round the house with clingfilm and Sellotape, sealing out the cold air. I'll get some tomorrow, she thinks, when we go to the supermarket. The list gets longer and longer.

Kicking her shoes off, she gets under the duvet, thick brocade curtains piled on top like an old-fashioned coverlet, fully dressed. Waits for the bedclothes to warm up, then struggles out of her jeans under the covers.

Normally she can't go to sleep unless she has at least brushed her teeth, but the prospect of facing the icy water in those taps is worse than the prospect of waking with a mouthful of fur. She stretches out on the mattress – it's not far off new, she notices, and comfortable. Her mattress in Streatham was so far gone – dimpled and stained from years of use – that she didn't even try to offer it to the second-hand man. Just left it to be the building society's problem.

We're going to be okay, she repeats to herself again. If you get a good night's sleep it will all look better. Switches off the light.

Darkness. Real, deep, velvet darkness of a sort she's never known. The bedroom curtains are thin, but nothing – no sign, even, that there is a village over the hill – penetrates the room. There's someone, she thinks. In the house, there's someone, I can feel it. They're hiding somewhere and I can only hear them when the lights are off.

Kieran used to do that: hide in the dark. He'd do it when they lived together, ambushing her from under the hall stairs, getting up in the night and following her, silently, when she went to pee or get a glass of water, jumping out and grabbing her from behind, hand over her mouth to stifle the scream. He thought it was funny, in the beginning. Hindsight's a powerful tool, isn't it? Allows her to kick herself for not noticing that his 'jokes' were the early signs of a bully's mentality. He thought a lot of what he used to do was funny. That was the excuse: you don't have a sense of humour. I can't help it if you can't take a joke. Christ, you wind me up. How can I live with someone who doesn't have a sense of humour? That's the thing with the abusers. If they did it from the off there would barely be a woman in the land who would let them stay. But it's the slow creep, the escalations so insidious that you don't see them, that get you, and trap you. Because he'd hold me, after, when I was shaking from the shock of it: he'd comfort me and soothe me and at the same time he'd laugh at me for being a baby.

And he'd never apologize.

What if it's him? What if he's here?

A sough of wind and a clatter and she's sitting up in bed, light on, heart pumping.

Don't be stupid. Don't be *stupid*. He can't get you here. He doesn't know where you are.

What was that?

The wind. It's the wind. Stop it.

So much house. That long, long corridor snaking from room to room. The shadowed attics. Anything could be happening and I'd never know. Anyone could be in here already and I'd never know.

You've locked the doors, Bridget. The doors to the outside and the doors that lead from the flat to the house. They're strong, stout doors and you'd hear if anyone tried to get through them. Stop it. *Stop it.*

Will I ever get used to this?

The clatter again, out in the yard. She jumps, bones rigid in her skin. Strains to hear. If I turn the light out I might be able to see what's out there.

And if I turn the light out I'll be in the dark.

Just stay here. Stay here where it's warm and tomorrow it'll be different. You'll see. In the daylight. It'll be fine.

Chapter Twelve

'They're here.'

Tessa drops her copy of *We Met Our Cousins* and trots over to the window. Stands on the window seat and leans her elbows on the sill, beside her brother's.

Hugh smells of roast beef again today, she thinks. Strange how boys always smell – *meaty*. Like they've taken a bath in dripping.

'Oh, horrid,' she says. 'Vaccies.'

'Euugh,' he agrees. 'If they think they're coming in here they've got another think coming.'

'Perhaps,' says Tessa 'they won't be *so* bad.'

'Not so bad? They're from *London*!'

'Oh,' says Tessa, 'yes.'

Cornwall is full of Londoners in the summer – well, was before the war started. Tramping about eating fish and chips and leaving gates open. And both the children have had experience of them at school: frightful name-droppers, overly concerned with dirt and fashion, at least until they're knocked into shape.

'Do you think we should go down?'

'Absolutely not,' Hugh declares. As both elder sibling and boy, his opinion counts for much in the Blakemore household. Even more so since Patrick Blakemore took his papers and went to join the war effort. 'Let's not set a precedent. They're not guests. They're evacuees.'

'Oh,' says Tessa. She feels a touch of disappointment. Rospetroc is isolated at the best of times – even more so now there's petrol rationing – especially as their mother has quite clear opinions (mostly based on size of house and decades of ownership) as to which of the locals one mixes with, and the summer holidays hang quite heavy on her hands. A little bit of her had been looking forward to the house filling up with children, even strange ones from London.

'Cuckoos in the nest,' says Hugh ominously.

'Look,' she says. 'Half of them've got their stuff in brown paper parcels. Haven't they heard of suitcases?'

'Maybe their suitcases got blown up. There *is* a war on, you know.'

They watch as their mother emerges from the front door and makes her way up the path. She has donned her best tweed skirt and a twinset in alpaca, once yellow, now faded to a sort of *café au lait* sepia.

'Look at old Peachment,' says Hugh. 'Do you think that's her best hat?'

'Can't be, surely?'

'I don't know. After all, it's not often she gets an invitation to Rospetroc, is it?'

Tessa glances at her brother. She's at an age where it's beginning to dawn on her that her family's assumption that it has been chosen by God and is therefore empowered to make any judgements it wishes on its neighbours might not actually represent the whole of the story.

Still, she thinks, Mrs Peachment is a frightful busybody. Says 'toilet' and 'pardon'. And it's an awful hat.

Silently, she cons her new housemates. Wonders if, despite the family's misgivings, one might turn out to be a friend: a companion to take the boat out, dam the stream, go hunting for birds' eggs in the hedges that form the boundary between the farm and the moor. Perhaps, she thinks, we'll end up making friends for life, even if they are Londoners. You can have things in common with people even if it doesn't look like it on the surface. Why, at school, I go on exeats with Susannah Bain when her mother comes down, and her father owns a brickworks in Manchester . . .

They don't look like a hopeful bunch, red-faced in their winter overcoats even though it's summer, their faces streaked with tears and the smuts from the train-stack.

One is even crying now. A stocky little girl with two thin plaits and drooping knee-socks, rubbing at her eyes with her sleeve.

'How pathetic,' she says. She didn't cry when she went to school, not once. Well, not where anyone could see her, anyway.

Then: 'Hang on,' she says, 'weren't there meant to be four of them?'

'Golly,' says Hugh. 'You're right. And look at the mater! Open the window! Hurry up!'

'No!' says Felicity Blakemore. 'Absolutely not! No!'

Margaret Peachment has been expecting this response. She is also at her wits' end.

'I'm sorry, Mrs Blakemore,' she says, 'but there really isn't anywhere else to put her.'

'Surely someone in the village . . .'

Mrs Peachment shakes her head. 'Believe me, I've tried everywhere already. The entire village is heaving with evacuees. If there was anywhere, I'd have left her there.'

Were anywhere, thinks Felicity Blakemore. *Were* anywhere. If you're going to impose on me in this manner, at least remember your grammar. This war is ghastly: suddenly all the Women's Institute-Mother's Union bourgeoisie are climbing all over us, chuffing about the place with their well-ironed chest bows and their Robin Hood hats, bossing people in the name of patriotism.

'I'll do my best,' says Mrs Peachment, 'to find somewhere else for her as quickly as possible.'

Which means never, of course. Once I accept her, that will be it. A fait accompli.

'But the fact is, Felicity, you are the only one with the spare capacity. Tregarden's been turned into an officers' mess and Croan is a convalescent hospital. You're just going to have to help me out.'

Spare capacity? What is she talking about? This is my *home*, not a tyre factory.

And I don't remember that we were ever on first name terms, for that matter.

'Well, if we're all supposed to be doing our bit,' she says pointedly, 'I don't see why you can't you take her yourself.'

Margaret Peachment sighs. She's known that Felicity Blakemore would be difficult. At least we've managed to get here before lunch, she thinks. Everyone knows there's no persuading her to do *anything* she doesn't want to do once the pre-prandials have started slipping down. 'I think you know very well that I already have a family of Jews from Stuttgart. Where precisely would you like me to put her, in a three-bedroomed cottage?'

'I don't know . . . surely you must have an attic . . .?'

Felicity Blakemore sneaks a look at the child. Lank mousy hair that clings in greasy tendrils to a sharp, foxy face. Her complexion is a pasty grey that speaks of underfeeding and lack of baths, and her clothes . . . the only thing she can think of when she looks at them is the furnace in the west kitchen.

There is what looks like a cold sore on her upper lip: the size of a farthing, cracked and suppurating. The child's expression is a mixture of suspicion, indifference and – something nasty. Something which tells Mrs Blakemore that she's spent her life so far fighting for scraps with the ferocity of the viciously neglected. In contrast, the other arrivals look well fed, well cared for, despite their much longer journey. One of the girls is crying and all four clutch toys and teddy-bears as though their survival depended on it, but their suitcases are bulging. This child has a suitcase, too – a half-rotten, cardboard one – but it's clear from the way it dangles from two of her fingers that it contains virtually nothing. How is she going to absorb someone like this into a decent household?

'This is intolerable,' she says. 'Simply intolerable.'

The child, realizing she's being studied, suddenly comes to life. Turns ice-chip eyes on her putative hostess and holds her gaze. And then she smiles with a mouth full of grey, snaggled stumps. *Intolerable,* thinks Felicity Blakemore, and allows herself a quiet, ladylike shudder.

'Well, I'm sorry about that,' says Mrs Peachment, 'but we all have to make sacrifices at the moment. There *is* a war on, you know.'

Mrs Blakemore takes two steps to the side of the group, as though doing so will cast a blanket of silence around her. Whoops, thinks Margaret Peachment. I'm not so sure the sherry decanter hasn't come unstoppered already. She's not a hundred per cent steady on those feet and it's only just gone midday.

'Don't tell me there's a war on! Do you think I don't know, with my husband away fighting it? And not a scrap of bacon or butter or a gallon of petrol to be had for *weeks*?'

'As I say, Felicity –' Margaret adopts her best matronly tones. It works in the village, after all. In the village, she is Someone – 'we all have to make sacrifices. And my own husband is at Biggin Hill, I would remind you.'

Privately, she thinks Felicity Blakemore the worst sort of snob, the sort that will be wiped out once this war is over and the new world order makes way for the hardworking salt-of-the-earth like herself. But in the meantime she needs to harness these qualities or be stuck with the problem. The entire village has found itself crowded out when faced with the prospect of this child from the Portsmouth docks. Even the vicar took one look and lost the milk of human kindness.

Besides, a small, ugly part of her wants very much to leave the girl here. It would serve Felicity Blakemore and her limited guest lists jolly well right.

She modulates her tones accordingly, realigns for a different angle of attack. 'I'd've thought,' she says, 'it was essential that the people who . . . the better part of society . . . would want to set an example. How am I going to persuade the rest of the neighbourhood to do their bit if its leading inhabitants . . .?'

The question hangs in the air.

The dirty girl scratches at her scalp and stares at the two of them.

'I *am* doing my bit.' Felicity, knowing she is fighting a losing battle, summons her last shred of patrician dignity. 'Four of them, I'm taking already. Four children and not *one* adult to help me with them. And the Glovers have handed in their notice.'

'Well, I daresay they can pull their weight,' says Mrs Peachment. 'You can have them doing chores in no time.'

'Oh yes,' says Felicity. 'They'll certainly be doing that.'

The weeping girl's neighbour bursts suddenly, and noisily, into tears as well. 'I want my mummy,' he bawls. 'Want to go *home*!'

'This is your home now, Ted,' says Mrs Peachment firmly. 'And this is Mrs Blakemore. She will look after you until your mummy can come and get you.'

Felicity has never been the most demonstrative of parents. That, after all, is what nannies are for.

'Do stop crying,' she says.

The volume increases. Ted punches at his eyes with clenched fists, draws streaks of train-smut down ruddy cheeks.

Felicity Blakemore, heart sinking, holds out a hand. 'Come on,' she says. 'Let's go to the kitchen. There's lardy cake.'

'Good, well, thank you,' says Mrs Peachment. 'Here are their ration books.'

Mrs Blakemore takes the documents, glances through them. Edward Betts. Pearl O'Leary. Geoffrey Clark. Lily Rickett. Vera Muntz. 'Which one is that?' She gestures toward the unwelcome newcomer.

'Lily,' says the girl. 'I'm Lily Ricke'.'

The accent is a strange amalgamated West Country cockney.

'Right,' says Mrs Blakemore. Turns her back on the children and commences leading them toward her house.

'I don't want you using the front door,' she tosses over her shoulder at the straggling crocodile that's formed behind her. 'You can come in through the scullery.'

'Eugh,' says Hugh. 'Even worse than I thought.'

'Pathetic,' says Tessa, 'cry-babies.'

'I'd keep away from the one at the back if I were you,' says Hugh. 'I'll bet you five bob it's got nits.'

Chapter Thirteen

Oh to sleep like a child again, so deep and sound that the world cannot intrude.

I guess I must have been sleeping more soundly than I'd expected myself, thinks Bridget. I didn't notice her come in during the night at all, but she must have been here, curled up next to me, for a while.

Yasmin barely moves when she kisses her on the head, strokes a lock of damp hair back from her face and creeps from under the covers. It doesn't seem so cold today. Of course it doesn't. There's watery sunshine leaking in round the curtains. The storm must have blown itself out in the night.

Bridget retrieves her trainers from under the bed, picks up the overnight bag she had the sense to pack with a few odds and ends of clothing and washing equipment, and carries them through to the bathroom. By her watch, it's half-past seven, and the sky is only just beginning to bruise through the window. Too early to call Tom Gordhavo and find out about the boiler.

Her teeth sing as she brushes them. She doesn't bother with much else: a spray of deodorant under the arms in place of soap and a rubber band in the hair in place of brushing. She feels grimed and greasy, sludged with unsatisfactory sleep, but her mood is better today: more hopeful. It's a new life. Not a satisfactory one yet, but change brings possibility and possibility is a start.

I'll have one more look for the boiler, she thinks, before Yas wakes up. It must be easier to find in daylight.

Everything is easier to find in daylight. The boiler turns out to be round the back of the flat door, in the junk room. She would have seen it immediately had the door been closed once she'd got the lights on, except that she had assumed that a boiler would be on an outside wall.

Sellotaped to the boiler door – not the most obvious place for it – is an envelope with her name scrawled on the front. Her new-old name, 'Ms Sweeny'. For a moment she doesn't even recognize herself, wonders who the envelope is intended for, then smiles wryly as she pulls it off, opens it. I'll be really free, she thinks, when I stop thinking of myself as a Fletcher. Let it be soon.

The hand is scrawly but clear: the sort of handwriting which comes of expensive schooling. It's from Tom Gordhavo, of course: a letter and what looks like a contract.

Dear Ms Sweeny, the letter reads, *welcome to Rospetroc. I would have been here to see you in in person but have had to go to Penzance for a few days. Please find enclosed our contract of work. Strictly we should have signed this before your arrival, but given the speed at which everything has happened, it wasn't really practicable. Anyway, I shall drop in on Wednesday afternoon: if you could have it ready for then, I would be greatly obliged.*

The house is still in something of a state, I'm afraid. Frances Tyler seems to have left halfway through clearing up after the last bunch of guests. I am sorry to have left it for you, but I've been busy with the estate myself, and – hence the need for a housekeeper in the first place – finding reliable help in the village, even on an ad hoc basis, isn't easy. Anyway, the first guests aren't due until Christmas week, so I don't doubt you'll be able to get the place shipshape again in the time. Some beds have been stripped, but all will need laundering and airing, and making up again closer to the arrival time. Otherwise it's really a matter of the duties we discussed when we met: cleaning, hoovering, dusting, re-laying the fires, giving the kitchens a thorough going-over. Basically getting everything into a state that holidaymakers will be happy with. If there are any obvious issues you're unclear about, we'll go through them on Wednesday. Yours sincerely, Tom Gordhavo.

Yours sincerely, she thinks. Well, there's posh. In the modern world you usually only get Yours Sincerely-ed when you're in some sort of trouble. She lays the letter down on a mahogany card table whose hinges have worked loose so the leaf lies slightly askew, and turns her attention to the boiler. It's old, but not as old as the monster which heats the main house. It has a thermostat, at least, and a tap at the side for the oil feed rather than the two-handed valve with which she struggled last night. She turns it and, frowning, presses the button to fire the pilot light.

A distant boom, like a bird scarer in a neighbouring valley, is followed by a grumbling roar.

'Yessss!' says Bridget out loud, punches the air. Small triumphs. The flat will begin warming itself soon: she tried one of those last-ditch hopeless acts of the despairing last night, and went round the whole place turning the radiators on in the hope that they would warm themselves by willpower alone. Hopefully Yasmin will sleep on in her cocoon of curtains, leave her time to explore her new domain.

The house is unchanged, it seems, since her visit two weeks ago. In the dining room, she notices that a line of china figurines on the dresser has been turned inwards, so that they stare out at her from the mirror which forms its back. It gives one a nasty feeling, the sight of these frozen faces, tiny shoulders hard and unforgiving. Their eyes, like those of a good portrait, seem to follow her as she crosses the room.

A tumble of bedclothes lies at the bottom of the dining-room stairs, thrown there by her predecessor in preparation for laundering. Pure cotton, she notices – her heart sinking at the thought of all that ironing – and sprinkled now with a coating of the dust that lies on all the surfaces.

It looks like it's been an eternity since Frances Tyler left. She churns the pile with a toe, kicks it further into the corner and goes on through the house.

In the drawing room, on the gargantuan teak coffee table, a dozen mugs and wine glasses, their contents dried to stains with sitting. Two ashtrays overflow on to the wooden surface. A half-burnt log lies in a bed of ash. Cushions lie scattered and squashed as though the house's occupants had merely gone to bed after a big night rather than packed up their suitcases and driven back to London. The mugs have had milk in them. Even in a room the size of her old flat, she can smell their yoghurty must. She finds a tray – sticky, with ring-marks bleached into the wood by bottle bottoms – on the side table, clears everything on to it. No point in leaving something as vile as this lying about when there's a dishwasher near at hand. If nothing else she can at least put them out of her eyesight.

In the scullery, she rifles in the undersink cupboard and finds a roll of black bin-liners, a quarter pack of Persil and a can of spray starch. Something, at least, to be going on with until Wednesday. Presumably there are stocks of cleaning stuff somewhere, but she's damned if she's found them yet. Anyway, at least she can do a rinse cycle on the dishwasher and get the bin up and running. She tears a bag off and takes it through to the kitchen.

The bin is already running. Another couple of days and it would be doing it literally. When she lifts the lid off the chrome dustbin, the stench is enough to drive her back a couple of paces, force her to take the Lord's name in vain.

'Jesus God,' she says. Gulps, gags.

Despite the cold, the smell is vicious. The bin is halfway full. She glimpses a chicken carcass, green, nestling on a bed of blueish, orange-streaked fur before she slams the lid back down.

Bridget scurries across the room, slams the taps on full and grips the cold china edge of the butler's sink while her stomach does its best to rip its way out of her body via the navel. She gags, once, twice, feels a chill sweep down her upper arms. Her tongue seems to have doubled in size, to be blocking her airways. She coughs, from the diaphragm. The chill has been replaced by a fine sweat, now.

She bends down, takes a deep draught from the cold tap. Delicious well-water, soft and peaty.

'Christ, that was close,' she says out loud. Turns back and looks at the bin as though it were a troll in the corner. She'll have to do it at some point. But not until she's fully prepared. How can someone just leave a house like this? This Frances must have been a total slut. Total. I'd never leave a house like this for someone else to find. I even scrubbed down my skirting boards when I left Streatham, and that was for the building society. She must have been a total slag.

Or she left in a serious hurry.

She eyes the fridge. It hums gently beside the bin, getting its temperature back down after the power outage.

Don't let there be food in it.

Of course there's food. People always leave food at the end of short-term rentals. It's a form of tip. Often the only form of tip. And anyway, the vegetable basket under the sink contains potatoes, carrots and an onion, all sprouting, all blackening.

What have I let myself in for?

Crossing the room feels like crossing the steppes on the way to battle.

Bridget pulls down a sleeve and holds it across her face. She's had enough nights without electricity to know how quickly a fridge can turn. Especially when it contains . . .

Milk. The remains of some salad vegetables, little more than an auburn sludge in the drawer. Phosphorescent bacon. What was once pâté, probably, but is now merely something that lurks.

I think that might have been trifle.

Oh, God, no. It's fish pie. Oh my God.

Whatever is in the freezer, it's melted, collapsed, melded together, frozen again. It's black and faintly viscous. She slams the door, leans against the top. Breathes.

She knows already what the dishwasher will contain. Doesn't put herself through the ordeal of verifying it. Simply checks that the door is firmly closed and sets the dial to a full-heat pan wash. Even if it is empty, the machine itself will benefit from a cycle after sitting unused for so long. But she's pretty certain that it isn't, that whatever has been left in there will take more than one cycle to become safe.

I'll buy a face mask in Wadebridge. Food, bedclothes, fan heaters, face mask, washing powder. Wellington boots. Disinfectant.

She takes another drink from the faucet, waits while her churning stomach comes to a rest. Goes to see what other horrors the house holds.

Soap rings in the bathrooms. Mildew on unaired shower curtains. Carpet slightly crunchy underfoot. A window sill full of dead flies in the pink bedroom. Frances must have been letting things go long before she left. There are signs everywhere: dried flowers on the landing whose predominant colour scheme is dustbath grey; fingermarks by the light switches. The door to the attic lies slightly ajar. She pushes it to, makes her way up the corridor. Glances in at the bedrooms as she passes them. Not too bad. Quilts stripped back, hanging over bed-ends; pillows stacked on chairs. Some of the mattress protectors look like they've seen a bit of use, but there's nothing here a bit of Oxi-Action won't shift. This'll be okay. Once I've got the first dreadful push over with I'll be able to –

She stops dead in the doorway of the final bedroom, the one at the end of the corridor, just before the door to her own flat. It's the room with the four-poster. The one which must always be claimed by the alpha couple when they arrive, because it has the obvious look of a master bedroom about it.

'Good God,' she says.

Someone's had a riot in here. It looks like someone's gone down to the village and brought back a gang of bored teenagers and a couple of gallons of scrumpy. The tester is ripped from its hooks and has been thrown across the back of an upturned armchair. Curtains hang crazy from a sagging pole. Someone's taken a vase and simply thrown it into the middle of the bed. The mattress is stained, from the looks of it irrevocably, where the contents – melted, blackened arums and a couple of pints of brackish water – have landed and been left to rot. Bedclothes lie heaped on an upended armchair. A portrait has been knocked off its hook: hangs diagonally, its surprised subject teetering over a chest-of-drawers, cast-plaster frame chipped and scratched.

In the far corner, a door hangs open. She didn't notice it, when she was doing the tour with Tom Gordhavo; unpanelled, it is covered with the same paper that decorates the walls, has a handle of glass. Beyond, the space yawns pitch-black. It's a cupboard of some sort, dug into the thick outer wall of the house. She steps over, peers inside.

Black. Damp-smelling. You wouldn't want to store anything that might decay in here. It's the sort of cupboard where they lock children in early Victorian novels. Bet there are spiders, too.

She closes the door. Now she is looking, she sees that there are bolts on it, top and bottom. She shrugs, shoots them, turns back to survey the devastation.

What do I do here? Nothing I can do, really, except perhaps clear up that vase. I'll have to show it to Mr Gordhavo before I do anything or he'll be blaming me for the damage.

Outside the door, she catches the scutter of running feet. Someone – someone small and light – is running down the corridor, into the depths of the house. Bridget checks her watch, is surprised to find that almost an hour has passed since she got up. Yasmin must have woken and come through the flat door looking for her.

'That you, darling?' she calls.

The footsteps stop. Silence.

'Yas? I'm in here. In the big room.'

Silence. Yasmin is listening. She can feel her listen. It's unlike her not to speak. Yasmin is a great talker.

'Yasmin?'

She approaches the door, pauses just before she passes through. Something stops her from going out. She listens. It's quiet out there. No movements, no rustles. Maybe I'm hearing things. 'Yasmin?'

Someone giggles.

Bridget leaps through the doorway, hits the carpet, fingers splayed like a leaping lion.

'Boo!' she shouts.

The corridor is empty.

Chapter Fourteen

I don't believe it. I don't *believe* it. I feel – *invaded*. There's no other word for it. *Invaded*. My house will never feel clean again. It's as though she's brought the war *with* her. I might as well have a house full of Nazis. Worse. At least a Nazi would have the self-respect to be ashamed. This one – my God, I open up my home and not an ounce of gratitude do I receive. Not even the tiniest bit of embarrassment.

God knows what else she's brought with her. Syphilis, probably, and consumption. I can't believe I actually have a *prostitute's* child under my roof. We'll all be going down with nameless diseases carted in from the Portsmouth docks. There have *never* been lice at Meneglos school. Never. We'll be a laughing stock.

'Disgusting,' she says out loud. 'You're disgusting.'

Lily Rickett, hair tangled and sticking out from her head like a bird's nest, glares at her from the other side of the scullery. Her cheeks are livid with colour, but despite the foregoing ten minutes' manhandling, there is no sign of tears. Lily doesn't cry. Hasn't since she was five years old. Crying, she has discovered, gets you nothing, apart from a slap round the ear, most times. 'Give it a rest,' she says.

'Come here.'

'No.'

'Come *here*, Lily.'

'No. You're not coming near me with that thing.'

Felicity Blakemore glances down at the nit comb, a mat of ripped-out follicles wound round the metal teeth. They look like the pelt of some feral animal. They look, in fact, exactly like the sort of thing that would come from the head of this feral child. How do people manage to bring their children up wild like this, in this day and age? She hasn't noticed that she has been gripping the comb so hard that her palm is indented with two dozen sharp little pinpricks.

'Come on,' she says. 'This is all your fault in the first place. If you hadn't imported nits into this house –'

'Come one step nearer,' says Lily, 'and I'll bite you.'

'Don't be ridiculous.'

'I mean it.'

'It has to be done. You can't walk around like that for the rest of your life. I've already had to do it to the others, thanks to you.'

'Yeah, well,' says Lily, 'bet you didn't try and rip their hair out by the roots while you was at it.'

She feels a surge of rage. 'Well, *they* didn't give their – *parasites* – to everybody else.'

'How d'you know? Why you blaming me? Coulda been any of 'em. I'm not the only kid in this house, you know. Coulda been one of *your* precious kids.'

'Don't be ridiculous.'

'What?'

An eyeballing pause. Faced with such naked insolence, Felicity Blakemore struggles to hold on to her training. Has to wait and grit her teeth before her voice is controlled enough to speak again.

'The others may not come from the best walks of life,' she says, 'but it is quite evident that there is only one of you who has never been familiar with soap and a flannel. Now, come here. The sooner you do, the sooner it will be over.'

Lily folds her arms, glares out her defiance. 'No.'

'If you won't do it voluntarily, I shall have to make you.'

'Be my guest. Like to see you try.'

'Very well,' she snaps. Shoots the upper bolt on the garden door, out of child's-arm-reach. Lily makes a lunge for the kitchen door, but too late. Felicity Blakemore has her skinny arm in a grip of steel, swings her round behind her as she calls.

'Hugh! Hughie, come here a moment!'

Lily flails and kicks uselessly at her jailer. 'Get off! Get off get off get off!'

The door is pushed open and Hugh appears. 'Hello!' he says. He's five years older than Lily, and almost twice her size. A lifetime of chips and dripping has left Lily small and pale in comparison with her peers.

'Hold this child,' orders his mother.

'With pleasure,' replies the son. He enjoys a bit of rough-and-tumble. Always has. He already had a reputation for toughness at his prep school which stood him in good stead when he went up to Eton last year. He stands, meaty hands on chunky hips, and cons his houseguest. 'Giving you trouble, is she?'

'Apparently she thinks she's too good for the nit comb.'

'Right,' says Hugh. 'We'll see about that.'

'Please,' says Lily, a little too late, 'it hurts.'

'Well, perhaps,' says Mrs Blakemore, 'you should have thought about that before you brought lice into this house.'

Even Hugh can see the faulty reasoning behind this statement. But he's at an age where the stupidity of adults is more useful than contemptible, and he lets it pass. 'If she doesn't want her hair combed out,' he tells his mother, 'there is an alternative.'

It takes a moment for the statement to sink in, then Lily dashes for the outside door. Jumps for the bolt, fails, jumps again, then turns, teeth bared, back pressed to the wall. Like a cornered rat, thinks Mrs Blakemore. In the stables, when we set the terriers on them.

Hugh crosses the flags in two strides, is on the girl like a ferret on a rabbit. Lily plummets sideways against the sink, kicks out with naked feet, screams like an angry ape. The ferocity of her self-defence is enough – almost – to make him loose his grip. But then, blood up, he tightens up again. He's had plenty of practice – on his sister, on the village boys, on the younger pupils at school – and he enjoys the fight. Enjoys, if he were to admit it, physical confrontation more than anything else in the world. It makes him feel strong, vital, *alive*. And in the last year or so, there's been another element creeping into his enjoyment.

'C'mere,' he says.

She scratches at his face, receives instant punishment with the back of a hand. 'Stop it!' he hisses. Gets a wrist in each hand and hauls them backward into a full nelson. And now she's panting and wriggling, bent double, and he is looking triumphantly at his mother. Only he and Lily know that the struggle, the animal smell of her, has given him an immediate and urgent adolescent erection.

'Good boy,' says Felicity. 'Good. Now, you just hold her there while I fetch the scissors.'

She's bony in his grip. Her body heaves as she pants, rubs inadvertently against him. 'Bastard,' she says. With a mother like hers, she knows all too well what it is that's pressing into her buttocks. 'Dirty bastard.'

Hughie smiles. 'You'd know all about dirty bastards,' he says. 'After all, you're a *real* one. If you'd bothered to have a wash, ever in your life, you wouldn't be in this position.'

'Oh, but I would,' she says. 'You'd make sure of that, wouldn't you?'

He's annoyed. Tugs at her arms until she squeals at the pain, then pulls her harder against him to show her who's boss.

Hughie likes having evacuees. Once you're at the top of the pecking order, your ambitions have to turn to expanding the number of people below you.

His mother comes back, comb in one hand and kitchen scissors, sturdy for cutting up the carcasses of dead birds, in the other. Lily, catching sight of her, bucks hard against her jailer, kicks out in futility.

'Now, don't struggle,' says Felicity Blakemore. 'Struggling will only make it worse.'

Chapter Fifteen

It's not that they're unfriendly, exactly. More – silent. If this were Streatham, she knows that the silence would mean that the staff were checking them out as potential shoplifters, but here . . . Bridget thinks the middle-aged woman behind the till is more interested in whether she's holiday or home. It's not worth wasting much breath on someone who will never come back, after all.

She can't help thinking of *The League of Gentlemen* as she finds herself the subject of such scrutiny. *It's a local shop, for local people* . . . the phrase keeps circling her head as she circles the shelves. Meneglos is not a centre of culinary greatness, of that much she is certain. If the village has been invaded by second-homers, they must go up to Padstow or Port Isaac for their polenta and sun-dried tomatoes because there is nothing here that you wouldn't find in the average school kitchen. Then again, there's nothing here that Yasmin would refuse to eat, which is something of a bonus. And nothing with an eat-by date that actually requires attention. Even the fish, five miles from the sea, is tinned: tuna in brine and two types of sardine.

She wanders the aisle – there is only one, with a fridge to the right and a display stand of postcards teetering in the middle – and looks at what's available. Yasmin, her eye caught immediately by a display – well, pile – of clotted cream fudge, stays by the door, huge eyes drinking in the child-snatching prints of puppies and kittens which decorate the boxes. Probably, thinks Bridget, thinks there are actual kittens nestled in among the sugary treats inside.

Things in tins and things in packets. Lots of them. It's a Seventies convenience retail dream. Fray Bentos steak and kidney pies. Baked beans: plain, curried, BBQ, pork sausage, all-day breakfast. Green Giant niblets. Soupernoodles. Sandwich Spread. Shippam's paste. Tinned carrots. Marrowfat peas. Angel Delight. She half-expects to see a selection of dust-covered sachets of Rise 'n' Shine and Vesta just-add-water freeze-dried chicken curry, but instead the chiller cabinet bows to twenty-first-century ill health with stacks of agent orange Sunny D and cook-chill lasagne. Cottage cheese with pineapple. Ski yoghurt. Mattesons smoked pork sausage. Try saying *that* without saying mmm . . .

There's a lady sitting on a bar stool behind the toughened glass of the post office counter. It's more there in order to show where the counter is than as an actual security measure. If anyone wanted to rob the place, all they'd have to do would be to step through the open door to her cage. Bridget looks up from the lackadaisical display of lettuces and onions and catches her eye. Smiles.

'If there's anything you can't find,' says the lady, 'just ask.'

'Thank you,' she says. 'I think I'm fine at the moment.'

'Well,' says the lady, 'you know we're here.' Goes back to leafing through her big book of picture stamps.

Bridget lines the bottom of a wire basket with a copy of the *Mirror*, starts loading up. She won't bother with Wadebridge Tesco until Monday. Figures there won't be so many crowds. Beans. Bacon. Eggs. Spaghetti. She almost goes with spaghetti hoops until she notices that there are three pots of pesto on the top shelf, in among the cook-in-sauces. Pesto: the Marie Rose sauce of the Nineties. Even Meneglos would have caught up.

She needs to hurry up. Yasmin has moved on to the rack of chocolate at the front of the till. In the chiller, three types of pasty. Gosh, she thinks, I really am in Cornwall: I can't think of a time when I last saw a pasty that wasn't made by Ginsters. She decides to try each of them for supper tonight, with the beans: drops them into the basket. And then she thinks: sod it. Let's have some clotted cream. Life can't all be subsistence rations. Scoots back to pick up flour and jam and cream of tartar. This afternoon Yasmin will be introduced to the delights of scones. Now that she doesn't have to worry that the oven will make the meter run out quicker. Frozen peas. Fish fingers. Oven chips. A big loaf of Hovis. She has more than enough for the weekend, now.

The lady at the till takes her basket, begins, very slowly, to ring the items up and stack them, one by one, in a blue-and-white-striped plastic bag. 'Staying locally, are you?'

It's a local shop, for local people . . .

'Yes,' says Yasmin.

'Yes – well, no,' says Bridget. Sees her London accent noted, sees the information disappoint. 'We've just moved in, actually. Up the road.'

The woman perks up. 'Really? I hadn't heard anything had been sold . . .'

'No, I'm caretaking. Up at Rospetroc. Rospetroc House.'

She shifts on her stool. 'Oh, *right*.'

She rings up the bread, the peas. Giving herself some thinking time, observes Bridget.

'And how you settling in, then?'

'Fine,' she answers. 'Well – we only got here last night. Didn't find the boiler till this morning, though.'

'Bet you were freezing, big old place like that.'

Bridget laughs.

The woman leans round her. 'Ivy! Come out here! We've got the new housekeeper at Rospetroc come in!'

Ivy closes her book, comes out to greet her.

'Hello!' she says. It's a quizzical hello, as though Bridget were an old friend who'd suddenly turned up somewhere unexpected. 'How you getting on, then? Ivy Walker.'

'Hello.' She shakes her hand, surprised by the friendliness. She used the same corner shop in Streatham for seven years and the owners had only graduated up to a faint nod of recognition by the time she left. 'Bridget. Bridget Fl— Sweeny.'

Kicks herself inwardly. I'm going to have to get a lot better at this if it's going to work.

The woman behind the till reaches out and shakes her hand as well. 'Chris Kirkland. Welcome to Meneglos.'

'Thanks.'

Ivy bends at the waist, brings her face down to a level with Yasmin's. 'And who's this?'

'Yasmin,' says Yasmin, taking a rapid step back. She's not used to strange adults coming so far into her space. Bridget's not thought about it before, but people in London are scrupulous about keeping their distance from children for fear of being strung up.

'Hello, Yasmin,' she says. Reaches up to the counter and gets down the giant sweet-jar of lollipops. Unscrews the lid and offers them. 'Would you like one of these?'

Yas's eyes are out on stalks. Then: 'No, thank you,' she says.

Ivy looks taken aback.

'Mum says I'm not to take sweets from strangers,' says Yas.

Chris laughs. 'Too right,' she says. 'And you've got your manners, too, I see.'

'It's all right,' Bridget assures her. 'They aren't strangers any more. You can have one.'

The jar is lowered to within her reach again. Yasmin takes her time about her choice. Considers each sweet in turn before finally reaching in and plucking out a blue one.

'Thank you,' she says, unprompted.

Oh, bless you, my little darling. You don't know how grateful I am for this first impression. It'll be all round the village about us in no time; thank you so much for choosing this moment to not have a screaming tantrum.

'So are you at school, then, my love?' asks Chris. Yasmin, mouth clamped round her lollipop, nods, deep and long.

'She's in Year Two.'

'Sending her to the village school, are you?'

'Well, I was hoping . . . what do you think the chances are?'

'Oh, I daresay. It's not exactly Eton. You don't have to put them down before birth *here*.'

'Put 'em down,' says Ivy. 'I always liked that phrase. Always gives me an image of the upper classes drowning their young in a bucket, like kittens.'

Please don't let Yasmin have heard that. We've quite enough trouble with kittens as it is.

To her relief, Yasmin has found a pile of Barbie magazines, has lost interest in the grown-ups.

'Just pop in Monday morning,' says Chris. 'They break up Wednesday, so you're in luck. If there's no one in the office, go and knock on the headmistress's door: it's the house by the school gates. Blue door. You can't miss it. Mrs Varco, that's her name.'

'Will she get in, this late in the year?'

'It's the law,' says Ivy simply. 'You're in the catchment area. They'll just squash another chair round a table and away you go.'

'Thing is, there isn't a choice down here,' says Chris. 'Not like in London. No worries about avoiding the sink schools. Here it's whatever there is or there's private. Lucky for you, Meneglos is a good one.'

'Well, they don't come out swearing like pirates, anyway. Not like over at Wadebridge.'

The pair of them fall quiet in contemplation of the urban degeneration of the local market town. Tut and roll their eyes.

'So what sort of state is the old house in, then?' asks Ivy Walker. 'I heard Frances Tyler left in something of a hurry.'

The two women exchange a barely perceptible mutual eye-flicker. Bridget only just registers it before it's gone.

'Not great,' she says. 'She obviously left halfway through pretty much everything.'

'That'll be a lot of work for you, then.'

'Mmm. Well, it's what I'm paid for.'

'True enough,' says Ivy. 'He was down here trying to get someone to come up and do it before you arrived. Didn't have much luck, I expect.'

'I'm surprised,' she fishes, 'that no one round here wanted the job.'

The flicker again.

'Oh, I wouldn't be, dear,' says Chris, slightly hurriedly. 'It's not much of a salary, if you think about it. It's okay as a live-in wage, with all your bills covered, but everyone around here's got somewhere to live anyway, or they wouldn't be here, would they?'

'Yes,' says Ivy. 'And besides, that isolation thing's more of a city-folk fantasy than it is for people like us. Most country people would rather live in a village. A bit of life. Someone around. You know.'

'You're very cut off up there,' says Chris. 'You need to watch it. You can get cut off completely if it snows, with that hill to get up. And the power's not exactly reliable up there. You must make sure you've got plenty of candles and stuff because you can lose it altogether for a couple of days, sometimes.'

'Oh, I don't mind,' she says. 'After London it feels like a luxury.'

'I daresay it does,' says Ivy. 'You couldn't pay me to live up there, personally.'

Chris laughs. 'Well, someone *is* paying her, Ivy. I don't suppose she'd be there if they wasn't.'

Chapter Sixteen

The car alarm goes off and she knows he's back. It's taken months for her to realize that there's a correlation between the alarm going off and Kieran's visitations, but of course there is. That bloody idiot in the first-floor flat must leave the door open when he goes down to switch it off, and then Kieran must use the opportunity to sneak in and hide in the understairs cupboard.

Shit, she thinks. I knew it would come down to me in the end. I told her I didn't mind, but I do. He's going to be really, really angry and I'm going to have to deal with it.

The guy downstairs always takes five minutes to come down and sort his alarm out. Carol has a faint suspicion that it might be deliberate, that he wants his neighbours to know exactly who owns the Audi parked in the street, but it's more likely, she supposes, that he sleeps in the nude and he's lazy. She's seen him a couple of times, trying to turn the alarm off with the remote control on his key fob, though doing so has only ever unlocked and locked the doors in the hundred or so times he's woken up the street with his show-off security. She needs to flush Kieran out before he jogs down the steps, Calvin Kleins and black satin robe covering his fake-tan gym skin, and leaves the door hanging open while he does it. It's hard to credit that he wouldn't have noticed his former neighbour lurking when he came in, but he never has. Can't see beyond his own self-interest, that one.

She goes to the window, throws back the curtains.

Someone ducks down into the dark spot formed by the wheelie bins and the hedge. So that's how he does it. Of course.

She slides the window up. Leans out.

'Kieran?' she shouts.

No voice in response, but she feels a freezing in the dark place behind the bin. He is there: I know he is. And he's heard me, but somehow he thinks that if he stays still enough I won't know he's there.

'Kieran?' she shouts again. 'I know you're down there.'

Still no reply.

'Get the fuck away from here, Kieran,' shouts Carol. 'She's not here.'

Now there's a definite stir behind the bins. He heard that all right.

The front door opens and her downstairs neighbour appears on the step. Looks up at the sound of her voice and sees her leaning out of the window. Folds his arms, stares up. Carol struggles to remember his name. He has never, after all, introduced himself to her or to any of his neighbours. All she has to go by is the sheaves of junk mail – credit card offers, loan offers, brochures for expensive holidays – that pile up on the front doormat.

'Nick,' she says, 'shut the door behind you.'

He looks a bit surprised that she has called him by name. Goggles at her like a blowfish, starts down the steps.

'Seriously,' says Carol, 'close the door. You may not realize, but there's someone behind the wheelie bins.'

He jumps. He actually left his skin for a second there, she thinks. If there's one thing a yuppie is more scared of than car thieves, it's muggers.

'Shit,' says Carol. 'Come out from there, will you?'

Kieran stands up, steps out.

Nick bolts up the steps. Stands half-in and half-out of the door, wrapped around it like small child in desperate need of the lavatory. They both look at Kieran. Carol suppresses an urge to laugh. He looks absurd tonight. He's always suffered from man-of-action fantasies – action that never got further than a spell in the TA – and tonight he has dressed for it. He is wearing black. Black jumper, black jeans, black shoes and – she almost shouts with laughter when she sees this – a black beanie hat covering his black hair. My God, she thinks: all he needs now is a few stripes of mud on his cheeks and he'd do as a stand-in for Ross Kemp.

'Fuck off, Kieran,' she says.

Kieran walks forward, stands on the path, arms crossed defensively across his body. 'Don't tell me to fuck off,' he says.

'Fuck off,' she repeats.

'I just want to see my little girl,' says Kieran.

'Not at one o'clock in the morning you don't,' says Carol.

The car alarm is still shrieking. Nick appears to be at a loss as to what to do. He glances at the car, glances at Carol, glances at Kieran standing between him and the street, stays rooted to the spot.

'You don't know anything about it,' says Kieran.

'Yes I do,' says Carol, 'believe me, I do. You've got a restraining order out on you, Kieran, and you just won't pay attention to it, will you? You've only got yourself to blame.'

'I just,' repeats Kieran, 'want to see my fucking kid.'

'Well, you can't,' she says. 'She doesn't want to see you. And anyway, she's not here. Neither of them are.'

She knows that she's being harsh, but she is so angry – with him, with the situation, with his pig-headed thuggery, the way he thinks his wife and child are his belongings to do with as he will, with the fact that she's been left to break the news because Bridget is too afraid of his reaction to do it herself – and she can't help it: she feels like he's getting everything he deserves. Everything. No, not even half of everything.

'They've gone away,' she finishes, spitefully. 'Gone to get away from *you*.'

For a moment, the only sound is the shriek of the alarm. Then: 'What do you mean?' he asks, and his voice has suddenly dropped. No longer the wheedling, no longer the mistreated Daddy. Both she and Nick hear the edge of threat in his voice.

'Gone away,' she repeats. 'Moved away. Moved out. Handed the keys back and buggered off.'

'What do you mean?'

'You heard me,' she shouts. 'Now piss off and leave us all in peace.'

I'm not handling this well, she thinks. It's one in the morning and I'm knackered, and I'm probably making things worse. But fuck it. Since when did Kieran deserve the softly-softly approach?

A window goes up next door. A voice, heavy with sleep, bellows: 'Shut the fuck up, all of you! Do you know what time it is? There are people trying to sleep here!'

'Sorry,' Carol shouts back, 'this won't take long.'

'What do you mean, won't take long?' Another voice, a woman's, emboldened by her neighbour's intervention, drifts down from the attic window two doors up.

'What do you mean, won't take long?' asks Kieran.

'Shut up! All of you! Go to sleep!' bellows the first voice. 'And turn that faahking car alarm off!'

'You can fuck off and all,' shouts Kieran. Starts toward the door.

Nick, seeing him approach, darts back inside the hall, slams it shut in his face. Carol, now that there's a barrier between her and the street, goes to her own front door, comes out on to the stairs. Nick's physical presence emboldens her. He may be a useless bugger, but now he's here there's no way he can wriggle out of being involved.

The banging starts. Kieran hammering on the front door. Nick leans against it, eyes bulging, sweat on his Youth Serumed forehead. He looks more scared than I feel, thinks Carol.

'Call the police,' he stutters. 'For God's sake call the police. He's trying to get in!'

Great, she thinks. There were a few times when we would have been grateful if you'd done that yourself.

Nonetheless she sets off down the stairs as the hammering goes up a notch, the sound of kicking adding to it. Kieran's rage is mounting. She steps past Nick, puts a finger on the intercom button. Should've got those mortise locks, she thinks. Should have got that burglar chain.

'Go away, Kieran,' she says again. 'They're not here any more. They've gone away. There's nothing here for you any more.'

A renewed bombardment shakes the door. Kieran's voice, all control gone now, howls like a wolf through the wood. 'Let me in! Let me in! I wanna see my kid! Let me in, you bitch!'

The hall light timer switch goes off. Even in the dark, she sees the whites of Nick's eyes. He's going to have handled this totally differently by tomorrow morning, she thinks. By the time he's in the office, he'll have seen Kieran off single-handed.

'Let me in!' bellows Kieran. 'Let me fucking in!'

And further away, off on Streatham High Road, the sound of an approaching siren.

Chapter Seventeen

She's locked back in the old dream. The reliving. Night after night, over and over, like a video image stuck on loop: his teeth bared, the fist drawn back, the crunch of contact, the red. Over and over. His vulpine face looming at her out of the dark, rushing at her, pouncing . . .

She thinks she might have screamed. Something has woken her. And then she remembers.

He was here, she thinks. He was here. I heard him hammering on the door, shouting to be let in. But now there's nothing but the wind. And the sweat on the bed-sheets. And the darkness. Velvet, enveloping darkness. The sort of darkness she imagines the blind see. She can make out nothing in her bedroom: no streetlight filters round the curtains, no red alarm clock LED creating its own tiny oasis of normality. No sounds: just the sobbing of the gale and the sound of her own breathing.

He's here. He's here.

She reaches into the darkness to turn on the light, clutches only air. Feels the panic grip once again at her throat. *It's gone. It's gone. The world has gone while I was asleep . . .*

And then she remembers. You're not in Streatham any more. You're in Cornwall. The light is on the other side of the bed.

She reaches out again, to the left this time, finds the familiar shape of her bedside lamp and presses the button. Breathes again. Collapses against the pillows.

Suddenly, the room, which felt cavernous as Hades

when she couldn't see its boundaries, closes back in again, becomes comforting. She likes this room already. With its tongue-and-groove panelling and the sound of the wind tossing the foliage outside, she feels as though she is on a boat, way out to sea, safely distant from London, from Kieran, from fear. This will be our haven. I know it. This will be our sanctuary.

Bridget begins to relax against the pillows. He cannot find us. We are safe and he can only find me in my dreams, and I am awake and we are safe again.

She picks up her watch from where it lies on the bed-side cabinet – the clock is still buried somewhere, at the bottom of one of the bin-liners in the living room – and checks the time. 1.30 a.m. Here I am again, awake, in the small hours. How long will it be before I learn to sleep again? When will I go to bed and close my eyes and stay here, resting, without one ear open for invasion? I've got out of the habit. So many nights spent waiting for the bang of the door, the thunder of fists, the bay of his voice.

It'll take time, Bridget. It'll be a long, long time before you sleep the whole night through.

There's a packet of valerian tea by the kettle, bought in the health food shop in Wadebridge under the advice of a girl who looked as though she were barely old enough to be reading, let alone prescribing to strangers. She throws the covers back, gets out of bed and pads through to the kitchen.

The wind is very strong tonight. It hadn't occurred to her that warm, friendly Cornwall, the destination hundreds of thousands of the British dream of for its Riviera delights, could be so inhospitable in the winter. But of course it is, locked between the Bristol Channel and the wild west-English one: on the edge of a wasteland famous for treachery and exposure deaths. These rocky shores have always provided a rich shipwreck harvest. Only an untamed part of the country could have gone on for so long, cutting the throats of floundering sailors and plundering their cast-up cargo to supplement their scratch-farm existence. When she was a kid – before reading became uncool, before the death of her parents threw her prematurely into a world of adult cares, before Kieran – she used to devour the books of Daphne du Maurier, swallow with relish those tales of distance and derring-do. Funny, really, that she has only just noticed that she is living in the place where many of those tales were set. They even passed signs for Jamaica Inn on the road down here.

She fills the kettle, presses the tit and sits at the kitchen table to wait for it to boil. Sitting there, she realizes that she is actually, for the first time since the plan to come down here was put into action, hungry. Genuinely hungry. Not just knowing-she-needs-to-feed-herself-to-keep-going hungry, but hungry with a relish and a longing so intense that she barely remembers the last time she felt a feeling so strong.

Poached eggs on toast, that's what she wants. Her mouth waters at the thought of runny yolks exploding into a warm pool of butter and Marmite, the farinaceous comfort of heavy wholemeal bread fresh from the toaster. Extraordinary how the simplest of pleasures can have such intense sensuality at their very core. She goes to the fridge, gets a couple of slices of bread from the bag and pops them under the grill.

The wind raises its voice, blats against the window like a passing express train. Involuntarily, though the room is warm and she is well wrapped up, she shivers. Then she smiles. Gosh, this is nice. I can't remember when . . . oh, Yasmin, this will be good. It will be a happy time. Our first good winter: we can do all those British winter things: toasting crumpets in front of an open fire; snowballing; running through the rain in hats with ear flaps, wind-chapped cheeks and eyes bright with the cold. This is so right. It's so right . . .

The kettle clicks off. She stands once again, starts her tea off brewing and fills a pan with boiling water ready for the eggs.

It can all be this simple, she thinks. Here, in our haven:

we just do an honest day's work for an honest day's pay and enjoy the pleasure of the simple life.

It is wonderful. Almost heavenly. How did I go this long without realizing that a poached egg was proof that there really is a God? The eggs, free range, have yolks bigger and more golden than any she can remember seeing in London. They burst under her knife, trickle in peppered golden perfection across the toast, soak in. Bridget takes a sip of her tea, cuts a corner off, spreads it with yolk and pops it into her mouth. Closes her eyes and suppresses a surprising moan of pleasure. She feels as though she is beginning to wake from a long, long slumber. Suddenly she is noticing things around her – food, colours, heat and cold – against which she thought she had been anaesthetized, possibly forever.

There is a proverb – Spanish, she thinks – that goes 'A life lived in fear is a life half lived,' and she thinks she is beginning to understand the full truth of it. Life with Kieran – the trepidation, the walking on eggshells, the care with words and looks and actions, even with thoughts lest her expression should betray them, in order to avoid starting off another round of punishment – was a life lived in black and white and shades of grey. She never dared to taste the colours, see the heat, feel the music.

I never had a second to myself, even when he wasn't there, she thinks. It would have been unthinkable, sitting down like this by myself, enjoying this simple moment, when I knew he might walk back through the door at any time, find me idle, be angry. It was survival, she thinks: it wasn't life. She cuts off another slice of egg-soaked bread, closes her eyes and savours its salty, fatty goodness.

'I can't sleep.'

Bridget opens her eyes. Yasmin – pink woolly pyjamas and bare feet, manky old monkey clutched against her chest – stands in the doorway, tousled hair and big brown eyes.

'I'm sorry, baby. Did I wake you up?'

Yasmin rubs a tired fist across the bridge of her nose.

'I don't know,' she states. 'I think I've been awake forever. What are you eating?'

'Eggs. Do you want some?'

'Eeugh,' says Yasmin, 'eggs.' She pulls a face that involves a lot of tongue. 'No, *thank* you.'

'Not eeugh,' she says. 'Eggs are lovely. Especially with soldiers.'

'Yukky,' says Yasmin unequivocally. Yesterday she ate three bowls of home-made custard without a murmur of disapprobation. The mysteries of children's ever-changing appetites will always be unfathomable.

'I've nearly finished,' says Bridget, 'then I'll take you back to bed.'

'Don't want to,' says Yasmin.

'Yes, but,' says Bridget, 'it's bedtime. Well after, actually.'

'Can't I come in with you?'

'No, honey. You've got your own bedroom now. That's where you sleep.'

'Yes, but,' says Yasmin.

'No, but,' says Bridget. 'You're a big girl now. Surely you want to sleep in your own room? Only babies want to sleep in with the grown-ups.'

Yasmin looks torn. Appealing to her sense of her own maturity always works. Up to a point. Her pleasure in having a space all of her own is obviously fighting a big battle with the memory of all those fuggy nights in with her mother. Bridget knew it would be an issue, parting company like this. She's been surprised she's got away with it for six nights already.

Yasmin frowns. 'Yes, but if I can't sleep, then I'll be tired in the morning and you won't like that,' she threatens.

Bridget scoops the last of her midnight feast into her mouth, does a couple of chews and washes it down with the dregs of the tea. Time to be decisive. If I hang around discussing it with her, she'll think there's room for manoeuvre. 'Yes,' she says, holds out her hand, 'and you know we've got the first lot of guests coming tomorrow.

Which means we've both got to be on good form. Come on. I'll take you back.'

And suddenly, there are tears in her daughter's eyes. 'Mummy, *please*! Please? Can't I come in and sleep with you? Just for tonight?'

'Honey,' says Bridget, 'if we do just tonight, then it'll be just tomorrow night and then just the night after as well. Come on. Be grown up. Do you know how many people *long* for a bedroom all to themselves?'

'But it's not! It's not!'

'Not what?'

'Not all to . . .' She pauses, looks a bit confused by what she's been about to say, changes tack. 'I just can't sleep tonight! Please, Mummy! I've not been – I've not been in with you since we got here, have I?'

Bridget has to acknowledge that this is true. Sort of. Yasmin has always waited, at least, until she herself was sound asleep before creeping in with her under the covers. 'So what's so different about tonight?'

'I don't know,' says Yasmin reluctantly, 'I just can't . . . I feel like there's . . .'

'It's just the wind. It's nothing. It's just a bit blowy out there tonight.'

They reach the bedroom door. Yasmin, hand still clutched in Bridget's, pulls back, hard, attempts to drag her mother back into the corridor. '*Please*, Mummy!'

I've got to be firm. We can't carry on sharing a bed till she's a teenager. She bends downs and picks her daughter up, hugs her to her side. Yasmin's legs automatically wrap around her hip, pubic bone balancing on the bulge where encroaching age and cheap food have started to expand her flesh. 'Please!' she pleads again.

'I'll tuck you in,' says Bridget.

She turns the light on, notices that both of the beds in the room are unmade. The spare bed, the one on the right, looks as though it's been tossed apart by a fault-finding sergeant-major in a cadets' dormitory. Pillows, quilt and bottom sheet lie rucked up against the wall. Bridget sighs.

'You *have* been having trouble sleeping. And did you decide which one you want to be yours, in the end?'

Yasmin looks puzzled. 'Well – *that* one.'

She points at the one they had originally agreed would be hers, the one under the slope of the eaves. It is piled, as they arranged it, with her soft toys, dolls and books; just a small puddle of body space left in the middle. It certainly *looks* like the sort of bed a six-year-old would sleep in. 'Of course,' she finishes.

'Just trying the other one out for size then, were you, baby?'

Bridget rubs her nose against her daughter's cheek, inhales the scents of soap and baby shampoo. How I love you, she thinks. How I love you. However much work you are.

'I didn't –' says Yasmin.

'Well, somebody did.' Bridget laughs. 'Who was it? The Invisible Man?'

Her daughter stiffens. 'What invisible man?'

She's good at taking things literally when she thinks she might turn them to her advantage.

'A joke,' says Bridget. 'A *joke*, Yasmin. There is *no* invisible man. Not one. It was a *joke*.'

'Well, *I* didn't do it!' she says. '*Someone* must've, because it wasn't me!'

Yeah, yeah, yeah. And that mirror jumped off the wall all by itself this morning.

'*Stop* it, Yasmin! Right now!' she barks. 'You're not getting out of bedtime by playing games. Into bed, now, or you'll –' she casts about for a punishment – 'you'll be making that bed *all by yourself* tomorrow.'

'No, Mummy!' Yasmin clings tighter round her neck, digs her knees into her stomach and back like a cowboy hanging on to a bucking bronco. 'Nonono*please*, Mummy! I promise I'll go straight to sleep!'

'You bet you will,' says Bridget, unpeels the clutching arms. The valerian tea is working and she feels too tired to reason, too tired to do anything but stumble back to her own room and get under the covers. She made eighteen beds today and hoovered the public rooms from top to bottom. Tomorrow she's got to be friendly and welcoming and hand out eighteen sets of bath linen, show half a dozen adults round wood stores and laundry rooms and car ports. 'I don't have time for this, Yasmin. *Go to bed.*'

She's surprised how firm and determined she sounds. 'No more nonsense,' she says. 'Go on. Get in.'

Yasmin lets go, flops down on to the mattress. Her eyes are still tearful. 'Please don't leave me,' she says. 'Please, Mummy.'

'Come on,' says Bridget. 'Close your eyes and when you wake up it'll be morning. I'll leave the passage light on.'

A single sob. Blackmail, thinks Bridget. She knows she can always get round me by playing for tragedy. All my guilt, my big soft heart: I find it so difficult to say no to her because I feel so bad about the start I gave her. Not fair. I have to be tough. She pulls the duvet up so it covers her daughter's body, tucks it in around her neck and shoulders while Yasmin continues to sob. 'It won't work,' she says. 'Everybody has to go to sleep.'

She strokes a strand of hair away from Yasmin's face. 'There you go,' she says, forces her voice to lilt soothingly. 'Nice and warm. Isn't that better?'

'No,' says Yasmin. 'I want to come and sleep with you.'

'Well, the whole point of you having your own room is that you actually sleep in it. Come on, baby. Give it a little while. You'll get used to it, I promise.'

Yasmin gives her the silent treatment.

'Now, you just roll over and go to sleep,' she orders.

Obediently, pointedly, Yasmin turns her back on the room, assumes a position somewhere between foetal and prayer. Bridget leans over her, plants a kiss on her hairline, just in front of her ear. 'Nighty night,' she murmurs. 'Sleep tight, darling, and mind the fleas.'

Yasmin says nothing. Sniffs.

'Now don't sulk,' says Bridget. 'I'll see you in the morning. Remember that I love you.'

No answer. It's amazing how early people learn that not responding to words of love is one of the most effective punishments there is.

Bridget retreats from the room, stands in the doorway and switches off the light. 'Night night, sweetheart,' she repeats. Still no answer.

Her feet feel as though they have been glued to the sisal in the passage. Whatever she thought of the teenager who sold her the tea, it's clear that she knew what she was talking about. She clomps back to her own room, drops her dressing gown on the floor and falls wearily into bed. The sheets have cooled while she's been in the kitchen. Still clean from their packaging – she couldn't resist buying new, in the market, to mark the new life – they feel crisp and luxurious. She burrows beneath them and listens to the wind. Enjoys the feeling of being warm and dry when the night is cold. It'll be okay, she thinks. It'll be okay . . .

The door opens. She doesn't need to look toward the light to know that Yasmin is standing there. Determined little sod, she thinks. Won't take no for an answer. Must've got that from her dad.

I'll deal with it tomorrow. I'm too tired now. Tomorrow . . .

Small feet pad across the carpet. The bedclothes are drawn back, letting in the cold night air. Bridget moves over, makes room. I can't do a tantrum tonight. Just tonight . . .

Yasmin gets in beside her. Crushes up against her and pulls an arm over herself. 'I told you I couldn't sleep,' she says. Presses her nose into Bridget's armpit.

And Lily watches, and waits, as their breath slows, drops, turns to snores.

Chapter Eighteen

'So have you seen the ghost yet?'

Bridget, grateful that her face is hidden by the cupboard door, laughs. Half-laughs. A sharp, nervous titter. Because it's not the sort of question you expect to be asked when you've barely settled in.

'No. Is there one?'

'Of course there are ghosts. Dozens. You'd hardly expect a house to be four hundred years old and not have a *few*, would you?'

'I suppose not.'

Dozens I can handle. That's like having spiders.

'I thought you said "ghost" not "ghosts".'

It's Ms Aykroyd's turn to titter. 'Oh, don't mind me, darling,' she says. 'I'm numerically dyslexic. I'm surprised I didn't say millions.'

'Well, no,' says Bridget. 'The only thing that's gone bump in the night since we got here was Yasmin falling out of bed.'

Ms Aykroyd – CallmeStella as she refers to herself – laughs again. 'Well, that's good. It wouldn't do to be too psychic around here, I'd've thought.'

Bridget hears the jangle of gold bracelets as she leans a hand against the door jamb.

'I don't know anything about ghosts,' she says, hears the Old Retainer in her voice as she speaks.

'Darling,' says Ms Aykroyd – she's the type who calls everyone darling because it saves having to learn their names – 'that's the spirit. Didn't he tell you about them? Tom Gordhavo?'

Bridget shakes her head. 'I can't say he did.'

'No, I suppose he wouldn't have. I should think he'd have a hard enough time finding someone to come and work here as it is without filling their heads full of notions.'

'I daresay he did,' says Bridget. 'And that was why he got me. Still: take more than a few ghosts to scare me off.'

Ms Aykroyd laughs again. 'Oh, I know,' she says. 'I've been here every year for the last fifteen years. I do hope you'll stay, though. It would be nice not to have to get to know a new person every time we come down. More like coming home. Anyway, ghosts just add to the atmosphere as far as I'm concerned.'

Bridget glances up. She's not sure if this last statement was for real or a joke. These arty types will tell the story of their granny's deathbed as though it were a theatrical anecdote. It's hard to tell which way the Aykroyd party go. They're Creative certainly – that's easy to spot, what with the kaftans and the head-wraps and the oversized junk jewellery hanging from every extremity, and the complicated facial hair that sprouts from the men's (and one or two of the women's) chins like topiary. And the fact that it's difficult to distinguish which of the twelve children belong to which of the six adults. At least two of them, she's worked out, seem to be related in one way or another to at least three of the grown-ups, and a couple to only one of them. But whether they're the sort of artistic that actually believes in horoscopes and phantoms and the power of the ouija board or sees them as entertainments to be consumed with cocktails, she's uncertain.

'The children are a bit of a pain, though. It's a good thing there are a lot of them, what with one thing and another, or we'd never get them to sleep in that attic.'

'The attic?'

'Silly. Nothing, of course, but they've got a thing about it being haunted. Camilla and Rain started it off, I'm afraid. I could brain Camilla, filling their heads up with spook stories and then taking off to university. Now Rain won't go up there by herself at all.'

'Oh dear,' says Bridget.

'Oh, it's fine. In a way they quite like it, I think. Gives them an excuse to get overexcited.'

'What do they say they see?'

'Oh, nobody's *seen* anything. Well, except for Camilla, and she's always had an overactive imagination. She claimed she saw a girl up there once. Came screeching down the stairs. In the middle of a dinner party, of course. The way they do. You know what they're like. Any excuse.'

Dinner party. As if. Imagine if we'd had dinner parties. Who would we have asked? His friends from the dealing floor? Crammed round the four-seat table in our living room? A gram of coke and a trip to Spearmint Rhino was more their style, the Big Swinging Dicks of Capitalism.

'Anyway. It just adds to the atmosphere,' says CallMeStella. 'You can't have a house as old as this without a few ghosts.'

I don't think I want to hear any more of this stuff. I've got to be here by myself, remember? Bridget digs deeper in the cupboard, concentrates on finding the Windolene so she can change the subject. It's there, of course: right under her hand all along. Funny how you can see things and yet not see them. Happens all the time.

'Here it is,' she says. She knew she'd seen it somewhere. She emerges and hands it to CallmeStella.

'Oh, darling, thank you,' she says. 'You *are* a star.' And stands there holding the bottle in a lost sort of fashion, as though it were some ancient artefact whose purpose she doesn't understand.

'I'll give you a hand,' says Bridget, resignedly.

'Oh, darling,' says Ms Aykroyd again, 'thank you.'

Bridget follows her into the dining room.

She hasn't been able to work out much about the party, to be honest. It took her a full twenty-four hours to work out who the Aykroyd of the booking form was in the first place. It doesn't help that, although they have twelve children – she thinks it's twelve; isn't entirely sure as the house and yard seem to be swarming with visitors from the village and the county most of the time – between them, none of the adults seem to be actually married to each other. And none of them seem to mind. And though she thinks a couple – the parents of the many-parented children – might have been married to each other in a different combination at some point in the past, it doesn't seem particularly relevant to any of them now.

That's what I should have done, she thinks. Illegitimacy doesn't seem to matter as long as you talk posh enough. Or common enough. It's only us lower-middles, with our fear of slipping down into the underclass, who give a damn these days. There I was – I only married Kieran in the first place because I didn't want my Yasmin to be a bastard – and obviously what I should have done was start talking lah-di-dah and wearing velvet and smoking through a holder. No father on the birth certificate and he wouldn't have had half the weaponry to pursue us with. No one would have minded if my daughter grew up feral if I talked posh, like this lot, and the social would never have dared to get involved. Upper-class bohemians seem to get away with stuff that the rest of us would never be allowed to do: flicking ash wherever, swapping bedrooms, dropping into the village and coming back with an entire houseful of people for a party. CallmeStella seems to know everyone around here: was born, she says, in the next valley and decamps down here for Christmas every year 'visiting the haunts of my tortured adolescence without having to actually live with it'.

Bridget doesn't mind, though. They're jolly enough people, and friendly enough, and undemanding enough, as long as you don't mind the fact that you'll be finding discarded fag butts in odd places for weeks to come. It's nice, as a point of fact, after a week in which the silence of the house was not exactly oppressive, but brought home to her just how large it was, to hear the building full of the sound of talk and childish disagreements and at night, the sound of singing. A couple of the guests are something to do with the stage – Bridget thinks she even recognizes one of them from those BBC2 drama series where people hang about maundering over storm-tossed landscapes and nothing much actually happens. The piano in the drawing room has been opened, found to be in tune, and is sparked up every night. She likes it, the drifting small-hours sound of Fifties jazz, show tunes and – when local fervour, or local scrumpy, gets powerful enough – bellowed choruses of 'Trelawny'.

A bit of her feels cheered up. Another bit feels even lonelier than before. Bridget has never had enough friends to have a huge house party like this: tables of twelve or twenty all in a row scarfing vegetable lasagne and talking themselves hoarse. It's not the way her parents lived, and it's not the way anyone she knew lived. Parties, pre-Kieran, were the sort of parties where you couldn't actually hear yourself shout, let alone sing, in corners of whatever the coming venue was that year. She's a child of the club boom. Has the tinnitus to show for it. Even when they weren't in cavernous aircraft hangars where the speakers were a million watts and the humidity was over a hundred per cent, it was taken for granted that, if you had people round, the first thing you did was turn the stereo up to full.

She's not sure if she can remember ever having a conversation with more than one person at a time. Everything she's ever known in terms of social talk has involved swapping over: pressing your lips against someone's ear and bending your head for them to do the same to you; never seeing the expression on their face when they heard your bellowed words.

How ironic. There we were, having fun, and we never got round to making any friends. The only person apart from Kieran I've ever really had long talks with as an adult was Carol, and that was because she came from upstairs rather than from my social life. I didn't even talk to Kieran much, really, not even at the beginning. We were always loved-up, or hung over, and then later I avoided talking to him because I never knew where it might lead. Stupid, isn't it? How people base their entire future happiness on things like whether they like going out to the same sorts of places, or whether their friends are impressed when a guy turns up in an Audi; that they never think about what will happen when fashion moves on and you can't do the e's any more because it'll harm the baby.

But they've been lovely with Yasmin. Included her in everything. She seems to have spent every waking hour running up and down the corridor with one child or another: or sometimes a dozen. She's met some children from the village, and the prospect of school doesn't seem so bad to her any more. Maybe some of them will be real friends in the course of time.

'I'll tell you what,' she says to Ms Aykroyd's back, 'I'd be grateful if you'd mind not doing too much ghost talk around Yasmin. She's only six and I could do without her getting ideas to scare herself with when the place is empty.'

'Oh, darling,' says Ms Aykroyd. 'It's only games.'

'And she's only six,' she repeats, trying to sound kind but firm. 'Six-year-olds can't always tell the difference.'

'Well, you can never start too early on training their imaginations. It's all part of helping them become free spirits.'

They stop in front of the dresser. On the mirror, a childish hand has scrawled FUCK OFF in bright red lipstick.

If that's an example of free-spiritedness, thinks Bridget, I'll go for inhibition any day. She doesn't say anything, of course. Not her place. She's a housekeeper, she must remember that. Discretion is what she's paid for. Discretion and the sort of incurious efficiency that makes paying guests feel secure. She is, after all, only among these people, now that they're settled in, when someone comes and finds her and asks for her help.

She starts to move the figurines. They've been turned round again to face inward, she notices. A bizarre obsession, and one that seems to be shared by everyone who passes through here. Perhaps the Gordhavos actually keep them like that – some family custom – and it is she who keeps setting them wrongly.

Ms Aykroyd hovers. 'Frightfully sorry,' she says.

'That's all right.'

She's obviously hovering in the hope of dismissal. Bridget gives it her. Doesn't really want to get drawn into lengthy chat, anyway. 'You get off,' she says. 'I'll do this.'

'Are you sure?' She sounds relieved. Though she'd be right hacked off if I said I wasn't.

'Of course. That's what I'm here for.'

'Well . . .' Ms Aykroyd makes a show of looking at her watch. 'I suppose I *should* . . . lunch coming up. If you're sure you don't . . .?'

Oh, do go away, thinks Bridget irritably. 'I'll get it done much faster if I'm by myself,' she says.

A crash upstairs, followed by the sound of wailing. Too heavy, thinks Bridget. Too large to be mine. 'Oh dear,' says Ms Aykroyd. All the other adults have gone on a day trip to Tintagel. 'I'd better go and . . .'

'Yes,' says Bridget. 'It sounds like that'd be a good idea.'

CallmeStella shuffles off, disappears into the dining room. Bridget unfurls a duster, leans toward the glass with a cloth-wrapped finger. The lipstick is thick, as though it's been heated and painted on with a brush. Amazing. If a kid of mine did something like this, I wouldn't just . . .

Suddenly, from upstairs, the sound of voices. United voices: raised and organized. They are counting, slowly, deliberately.

One . . . two . . . three . . .

She hears a door open, and the sound of running feet. There's a game of some sort afoot.

The footsteps scutter back and forth for a moment, as though their owner is undecided as to which way to go, then make their way up the corridor toward the dining-room stairs. As they begin to descend, she stays her polishing and turns to see who's coming.

It's Yasmin. Looking almost as unkempt as an Aykroyd. Someone has put half a dozen plaits in her long dark hair and tied them off with strips of rag so that she looks like a small and rather giggly Medusa. Barefoot, she seems to be wearing what looks like a party dress: powder-blue satin, gone to holes, several sizes too big and several decades too old for her. She reaches the bottom of the stairs and, in that childish way, only notices her mother's presence when she gets there. Jumps, laughs at her own foolishness and then grins.

Twelve . . . thirteen . . . fourteen . . .

'What on earth are you wearing?'

'Oh,' she says distantly, looking down and rubbing the cloth between thumb and forefinger, 'dressing-up clothes. I found them in the attic. There's a great big trunk. Lily showed me.'

Bridget doesn't have the faintest idea who Lily is. Doesn't even know if there's a Lily in the Aykroyd party, who all seem to rejoice in names like Summer and Moonlight – she wonders if somewhere in an alternative universe there's a sort of anti-hippy culture which rejoices in filling in tax returns and gives its children all the nature names like Winter and Mudslide that the flower people eschew – or if she's one of the village kids.

'I'm not sure if you ought to be wearing those,' she says. 'I'm not sure if Mr Gordhavo –'

'Lily said it was all right,' Yasmin assures her. 'She says she wears them all the time.'

Twenty-three . . . twenty-four . . .

Yasmin looks wildly over her shoulder. Bridget has forgotten the intensity of feeling that a childhood game can arouse.

'Never mind,' she says. 'We can talk about it later. What are you playing? Hide and seek?'

'No,' says Yasmin. 'Sardines. I have to hide and everyone has to find me and get in with me.'

'Oh, yes,' says Bridget. 'I used to love that one. Where are you going to hide?'

'I don't know.'

'Well, how about under there?' She gestures with her duster toward the huge cloth-covered table.

'Tchuuch!' groans Yasmin. 'You've only gotta be thick, Mum! That's the *first* place they'll look!'

How funny, thinks Bridget, she's already losing her London accent and she's just been hanging around with these kids for a few days. She'll sound like a proper Cornish Pisky by the New Year.

'Well, I don't know.'

Thirty-one . . . thirty-two . . .

Yasmin leaps from foot to foot as though she's suddenly found herself standing on hot coals. 'Hurry up! I've only got to fifty!'

Bridget casts about her. Behind the curtains? Behind the sofa in the second salon? Too easy. Not enough room.

She gets it. 'Come with me! Quickly!'

She's noticed that the window seat in the drawing room, which runs the whole length of the south wall, is hinged for storage. Not that there's anything in there apart from a few Hoover attachments, some half-burnt church candles, a box of bulk-bought china plates and a lot of dust. It's these sorts of details that make a house a holiday home. Anything of any real value – sentimental or fiscal – will have been taken away from here years ago.

She holds her hand out to her daughter and they jog quietly into the drawing room. Bridget lifts the lid on the central part of the seat.

'Come on!' she says. 'There's loads of room in here.'

Yasmin looks at her in amazement, as though she's only just discovered that she has the ability to think independently. 'Star!' she says. 'How did you know that was there?'

'I know everything, darling,' says Bridget. 'You know that. Now hurry up and get in.'

Forty-three . . . forty-four . . .

There's room enough inside to house an entire army. The only thing that will give Yasmin away is her tendency to giggle. She climbs inside, lies down like a princess in a glass coffin and crosses her arms over her chest. 'Okay,' she says.

Bridget drops the lid down, strolls casually back to return to her cleaning. There's only the final F of OFF to get rid of now. She picks up the palette knife and scrapes the top layers away, sprays Windolene over the patch.

Coming ready or not . . .

A herd of water buffalo stampedes from the master bedroom.

Bridget rubs. It must have been very greasy lipstick: theatrical lipstick, the sort of greasepaint you see on movie stills from the Thirties and Forties. The smears are taking ages to dissipate.

The sound of feet and voices scatters, dies away. She imagines Yasmin, lying in her wooden coffin, wriggling with the effort of suppressing the urge to leap out and show everyone how clever she has been.

A couple of the Young thunder down the stairs, shriek to a halt when they see her.

'Hello, Leo,' she says. 'Hello, Rain.'

She doesn't like Leo much. He's one of those thickset boys who tend to tell people how things are in a stern, unsmiling fashion. She suspects he might be a bit of a bully: certainly, most of the other children seem to obey him at speed when he issues an order.

'Hello,' says the boy. Puts his hands on his hips and looks anywhere other than at her. Some kids are like that. It's not a social comment, they just don't think of adults as being worthy of their attention unless they want something from them.

'Are you playing a game of some sort?'

'Yes.'

'Hide and seek?'

His eyes flick over to her. No, she sees him think, she's a grown-up and someone we won't see again after this week. Not worth the effort of explaining.

'Sort of,' he says. 'Have you seen Yasmin?'

Well, at least my daughter's not infra dig. 'I'm not sure if I ought to tell you,' she teases.

He thinks I'm quite, quite mad. Funny how people with no sense of humour always assume that other people's attempts at joking are signs of stupidity, even when they're nine years old.

'It would spoil the game, wouldn't it?' she finishes.

He gives her a look, ignores what she's said. 'Which way did she go?'

'If I told you that, I'd be a snitch.'

Rain – droopy hair that looks, appropriately enough, permanently damp – sticks her head under the tablecloth. Comes out, combs her bangs back down with greasy fingers. 'Not here,' she announces, and trots off to the kitchen.

Leo thinks for a bit. God, I hope Yas doesn't end up shut up alone with *him* for too long. 'Right-oh,' he says. Takes off in the opposite direction from the one his sister's taken.

An eruption of shrieking upstairs. Someone's obviously found *somebody*. Half a dozen sets of feet rumble off up the corridor toward the far end of the house. They must be well scattered now: this is the perfect house for hide and seek. You could hide anywhere here. All those dark places and hidden doorways. I'm glad we've got good locks on the flat door, for the night-time.

She turns back to the mirror, resumes her polishing. Once this is done, she thinks, I'd better go and re-lay the drawing-room fire. Not so much out of a wish to provide the guests with cosy snugness for tonight, but because I know no one will sweep the grate out before they rebuild it themselves, and that grate can't really take more than one fire before it's full. It's amazing how much ash you can get on a Persian carpet if you don't know what to do with a dustpan. Earlier this morning, she saw Humphrey – the one she thinks is probably CallmeStella's partner – and the one she thinks is probably his ex-wife, carrying a log the size of a crocodile across the garden from the woods beyond the pond. If they try and burn that tonight, damp and green as it is, there'll be bits spitting all over the place. Best not to set things up so any more damage can be done.

Another clutch of children barrel through from the drawing room, skid across the floor, launch themselves beneath the table and emerge disappointed. They don't even look at her. Adults, in a child's world, only really exist when they are providing the entertainment or putting a stop to it. All of them are in some form of fancy dress, she notices, though how much has come from the attic trunk and how much is their normal everyday clothing, she couldn't say. She's so used to the sight of seven-year-olds with belly-button rings and platform shoes that nothing much seems odd to her these days. Kieran wanted to get Yasmin's ears pierced the week they came home from the hospital and she had a bruise on her shoulder for weeks that proved she'd said no. Ear piercing. the Chav equivalent of circumcision. I always wanted more for her than that.

They throw back the curtains, look behind them and then, with a cursory hello, they trot on to the stairs and disappear. That's one good hiding place I've picked there, she thinks. I hope it's not too good: that they don't just get bored and wander off and leave Yas lying there all afternoon.

She can't believe how powerfully this lipstick has adhered. Bridget squirts another dose of window cleaner on to the glass, looks at her misted reflection and sets to polishing.

A movement behind her makes her jump. A small figure, emerging silently from the anteroom. She hasn't heard anyone go in there. She turns, looks.

A small girl. Not one she recognizes. Must be one of the village kids: probably one they picked up in the playground because she certainly doesn't have the pink-cheeked, vitamin-fed, nightly-bathed look of the Aykroyd friends' spawn. This one is sort of greyish-yellow if she's anything: hollow cheeks and big dark patches round the eyes, and arms bleached like flotsam. Someone's given her a bad home haircut with the kitchen scissors, by the look of it. And dressed her from Oxfam.

'Where on earth did you come from?' she asks.

The girl stops dead in the doorway and stares at Bridget as though – a small shiver of shock runs through her – she hates her.

She's got a nasty little mouth. Ill-tempered, judgemental.

'Are you looking for Yasmin?'

The child folds her arms and narrows her eyes. Juts her jaw and gives Bridget a look of pure poison.

'It wasn't me,' she says. 'I didn't bloody do it.'

Chapter Nineteen

She doesn't wait for the others. They wouldn't wait for her, and anyway, she is too happy. She doesn't want them bursting her bubble. This is my day, she thinks. My day. Today, I won a prize, and nobody's ever given me a prize before.

Fighting her way through the school doors, jostled by end-of-term pupils eager to start the long summer holiday, she is momentarily dazzled by the brightness of the light. The sun, as they sat cross-legged while the hour-after-hour of assembly – even a sixty-pupil school can drag prize-giving out till lunchtime – crawled past, has burst through the clouds, bathes the fields around Meneglos in gold.

I won, she thinks. I won a prize. Clutches against her chest the first – and last – handwritten certificate bearing her name since her birth was registered as she wanders away from the group. No one notices her go. No one wants her to stay. There's a game of rounders starting up on the common and no one will want her on their team. She knows without having to put herself through the humiliation of the selection process. But Lily doesn't care. She doesn't care. She's been the outsider all her life; she barely notices any more.

They can't take it away from me. This is one thing they can't take away. I'm the best drawer in the whole school and no one can take that away.

Suddenly she sees a world of possibility. I can be an artist. When I grow up. People pay money for that. Good money. Biddy Blakemore's always going on about how much her stupid paintings are worth, and mine are much better. At least my children look like children. Hers look like tiny little grown-ups with great big pumpkin heads stuck on top. Like dwarves. Mine look like they can move. Mrs Carlyon said so. In front of the whole school. She said I was the best painter she'd ever taught and they can never take that away from me.

Her cheek muscles, unused to smiling, ache slightly as she walks up the lane. There are flowers on the hedges – Lily never saw a hedge in Portsmouth, never even made it to the clipped-and-tonsured suburbs, so she doesn't know that the Cornish hedge, banks of soft moss disguising steel-cold slate walls, is not a hedge as the rest of the country knows it – and she suddenly notices their beauty for the first time in her life.

I'll practise all summer, she thinks. Someone'll let me do a job for them, earn enough to buy some pencils and some paper, and then I'll spend the whole summer . . . maybe Tessa will let me use hers, if I ask her. If I'm nice. She's got more than she needs. She's got two sets. She can't want all those.

I'll go everywhere. The lanes and the hedges and the moor and down by the stream, and I'll draw it all. All those colours. That big tree in the garden, the one with the swing hanging off it. It looks black when you first look at it, but when you look some more, it's full of colours: black and blue and green, and the trunk's not brown, like little kids draw it: it's grey and silver and there's yellow as well: great stripes of it, all down one side. And other people don't notice these things, but I do, and that's why I'm better than them.

She pauses at the junction where the Meneglos road crosses the St Mabyn road, turns, on the far side, into the unmetalled track that runs down through arable fields to Rospetroc. The wheat is knee-high. It ripples in the breeze as she looks down at her destination. Lily takes a moment to untie the ribbon that binds her certificate, to unfurl it and look once again at the proof of her triumph. She can barely read it – Mrs Carlyon says her reading's a disgrace – but she can make out the words 'First Prize' copperplated across the top, inside the scrolled margin which runs all the way round, and her own name, written carefully in Indian ink. Lily Rickett. That's me. Prizewinner Lily Rickett.

And I'll get good enough, and the war will finish next year, and I can slip away while no one's looking. I'll go a long long way away, where no one knows me, and I'll find a little cottage somewhere, in the middle of the country where no one wants to live, and I'll draw and draw and paint and paint and paint, and people will come. They'll come. They'll hear about me and they'll come and they'll see my pictures and they'll give me money and it won't be like the old days. And I'll be famous, and then they'll all want to know me. And when I'm rich, I'll go back. I'll go back to Portsmouth and I'll find my mum, and I'll show her. I'll show her my good clothes and my car and my shoes, and she probably won't even know who I am till I tell her. And she'll be sitting there in the pub, and I'll just walk in and . . .

She rolls it back up with greater care than she has ever treated any other possession, reties the ribbon, walks on. A few feet on to the track, she kicks off her shoes – the holes in the soles make them more uncomfortable, strangely, than walking barefoot – and steps on to the verge.

Just think. They'll all be sorry they didn't make friends with me then. They'll say, I lived with her once. With Lily Rickett. We were evacuated together during the bombing. I wish I'd been nicer to her. I saw her in the street the other day, and she didn't even know who I was. Ted and Pearl and Vera and Geoffrey: think they're a cut above, won't talk to me, Pearl crying all the time and Geoffrey telling everyone they'll catch things off me. And I'll see him in the street one day, and he'll want to know me then. And I'll just look at him, and I'll toss my head, and I'll say: no. I don't remember you. Who did you say you was again?

The grass is soft, prickly, the earth beneath damp from last night's rain. I like the smell here, she thinks. Not like Portsmouth. No coal-fires or glue works or spilled fuel. No smell of mushrooms in the bedroom or shit in the yard. No fags or port-and-lemon as she comes in with whoever, turfs me out of my nice warm bed so she can make noises like an animal, and that smell when she lets me back in: salt and old milk and sweat . . .

Lily stops and sups the air. Smells are colours to her: the ones on this hillside green and brown and gold, with something soft and purple drifting on the breeze from the moor. She digs a toe into the soft broken surface of a molehill, feels a tiny shiver of pleasure at the cool, slimy, crumbled texture. And suddenly she has a thought she doesn't remember having had before. It catches her by surprise, shocks her.

I could be happy.

The thought disturbs her, thrills her at the same time, the way early moments of sexual attraction take the young. She is rooted to the spot, frozen with fear and exhilaration. Looks wildly around her as though she is afraid that someone might have overheard the thought.

My God, I could be happy.

It's too much. Too much for her untrained mind.

Lily takes to her heels, bolts down the hill. But as she runs, she feels the breeze, feels the earth beneath her feet, feels the world reel on its axis, and the surge returns.

I could be happy. It could all be all right. I could be . . .

Hugh is home. She's caught unawares, hasn't expected him. Of course he's home. Eton breaks up just like other schools, and the long summer holidays would justify the search for the space on a train.

He is standing in the dining room, by the dresser, with a cricket bat in his hand. He has his back to her, but by the time, running in from the sunlight, she realizes he is there, shrieks to a halt and tries to back out, it is too late. He has heard her. Starts, whips round with a look on his face made up of fear, guilt and defiance. And when he sees who has caught him, his expression changes.

Oh God, she thinks. He's just the same.

She backs away, tries to make her way toward the door and the possibility of escape.

'Oh,' he says. 'You're still here, then.'

Lily doesn't answer. Just looks at his face, at the gloat that has started to play across it.

'If you tell,' he says, 'you'll regret it.'

'I won't tell,' she says reflexively. And then she sees what she's not supposed to tell about. On the floor by his feet lies a cricket ball – hard, scuffed oxblood leather, a fray in the string which binds it – and the shards of half a dozen figurines. The stern features of the Duke of Wellington stare up at her, the baleful half-face of Queen Victoria, the tragic simper of Nell Gwyn, orange still gripped in her graceful hand, basket lying three feet away.

And then she sees something else pass across his face. A new thought. And then a gleeful decision.

Oh, God. I'm in for it now.

'Mummy's going to be very, very angry,' he says.

Again, she doesn't say anything.

He steps toward her. 'It would be better for you,' he says, 'if you just owned up straight away. I know how her mind works. She'll be furious, of course, but what she really can't stand is a liar.'

He steps toward her, and she closes her eyes.

Chapter Twenty

They're late. The congregation are already singing 'As Shepherds Watched Their Flocks'. So much for relaxed country timings. Nothing in London starts less than ten minutes late, to allow for the Tube.

They're all going to look at us.

She pauses beneath the lych-gate, almost turns back. Then she thinks: no, this is right. I'm going to be part of this community if it kills me. Hurries, clutching Yasmin's hand, up the graveyard path.

Yasmin looks up at the tower, dark and squat and Saxon, with open mouth. 'Why are we going here, again?'

'It's church,' says Bridget. 'It's what people do at Christmas in the country. They go to church.'

Damn Lambeth Council. No Little Baby Jesus in its schools for fear of offending the minorities. I should have thought about it before now, instead of worrying about how to afford the presents. She won't even know any of the songs. I barely remember any myself.

'So what do you do in church, then?'

'You pray. Talk to God. And sing. And then everyone listens to the man with the dress on when he gives you a lecture about how no one remembers the meaning of Christmas.'

'What if I don't know the tunes?'

'Doesn't matter,' says Bridget. 'Just mouth the words. And, look . . .'

She squats down just outside the door, looks her daughter in the eye. 'All you have to do is be as quiet as possible, and stand up and sit down when everyone else does. And if you're not sure what to do next, just close your eyes and clutch your hands together like this.'

'Oh right!' says Yasmin. 'Like *here's the church, here's the steeple* . . . I get it!'

'Yuh, that's right. But just stick with the "church" bit till I nudge you.'

'Okay,' says Yasmin. Holds still while Bridget smooths her hair down and checks her own hemline.

'All glory be to God on high, And to the Earth be peace,' sing the congregation. Blast. I'm sure that's the last verse.

'Christmas is weird in the country,' says Yasmin.

'I know,' says Bridget. 'People have all sorts of different ways of doing things. That's why they call it multicultural.'

'Hmm,' says Yasmin.

They push open the door. The pine and candlewax and damp stone smell fills her nostrils, half forgotten but familiar from her own childhood. Like riding a bike, she thinks. I'll remember how to do this.

'. . . begin and never cease . . .'

'In the country,' says Yasmin loudly into the post-hymn pause, 'don't they do presents, like at *real* Christmas?'

A hundred pairs of eyes fix upon them. Sunday-best wrapped in anoraks. Old ladies down the front in hats. Sulking teenagers. Respectability emanating from every pore. Yasmin looks up at her mother, enquiringly. 'Don't they believe in Santa Claus?' she asks.

'She's a one, that kid of yours.'

'Don't,' says Bridget. Feels herself flush again at the memory.

'Never mind,' says Chris Kirkland. 'That's what we have them for, isn't it? To remind us how fragile dignity is?'

'Oh, God,' says Bridget. 'What a way to introduce myself.'

'Don't worry about it. Better to stand out than have no one know you're there.'

'What are they going to think? Can't even teach my child the basics of Christianity.'

Chris laughs. Snags a couple of glasses of sherry from the cloth-covered trestle table that stands against the wall. Hands her one. 'I don't know what sort of place you think you've come into, but I should think it's exactly like the rest of the country. Most of these people don't see the inside of a church from one year's end to the next. I shouldn't think the congregation's bigger than twenty on a normal Sunday. Rest of them are down the pub, or watching the telly. Anyway. Bottoms up.'

'Cheers,' says Bridget. 'Happy Christmas.'

'Yes. Happy Christmas. What are you doing to celebrate?'

'Oh, it's just us. We'll be doing it quietly, in our kitchen. House is full of renters.'

'Ah yes. Stella Aykroyd and her lot. Don't suppose we'll be seeing *them* down the church in a hurry.'

Bridget laughs.

'So you've not got family coming or anything?' asks Chris.

Bridget looks over at her daughter, who has found a couple of playmates and is busy rearranging the nativity scene in the corner. It has, she notices, a Celtic cross and a small fleet of fishing boats included, and the countryside surrounding the stable is surprisingly green. Camels on Bodmin moor. No odder than snow in Bethlehem, really.

'No,' she says vaguely. 'No family.'

Then she realizes that she's probably causing more curiosity by being vague than being talkative. 'No,' she says hastily. 'My mum and dad died in a car crash when I was seventeen and I didn't have any brothers or sisters.'

Chris assumes the customary expression of neutral sympathy. 'I'm sorry to hear that.'

Bridget shakes her head. 'It was a long time ago. Half a lifetime.'

'All the same.'

She can tell that this isn't going to be enough. 'And I split up with her father quite soon after she was born,' she explains. 'We don't really have any contact any more.'

'Ah,' says Chris. 'You'll find there's a few like that in this village. You'll be in good company. Mince pie?'

'Yes,' says Bridget.

'Don't really like them without brandy butter myself. Not with short pastry, anyway.'

'I know what you mean.'

'Vicar's wife makes them, though, so you have to seem willing.'

'Absolutely.'

They bite, and chew. The pies are heavy, like someone's made them from Potty Putty, and contain little more than a half-teaspoon of filling. Chris splutters a few crumbs as she begins to speak again. 'So have you met anybody much yet, then?'

'Not really. Haven't had much chance. Mrs Varco. You. Mrs Walker.'

'Everything all right with the school?'

'Yes. She's starting in the New Year.'

'Good. She'll be fine there.'

'I hope so. I worry, you know, that she'll be behind everyone. You know. London schools . . .'

'Well, given that she'll be in with three kids with webbed toes that I know of,' says Chris, 'all theoretically from different families, I wouldn't be too concerned. She's as bright as a button, that one.'

'Thank you.'

'Don't mention it.'

A woman in navy blue sackcloth approaches. She wields a cup of tea with its saucer. 'Merry Christmas,' she says.

'Merry Christmas, Geraldine.'

'All well?'

'Delicious. Thank you. Must have taken you ages.'

'Nothing,' she says, smiling modestly, 'is too much when it's the Lord's work.'

This must be Mrs Vicar. She turns to Bridget. 'I don't think we've met before,' she says. 'Staying with the Kirklands?'

'No –' begins Bridget, but Chris cuts across her.

'This is Bridget Sweeny,' she says. 'She's taken over as caretaker at Rospetroc.'

The woman raises her eyebrows. 'Ah! I'd heard he'd found someone.'

'That'll be me.'

'And how are you getting on?'

'Fine. Thank you.'

'Not too lonely?'

'Not in the least. We've a houseful at the moment, anyway.'

'Yes. I imagine. Much better at Christmastime. Horrible big empty place otherwise.'

'Oh, it's not too bad,' says Bridget. 'I've got good locks on the flat, anyway.'

'Good,' she says vaguely, not really interested. 'Good. Now, do you have a family or are you here by yourself?'

'Just my daughter.' She gestures toward Yasmin. 'She's starting at the school in January.'

'Good, good,' repeats the vicar's wife. 'Have you met my husband?'

'Not yet. Hello.'

'How do you do?' He is a spare, bespectacled man, a line of white hair hugging the nape of his neck, who looks as though he might take the vow of poverty quite seriously. 'And a very happy Christmas to you,' he adds with the reflexive goodwill of a royal on walkabout, and pumps her hand with both of his, actor-style.

'And to you,' she replies automatically. 'Lovely service. Thank you.'

'No,' he says, 'thank *you* for coming.'

'Ms Sweeny has just taken over at Rospetroc,' says the wife.

Again, the raised eyebrow. *'Really?'*

'Yes,' says Bridget.

'Well, well. I do hope you'll be happy there. We never saw much of your predecessor, I'm afraid.'

'Frances Tyler.'

He looks a bit unsure. 'She wasn't here for very long, of course.'

'No. So I gather.'

'Never managed to settle.'

'No.'

'Nice lady,' says Chris. 'Ate a lot of toffee.'

'Happy Christmas,' says the vicar. Gives her the Meneglos hand-press.

'And to you.'

'And how are the little ones?'

'Not so little,' says Chris. 'Hence the hangovers.'

'Ah, yes,' he says. 'Have you met Ms . . .'

'Sweeny,' says Bridget. 'Yes, we've met.'

'Good,' he says. 'Good.'

She has another look for Yasmin. She's talking to a girl of about her own age in pink dungarees and an orange jumper. The hall is thinning out, now. Everyone with a life is going home to baste the turkey. The only people left seem to be over sixty, or on their own, or to have a blemish or a disability of some sort, or to have tucked their trousers into the tops of their green wellies, which is a sure sign that there's something wrong with them. There's a normal-looking man in his mid-thirties, but he's on the floor wrestling a plastic pony from the grasp of a six-year-old boy. Obviously a bully or an inadequate of some sort. Shame, really: he'd be quite good-looking otherwise. Well-built, large shoulders, narrow hips, a well-shaped skull under a number-two cut, humour lines around the eyes. I bet he's a hit down the pub, she thinks bitterly. A rural Lothario if ever I saw one.

'Zat your little girl playing with mine?'

She drags herself away from her reflections. She's being addressed by a woman in her late twenties. Light brown hair streaked with clumsy home highlights, multi-coloured jacket made of blanketing, jeans, a welcoming smile.

'I don't know. Yours is the one with the dungarees?'

'That's right. Chloe.'

'Right. Yes, then. Mine's Yasmin.'

'Now there's a pair of aspirational names,' says the woman. Sticks a hand out. 'Tina.'

'Bridget.'

'Still,' says Tina, 'not as bad as my nephew Jago.'

'Now, there's a name.'

'Cornish for Iago, of course. Like in *Othello*. A leftover of the Spanish who fetched up on our rocks after the Armada. Not that they'll know that in the fleshpots of wherever he ends up. Jago Carlyon. Sounds like a character in a Mills and Boon. I hear you've taken over at Rospetroc?'

'That's me.'

'Great,' she says. 'It's great up there. What a lovely place to grow up.'

'You're the first person to say anything positive about it.' Bridget gives her a smile, warmed by her enthusiasm.

'Oh, you don't want to go paying attention to any of those old biddies,' says Tina. 'They think buying into all the old superstitions makes them more country, so to speak. It's nothing but signs and portents with them.'

'It does seem that way.'

'So how you settling in? Yasmin coming to the school, is she?'

'Uh-huh.'

'Good. Looks like she and Chloe are getting on like a house on fire, anyway.'

'Yes,' says Bridget. 'I'm glad to see it. I was a bit afraid she'd end up being one of those weird children who never have any friends.'

'Don't you worry about that,' says Tina. 'Much harder to keep people out of your business than get them into it. That's the country way. Jago!'

The last word is shouted. The small boy looks up.

'You give that back to your cousin *now*!' she shouts.

The man, looking up too, lets go of the plastic pony and the boy trots obediently over to Chloe, pushes it into her hands. 'He's got no control,' says Tina. 'Doesn't see him often enough, that's the problem.'

He approaches. Grins a sheepish grin. 'Five minutes I've been trying to get that off him,' he says.

'I've told you before. There's no point reasoning with them. They're children, not people. They need to be treated like puppies. Give them clear orders and they'll usually do what you say.'

'Whatever,' he says. He's looking at Bridget with a shy sort of curiosity. It's a nice face, she thinks. One of those clear country faces. Innocent. Not a Lothario at all. I'm just over-cynical.

'Hello,' he says. 'I'm Mark.'

'Carlyon. My brother. Bridget,' says Tina. 'She's just taken over at Rospetroc.'

'Oh right. Hello. How's your electrics?'

'Dodgy, as it goes,' says Bridget, rather taken aback.

'He's going to have to face up to it and stump up in the end,' says Mark. 'Tom Gordhavo. Tight as a gnat's chuff when it comes to that house. Pardon my French. Don't let him fob you off. I'm sure that's why Frances left in the end. Couldn't stand the lights going out without warning like that.'

'I'll remember that,' says Bridget.

'My brother's an electrician,' says Tina.

'Ah.'

'I'm down in the village,' he says. 'Just give me a ring if there's any trouble.'

'Okay,' she says, wondering how she's going to do that without a phone number. 'I will.'

'Come on,' says Tina. 'We'd best get back or there won't be any dinner this side of Boxing Day.'

'Okay,' says Mark. 'I'll get the kids.'

'Nice to meet you, Bridget,' says Tina. Shakes her hand again. Begins to walk away, then turns back. 'Perhaps we should get those girls of ours together again before term starts. So Yasmin's not all by herself when she goes to school.'

Bridget is pleased. 'Yes,' she says. 'Yes, that would be nice.'

'Bring her over. In the New Year.'
'That would be great.'
'Good-oh,' says Tina. 'We're down at the other end of the village. In the modern bit. Well, modern-ish. Four Betjeman Grove. Just come down any day. It's not like I've ever got anything to do. Single mother dole scum scrounger, that's me.'
'Cool,' says Bridget. 'We've already got a lot in common, then. How do I find it?'
'Just ask,' says Tina. 'Everybody knows me.'
'Okay. What's your surname?'
'Teagle.'
'Teagle.'
'Don't start. My mum and dad didn't know I was going to marry a Teagle, did they? Anyway. It could be worse. Our mother's maiden name was Bastard, if you want to know. She was glad to get rid of that. Probably why she married Dad the minute she was legal.'
'Bastard?'
'Bastard. It means High Dwelling, apparently. What's yours, by the way?'
'Fl— Sweeny,' says Bridget.

Chapter Twenty-One

'Hello?'

There's no noise at the other end, then some breathing.

She tucks the phone into the crook of ear and shoulder, stirs the bread sauce.

'Hello?'

Yasmin is sitting at the kitchen table, drumming her heels against her chair legs with her knife and fork clutched in her fists like a hungry cartoon child. She chews on a lock of hair which has drifted loose from her tiara. She's been dressed as a princess – pink tutu, pink costume jewellery, pink shoes, all found at the end of her bed when she woke this morning – since they got in from church. Bridget is still surprised that she managed to persuade her not to wear the clothes *to* church.

'Hello?'

'Fucking bitch.'

He's drunk. The two simple swearwords are slurred, but the venom is no less palpable.

She doesn't say anything. Thinks: I should hang up now, cut him off. But she is frozen, powerless, as though he were actually in the room. The very lights seem to dim as she fights to breathe.

'Happy fucking Christmas,' he says.

A gust of laughter bursts through the floorboards. There are eighteen to dinner downstairs.

He can't get you. There are people here.

He doesn't know where you are.

Mustn't let Yas see me frightened.

She turns her back to her daughter, drops her hair over her face.

'How's my daughter?' he asks.

'F-fine.'

Don't engage with him. What are you doing? Don't speak to him. Hang up.

'Let me speak to her.'

'I'm sorry, but that's not possible.'

'Let me speak to her. I want to speak to my daughter.'

'No,' she says.

My God, I just said no to him.

'No,' she repeats more firmly.

He shouts: 'Let me speak to my FUCKING daughter! You can't do this! You can't run a-fucking-WAY and expect me to just – you'll fucking LEARN, Bridget! You'll fucking –'

She hangs up. Presses the off button and powers the phone down.

He can't get you, Bridget. He's miles away. He doesn't know where you are.

Her hands are shaking and she feels sweaty.

It's all right. It's all right. Breathe.

There's a smell of burning. The bread sauce, still on the heat, is catching. She takes it off the hob, stirs frantically. Breathes.

'Who was that?' asks Yasmin.

Two more breaths. She plasters a smile on to her face, turns back into the room.

'No one,' she says. 'Wrong number. Would you believe it? Christmas Day and they're still trying to sell things, eh?'

Chapter Twenty-Two

How can something so good go so bad?

She has asked herself this question a million times. Gone over and over her history. Relived times, incidents, words, looks, searching for the clue, searching for the truth.

Was it me? Was it something about me? Did I drive him to it, turn him from alpha male to rage machine?

Or was it that I couldn't see? That I was so blinded by my want, by my wish for love, by my arrogant belief in my own judgement, that I couldn't see signs that were always there?

Is it me? Is it just that I am stupid? Did I make some stupid, deliberate choice because I didn't want to see the signs? Can I ever trust myself again? Can I ever be trusted? How can I be trusted to take care of my daughter, protect her, show her how to survive and be strong, when I couldn't even see the freight train as it thundered up the track towards me?

Yasmin's gone downstairs to play charades with the Aykroyds and she's allowed herself the luxury of gin and crying. He was so beautiful. That's what she remembers. She was dazzled by his beauty the first time she set eyes on him. He had sensitive eyes. She remembers thinking that. Blue, they were, and surrounded by long, black lashes.

Eyes aren't sensitive. They're just a product of your genetic inheritance. I should have looked at his mouth. Not been carried away by lust into projecting on to him qualities he never possessed. It's the mouth, not the eyes, that is the window to the soul. Lips can be misleading, too, of course. Those downturned corners can denote great sadness as well as habitual petulance. That upward curve that leads to a dimple is as likely to be telling you that you're looking at self-satisfaction as good humour. But in the end, your mouth reflects far more of your habitual expression than your eyes do.

Kieran's upper lip was thin, but it was curvy. If she'd had her right mind in place she'd've seen that that curve was the sort of shape you get if you spend a lot of time sneering. But she didn't. She saw:

– the gym-toned torso
– the Armani suit
– the convertible Audi parked carelessly on the kerb
– the twinkle as he took her in behind the desk
– the thick mop of shiny Irish-black hair, just ripe for grabbing hold of.

And she thought:

– I want that
– I want to touch those arms
– I want to be in that passenger seat.

It's my punishment, she thinks. My karmic reward for my shallow ambitions. That I chose the father of my child on the basis of a flash car and a well-turned cheekbone.

But he was beautiful, and the breath caught in her chest as he approached the counter. Don't, she thought. He'll be wanting flowers for his girlfriend. That's the only men we see in here, outside Mother's and Valentine's Days: ones with something to make up for. Ones who are hoping to wheedle their way back into some angry woman's good graces. Bridget put on her most professional front, concentrated on picking over a big batch of baby's breath that had come in boxed from New Covent Garden.

He stopped in front of the counter. Put a hand on the stack of tissue paper laid out ready for the wrapping of bouquets. He was wearing a Rolex Oyster, she noticed. Six grand's worth of watch in a small shopfront on Lavender Hill. The nails had been recently manicured. She'd never seen a manicure on a man down here before, though plenty of the Chelsea bankers whose flats she kept filled with flowers had that never-been-dirty look to them.

Deep breath. Deep breath. She looked up, met those eyes. Candid, clear, full of naked admiration. He held her gaze for just that fraction too long. Her heart – she felt it – skipped in her chest. He is beautiful. The most beautiful thing I've ever seen. That smooth skin, the way his nostrils flare slightly. It's as though he's been carved from marble . . .

'Can I help you?'

It was as though the world had dropped away. The sounds of the shop – her assistant Gemma stacking oasis in the back room, the swish of traffic going down toward the Latchmere Road traffic lights – faded into the background and all she could hear was the whoosh of her own blood in her ears.

He smiled.

'I was driving past,' he said, 'and I saw you.'

Not me, she thought. My shop. It's a figure of speech.

'Uh-huh,' she said.

'I'd like,' he said, 'if you've got them, a dozen red roses.'

'Of course,' she replied, and her heart plummeted. No one buys red roses for themselves. It doesn't happen. They buy gerberas and peonies and lilies and alstroemeria. Not roses. Everyone knows that roses are for love.

Things like that don't happen to people like me. Who am I kidding? Get real, girl. You're not the sort who gets the beautiful ones. He's buying them for some well-groomed blonde up on Prince of Wales Drive. Buying them for someone who would look right perched there next to him with the top down.

Oh, but if it could be me, God. Just once, if it could be me. A man like that. If a man like that wanted me, I would be happy forever . . .

She went into the back room to fetch the bucket of roses. Black Baccara, delivered from Jersey that morning: scarlet so dark it was tinged with midnight, lush petals rich velvet like a royal evening gown. Gemma hovered just inside the door, eyes wide with excitement, a giggle barely contained by her lips. 'Omigod, *omigod*!' she whispered. Bridget threw her a frown. 'It's like having Brad *Pitt* walk in off the street!' she continued. 'Can I go out and serve him?'

'No, you can *not*,' hissed Bridget. 'You can stay out here till you've calmed down.'

And with shaking hands she picked up the bucket and returned to the Adonis outside.

'How about these?' she asked, tried to control her voice, to sound breezy and professional. 'The world's darkest rose,' she added. 'Classy.'

He reached out and caressed a petal. The sight of his fingers set off an involuntary shiver in her. Keiran glanced up, held her eyes, and once again he smiled. Looked fleetingly triumphant, had she but realized it, then covered the expression with complicity and warmth.

'Beautiful,' he said. And she couldn't tell if he meant the flowers or herself.

'How would you like them wrapped?' she asked.

A pause. Another look. He's flirting with me.

No he isn't. Some men just flirt, naturally. It comes as naturally as breathing.

'How would *you* like them?'

'Oh, quite simple,' she said. 'Just loosely tied to stop them spilling and wrapped in some of this black tissue.'

'Whatever way you like best,' said Kieran. Looked around the shop as she set about turning the roses – long smooth stems, vicious thorns – into a simple, stunning bouquet. Allowed herself the luxury of a brief daydream. Quashed it down deep.

'How come I've never noticed you before?' he asked. 'Have you been here long?'

Bridget shrugged. 'About three years now.'

'Business good?'

'Blooming,' she replied; what she always replied to that question. She had the strangest feeling: that time had gone into suspension, that things were happening at a third of their normal speed. 'Would you like a card with that?' she asked.

He shook that beautiful mane. 'Just one of yours,' he said. 'With your phone number on it. I have a feeling I'll be using it.'

She handed him a card and he handed her one in return: Platinum Amex. Very flash. Kieran Fletcher. A good name. Nothing too daunting about it. Bridget swiped the card, waited for a response from the clearing house.

'Bridget Barton,' he read out loud. 'Nice.'

She felt herself blush. 'Thanks,' she said.

'What time do you close tonight?'

The credit card machine bleeped, spat out the receipt for signing. Thirty-six pounds. Even back then, roses as special as this went for three pounds a pop.

She handed it to him. Waited as he signed. Big, cursive writing, a flourish on the F. 'Six o'clock,' she said.

'Great,' he said. Took the roses. Held them for a moment as he held her eye. Pushed them into her arms with a smile.

'I'll pick you up then,' he said.

Chapter Twenty-Three

Eighteen beds. Suddenly, the industrial washing machine doesn't seem large enough. It takes an hour and a half simply to strip them and get the linen down to the scullery, another three to make them back up again. And maybe I'll get better at it, or maybe I'll just get used to it. But I can't get much faster. These things – getting up and down the stairs without tripping over mountains of trailing fabric, turning duvet cover after duvet cover inside-out, making hospital corners because he hasn't had the sense to buy fitted bottom sheets – take a certain amount of physical time and I don't see how I'll ever shave that much off.

It's going to be a full day's ironing. People who stay in places like this expect Egyptian cotton. I'll do it up in the flat, where it's warm. Turn the radio on and set Yasmin up with the telly. Damn it. I didn't bring her down to the country to spend her days monging in front of the electronic babysitter.

She is bathed in sweat. The Aykroyds didn't all clear out until gone midday, and she felt inhibited about being too overt in getting started before they went. But they turned out to be nice people. There was almost two hundred pounds in tips scattered on the adults' bedside tables. She hadn't thought about the possibility of tips. Now she can get Yasmin a pair of decent wellies and herself a proper coat to see her through the winter.

She looks at her watch as she tidies the Hoover away. Five thirty. It's been dark outside for long enough that she'd lost track. There's still the kitchen to get shipshape.

The cooker top alone will take several aeons. Do they leave their kitchens like this at home? Probably not. At home they've not paid two thousand pounds plus tips to have it all done for them.

She unloads a batch of sheets from the washing machine, dumps them in the dryer, starts another wash cycle and hastens through to cover it in Fairy Power Spray. Turns the oven on to give its self-clean lining a blast of heat. Goes back and pops her head into the flat staircase.

'You all right up there, Yas?'

Her daughter seems to be talking to someone. She has a whole stableful of My Little Ponies now, and spends a lot of time brushing their manes and telling them to stand in corners. There's a pause, then she calls back: 'Yes. When's tea?'

'In a bit. Get yourself a biscuit if you're hungry.'

'Okay,' calls Yasmin. 'We'll have a tea-party.'

'All right,' she calls. 'Use the plastic mugs, not the china ones, okay?'

'D'oh.' Yasmin makes the universal sign of stupidity. Adolescence starts earlier and earlier these days. 'Of *course*.'

The dishwasher lets off an explosion of greasy steam as she opens it. I must start a list, she thinks, of things to buy in Wadebridge. Dishwasher cleaner. Cillit Bang. A gross of kitchen towels. One of those five-kilo packs of washing powder. Furniture polish. Window wipes. It's amazing how much glass can get smeared by a houseful of children. Oh, damn, I forgot to replace the bog paper in the bathrooms. I'll have to do it once I'm done in here. I just hope he'll stump up for whatever I buy. To be honest I don't care about some of it. If it saves me five minutes it'll be worth the tip money.

She leaves it to air, goes back to scrub at the cooker. There's melted cheese on here, and loads of blackened crumbs. And something viscous that someone's been scraping at with a knife. She finds a scouring pad under the sink and lays into it. No time for the gentle way.

Anyway, it's stainless steel. It should be tough enough to take it.

Fire. I need to get a fire laid and lit in the drawing room. He's really keen on that. Says it makes the place welcoming. And there's a vase of flowers on the dining-room table that's gone brackish. Oh, God.

She grabs a cloth, rinses it under the tap, wipes the cooker surface off. It'll have to do. It should look like a restaurant cooker, but I don't have time, I'll give it another polish once they're here. Hopefully they'll be too busy checking out the bedrooms to notice. I can unload the dishwasher at the same time.

She dumps the flowers in the scullery, on the top. The room is filling with thick damp warmth from the dryer; smells pleasantly of fabric conditioner and cleanness, the windows fogged against the cold night outside.

Bin. I need to empty the bin. And check the fridge. You never know, there might be something in there we could have for our tea, because otherwise it's beans on toast again and she's going to start grumbling. Fish fingers? Maybe fish finger sandwiches. And sweetcorn on the side. I'm sure there's a tin . . .

The bin is almost at repletion. Takes a couple of goes, clamped between her knees, before the vacuum breaks and the liner comes loose. There's been a leak. Something brown. I don't have time. A spray of Flash and a wipe-round with a kitchen towel, and I'll get it out to the scullery and deal with it later.

She's on her knees, cleaning up the remains of the leak from the floor – thank God for kitchen towels – when headlights play across the ceiling. My God, it can't be six o'clock. What happened to the day?

She leaps to her feet, runs her hands under the tap, flicks her hair down from the greasy ponytail it's been up in and goes to the front door.

He's tall. Has hair that has balded in a double V back over

the temples, which he's shaved in an attempt to cover it. He's wearing a black polo-neck sweater and overtight jeans: a middle-aged man dressing trendy to match the trophy wife who totters up the pathway behind him in fur, stilettos hazardous on the flagstone path.

'Good evening,' she says. 'Mr Terry?'

'Yes,' he says.

'Bridget Sweeny. I'm the housekeeper.'

'Right,' he says.

'Find it all right?'

'Of course, with satnav,' he says. Walks past her into the hall without really bothering to look into her face. Stands in the drawing-room door and looks around. 'Well, this is okay,' he says.

'It's not a hundred per cent done yet,' she says. 'I'm afraid the previous party were a bit late getting off.'

She sees a little flicker of the jaw. 'Not my problem,' he says. 'It was supposed to be ready.'

Not my place to argue, she thinks. 'No, I'm sorry. I've just got the fire to lay and the towels to put out . . .'

'Well, I want a bath right now,' says the trophy wife. Now she's in the light, Bridget sees that she's not as young as she looked coming up the path. She's got the facial lines of someone who's kept themselves unnaturally thin throughout their life.

'There's plenty of hot water,' says Bridget. 'I'll just go and –'

'No,' he says. Holds a bunch of keys out to her, sideways. 'We'll have our luggage first. There's quite a lot, I'm afraid. New Year and all that.'

Bridget looks at the keys.

He wants me to go and get it for him, she thinks. Feels herself get a little red about the face.

'Um . . .'

How do I handle this? I don't want to come across as unwilling, but . . .

'Perhaps you'd like me to show you around?'

'No, you can just get the luggage and do that in a minute.'

What do I say?

'Yes, we don't actually have a . . . um . . . porter . . .'

Michael Terry sighs, finally turns to face her.

'Just do your job, will you?'

Bridget fights the urge to sock him one. Rude fucker. Presumptuous dickhead. Who the hell do you think you are?

'Yes,' she says, 'I am.'

There's a short silence. 'I've been on the road for six hours,' he says.

And I've been working my arse off for eight.

She looks at him. The wife totters away and slumps on a sofa, unzips her boots.

'It's just a few cases.'

'I'm sorry, but I've still got the house to finish up. I'll be out of your way as quickly as possible.'

He throws the keys down on the hall table. Petulantly.

'Great,' he says. Turns away from her. 'Great start to my holiday.'

'Any chance of a cup of tea, at least?' calls the wife. 'Or is that too much for you as well?'

Chapter Twenty-Four

'Hello?' she shouts.

'Happy New Year! Jesus! What's that noise?'

'Jesus is about right. They're having a party. The tenants.'

'Are they allowed?'

'God knows. By the time I realized what they were up to it was a bit late to do anything about it.'

Monsters. They are monsters. They couldn't be more monstrous if there were horns sprouting from their heads.

'Where's Yas?'

'In my bed,' bellows Bridget. 'But she's not asleep, funnily enough.'

And their music. Most of these people – most of the men, anyway – are in their forties. What are they doing, playing bone-shaking doom-bada-doom-bada-doom-bada-doom club anthems when they should have graduated to something with a tune by now?

'Jesus,' says Carol. 'It's worse than those bastards downstairs.'

'For all I know it *is* those bastards downstairs. It's not like we ever saw them, is it?'

'Well,' says Carol, 'they're certainly not at home here tonight . . .'

Outside, below the living-room window, someone is throwing up, copiously and without inhibition. Lovely. I just *know* it's going to be *me* out there with the hose getting that off the wall in the morning. Oh, you bastards. You utter, utter bastards. It's been hard enough steering Yasmin's attention away from your car key parties and the fact that half your blonde popsies aren't wearing pants under their miniskirts without having to explain why you can't vomit in lavatories like normal people.

'So . . . if she's still awake, can I say Happy New Year to her as well?'

'Of course,' says Bridget. 'Hang on.'

She walks up the corridor, pushes open the bedroom door. Yasmin is kneeling up, looking out of the window. Her eyes are wide with fascination and fatigue. I'm going to have a *great* day with her tomorrow. Just great. Tantrums *and* buckets of bleach. Happy New Year, Michael Terry, you pompous puffed-up wanker.

She holds out the handset. 'Auntie Carol.'

Yasmin scoots across the bed, presses the phone to her ear. 'Auntie Carol!' she says. 'There's two people playing the Beast With Two Backs in the alleyway.'

Beast With Two Backs? Where does she get these things from? And how does she know what it is? Good God. I got her out of London just in time.

Yasmin settles back, pulls the bedclothes around her. 'Yes,' she says. 'Thank you.'

Bridget goes through to make a cup of tea. Might as well. It's not like the caffeine's going to make much difference to her sleep tonight. The kitchen is literally shaking. They've turned the bass up on those damn speakers so high that the ceiling light dances above her head. Old Skool bollocks. Stuff she hasn't heard in years. Stuff she sort of hoped she'd never hear again. A woman's voice, shrieking, barely in tune: *RAYd on tahm, ruh-ruh-ruh RAYd on tahm . . .*

She looks at the clock on the cooker. Nearly midnight. Will they stop, at least, for the bells?

God, let's hope not. These people, the New Year kisses will probably turn into some revolting full-on orgy. I had to clear a condom out of the library waste basket yesterday. Disgusting. Animals. Get a bit of money, and they turn into monsters.

Maybe I should try some of that valerian stuff. Maybe

it'll even override this. No. It won't. I'm in hell. They're going to go on all night. Jesus God. They could have warned me. Let me get my daughter off the premises. But they wouldn't, would they? If they'd given me some warning I could have got Tom Gordhavo to put a stop to it.

The sound of breaking glass.

Well, they're certainly losing their deposit.

She goes back to the bedroom.

'Okay,' says Yasmin. 'I will. Night night, Auntie Carol. Sleep tight. Happy New Year.'

Bridget takes the phone back.

'Well, she certainly sounds like she's enjoying herself,' says Carol.

'I wish the same could be said of her mother. Can you imagine what sort of a day I'm going to have tomorrow?'

Carol laughs. 'Happy New Year,' she says.

'So what have you got up to?'

'Nothing, actually,' says Carol. 'I'm sitting here with a bottle of Muscadet burning candles and casting spells. Trying to attract a bit of luck.'

'We could do with some of that.'

'That's what I thought.'

'So what are you wishing for?'

'A job,' she says decisively. 'I'm going to get a job this year if it kills me. And a life. Now you've gone I don't speak to anyone from one day to the next. I swear, I could vanish and no one would notice.'

'I'd notice, Carol,' says Bridget.

'Not for a while, let's face it.'

There's a tiny, uncomfortable pause between them. Bridget's busy, now, with her new life, and not so dependent on Carol. It *would* take a while, it's true. She hasn't rung her since before Christmas as it is.

'Anyway,' Carol hurries on, 'I've got the candles still lit. Anything you want me to wish for for you?'

'Yes.'

She ducks, instinctively, as something else smashes on the garden path.

'Yes,' she says. 'Put a bloody curse on these people.'

'No sooner said than done,' says Carol. 'Happy New Year, honey. Have a good one.'

'You too. Thanks for calling.'

Carol goes. Bridget gets into bed with her daughter and her tea. Cuddles up and strokes fuzzy hair.

'People,' says Yasmin, 'are weird.'

'Sure are, baby,' she says.

'Why would you want to make that amount of noise, anyway?'

'You know what I think? It's to drown out what they're saying. Because if anyone could hear what they were saying they'd realize they were completely *schtoopid*.'

Yasmin giggles. You won't be giggling soon, thinks Bridget. I can see it in your eyes. Give it an hour – less – and you're going to be climbing the walls. You're going to be crying your poor little eyes out because they won't let you go to sleep.

A brief pause, then the music starts again. Bloody Keith bloody Flint. I'll give him Twisted bloody Firestarter.

Someone pumps up the volume.

The lights go out.

Chapter Twenty-Five

'It was hilarious. Couldn't have happened to nicer people.'

'So what did you do?' Tina Teagle puts her mug down on the kitchen table, sits back and looks at her.

'Well,' says Bridget, 'we were in bed already. And obviously our lights were out, too, because we *were* in bed. So we just stayed there.'

'And?'

'They came and banged on the door. Downstairs one first, and then he came and rattled at the one on the upstairs corridor.'

'Lucky you'd locked them.'

'Too right. Imagine having a load of –' she lowers her voice so Yasmin and Chloe can't hear her – 'coke-fuelled superannuated models wandering in and shagging wherever they fetched up. It was difficult enough keeping madam distracted while they were outside without them coming in and doing it in her bedroom. As it is I'm going to have my work cut out with the laundry this week.'

Tina pulls a face. 'Ewww.'

'I swear,' says Bridget, 'they've been doing key parties down there.'

'Ewww,' says Tina again. 'Do people still do that?'

'Apparently so. In the more expensive parts of North London.'

'Which keys go first, do you think?'

'Not the Ferraris, that's for sure,' says Bridget. 'Or maybe it's only me that's noticed that Ferrari drivers always wear pony tails to make up for what's missing on top.'

'Baseball caps,' says Tina.

'Lettered bomber jackets.'

'Ewww,' says Tina again. 'When did you say they go again?'

'Day after tomorrow. Although half of them have gone already. That's how come I know about the laundry. It's going to take me a week to clear up properly once they're finally gone.'

Tina hisses in through her teeth. 'Happy New Year,' she says.

'Cheers,' says Bridget and raises her glass. 'Fortunately there's no one else booked in to come for a bit so at least I've got time to do it.'

They're drinking cider. In the middle of the afternoon. Bridget feels louche and liberated, even though she's keeping an eye on her intake for her driving licence's sake. In London, if she drank before Yasmin was in bed – not that it was something she could afford to do much of – she spent so much time worrying about Social Services she could never enjoy it. Here, with rain pouring down from the gutter outside and her daughter engrossed in a game of Snakes and Ladders (Snakes and Ladders! When did a London child last play something which didn't have explosions in it?), she just feels – warm.

'Nice cider,' she says.

'Scrumpy, actually.'

'Scrumpy.'

'Mark makes it.'

'That's a useful skill.'

'Nicked the apples from your garden, matter of fact. From that old orchard bit beyond the pond.'

Bridget laughs. 'Bet that'd make Tom Gordhavo happy.'

'I daresay he won't have noticed. Nobody goes in there as far as I know, and he avoids the place like the plague if he can help it.'

'Well, he's welcome to do it again next year,' says Bridget. 'As long as I get a cut of the product.'

'I'll tell him,' says Tina. 'So you're planning on being here next year, then, are you?'

'Don't see why not.'

'Good for you.'

'Why would you think I wouldn't be?'

'I dunno,' says Tina. 'He just doesn't seem to have much luck keeping staff up there.'

'So I hear.'

'So what,' asks Tina, 'brought you down here, anyway?'

Bridget looks at her, calculates. Am I ready to be telling everyone my business? Is it wise? From what I've seen of this village, nobody gets to keep a secret for long.

'Oh, you know,' she says. 'I split up with my husband. Money was tight. And I looked around and wondered what on earth I was doing, bringing a kid up in the city. It made sense.'

'You bet,' says Tina, with all the complacence of the inveterate country-dweller. 'So what did your ex think, then? You going such a long way away?'

'He . . .' He rang me up and threatened to get me. 'I haven't the faintest idea,' she finishes. 'He wasn't exactly Mr Regular, you know what I mean?'

'Deadbeat Dads,' says Tina. Seems satisfied by the answer, assumes she knows the whole story. 'You should get the CSA on to him.'

Yeah. That would be a good idea. Get them to give him my address and all while I'm at it. Mind you, from my experience of them, when I was desperate to get some help, get some child support to stop us being made homeless from the flat where my husband thought he still had right of entry, the best way of making sure no one ever finds out where you are would be to contact the CSA and give them all your details, in triplicate, in writing. That would make damn sure no one ever got in touch with you again. Kieran didn't pay a penny from the day he left to the day she and Yasmin did, and all the CSA could say was that they'd lost her file and would get back to her.

'Her dad was the same.' Tina gestures at Chloe. 'Went to St Austell looking for a job three years ago and we haven't seen hide nor hair of him since.'

'Good God.' Bridget is shocked. 'Did you report him missing?'

'Course not,' says Tina. 'Just 'cause we haven't seen him doesn't mean we don't know where he is. Anyway, Justine Strang saw him on Darky Day in Padstow a couple of months later with his hands down some fat bird's blouse. Complexion like a boiled potato and an arse like a ro-ro ferry, she said. Good luck to her, I say. He was never much good for anything anyway. He'll probably have spawned another one by now and moved on to Newquay.'

Bridget looks at her speculatively. Her face has one of those defiant expressions on it: the I'm-okayness of someone who probably isn't but has to make the best of it. A bit like me, she thinks. A bit like most of the world, I sometimes think.

'I'm sorry,' she tells her.

'Not your fault. Anyway, at least the lease was in my name, thank God, so we didn't end up homeless as well. And when Mark's girlfriend did the same thing he moved in here, so at least we've been able to pool our resources a bit. It's not ideal, but it's better than nothing, eh?'

They drink. Think.

'I don't suppose it was exactly what either of us was thinking about,' says Tina. 'When I'm twenty-seven I'll still be living with my brother. At least I was able to save him from going back to Mum and Dad's, anyway.'

'Where are they today?'

'Cinema. Bodmin. Said they'd get out of our hair so we could have a proper women's afternoon.'

She feels a twinge of disappointment. Realizes that a tiny bit of her has been hoping that he'd turn up. So tiny she has barely registered it. The last thing she needs right now is a man; not after the last one. What she needs first is a life. And some understanding of how she managed to make such a bad choice last time.

'What have they gone to see?'

'James and the Giant Peach.'

'It's about a boy,' calls Yasmin, 'and a giant peach.'

'Mmm,' says Bridget. You don't say.

'Can we go?'

'We'll see,' she says. God, I'm tired of saying 'We'll see.' If this lot turn out to be good tippers, I'll take her. I'll take all of us. We need a treat. And if anyone deserves a good tip, it's me after this week.

'So what's it like, then,' Tina changes the subject, 'up at Rospetroc? When you haven't got a load of yuppie wife-swappers to contend with?'

'Yeah. Yeah, it's okay.'

'Not too cut off for you, then? I wouldn't like to live so far out of the village.'

'God, it's not that far. Everybody talks about it like it's the North Pole or something.'

'Yeah,' says Tina. 'I suppose in a way everybody thinks of it as being further away than it is. It's 'cause no one's lived there in so long, I suppose everyone's stopped thinking of it as part of the community.'

'Oh, right. So when did the Gordhavos move out, then?'

'The Gordhavos?'

'Yes.'

'Bless you, love, the Gordhavos never lived there. That was a Blakemore house.'

'Sorry,' says Bridget. 'You have to remember I've only just arrived.'

'Sorry,' says Tina back. 'I forget everyone doesn't know everything about Cornwall. Blakemore. Big family they were, once, round here. Name means bleak moor. Very Emily Brontë.'

'So who are they?'

'The people who used to –' She laughs at herself, continues. 'Mrs Gordhavo was a Blakemore. Teresa Blakemore. Tom's mum. He inherited it through her. Well, technically it's still hers seeing as she's still alive, but she's not set foot in there in decades.'

'Oh, right. I thought the Gordhavos were –'

'Yes, they are,' says Tina. 'Land still marries land around here, believe me.'

'So that's why they don't live in the house, then? They've got other houses?'

'Sort of. Yes, I mean. But also, I don't think they like the place much. It's not brought them a lot of luck, what with one thing and another. She only inherited because her brother did himself in. He'd be living there now, otherwise.'

'Did himself in?'

Each of them glances at her daughter. They lower their voices again. Neither wants to be the one who plants ideas in their heads. But nor does Tina want to miss out on the opportunity to share a bit of local gossip.

'Yes,' she says, conspiratorially. 'Ages ago now. Old Mrs B must be dead nearly twenty years, and it was before that he did it. There was some of that mother-died-of-a-broken-heart speculation hereabouts, but I don't think so. More like a loose stair rod and a worn carpet and a skinful of whisky, by all accounts. Hanged himself. Down in that old boathouse. With his own tie, slung round a hook. Horrible sight, apparently. Took 'em a few days to find him. I don't think anyone had been in that boathouse since before the war, so it wa'n't the first place they looked, exactly. All I know is, he'd turned black by the time they found him.'

'Lovely,' says Bridget. Checks the girls. They have their backs to her, are riffling through a tub of old beads and sequins. Yasmin seems to have found a kindred spirit on the princess front, at last. Sparkly things will keep her distracted for hours.

'What made him do it?'

'No idea. I don't think anyone cared much. He wasn't popular, I remember that. A bit of a bully. My mum used to keep us away from him. Made out it was because he had a bit of a temper. But you know what grown-ups are like. Don't want to scare you with bogey-man stories. I wonder, sometimes, now I've got one of my own, if that was what she was really going on about, you know.'

'You mean . . .?'

'Well, it doesn't do to speak ill of the dead, of course, but you know. You can't help wondering.'

'Well,' says Bridget.

'I don't think they were a very happy family, living there. Even before he did himself in. Mrs Gordhavo's father disappeared at Tobruk and they kept themselves to themselves in the village, except for paying people to come in when they could get them. The old lady was one of those old-fashioned snobs.'

'Snobs can be happy.'

'Well, yes,' says Tina. 'Until you get old and no one comes to keep an eye on you unless you pay them.'

She smiles as she speaks, with that glee with which people often greet the misfortunes of the wealthy.

The back door opens and Jago barrels through it. Stops dead and stares at the visitor. 'Allo,' he says.

'Hello,' says Bridget.

'You're Yasmin's mum, aren't you?'

'The very same.'

'That mean Yasmin's here?'

'It does.'

'Cool!' he says.

'Jago,' says Mark, coming in in his wake, 'take off your boots before you go in the other room. Oh, hello, Bridget. How are you?'

'Good. Thanks,' says Bridget. He gives her a friendly, lopsided grin, bends down to pull his son's footwear off. 'So I hear you had a bit of a do up at yours at New Year,' he says.

'Oh, don't,' says Bridget.

'She's just been telling me,' says Tina. 'Quite a party.'

'Bet you've been having fun clearing up.'

'Well, actually,' says Bridget, 'I did get my own back, a bit. In the morning. Couldn't stay awake after eight, so I went down to see what the damage was like.'

'Uh-huh?'

He's got a lock of hair loose, flopped over one eye. She feels a sudden urge to reach out, brush it back. Blinks, gets hold of herself.

'Well, you can imagine. Broken glass, streamers, great puddles of spilled stuff, ashtrays all over the carpets.'

'Great.'

'And half a dozen dead bodies.'

'No!'

'Yeah,' says Tina, 'you don't have to be so literal. They'd just passed out, dumbo. Drunk.'

He grins.

'So you know what I did?'

'No.'

'I got the Hoover out. Switched the electricity back on and started cleaning round them where they lay. Made sure I bumped into everything I went past.'

'Brilliant,' he says.

'They won't be coming back here in a hurry,' says Bridget.

'I shouldn't think they will.'

'Weird people, though. No, I mean, apart from that. You know what I found?'

'What?'

Jago, released, runs off into the interior of the house to look for the girls. Mark comes and sits with them at the table.

'Well, I went to clear the fireplace up and someone had taken all the ashes and spread them all over the hearth-stone, and then they'd written a whole load of swearwords in them. Like "Fuck off" and "Bugger" and –' she lowers her voice – 'the c-word.'

'The c-word?' He raises his eyebrows and she suddenly realizes he's amused that she's turned to self-censorship when it comes to that word when she's said the first two without thought.

'No, but,' she says, 'don't you think that's weird? I mean, how bored do you have to be to do something like that to keep you entertained?'

'Londoners,' says Mark, as though the word is an explanation in itself. 'Oi! Is that my scrumpy you're drinking?'

Chapter Twenty-Six

'It wasn't me,' says Lily. 'I didn't bloody do it.'

'You see?' says Felicity Blakemore. 'Defiant. Defiant *and* a liar.'

Margaret Peachment holds her counsel. The tickets for Canada are practically burning a hole in her pocket. It'll be someone else's job in a few weeks, she thinks. Anything for a quiet life.

Behind her, Hugh Blakemore stands with his hands in the pockets of his grey tweed shorts. Grins at Lily Rickett like an ape.

'Well, who else is likely to have done it?' asks Mrs Blakemore. 'Answer me that.'

Lily shrugs.

'What's *that* supposed to mean?'

His eye catches hers. Hugh raises a triumphal eyebrow, grins again. There is more, the smile says, where that came from. You'll never get away from me.

Lily touches the burgeoning bruise through her sleeve. 'I don't know,' she snarls. 'But it wasn't bloody *me*.'

The women stare down at the shards on the floor, a poker clutched like a lance in Mrs Blakemore's right hand. Hugh put it there right after he popped his cricket ball into the window seat. Right before he grabbed her by the scruff, raised his voice and called for his mother.

'It's too much,' she repeats. 'I cannot be expected to just – accept . . . Look!'

She bends down and takes the head of a King Charles spaniel between thumb and forefinger, brandishes it in

Mrs Peachment's face. 'Staffordshire. Over a hundred years old. Not, I suppose, that one should expect a guttersnipe from the slums to be able to discern such a thing.'

'Oh dear,' says Margaret Peachment. 'And are you sure it can't have been –'

'Worth five pounds each, some of 'em,' says Felicity, dropping the head back among the broken remains of W. G. Grace, of Gladstone and Wellington, of Queen Victoria as a young bride and a nameless flower-seller with pink and dimpled cheeks and a skirt full of posies. 'But that's beside the point. They're *family* things. *Family*.'

'I do appreciate that,' says Margaret Peachment. 'I feel the same about –'

'Yes, well,' snaps the lady of the Great House, 'I'm sure *your* heirlooms go back *several* generations.'

Little spots of pink appear on Mrs Peachment's cheeks. Mrs Blakemore fails to notice. They do, actually, she thinks. Some of my things came down from my great-great-grandmother, not that someone like *you* would care. That's the trouble with this country. Old families . . . It will be better once this war is over. Things will be different then.

'I do sympathize,' she says sympathetically. She needs to emanate as much sympathy as she can at this moment without actually giving ground, because it is she who will have to pick up the pieces if this arrangement falls apart. For the time being.

'You would have thought,' says Mrs Blakemore, 'she would be grateful, but oh, no. I feel,' she continues, 'as though she's brought the entire bally war into my house with her.'

Mrs Peachment sees a brief flash of the events six months ago, the Channel awash with young men's blood, the brave little fishing boats that never returned, and holds her peace.

'I'm sure she didn't mean it. You know how children are. Thoughtless . . .'

'Yeah, but,' says Lily, 'I didn't bloody *do* it.'

Felicity snaps round to glare at her. The pinched, defiant glare, the skin that looks dirty however much carbolic you waste on her. I hate her, she thinks suddenly. Hate her. I can't help it. A cuckoo in my nest, taking over, with her dirty mouth, teaching the others her vile language, no control, no discipline. If Patrick were here, he'd know what to do. Damn this war. Damn Hitler and Chamberlain, scattering slum dwellers through our countryside, taking my husband away.

'Be quiet,' she orders. 'You're in enough trouble already.'

'Yes, but I didn't bloody *do* it!'

Felicity Blakemore loses her temper. Advances on the child, fist clenched, teeth bared. 'Get out! Get *out*! I'll – I'll –'

'Felicity!' cries Mrs Peachment.

She catches herself. Doesn't do to show temper in front of the village.

'Yes, well,' she says, after five ragged breaths. 'You can't expect something like this to go unpunished.'

'Of course not!' says Mrs Peachment. 'Naturally not!'

'She is defiant, Margaret, and it cannot be tolerated.'

Lily's eyes fill with tears, but no one notices. Except Hugh. And when he sees it, he grins again. Does the boohoo gesture with his clenched fists. I was so happy, thinks Lily. I was so stupid. More fool me, to think that anything that good could last.

'It wasn't me,' she says one more time, hopelessly.

'I'm too angry at the moment,' says Felicity Blakemore. 'I can't cope with it just now.'

'Yes,' says Mrs Peachment. 'Let her stew on what she's done for a bit.'

'Yes,' agrees Mrs Blakemore. 'We'll shut her up and let her think about what she's done.'

'Good,' says Mrs Peachment. 'Good thinking.'

She is thinking of a bedroom, of course. Thinking about how she would send Julia and Terence to their rooms to await punishment. She doesn't know about the cupboard in the four-poster room; the black, the flaking plaster, the spiders, the bolted door.

'You can deal with her when you've calmed down,' she says encouragingly then, quickly, to extricate herself before she gets embroiled again: 'Well, I must dash, Felicity. I have to get down to the Home Farm. Some trouble with the land girls, I'm afraid.'

'Oh, yes,' says Mrs Blakemore, and Mrs Peachment catches the edge to the comment. 'Mustn't keep the *land girls* waiting.'

'No,' she says. 'Well, bye-bye.'

'*Good*bye, Mrs Peachment,' says Mrs Blakemore, pointedly. 'If you wouldn't mind letting yourself out.'

It's a slight, and she knows it. Flusters her way out of the room. Finds her hat and her gloves on the hall table and scurries from the house without putting them on.

She really is the giddy limit, that woman, she thinks as she walks to her bicycle. *Such* a snob. I'm so glad I'm getting away from here.

She has to wheel the bicycle up the track; it's too rutted to get up the speed to make the hill. The heat of the day combines with her embarrassment, turns her face scarlet as she walks.

I've half a mind, she thinks, to do something to make sure she can't get rid of that girl. Thinks she can tell everyone what to do just because she's Lady Muck. And the fumes coming off her, at this time of day. She'll run out of Floris soon and then she won't be able to cover up her habits by drenching herself.

It would serve her right, it really would.

And then she smiles.

Why not? It's not as if anyone will be coming after me, she thinks. They're far too busy to go chasing off to British Columbia in search of administrative errors.

And suddenly the hill seems far less steep.

No one speaks for a minute after she leaves. Lily, tempted to bolt for the door, sees that Hugh has walked across and blocked it off.

Mrs Blakemore looks down at the floor, stirs the pieces of the figurines with an elegant toe. Takes a breath and looks up.

'Well,' she says.

Lily is ready to spring. Feels like a trapped animal. Wants to cry.

'Hugh, would you mind?' says Mrs Blakemore. 'I think it's time for the cupboard, don't you?'

'Yes, Mummy,' says Hugh. Steps across and takes Lily by the arm.

The cupboard. Nonononono! I'm scared! Shut in! Don't! Don't! My mum shuts me in, under the stairs . . . Don't!

Lily struggles. But Hugh has grown since he went away. He seems even larger than he was at half-term. He's got her by both arms, now, simply lifts her off the floor and carries her toward the stairs.

'Please!' shrieks Lily. 'Please . . . don't! I'm sorry! I'm sorry!'

'Sorry?'

'I'm sorry! I didn't do it! It wasn't me!'

'Well, what are you sorry for, then?'

'It wasn't . . . *please!*'

'Make your mind up,' says her jailer. 'You didn't do it, or you're sorry?'

Lily slumps in his grip. Hopes that the dead weight will be too much. Hugh, enjoying himself and strengthened by adrenalin, arrives at the stairs, humps her on to the first step. Takes pleasure in inflicting punishment for his own crime.

Felicity Blakemore turns away, walks off through the drawing room toward her study. There's a decanter of whisky in there. She feels she deserves a dram, after this terrible start to the afternoon.

They both wait until she has gone. Both know the ante will be upped the minute they're alone.

Lily starts to swear. 'You bastard,' she says. 'You fucking bastard. I'll get you. I'll fucking get you, you bastard.'

Hugh laughs. Shows her how much bigger he is than

she. Gets his hand into her armpits, pokes hard digits into tender flesh. Hauls her to the top of the stairs and, once they're in the corridor, digs his fingers into her sketchy scalp and begins to drag her, flailing like a fish on a hook, along the carpet. She is screaming, now. With the pain and with the fear. 'You fuckingfuckingfucking . . .'

She manages to twist her head around, bite him on the wrist.

'Christ!'

And now he's kicking her. Slapping her about the head. No one here to see. No one here to hear. And he gets her by the hair again and drags her into the four-poster room. Daddy's room. What must have been, he thinks, the room where he was conceived, though his mother moved down to the facing bedroom in the far wing so long ago he barely remembers them using it as a couple. No one has slept here at all since his father went off to serve King and Country. Even though it's the best room, with the best bed, in the house.

Hugh grabs Lily round the waist, throws her on to the heavy family bed, flings himself on top, pins her down. Enjoys the feeling of her body bucking beneath him. Gets her by the wrists and waits.

'Please,' she begs again.

'Please what?'

He smiles. Feels her breathe. Smiles wider. Grinds his body down on hers. There's been a lot of that, in this room, in this bed, over the centuries. It's a strong bed, a grand bed: a bed made for subjection. Ancestors taming the peasantry by whatever means they had to hand. Lily looks appalled. Looks sick. Tries to kick.

'Oh you – you fucking . . .'

Now he's got her by the wrists, grins the victor's grin. She subsides. Fight and you make it worse. Isn't that what she's always learned? Fight, and you just make them more aggressive.

He leans forward, whispers into her ear.

'I can always come back, you know,' he says.

She turns her head away from him, finds herself looking at the cupboard. It's built into a deep recess in the wall, windowless and soundproof. She doesn't know which is worse: to stay out here with Hugh, or the prospect of that scratching, creaking blackness.

'Please,' she says. 'Don't make me go in there.'

'Too late,' says Hugh. 'Got to do what Mummy says.'

'Please . . .' she says. 'I can't . . .'

And he moves against her. He is heavy for his age, despite the privations of rationing. Heavy and strong. She can smell the smell of him. He is Papal Scarlet.

Down below, in the courtyard, they can hear the sound of the others returning from the village. They are laughing, carefree. Lily feels despair soak her bones. They won't come looking for me. Won't ask where I am, even. I'll be shut in there and none of them will give a damn. Why was I born? Why did you make me be born, if life was always going to be like this?

Hugh dips his head down, sniffs at the scalp by her ear. Winning is good, he thinks. Especially here. In Daddy's bedroom. I'm the man of the house now, I'm the one in charge.

'Never mind,' he says. 'It won't be for too long. Just a while. And once you've learned your lesson, then I'll come and get you.'

Chapter Twenty-Seven

Michael Terry, I hate you. You *and* your skanky wife.

It's not just the stained sheets, or the upended ashtrays on the Persian rugs, or the streaks of oil-based make-up on the sofa cushions – where, presumably, someone's been sweating face-down – or the broken glasses – three of them at least if you count the stems – on the front path where my daughter could have gone to play, or the great gash in the paint on the drawing-room door-frame where you and your friends imported thousand-watt speakers to keep me and my daughter awake at night with, or the bleached stain on the dining-room table where one of your friends tipped over a drink and nobody bothered to mop it up, or the fact that you used every single utensil – pots, pans, plates, bowls, glasses, mugs, cups, platters, cutlery, cooking irons, steamers, Tupperware – in both kitchens to save yourselves the terrible ordeal of having to load the dishwasher and left it for me to do once you'd gone, or the white powder – oh you are *so* Primrose Hill – I just spent an hour scraping out of the cracks in the coffee table, or the used condoms I had to pick out of the trap on the septic tank with rubber gloves, or the great big burn on the work-surface in the far kitchen where you put a casserole dish down without bothering to use a trivet, or the skid marks you feel it's okay to leave in your lavatory even though there's a brush *right there*, or the way you all balled up your towels and left them, damp, to suppurate rather than hanging them up, or even the fact that, after the way you treated us all week, the high-handedness and the order-throwing and the never-say-pleases-or-thank-yous, you didn't bother to leave even the tiniest tip, not one of you. You're probably the sort of people who use the minimum wage as a justification for not tipping in restaurants.

No, it's none of those things, hateful though they make you. It's the way you've treated your room.

No one behaves like this. The Gallagher brothers don't behave like this. What is it with this room, that it obviously makes its inhabitants mad? Turns them into some weird hybrid of human being and pig?

They've torn the place apart again. It's all back the way it was when she first arrived, the tester torn down from the four-poster again, the paintings awry, the bedclothes ripped off and tossed through the open cupboard door. Only, it's worse. I don't know what they thought they were doing. There's a red wine stain on the naked mattress. And what looks like a patch of dried blood, to boot. And there's more. It looks as though they've gone through the contents of the jumbo-sized vanity case Skanketta Terry had with her when she arrived. Face cream. Body scrub. Shampoo. Poison by Calvin Klein. Palmer's cocoa butter. Talcum, in a pot with a fluffy pink puff. Foundation. Fake tan. All of them, squeezed and shaken and ripped open and *thrown* around the room. There's eyeshadow trodden into the carpet. Conditioner – at least, please God let it be conditioner – sprayed all over the curtains.

You are *so* losing your deposit.

What makes people do things like this? Do they do it in their own homes? Do they?

It's ten o'clock. At night. And she's only got as far as clearing all the plates and glasses – dumped down and left, their leftovers unscraped, wherever the eaters ran out of steam – out of the rooms and into the kitchen. Yasmin starts school tomorrow, and then she'll be alone all day, in this big empty place, with all the time in the world to be methodical, to blitz from room to room, disinfecting the surfaces and oiling the wood. But now she's seen this, she can't leave it alone. All she was going to do was strip the sheets, but now that Yasmin's asleep, she's on her hands and knees on the mattress, dabbing at their disgustingness with stain remover because a lot of these stains need tackling before they settle for good.

What sort of person?

And the weird thing is, she feels as though she's being watched. Keeps catching herself, gasping and flipping round to look at the open cupboard door. *He's coming*. That's what keeps going through her head. *He's coming*. And when she looks more clearly at the shadows, distinguishes dark from semi-dark, of course there's no one there.

Did I lock the door?

Of course you did.

Did I?

I don't remember.

He'll be back.

He can't be back. He's never been here.

He's coming back and I can't get away.

She checks her watch. Quarter past. Will there come a time when I don't automatically recheck? When I just get into bed and stay there? It's not only the Kieran thing: it's the country thing. People round here don't spend their lives lying awake listening for the sound of breaking glass.

Better go down and check. I don't remember. Don't remember shooting the bolts. Don't remember rattling each of the ground-floor windows, one after another. Don't remember turning the big heavy key that sits permanently in the scullery door.

She goes down via the flat. Puts her head into Yasmin's room. She is fast asleep: way gone; limbs splayed with such abandon she looks like a rag doll. She's been trying the spare bed again. The sheets are all piled up, thrown back as though she got out of it in a hurry, the pillow slipped over the side between bed and bedside table. Never mind. She'll decide one day. She'll settle. Maybe I'll just leave it like that; not bother to remake it. She's just going to unmake it again.

The dining room still smells: fag smoke, stale wine. She

passes through the ground floor slowly, methodically. Ante-room windows. Drawing-room windows. Far kitchen. It's only got a Yale, this one; she'll have to ask Tom Gordhavo about beefing up the locks. It's only fair enough, really. East wing door. Front door. There's a bolt undone at the top, but of course the key has been turned. Of course. I remember it now. I remember, because I had that stupid thought as I turned it: *Locking out is also locking in.*

She glances over her shoulder. The trouble is, a house like this is meant to be full of people. Not people like the Terrys, perhaps, but without them, with their noise gone when they took off the way they descended, like a flock of starlings, the contrast is even greater. Without them, the shadows are thicker, the dark places darker. Without the restlessness of human presence, every sound, every adjustment in the building's four-hundred-year-old frame resonates like gunfire. When they go, because they were there, I am more aware that I am alone.

She peers out into the garden and the yard beyond as she rattles the dining-room windows. She has never seen darkness like it. Hills on every side hide the lights from the village, and clouds obscure the moon. The only illumination comes from her own windows: the lights in here and in the four-poster room show winter privet as crouching trolls, the old yew a hunchbacked giantess, the knot where a branch must have been removed years ago a single, staring eye.

It's beautiful. Come on, it's beautiful. People would give their right arms to be living like this.

The windows are secure. She draws the curtains to shut out the night.

Half past ten. Up at seven to get Yasmin fed and tidied in time for school. She needs a proper breakfast inside her: needs to make a good impression. The last thing she needs is to be a labelled an attention-deficient townie before they've had a chance to get to know her. Her reading's bound to be behind the others'. They didn't seem to do much at that last school apart from refuse to exclude people and send the kids who came in carrying knives to the counselling team.

She turns off the dining-room light, quickly pulls the door to. Kitchen windows. Scullery. All fine. The tap is dripping and she twists it closed. Maybe I should put those curtains on to wash. One of them, anyway. Before I go to bed. They're so heavy they'll take a week to dry. Damn those Terrys. I'll call Tom Gordhavo in the morning and give him the full run-down. He needs to know, or I'll be paying for the breakages myself. Imagine. What can have got into their heads that they thought it was – what? Funny? – to vandalize their room like that? How long did they stay in it after they'd done it?

She remembers the discarded slips of origami'd paper she collected from the carpet; pages from porn magazines cut down to size so they showed lips and breasts and unmanned penises, folded over and over again; a drug dealer's ugly little joke. Of course I know what got into their heads. It doesn't take a rocket scientist.

She feels surprisingly weary as she mounts the flat stairs. The way she used to feel, in London, when lack of sleep weighed heavily. People like the Terrys, she thinks, are bullies. They get as much pleasure from dominance, from causing trouble to other people, as they do from their behaviour itself. I lived like that for too long. It wears you out. I'll be glad of my bed tonight.

The room stinks of spilled perfume. It'll take a steam cleaner and a pint of Febreze to get that out. Vile. Vile people. Thank God they're gone. Thank God, she thinks, we're alone at last.

She takes the dressing-table chair over to the window, stands on it. The pole is a long way ahead, at the full stretch of her reach. She knows she should wait until the morning and fetch the stepladder, but tiredness makes her obdurate. She wants the Terrys expunged from the house, and she wants it done as soon as possible. She strains, gets her index finger on to the bottom of the first hook and pushes. It pops out. There, she thinks. Drops her hand down to shake her arm out. It is aching already from working above her head. Damn you, Michael Terry.

It takes five minutes to liberate, hook by hook, the curtain from the rings. By the time it's done, she is sweating. Her calf muscles ache and so do her shoulders, the arches of her feet cramping from too long on tiptoe. I must look crazy, she thinks, from outside; teetering on a chair at eleven o'clock at night. The thought makes her glance down at the empty garden. Silver moonlight is beginning to break through the clouds, dappling the dewy lawn.

Bridget drapes the curtain over her forearm. There. It's all worth it. The light is so strong, now, that she can see the relief on the monochrome landscape below her. Flecks of silver in the granite walls of the house catch the light, glitter. Everything is shiny, polished, as though it has been washed by rain.

A light comes on in the east wing.

Chapter Twenty-Eight

Bridget has an out-of-body moment. Sees herself wobbling on the chair, curtain beginning to slip from her arms. How funny, she thinks, calmly, observing herself. My ears are cold. Like someone's rubbed them with ice.

And then a rushing sensation and she's back in her own nervous system. And the cold has become burning heat and then cold again, and then with another rush she's boiling. Can feel just how cold the winter night is, coming off the window. Swallows. Blinks to clear her eyes, hopes that what she's seeing is an illusion.

The light is still there, in the first-floor window opposite the one where she stands, in the blue room. Filtering, warm and gold – Tom Gordhavo insists on yellow-tinted light bulbs for atmosphere – round the drawn curtain.

I locked the doors. I locked them and there's someone in the house.

The strength deserts her thighs and her knees give way. She has to grab at the window latch to stop herself tumbling to the ground. Yaws like a sailor in stormy seas, leans her shoulder against the panes.

The light is still there.

What do I do?

She stares and feels the prickle of hair on her shoulders. She's cold again, now.

Is it moving? Or is it me? It looks like it's swinging side-to-side, like someone's walking up and down with it. Or maybe it's me. Maybe it's the rush of my pulse, screwing with my vision.

It could be anything, Bridget. It could be a timer switch. You've never looked out of this window at this time of night before; maybe it goes on every night and you just didn't notice.

No, but . . . I cleaned that room today. I would have seen it. Surely I would have seen it?

There's someone in the house. Someone in the house with us.

What do I do?

Call the police.

Come on. What if it *is* a timer switch? You'll get a reputation for crying wolf and then if you need . . . really need them . . . Go and look. Go quietly and listen, and if you hear anything, come back and barricade the door and call for help.

But what if that's what he wants? What if he's waiting for me, if he's turned the light on to lead me up there, away from Yasmin, if he's waiting and when I come. . .

He can probably see you now. Silhouetted in the window.

She gets off the chair. Crouches below the sill. Struggles to contain her breath.

Okay. Okay. Think.

Maybe if I just ignore it. Assume it's nothing. Lock myself into the flat and get into bed and in the morning . . .

With all my clothes on.

Like I'd sleep.

I have to go and find out.

Like a stupid girl in the movies. Walking alone through a darkened house toward the sound in the cellar.

Or what? Or wait for him to come to me?

After the light in the bedroom, stepping into the corridor is like being bathed in pitch. The urge to turn, and run, is intense. She longs to put a hand out and flick the switch as she finds herself standing beside it.

Yes. And let him know you're coming.

I should have something. A weapon. Even the chicks in the movies find weapons before they go into the dark. A fire-iron or something. The iron. A statue or a vase. Something heavy. Everything I can think of is downstairs. There's nothing here.

Yasmin's here. All alone in her room. I should lock her in. Keep her safe if anything happens to me.

She glances back over her shoulder at the darkness beyond the bedroom door.

If I lock her in, I'll be locking myself out and I'll stand no chance.

I need somewhere to run to.

She looks forward again. Into the dark. Struggles to swallow. Her mouth is dry. She can't see a light at the end; the two-door room in the middle of the house cuts it off.

Six rooms. Six gaping rooms between where I am and the light.

She casts her mind through them, sees herself exploring each room in the blackness, tries to remember what is in each, what she has moved and dusted and checked as she's cleaned. On the bedside tables. The dressing tables. The window sills. A house like this should have alabaster table lamps, brass candlesticks, pokers. Except that Tom Gordhavo has taken everything that could be stolen and nailed down the rest. It has the look of gentility, Rospetroc, but it's as much of an illusion as a country house hotel: decorated with a mind to a light-fingered clientele and a writ-happy society. There's nothing there. In those gaping spaces.

Except . . .

He could be.

Just because he turned the light on in the blue room doesn't mean he stayed there. He could be anywhere. Waiting in the dark. To come from behind me.

She freezes. Feels sweat prickle from her scalp.

Go back. Go back and lock yourself in. Call for help. They'll understand. You're on your own. Better safe than sorry, they'll say.

She remembers the indifferent eyes of the Streatham police. The night after night of calling them out to a house where the threat was long gone. The gradual slippage down the priority list from five minutes, to ten, to twenty. The look. Attention junkie. Domestic timewaster.

I can't afford to do it. I can't, unless I know it's for real. I can't be the hysteric of Meneglos, coming here from the city and getting freaked out by a bit of silence and country stillness. Attracting attention to myself, having to explain . . .

She goes on. Puts her back to the wall and works her way forward. Listens to the house. Feels it listen to her.

Oh, Yasmin, I am frightened. I'm so sorry, my baby. So sorry.

Soft tissue injury. Such an innocuous phrase for so much pain. Nights without sleep because the swelling was so bad I could find no way to hold myself that didn't hurt. Lying there next to him, hearing him breathe and wishing him dead. Probing my mouth, the hole where my tooth used to be, with my tongue. Not crying, not ever crying, because salt makes wounds more painful. And because he took tears as reproaches, and reproaches made him angry.

Don't look at me like that. Don't you fucking look at me like that. I said I was sorry, didn't I? What do you want from me? What do you expect?

She reaches the door to the green room. It gapes, the space beyond unknown. She finds that she is trembling.

Why? Why am I so timid? I survived. I survived Kieran. I will survive again. He can't get me. It's only an electrical anomaly, a timer switch, something to do with the stupid fuses.

Bridget summons her courage, jumps into the gap. Snatches at the door handle and pulls the door closed. There. Now if he comes from behind me, I will hear him.

The pink room door is closed. She feels the handle, makes sure the catch is engaged, moves on.

The centre room. I have to cross it. There are hiding places here, places I can't see behind.

Lying on the bedroom floor, begging him to stop. The way time would slow to a crawl as I watched him draw his foot back, as I curled in to protect my face.

She's only little. It's so unfair. She's seen enough. She needs me.

She remembers: in the corner, she noticed it before. Tucked down between the wardrobe and the wall, a handle. What looked like an axe handle. Don't know why it's there. It's probably been there for decades.

It's better than nothing.

She crosses the room as quickly as silence will let her, plunges her hand into the space. Gropes among the dustballs until her hand closes on the reassuring warmth of wood.

It clatters as she pulls it out, as she whirls to face the room.

Nothing there.

She isn't comforted by her weaponry. Arming yourself makes danger more concrete. Pressure is making her sick. She has to swallow several times as she steps into the corridor, pulls the door shut to her left, to her right, advances toward the light.

Can I hear him? Is he there?

She pauses before the threshold. Strains to hear any sounds of movement, hears nothing but the sound of her own pulse. Thud, thud, thud.

I have to go. I have to do it.

Bridget steps forward.

The room is empty. The lamp lies on its side on the floor in front of the bedside table. It rocks from side to side, as though caught in a breeze.

Chapter Twenty-Nine

New Year, new clients.

Steve Holden is having a fruitful week. January always brings in a rush of work; a combination of Christmas resentments and New Year's resolutions. Women who suspect their old man is playing away. Men whose business partners have done a Michaelmas bunk with the contents of the company bank account. Adoptees whose opt-in families have become opt-out and who think they're going to get joy from the mother who couldn't be arsed when they were babies. They all want him at this time of year, and all of them are good for a deposit, at least, even if half will have changed their minds before he's done more than make a few phone calls.

Not this one, though. He can usually tell the keepers, and this is one of them. He has the look of a terrier about him, and everyone knows, once a terrier's sunk its teeth in you've got a job to make it let go.

'So what can I do for you?' he asks.

Kieran Fletcher shifts in his chair. He has difficulty sitting still, Steve notices. Hasn't stayed in the same position for more than thirty seconds since he got here. Crosses and uncrosses his legs, holds the arms of the chair and uses them to raise himself from the seat as though his back is hurting, slings himself from side to side as he takes in his surroundings with sweeping gaze.

Shifty, thinks Steve. Dismisses the thought. He's well dressed; obviously not short of a bob. One of those barrow-boy traders in the City, if my guess is right. And money is money, after all, and a lot of people look shifty when they first consult a private detective.

'I've got a problem,' says Kieran Fletcher.

You don't say. 'Most people who come to me have,' Steve says non-committally. 'I'm used to people with problems.'

Kieran Fletcher produces a cigarette lighter from his pocket, begins to fiddle with it, turning it over and over between thumb and forefinger. Steve gets the ashtray from where he keeps it in his top drawer – he doesn't like to have it there on show; it looks seedy – and pushes it across the desk. 'Feel free to smoke, if you want,' he says.

'Thanks,' says Fletcher. Gets a pack of Dunhill from the other pocket, removes a cigarette from the pack and sits there tapping the end, unlit, against the cellophane on the box.

'So perhaps,' says Steve, 'you want to tell me about your problem?'

Fletcher looks irritated for a moment. Arrogant, thinks Steve. Doesn't like being told what to do. Then he settles back into the chair, breathes heavily out through his nose and says: 'It's my wife.'

Now, there's a surprise, thinks Steve. He nods, encouragingly. 'Uh-huh?'

'She's vanished.'

'Uh-huh?' says Steve again. He doesn't want to offer the wrong reaction.

Kieran doesn't say anything more, so eventually, he asks: 'And when was this?'

'About a month ago,' says Kieran.

'I see. And have you reported it to the police?'

Again the look of impatience. He shakes his head, vigorously. 'Not that sort of vanished.'

'I see,' says Steve again,

'I turned up to see my daughter,' he says, 'and she was gone. I had to find out from her nosy neighbour. Took a lot of pleasure in telling me.'

'Aha,' says Steve.

'I wouldn't care,' says Kieran, 'fuck her. I got rid of her years ago.'

'Ah. *Ex*-wife, then?' This would explain why he's irritated rather than tearful. Men who haven't seen it coming are usually pretty shaky by this point in telling their story.

'Yeah. Useless – let's just say we weren't compatible, eh?'

'Okay.'

'It's not that. Couldn't care if I never saw her again. It's my daughter.'

'Ah,' says Steve. He understands now.

Fletcher finally jabs the cigarette between his lips, puts the flame to it. Inhales, exhales a long stream of smoke toward the ceiling. 'She's taken my daughter with her.'

Steve can't help but feel sympathy. He doesn't find him likeable, but he remembers how unlikeable he was himself, when Jo took off. Women. They may get the credit as the peacemakers and the home-makers, but there are plenty of avenging harpies among them. Not a week goes by when he doesn't get a visit from some kid's father. Bereaved fathers, angry fathers, tearful fathers, fathers who have all but given up hope. A certain type of woman will do anything to punish an errant husband. He has plenty of proof of that.

'That must be hard for you,' he says.

Kieran Fletcher's face tinges near the jawline. 'You have no idea.'

'So,' he clicks the clicker on his pen, sits forward ready to take notes, 'perhaps you'd like to start at the beginning. Name?'

'Bridget.'

'Bridget Fletcher?'

'Yes.'

He writes it down. 'Age?'

'Thirty-three.' He pauses, thinks. 'Maybe thirty-four. I'm not certain.'

He doesn't feel any surprise that a man wouldn't know his own wife's age. Women can be pretty vague about these things themselves.

'Okay,' he says. 'Thirty-three. And she was living at . . .?'

Kieran gives him the Streatham address. Looks sour. 'My flat,' he adds. 'Where I was living, till she thought better of it.'

Hmm, thinks Steve. Not the most watertight of back-stories. He'd got rid of *her* a minute ago. Still. You can't blame a guy for salving his dignity by pretending he was sacker, not sackee.

'And where do you live now?'

'A studio. Clapham.'

Steve feels a wave of sympathy. Isn't it always the way? He remembers the year he spent staring at the swirls on the carpet of his post-separation rental: the chipped laminate, the kitchen drawer with the front that came off every time you pulled it. He remembers the way he felt as he went to pick the kids up from his own house, the house where he was no longer welcome; looking through the windows as he waited in the car at the potted plants, the mirrors, the comfortable settee.

What he doesn't see, in his mind's eye, is Kieran's tubular-steel-and-black-leather reality. There are studios and studios, and Kieran's was built for one of the more successful of the Pre-Raphaelite brotherhood. It's been Bonus Central in the City over the past couple of years. And without the millstone that is Bridget round his neck, he's been back on his feet a while, now.

'Does she owe you money?'

'Well,' he says bitterly, 'I've certainly never seen anything back on all those mortgage payments.'

'And the flat?'

'Handed the keys back to the building society. No discussion. Just did it.'

'I see.'

'Do you?' says Kieran.

'Yes,' says Steve. 'You might have some legal recourse where that's concerned.'

'I doubt it. The deeds were in her name.'

'Oh.'

'I don't know how it came to this,' he says. 'I mean, I wasn't perfect, but who is? But all these lies she's told about me. It's like . . . she wants to punish me. She's . . . you know, you think you know someone, and then . . .'

'Yes,' says Steve. 'A lot of people get nasty shocks when marriages break down.'

'But you know,' he grinds the cigarette out, starts playing with the lighter again, 'I wouldn't care, but we've got a kid, you know? It's not just about her and me.'

'No. I understand that. We'll do what we can. Maybe . . .' The clock on the wall is ticking on. He needs to hurry this up; free initial consultations don't pay the rent. 'If you give me all the details you can think of, it'll be a start. So the name is Bridget Fletcher?'

'Yeah. Maybe Barton. She might have gone back to her maiden name, I suppose.'

'A lot of women do. And your daughter?'

'Yasmin. She's six. Seven in a couple of months. And I won't – at this rate I won't even be able to send her a card . . .'

His voice falters and he stares down at his shoes. Grips his hands into fists. Swallows.

It flashes through Steve's head: *He's not as upset as he wants me to believe. He's putting this on.*

Not my problem. I'm not here as an arbiter of how deep people's feelings should run. God, if we judged people's fitness for parenthood on shallowness, most of the media world would have children in care. It's probably more of a pride issue than anything else. He doesn't like having this woman call the shots. But fair enough. The guy wants to see his daughter. That's not a crime, is it?

'Okay, Mr Fletcher,' he says. 'What I suggest is that you have one more go at seeing if you can find anyone who might have an idea where she's gone.'

'That bloody Carol knows,' says Kieran. 'I know she knows.'

'Carol?'

'The neighbour. Upstairs. One of those bitter types.

Can't stand men. She was always interfering, even when we were together. She'll know. But she won't tell me.'

Mmm, thinks Steve. A few issues about the opposite sex yourself, I think. Not that surprising, though. You go on a steep learning curve when divorce enters the playroom.

'Has she got parents? Family? Where she might have gone?'

Fletcher shakes his head. 'Dead. Only child. No one to be in touch with.'

'And this neighbour?'

'She hates me. I think she thought she was in with a chance once. Woman scorned and all that.'

Do I like this man? No. But it's not my job to like my clients. It's my job to do what they pay me to do.

'Well, do you think you could try one more time?'

'Don't you think I've tried already?' His eyes flash, annoyed, like a teenager being nagged to clean his room. 'I told you! There's no way she's doing *me* any favours.'

'Okay. Okay. Well, look, I'll tell you what we'll do. You come back here in a couple of days and bring as much detail as you can. NI number. Health Service number. Driving licence details, if you've got them. Any other names. Bank account details. You must at least be able to get those from the CSA. And a photo would be useful.'

Kieran Fletcher looks astonished. Not one to hang on to sentimental treasures, then. After a moment he says: 'Yes. Yes, I've got one. 'Cause it's got Yasmin in it. But it's a couple of years old, now.'

'Better than nothing,' says Steve. 'Well, I'll need you to write down every detail you can think of. How they look. What they like doing. What her qualifications are. How she might be earning a living. Hobbies. All of that. Anything you can think of. She'll be having to make money somehow, and if she's not she'll be signing on.'

'She was a florist,' says Kieran doubtfully.

'There you go.' He scribbles another note. Florists use wholesalers, delivery people, the Yellow Pages. 'Now, look. It's not hopeless, by any means. People try to disappear all the time, but in the end there's usually a paper trail. Does she have a mobile?'

'Yeah, she can afford one of those all right.'

'Oh, right. And have you tried calling her?'

The flash again. 'Of course. She hung up. Of course she did.'

'And the bills go to . . .?'

'Pay-as-you-go.'

'Oh.'

Neither of them speaks for a moment. Fletcher gets another cigarette out, lights it, stares at the private detective. 'I want to know where they are,' he says. 'She can't be allowed to get away with this. Just find them for me, okay?'

Chapter Thirty

'Euugh.'

Bridget suppresses the urge to roll her eyes. The euugh phase will pass. It will pass, like Thomas the Tank Engine and Pingu and pulling down her nappy to see what's inside. It will pass.

'Rabbit shit,' says Yasmin.

'Rabbit *poo*,' says Bridget. 'It's rabbit *poo*.' Realizes too late that she's backed herself into a corner.

'Rabbit poo, then.'

'You used to love peas.'

'Lily says they're rabbit shit. She says the rabbits wait until night when no one's looking and then they shit it out and you eat it.'

'Well, Lily's wrong,' says Bridget, 'and she needs to watch her language. Doesn't her mum mind her talking like that?'

'She hasn't got a mum,' says Yasmin, as if it's the most obvious thing in the world.

'Oh, sorry.'

Yasmin starts picking the peas out, one by one, from the rice. At least, reflects Bridget, she's using her knife and fork to do it with.

'Eat some chicken, anyway,' she orders.

Yasmin waggles her pigtails, spears a piece of chicken nugget and chews.

'Mouth shut,' says Bridget.

Yasmin washes the food down with a gulp of squash, goes back to separating pulses from grains.

'Cauliflowers are cows' brains,' she announces.

'Lily says that too, does she?'

A vigorous nod.

'Come on, you've got to eat *some* peas.'

She pulls a face like a gargoyle. 'Euu-yachh.'

Bridget decides to wait a while between pestering. 'So which one was Lily, again? I thought she was one of the Aykroyd children.'

'No. *You* know. *Lily*.'

One two three four five. All children think that their concerns are the only concerns, believe that anyone who doesn't know immediately what they're talking about is stupid. No need to get irritated.

I need some adult company. I love her, but I've really got to make friends.

'No,' she says, 'I can't say I do.'

'Well, she knows who *you* are.'

'Have we met?'

'Yuh.'

'When?'

'The day we were playing pilchards.'

Bridget looks blank.

'Sardines,' says Yasmin.

'Eat some rice.'

She spoons up a forkful, spills half in the transfer to her mouth.

'What does she look like?'

'Taller than me. Brown hair. Sort of messy. Skinny.'

'Is she a bit older?'

Yasmin nods. 'Lily's nine,' she says. Then corrects herself. 'Sort of.'

Sort of? What's *sort of*?

She vaguely recalls the girl. Skinny and sallow with hair that looked like it had been done in the kitchen, with a blunt knife. *It wasn't me. I didn't bloody do it. Didn't do what? I didn't bloody do it . . .*

'And she swears like that all the time?'

'Oh, *Mum*.'

'I don't want you swearing like that.'

'Huh-huurrr,' says Yasmin.

'What do you want for dessert? Yoghurt or banana?'

'Banana.'

'So maybe she wants to come and play sometime?' asks Bridget.

Yasmin swivels to look at her. Damn me for desperate, using my child as a way of making friends for myself. The kid's got to have an adult attached somewhere.

'Maybe when Chloe comes tomorrow?'

Yasmin sounds suddenly condescending. 'I don't think that'll be necessary, Mum,' she says.

She's a bit offended. 'Oh. All right, then. Sorry.'

'It's okay,' says Yasmin. 'We see plenty of each other. It's just – she doesn't like grown-ups.'

'Fair enough.' There are a fair number of grown-ups who don't like children, after all. 'What doesn't she like?'

'Everything.'

'Everything?'

'Lily says you can't trust a grown-up any further than you can throw them.'

'I'm sorry,' says Bridget. 'You don't think that, do you?'

Yasmin pauses.

She feels a wash of guilt. Whatever you do, you're not going to be able to stop the stuff that's happened having an effect. I didn't do it myself, but I didn't stop him breaking her arm.

'I'm sorry, baby,' she says. 'I am. But you do know that there are some grown-ups you can trust, don't you?'

'Lily says you can't. Lily says they all turn on you in the end.'

'Oh, darling. She must have had a very tough life to think like that. Doesn't the school do anything?'

'No,' says Yasmin. 'She says they're the worst of the lot.'

'Oh dear,' says Bridget. 'Well, you can tell her, anyway, that she's welcome here any time she wants. Can't you?'

Yasmin pulls a face. Shakes her head. 'I don't think it'll

work. I told her already. That you're okay. But she – she doesn't want to be friends. With you.'

'Fine,' says Bridget. 'Whatever.'

'Sorry,' says Yasmin.

'Believe me,' says Bridget, 'I'm not upset if a nine-year-old doesn't want to be friends with me.'

Only upset enough to sound like a nine-year-old myself.

The mobile rings in another room.

'Phone's ringing,' says Yasmin.

'Thanks, smartarse. Where is it?'

'It's *your* phone,' says Yasmin. 'As you're always pointing out.'

'You're not getting down till you've finished.'

Yasmin shrugs and rolls her eyes, American-adolescent style. 'What*ever*.'

She can't help smiling as she leaves the room. That's the worst thing about disciplining children: the urge to laugh when cheekiness is done with flair and imagination. The phone's in her handbag, she remembers now. In the sitting room. It's on its third repetition of 'Chocolate Salty Balls' when she puts her hand on it, buried down in the bottom under the empty diary and the spare tights. She hits the on button as she pulls it out, puts it to her ear.

'Hello?'

'You are so in for it now,' he says.

'Kieran,' she says. Thinks about hanging straight up, stays on the line. I have to get a new phone, she thinks. Can he find me by my records?

'When I find you,' he says, 'you are so fucking in for it.'

'Go away, Kieran,' she says.

'Don't even *think*,' he says, 'about telling me to fuck off.'

'I didn't. I told you to go away.'

'Shut the *fuck* up! Shut it!'

'What do you want, Kieran?'

'I want to give you a last chance. Tell me where my daughter is, or I'll find out, and when I do –'

'That's why I'm not telling you,' she says.

'You've got to stop calling,' she says.

'Oh yeah? And what are you going to do about it?'

'I'm not going to answer. From now on, when I see it's you, I'm not going to answer. If you're going to call and threaten us, I won't answer.'

He ignores her.

'I want to speak to my daughter.'

'Tough,' she says harshly. 'she doesn't want to speak to you.'

'It's not up to you.'

'It is,' she says.

'I'll fucking – you wait, Bridget. Just wait. You can't stay hidden forever.'

She can't resist goading him. The distance gives her a sense of power she would never have had a month ago.

'You sound fucking pathetic. Little man. Little Hitler. Don't you know it was your threatening that made us go away in the first place? You're fucking pathetic. That's why you used to take it out on me, wasn't it? Beating up your family because you couldn't stand up for yourself when it came to people your own size.'

'Fuck you, Bridget,' he says.

'Yeah,' she sneers. 'That's good. You always had a way with words, didn't you, Kieran?'

'Aah, fuck *you*!' he repeats. 'You can't do this! You can't keep me away from my daughter!'

'Or what?' she asks triumphantly. 'Or you'll call the police?'

Silence.

'In case you'd forgotten, Kieran Fletcher,' she snarls, 'the police were already meant to be keeping *you* away from *her*. A small matter of a thing called a restraining order, yes? You remember?'

'You're a lying bitch,' he says, sulkily.

'Yeah, but I'm not, am I? Fuck you, Kieran. It's because you couldn't control yourself that we've had to go away, and you're never getting back into our lives. *Never*, do you hear me? You can go fuck yourself and you can threaten me all you want, but you're never seeing her again. Fucking free with your fists cunting *bastard*!'

Her voice has risen to a shriek as she speaks. She hates him, hates him with boiling rage. Hates him for the years of fear, for the broken skin and broken bones, for the look in her daughter's eye she's not seen for weeks now.

'You will *never* find us. Do you hear me? It's *over*! Go and find someone else to bully!'

Bridget stabs a thumb on to the off button, throws the phone on to the sofa. It bounces off a cushion, slips to the floor, skids under the chair. Bridget hugs herself, wipes a lock of hair from her eyes. She feels shaky, strong, weak, tearful, brave. She feels free and trapped, enraged and at peace. She has told him. Finally told him. All of it, to his face, no fear of reprisal, no repercussions. Right, she thinks. And now we go on with our lives. I'll get a new phone. Leave that one down there on the floor. Let it ring until it dies.

She turns round to return to the kitchen.

Yasmin stands in the doorway. She is shiny white. As if she'd seen a ghost.

Chapter Thirty-One

'Mummy?'

She swims up out of sleep, heavy as though lead weights have been attached to her limbs. The clock reads 3:17. Her mouth is dry and furry.

There's a small figure in the doorway.

She smacks her lips together, unglues her tongue from the roof of her mouth. 'What is it, baby? What's up?'

'Can I get in with you?'

'What's happened?'

'I saw Daddy in my room.'

'Oh, darling.'

She lifts the duvet, opens the bed up. Yasmin crosses the room and climbs in beside her. This is wrong. Supernanny would be wagging her finger if she saw me now. But it's after three and my baby's in a state.

Yasmin smells of talc and No More Tears. Bridget puts her arms round the frail body, breathes her in.

'He was standing at the foot of my bed,' says Yasmin. She sounds – defeated, exhausted.

'Oh, darling,' she says again. She'd been half-expecting this. Whenever there was an incident with Kieran in London, Yasmin would be clingy and nervous for days, following her from room to room and kicking up a fuss when they left the house. I can't expect it all to clear up in a few weeks. She's lived her whole life with the shadowy promise that one night he might get in; you don't shrug that sort of history off just by moving.

'You know it was a dream, don't you?'

She feels Yasmin's hair scrape across her cheek as she nods. 'But I dream about him.'

'I know. So do I, sometimes. But, darling, they're only dreams. Nothing in a dream can hurt you. It's just – stuff inside your head. Dreams are good. They're memories cleaning themselves out.'

'Then why do they have to be so scary?'

'Because . . .' She doesn't really have an answer for this. Except that she suspects it's something that afflicts most species. She remembers the way Jinx, the fat tabby they had when she was Yasmin's age, used sometimes to caterwaul in his sleep, legs pumping as though he were running. Hunting or being hunted? Either, or both: but it was plain that what he was seeing was real to him. 'I don't know, darling. It's just one of nature's little tricks.'

'Chloe says that if you die in a dream you die for real.'

'Yuh, I know. Everyone says that. Of course, there's no way to actually tell if it's true.'

But I've always saved myself, haven't I, in nightmares? Always come to just before I hit the ground, or summoned the will to soar upward again, an inch from the pavement.

'I don't want him to find us,' says Yasmin.

'I know, baby, I know.'

'He won't find us, will he?'

'No,' she says, definitely, defiantly. 'And he won't be calling again any more, either. I'm going to get a new phone, and then he'll never be able to call us again.'

'Do you promise?'

How can I promise? How can I promise something I can't be certain of? How do parents lie so blithely to their children, just for the sake of convenience?

She shifts, pulls her daughter closer to her bosom, kisses the top of her damp head.

'I promise, baby,' she says. 'You're safe here. There's nothing here that can hurt us.'

Chapter Thirty-Two

At least they're not rationing water, he thinks. Even though I can't have a bath more than three inches deep to save fuel and I've three sons I haven't heard from in weeks, at least my pansies don't have to suffer.

He's even managed to scrounge a sack of mature horse manure from the stables at the dairy, an unheard-of triumph and probably illegal given that everything is supposed to be going toward agricultural production, but the Bodmin Road flowers were his pride and joy before Adolf and his hordes and he'll be blowed if he lets them fail because there's a war on.

Arthur Boden replenishes his watering can for the fifth time from the greenish supply in the horse trough, and sloshes his way up to the far end of the platform. It's a beautiful day – a blazing day, perfect for watching the dog-fights further along the coast over the Channel – and he has taken his jacket off while he works. It's easier, in these days of shortages, to get the sweat stains out of a shirt than to get a uniform cleaned. He hums as he lugs the can, screws his eyes up against the light.

There's a small girl sitting on the bench behind the flower trough. His display is so grandiose and the child so scrawny and drab that he hadn't noticed her. He doesn't remember her coming through the ticket office, but he's only been on duty since noon. She has a battered brown suitcase with her which looks like it's made of cardboard. She wears a dress that may once have been made of red gingham, but its general greyness makes it hard to tell. It doesn't fit her, is far too large, and has been darned at the armpits, make-do-and-mend style. It's her hair that really attracts his attention, though. It stands out from her scalp as though it has been roughly shaved, and recently. Nits, he thinks. That one's had nits.

He pauses in front of her, feels the can bounce off his shins.

She gives him a look.

'What?' she says. Challengingly.

'There's not another train due in for four hours,' he says. 'Are you sure you're in the right place?'

'What's it got to do with you?'

Arthur Boden puffs himself out, annoyed that his authority should be called into question. 'I'm the station-master, that's what, young lady,' he informs her, 'and I've got every right to be finding out about people's business. There's a war on, you know.'

'Yer, yer, yer,' says the child. 'Change the record, mister. This one's got a scratch on it.'

'Well, there's no need to be rude,' he says. Walks off to water the pansies, muttering under his breath about young people and modern times.

She doesn't move from her spot on the bench while he drenches the half-tubs of compost, feels the plants breathe out gratitude as the water reaches their roots. It's funny, he thinks, how, once you're responsible for a garden, it becomes so much more alive. You can practically see plants taking a stretch, laughing with pleasure, when you give them a drink. A bit like people, really. In the Legion on a Saturday night. I must remember to tell Ena about that when I get home.

The child starts kicking her legs, swinging them into the space beneath the bench, fingers gripping the slats to give her better purchase. What a way to pass a summer afternoon. Just sitting on an empty platform finding grown-ups to be rude to. That's not country behaviour. I'd have got a clip round the ear if I'd spent more than ten minutes on the village bench. The country's going to rack and ruin, that's about the truth of it. The Blitz driving London slummies all over the place like rats off a sinking ship, bringing their city ways to places where they're not wanted. You can't turn your back on half of them or they'll be away with anything that's not nailed down.

He glances at her again. Nasty, mean little face, he thinks. Poor little mite. Probably hasn't stood a chance, wherever she's come from. Never seen a vegetable before she came here and not a breath of fresh air from one day's end to the next. He softens, reapproaches.

'You off somewhere?'

The child rolls her eyes insolently, lets loose a groan. 'I told you,' she says, 'it's got nothing to do with you.'

'Well, there's no need to be rude,' he says again. 'I'd be well within my rights to order you off this station if I felt like it.'

'Well, bully for you. Ain't you the big almighty.'

Arthur sits down on the bench beside her. He's a kindly man, really, beneath the veneer of officialdom. Doesn't like to see kiddies on their own. Doesn't feel it's natural. He digs in his pocket and finds the eighth of Mint Imperials he got off the ration at the beginning of the week, in their crumpled paper bag. Puts one in his mouth and offers the bag.

She looks at him suspiciously.

'Go on, have one,' he says. 'They're not poisoned.'

She gazes at the sweets, looks up at him, back at the sweets.

'They won't be here forever,' he says.

She snatches a sweet from the top, crams it into her mouth as though afraid he'll change his mind. Sits there with it pressing her cheek out like a gobstopper, and sucks and sucks.

'What do you say?' he asks.

'You ain't supposed to be giving sweets to children,' she says.

'And you're not supposed to be taking them,' he reminds her.

She shrugs. 'Well,' she says. 'Thanks.'

'You're welcome,' he says. 'Been evacuated, have you?'

She shrugs again. 'Ain't going to stay evacuated, neither.'

'Going back to London, are you?'

'Don't be stupid,' she says, 'Portsmouth.'

'Ah, right,' he says.

'My mum's there.'

'Ah, right,' he says again.

They sit, and suck, and she swings her legs in the sunshine.

'Missing her, are you?' he asks.

She shrugs again. Swaps her sweet into the opposite cheek. 'Dunno about that, but I bloody hate it here.'

'Ooh,' he says, ignoring the swearword, though his own children would have spent ten minutes in a corner for it, 'I'm sorry to hear that. You told anyone you were off, did you?'

'Course not. Ain't nobody spoken to me since Tuesday anyway. I'm in *Coventry*.'

Five days, he thinks. That's a fair old time to put a child into Coventry for.

'What, no one?'

'No one. Buggers. Snobs, the lot of 'em.'

'I daresay,' he says. He imagines some old-fashioned Cornish family, landed suddenly with this foul-mouthed larrikin. Chances are they wouldn't be too happy. But five days . . . 'Where you been staying?'

'Meneglos.'

'That's a fair old way. What did you do? Walk here?'

'Don't be stupid,' she says. Sneers. 'They was all going in to the cinema in Bodmin. Only when we got there she suddenly says Lily you're not coming in with us 'cause I'm *not to be trusted*, so she says I've got to sit in the car and not touch nothing for *two hours* while they're all in there watching *Pimpernel Smith* and I thought, bugger that for a game of soldiers, I'm making myself scarce.'

'I don't blame you. Don't you think they'll be worried, though?'

She's broken through to the mint's soft, powdery interior, concentrates on it for a second or two before replying: 'Course not. Glad to see the back of me, more like.'

'All right,' he says. 'You know best, I daresay.'

'She's told me so often enough,' says Lily.

'Has she? And who's "she"? The cat's mother?'

'Mrs Bloody Blakemore,' she says. 'Bloody Bitch Blakemore, I call her.'

'Do you?' he asks. The name has a familiar ring to it. One of the big houses around Wadebridge way.

'She's a snob and no mistake,' says Lily.

Probably not wrong, he thinks. Still, what am I meant to do? These people are *in loco parentis*. She'll probably be worrying herself sick.

'So you don't like it there, then?'

'I want my mum,' she says firmly. 'At least my mum didn't used to lock me in bloody *cupboards*.'

Mmm, he thinks. A vivid imagination, as well.

'And she hits me, and all,' she says.

'Hits you? What for?'

'Who cares what bloody for? I ain't done nothing bloody wrong but she blames me for everything.'

'Oh dear,' he says. 'It does sound like you've been having a hard time of it.'

'Can I have another one of them?' She nods at the mints.

That's my ration for the month. The cheek of it. Doesn't even say please.

'All right,' he says, unwillingly, regretfully. Offers the packet once more, sees his precious sugar allowance disappear into that snag-toothed maw.

'Tell you what. I was just about to make myself a nice cup of tea. Don't suppose you'd be interested, would you?'

'Don't mind,' says Lily.

'I'll take that as a yes,' he says. 'Tell you what. You wait here and I'll bring it out. It's a nice day. Might as well make the most of the sunshine.'

'Toodleoo,' she says.

Arthur Boden walks back up the platform to the station

house. He doesn't like it when he has to interfere. But what can you do? They all hate it, without exception, these poor mites, dragged away from their families and dumped in strange places, with strange people and their strange habits. He's had one staying who screamed the first time she saw a cow. She'd never even heard of cows, certainly didn't know they were where milk came from. But you can't have them wandering about willy-nilly all over the train system. Anybody could get them. There seem to be a lot of unsavoury types wandering about the place these days. And even if they did make it home, there's no guarantee that home would even exist any more.

The room behind the ticket office is fusty, sleepy in the afternoon heat. He takes off his peaked cap and lays it on the desk, beside the timetables. Fills the kettle and puts it on the single ring the company have provided as the sole source of cooking for their all-day-and-night employees. Sits heavily down on the chair and picks up the telephone. Rattles the nuggets on the top and waits for the operator.

'Ah, Bella, love,' he says. 'Arthur Boden at Bodmin Road station. You couldn't find out, could you, who's in charge of the evacuees over Meneglos way? I've got another one here. Trying to get to Portsmouth.'

He listens, chuckles.

'I know,' he says. 'I think it's the weather. This is the third one this week.'

Chapter Thirty-Three

The TV has been on the blink for nearly a year. The only way to turn it on and off has been to crawl round the back and switch it off at the wall. But tonight, when she has emerged on her hands and knees from turning it on, nothing has happened at all. She's tried taking the fuse out of the kettle and using that in its plug, but it's made no difference: there's no sound, no picture, and the red light on the front which shows that the set is connected remains obdurately dark. She's tried all the tricks which are usually so effective with delicate technology: banging it hard on its top; tipping it forward and rocking it back and forth on its stand; shouting at it. But nothing has happened. The machine has died.

It squats on the chair in the corner, laughing at her, reminding her that everything she owns is on its last legs, one way or another. You can only make do and mend for so long in a world where built-in obsolescence is the key to manufacturing growth. All her stuff, the accoutrements of modern adult life, will need replacing, bit by bit, as her money situation steadies. That's one of the miserable, crushing things about poverty: once you've been in it for a while, the distance between you and what other people would call a civilized level of existence gets greater and greater.

Never mind, she thinks. I saw a second-hand TV shop in Bodmin, in one of those pikey three-for-two, everything for a pound, discount streets the tourists never see. I'll buy one – just a small one, it doesn't have to be anything grand – when next month's money comes in, and that will tide us over until things are easier. And in the meantime, I'll use that fabulous entertainment centre down in the drawing room. It would be stupid not to. It's not like anyone else is using it, is it? I can't spend every night alone here with nothing to keep me company. I'm not the embroidering type.

As she's going downstairs, baby alarm and copy of the *Mirror* tucked into her armpit, mug of tea in her hand, blanket thrown over her shoulder, she glances out of the window and sees that it has begun to snow. Eddies of white circle beyond the pane, lit up by the security light, which she keeps on permanently at night since the scare. She pauses in the dining room and climbs on to the window seat, leans her elbows on the sill and presses her nose and forehead on the cold glass. I do hope it lies, she thinks. Yasmin's never actually seen snow lying on the ground, except in pictures. They do say you hardly ever get snow lying around here, but we're an island on the edge of the Arctic Circle, for heaven's sake. It's got to happen sometime.

She feels like a burglar. Feels strangely guilty, though she's never been told she can't use the house. The equipment is there, after all, sitting unused, and it's not as if she's having a wild party or anything. No one could begrudge her a night in front of the telly when her own has broken down. And yet – she feels like an interloper. Feels that Tom Gordhavo will somehow *know*. Is careful to put a coaster under the mug, as though he'd be able to tell the difference between servants' stains and those left by tenants.

The big sofa is more comfortable than she had expected. It looks hard and austere with its leather frame and kelim cushions, but feels like the firmest, most welcoming of beds when she lies on it. It's cold in here – she doesn't feel entitled to run the boiler above defrost level when there are no tenants because a house this size will eat heating oil – and she's glad of her blanket. She doubles it over and lies with her neck on a cushion, only her head and the hand that holds the remote control protruding. Hits the power switch and begins to flick through the channels.

He's got the full gamut of satellite. She feels a small surge of resentment. He's paying for this, no doubt advertising it as part of the attraction of the house, but of course there's no aerial outlet in the flat. People like me, she thinks, get five channels only. Even Freeview doesn't work down here without a proper aerial to feed the box. And all this time, there's been scores of channels just sitting there for the entertainment of people who are here on holiday and the least likely of all to need it.

QVC has a diamonique sale on. BBC4 has a documentary on Sam Johnson. BBC3 is playing *Four Pints of Lager and a Packet of Crisps.* UKTV is showing *Are You Being Served.* The History Channel is doing something on the Nazis. ITV3 is showing *Police Academy 4: Citizens on Patrol* again. Sky One has a drama series where no one wears clothes. E4 is doing a *Friends* all-nighter. FilmFour is in Czech.

Okay, she thinks. Forty channels and it's still all crap. She tries the movie channels. *Lord of the Rings.* Great. If I wanted to see what it was like to climb a mountain in real time I'd go and climb it myself. Kirsten Dunst, smirking. She doesn't even wait to see what the film is. *Twenty-Eight Days Later.* Zombies with their faces hanging off, running howling at the camera. She used to love zombie movies. Always cherished a secret ambition to be an extra in a Romero film. To sit around eating bacon sandwiches with half her head falling off.

Yeah, but. I'm so suggestible these days I'd never sleep again if I watched that. I'm seeing ghosts as it is.

Yasmin stirs in her sleep, mutters, goes quiet again. Beyond the window, a singing quietness tells her that the snow is still falling. She tucks herself further in, mesmerizes herself with an auction for a waterproof watch and a Star Wars fabric patch kit. Finds something with Shirley MacLaine in. Settles.

She's surprisingly tired, she realizes. All I need now, she thinks, is a nice warm cat on my lap and I'd be off to sleep in seconds. Shirley is wearing clashing fabrics and saying outrageous things while a younger woman rolls her eyes. This is fine. Good background. She unfurls her arms, opens the paper. Someone from last year's *Big Brother* has got drunk in a nightclub. A group of footballers have got drunk in a nightclub. Two young men have been shot in their car two roads over from the Streatham flat. Tom Cruise is barking mad. Madonna's got the builders in again. Nikola, 23, from Purley, thinks the government should be doing more about law and order and has taken her top off to prove it. Some actors from *EastEnders* have got drunk in a nightclub. There's been a dust-up at the first day of the Harrods sale between three people all after the same plasma TV. The TV was broken and all three were arrested. Ken Livingstone wants to knock down Admiralty Arch to make room for bendy buses.

I don't miss London at all, she thinks. All that argy-bargy and elbowing and thinking you *are* your consumer goods. She yawns, sips her tea. The young woman has stormed out of the house and Shirley is pulling 'so-what' faces and polishing a vase.

Mystic Meg says that someone from the past is thinking about her. And that Love will be found where friends share spicy food.

The newsprint begins to swim. I'm tireder than I thought, she thinks. Maybe I should've gone to bed rather than coming down here. I'd go back up now, but I can't be arsed. I'll wait a bit, rest up till I've got the energy.

She drops the paper on to the floor. Stares up at the ceiling. The rooms are low here, in comparison with their size. She can make out every detail of the knotting in the beams, illuminated in relief by the lamp on the side table. There are faces in the wood; long, despairing faces: the spirits of the trees, mourning the lives they once had. Bridget blinks away a batch of sleep-tears. Tries to watch the movie. Realizes that the actors might as well be speaking Martian for all she's taking in. She hits the mute on the remote for some peace and quiet. Closes her eyes, just for a second.

'I'm cold . . . I'm so cold . . .'

Bridget feels as though she is swimming underwater, as though she has fallen into a deep, dark lake, that the current is trying to suck her down. Who was that? Who just said that?

'Where is she? She's downstairs . . . don't worry . . . we have time . . .'

Whispering. Not speaking. I'm asleep. I've fallen asleep.

She kicks upward, struggles, breaks free. Something was holding me. I must –

She wakes with a start, all limbs jumping. Hears a croak break from her throat, looks around. Panics because she doesn't know where she is. Somewhere large and dark and . . . Rospetroc. I'm in the drawing room at Rospetroc. I was dreaming. I must have gone right off to sleep.

Her limbs are dead-weighted beneath the blanket, her body temperature down from lying open-bodied under such inadequate covers. She lifts her head and looks at the screen. It is black: white lettering scrolling up the centre. Gosh, I must have been asleep a while. The film's finished. What time is it?

Nearly eleven. Damn. I've been out for well over an hour. I'll be awake all night, now.

The baby alarm crackles, comes alive.

'It's all right . . . go on . . . touch it . . .'

Bridget frowns.

'She'll never know. She's downstairs, I told you.'

Yasmin sounds – different. But people do when they're whispering. What is she up to?

There's an urgency to the next one. *'Hurry up! Hurry up! I can hear her! She's coming!'*

Eleven at night. How long has she been awake? Bridget sits up, kills the TV.

'I'm cold. I'm so cold. Oh, don't . . . I want my mum.'

God. Is she looking for me? I'd better . . .

A harsh giggle. Spiteful. What's going on? What is she doing?

The voice speaks out loud. It doesn't sound like Yasmin at all. *'Stop it! Stop it! Oh, don't! Stop it!'*

Bridget is on her feet in an instant. It's okay, baby, I'm on my way. She leaves the mug, the blanket, takes only the alarm. Runs through the house, feels the beat of urgency. I'm coming, darling. I'm coming . . .

Another laugh. *'She won't know . . . don't you see? She won't know. She'll say it was your fault. It's always your fault . . .'*

She reaches the flat stairs. Calls up them. 'Yasmin?'

She's running up the staircase, bouncing off the close, tight walls. It's so cold in here. How could I leave her when it's so cold? It feels as though the air is freezing.

The corridor is quiet, empty. Bridget glances into the rooms as she passes them: the silent kitchen, the dark sitting room. My baby. I'm coming. Belts down the sisal carpet, puts her hand on Yasmin's bedroom door handle. It's almost frozen, like a block of ice. 'It's all right,' she says as she enters. 'I'm here.'

No movement. No noise. The night light burns on, in the corner, its thick mobile shade casting moons and stars and comets on the walls, the sloped eaves ceiling. She stands in the doorway, and her breath mists the air. It's as cold as the tomb in here.

'Yasmin?' she says, uncertainly.

The child sleeps on. Bundled up beneath the covers, only her forehead showing, a lock of dark hair curled across the pillow. The spare bed is rumpled again, blankets trailing like a mudslide to the floor.

Bridget looks down at the alarm in her hand. The monitor light, she notices, is off. She puts her thumb on the on-off-volume dial, feels the click and sees it light up. I must have turned it off while I was running.

She kneels by the bed. Peels the covers back from her daughter's face, to check. Asleep. Definitely. Not faking it. Her mouth is slack and her skin slightly damp.

'It's all right, darling.'

Yasmin screws her eyes tighter, unwilling to be disturbed, then opens them. Stares at her mother as though she doesn't recognize her. 'Wh—' she says.

'It's okay. Go back to sleep. You were having a dream.'

Yasmin stares at her, sightless, drugged by sleep. I'll get her another blanket. The heating must be shot in here. I've got to face up to telling Tom Gordhavo about all the things that are wrong with this place. It's no good letting it all go to rack and ruin because I'm scared of seeming troublesome. 'Sleep,' she orders.

Yasmin turns back on to her side, buries her face in her pillow. Bridget gets up, takes a blanket from the tumble on the spare bed, spreads it over her. Tucks her in. 'Night night,' she whispers.

In the corridor, as she makes her way to her own weary bed, the alarm crackles to life once more. 'Night night,' it replies. 'Nunnight.'

Chapter Thirty-Four

Carol – black ankle-length leather coat and four-inch heels – takes one look at the boardwalk and the steps beyond and stops dead.

'Sorry,' she says, 'but there's no way I'm going up there. Even if I did get to the top without breaking my neck, there's no way I'd get down again.'

'Townie,' says Yasmin. 'Auntie Carol's a townie.'

'Where does she get these things from?' asks Carol.

'School. I had to buy her some blue cords and a jumper on day two because they were calling her one. And an anorak. It's about the worst thing you can be, down here, a townie. Only thing worse is being one of the Conran yuppies at Rock.'

'How funny,' says Carol. 'It's like Trainer Wars in reverse.'

'I know,' says Bridget. 'It's the telly, I'm convinced of it. They don't watch half as much down here, 'cause people aren't scared to let them go out and play, and they're nothing like as materialistic as a consequence. Did you know, there's not one of them's got an iPod?'

'What's an iPod?' asks Yasmin.

'Nasty white plastic things, darling,' says Carol, 'that eat your records and make people want to mug you.'

'Well, why would I want one of them, then?'

'You wouldn't.'

'I rest my case,' says Bridget.

'By the way,' says Yasmin, 'I'm not going up there either, Mummy.'

'Oh, really,' says Bridget. 'What a pair of wimps.' She's

not going to admit it, but she feels faintly relieved that the others have done the cowardly thing for her. From this angle, rain driving across the isthmus, Tintagel does seem far off and high up. Dramatic and exciting and romantic with the waves beating at the foot of its black and ragged cliffs, but a long way away in this wild western weather.

'I thought Cornwall was meant to be sunny,' says Carol.

'We still get winter down here,' says Bridget. 'It's not blimmin' Tuscany.'

Carol slaps her upper arms with leather-gloved hands, stamps on the puddled granite.

'We've come all the way here now . . .' says Bridget doubtfully, though she knows she'll need more enthusiasm than that to drag an unwilling six-year-old several hundred feet upwards in the pouring rain. She can see two cagoule-wrapped figures huddled in the ruined gateway at the crux of the cliff, looking downward. A gust catches them and she watches them cling to the rock, capes whipping out in front of them like pennants.

'That's it,' says Carol, decisively. 'How about a nice cup of tea while we wait for the Land Rover shuttle?'

'Yes,' says Yasmin firmly and starts skipping back in the direction of the café. 'Chips!' she shouts.

The adults follow more sedately, Carol leaning on Bridget's outstretched arm as she hobbles over the rough ground.

'You really *are* a townie.'

'Yeah, well,' says Carol, 'if God had meant us to wear moccasins he wouldn't have given us pavements. Anyway. You never know when a nice farmer's lad mightn't come along.'

'Well, he won't want you looking like *that*,' says Bridget. 'The farmers' lads round here want someone who's going to be good with a spanner, not a trophy wife.'

'Who said anything about wives?' asks Carol. 'I'm only here on holiday.'

'There's a village disco on the first Saturday of every month, but I think they might be a bit young for you.'

'Thank you very much.'

'If you're looking for a husband.'

'Right.'

They burst out laughing.

'There are some nice surfers down in Newquay, if you can bear the vomit in the streets,' Bridget continues, 'but it's a bit cold for them at the moment. They'll be following the weather somewhere in Australia right now.'

'Ah, now, a surfer. Now you're talking. One of those nice long swimmers' bodies.'

Bridget smiles.

'So how are you doing on that front, anyway?' asks Carol.

She feels a twinge of irritation. 'Give me a chance. I've only been here just over a month. And besides, I don't think I'm going to be in that market for a good while yet.'

'Oh, Bridget,' says Carol, 'you can't tar them all with the same brush.'

I wish I had your confidence, thinks Bridget. Your brush-yourself-off-and-start-again sangfroid. That's the thing with Air Staff, isn't it? They're so used to being in strange places, to striking up instant relationships with unfamiliar long-haul crews, and it rubs off on their personalities.

'It's like falling off a horse,' says Carol.

'Nice analogy.'

'No, but . . . the longer you leave it the more scared you'll get.'

'Well, it's been over three years already,' says Bridget. 'Since . . . you know . . .'

'Is it really? That long? I'd forgotten. Seems like he's been around forever.'

'Well, I suppose he has, in a way.'

Yasmin has reached the café, is playing tightropes on the wall of the slipway outside. Bridget feels the familiar lurch, tries to rein herself in. It's probably at least a couple of feet wide, and if you stop her every time she takes a risk she'll end up being one of those scared little girls. One of those scared little girls like you, looking for a big man to take control and save her. She'll be fine. There are three people sitting on one of the bench tables. If it's really dangerous, they'll stop her.

'Yes,' says Carol, 'I suppose he has.'
I have to ask. 'Has he . . . you know, been back?'
Carol cackles. It sounds a bit bravado-ish. 'Oh, don't you worry. Nothing I can't handle.'
So he has, then.
'I haven't told him where you are, don't worry.'
'I didn't think you would for a second.'
'Actually, I let slip something about Derbyshire. Then pretended I hadn't said it. He's probably up scouring the north as we speak.'
I do hope so. No I don't. 'I'd rather,' she says, 'he gave up scouring anywhere.'
'Yeah, well, we can but hope. Has he been on the blower?'
Bridget nods. 'Several times. I think I'm going to get another one. Throw this one away.'
'Just get a new SIM card. That's all you need.'
'Yes, I guess so. It only seems to work sporadically down in that valley, anyway. Half the time it doesn't pick up a signal at all. That was why I didn't answer when you rang the other night.'
'Ah, right. Don't you have a landline yet?'
'No. There's one downstairs, but it's only for ringing in on. And believe it or not, it's still a couple of months on the waiting list to get another line into the flat.'
'Nothing surprises me,' says Carol. 'Oh, did I tell you? I think I might have got a job.'
Bridget stops dead. 'Carol! No! Fantastic! What?'
'Virgin,' says Carol. 'Transatlantic. Seems like they've realized that the odd fortysomething might actually be effective in keeping the drunks under control.'
'Oh, that's wonderful!'
'Yeah,' says Carol. 'There's life in the old dog yet. Not that I'm saying I'm a dog . . .'
Bridget smirks. 'So when would you start?'
'Sooner rather than later, hopefully. I've just to do the medical and a refresher course and hopefully I'll be in the air in a month or so. I can't wait, I'll tell you. I was beginning to think it was all over.'
'I know.'

They both think about the last year: the pair of them, savings dwindling, Carol trudging off to temporary filing jobs because trolley dollies don't really learn to type. Even Carol's impermeable cheerfulness was beginning to wear a bit thin. There were many days when they'd see each other on the stairs in the morning and the bags under her eyes were exaggerated by leftover tears.

'So it looks like we're *both* on the up, then,' says Carol. 'I'll tell you what, I'm getting out of Streatham as fast as I can once I've got some sort of income. I don't know why it didn't occur to me before, but I don't need to live in London to get to the airport. In fact it's completely stupid. I've been looking at estate agents around Crawley and places are half the price they are in London, even where we live. And without the crack dens round the corner and neighbours who won't give you the time of day. I'll tell you what, I've been missing you like crazy. That lot in our house now, they're so far up their own backsides they'd probably ignore the sound of gunshots in case it lowered the value of their property.'

'Has anyone moved into my old flat?'

Carol shakes her head. 'There's an auction sign up outside, now. It's going up in April.'

Bridget feels a twinge of – something – as she listens; is not sure what, exactly. She never wants to see the place again, but it was the scene of so much hope, and so much fear, that she knows she will never forget it.

'Tell you what,' says Carol, 'you've inspired me, though. London's not all it's cracked up to be.'

'No, it's not,' says Bridget. 'I don't think I ever want to go back.'

'Steady on.'

'No, I don't. I just look at –'

Yasmin teeters on the wall and she prepares to run. Relaxes as she sees her jump down on to the paved side and run towards a climbing frame. She nods in her direction. '– her. I mean. Brockwell Park or rockpools? Drive-by shootings or learning to surf? Winnie Mandela primary or Meneglos school? It's a no-brainer.'

'And no Kieran,' adds Carol.

'And no Kieran. Carol, he's not been bothering you, has he?'

'I told you. Don't worry about it. He wouldn't dare.'

I don't know, thinks Bridget. I don't know. Not while he had me to focus it all on, but now we'll have turned into a coven of witches in his head, conspiring against him, and she's the only one he can get to.

'You will be careful, though, won't you? He's not – balanced.'

'Stop it,' says Carol. 'I know what he's like.'

'I just – you know, you've got dragged into this and I don't want . . .'

'So what,' asks Carol, in a let's-change-the-subject voice, 'do you get up to for fun around here? Made any friends?'

'Mmm. Yes, I think so. Sort of. There's a girl in the village with a kid Yas's age. Tina. I like her. She's a laugh. And her brother's nice, too.' She glances over at her, hopes she won't pick up on the reference to a man. I'm not looking for a man. All I want right now is a life. She hurries on. 'And they're – yes, they're good people around here. Friendly. Careful, but friendly. I think they want to be sure I'm staying before they bother too much. But they're not standoffish.'

'So what do you do? Pub?'

'There is one. But it's no more child-friendly than the Bricklayers in Streatham. And anyway, there's babysitters.'

'So you don't go out, then?'

'I'm not you, Carol. You're good at this sort of thing. You pick up friends like they're going out of business. Me, it takes more time. I'm fine. There's things go on in the village and we go down to them, and we'll get to know people. The Beaver Scouts are letting in girls now and I'm signing her up for that. It's fine.'

'Sounds a bit lonely to me,' says Carol. Laughs. 'Says the sad old spinster.'

'Well, it's not,' lies Bridget. 'It's fine. I don't need other people around me all the time. And a sad old spinster is something you will never be.'

Chapter Thirty-Five

'Tea? Coffee?'

'Um . . . I'll have a coffee. Thanks.'

She stands awkwardly, hands in pockets, while the grey-haired stranger spoons Mellow Birds into a plastic beaker and fills it up with water. 'Black or white?'

'White, please.'

She spoons Coffee Mate on to the top, stirs vigorously until most of the lumps are gone.

'Sugar?'

Bridget shakes her head. 'Thanks.'

'So,' she says. 'Whose mother are you?'

'Oh,' says Bridget, 'Yasmin. Yasmin Sweeny's.'

'Ah, *right*. Lovely Yasmin.'

Bridget glows. There's only been a couple of weeks of term but she's glad if Yas is making a good impression.

'And where is Yasmin tonight? Not home alone, I trust?'

Bridget colours. *She's only joking. She doesn't really think you're a neglectful parent. Look, she's smiling.* She's so used to the faintly accusatory tone of Social Services – the Social Services who were supposed to be helping her – that she just automatically hears it from the lips of any authority figure these days. 'She's back at Rospetroc. I've got a friend staying. Her sort-of godmother. She'll be in the throes of sugar rush right at this moment, if my guess is good.'

The woman laughs. 'That's what godparents are for. Winding them up and giving them back when it gets out of hand. So how is life at Rospetroc? Nice to see a family settled in there at last.'

Look, this is all very well, but I don't know who the hell you are. 'Sorry,' she says, 'you are . . .?'

'Oh – gosh.' She sticks a hand out. 'I *am* sorry. You get used, I'm afraid, in small communities like this, to thinking everyone knows who you are. Sally Parsons. I teach maths and science. Well, you can hardly call it science. Sums and How Things Grow. Yasmin's very bright. You must be proud of her. We were expecting her to be behind, coming out of the London state system, but frankly I don't think she's going to have any problems.'

'Oh, thank God for that.'

'Were you nervous?'

'I don't know,' says Bridget. 'It's this Parents' Evening thing. It just makes you nervous even if you think everything's fine.'

'I remember,' says Sally. 'I used to spend about three hours getting ready for them, changing my clothes so I didn't look too – *fast*. It was like being lined up outside the headmistress's door waiting for a spanking. I wouldn't worry, if I were you. We're very soft here anyway, but I don't think anyone's got any complaints where Yasmin's concerned.'

'Phew,' says Bridget. Sips her coffee. Scalds her lips. I should remember that about instant. It's pretty much like drinking kettle water.

'So how's Tom Gordhavo? I haven't seen him in ages. Gosh, he was a naughty one.'

'Tom Gordhavo went to school here?'

'Standard practice. Primary level. Mix with the next generation of tenants until you go to prep school.'

'Oh, right. Well, he's fine, as far as I know. Though I've only seen him once since I got here. He's fairly – hands off, as bosses go.'

'Mmm,' says Sally. 'I can't say I'm surprised. He never liked the place.'

'So people keep telling me.'

'Yes, I'm sure they do. I'm surprised they didn't sell it,

to be honest, when old Mrs Blakemore died. Frankly, I think the poor old place probably deserves a new start.'

'What do you mean?'

'Well. Not a happy family. A house like that deserves a happier life. Not that I'm wishing you out of a job, obviously.'

'Obviously.'

'It's just a shame, that's all. Some families do seem to have these runs of bad luck, don't they? Even the rich ones. And anyway, a house can't sit there for several hundred years without getting a bit of history, eh?'

Funny how everyone seems to assume that I know everything about my employers. It's as though it's celebrity gossip published in the *Mirror* this morning. 'No,' she says. 'Not that I know all that much about it. I know about Mrs Gordhavo's brother, but really, the rest is a mystery to me. I've been having to make stuff up for the renters. Cavaliers and Roundheads and tin mines and Trelawny and that.'

Mrs Parsons laughs. 'Well done you! Not bad at all! And much less offputting than a hanging in a hay-loft, I must say.'

'Yes, I thought so.'

'Is the boathouse even still there?'

'Yes,' says Bridget. 'Though I've not been down to it apart from to check the padlock's strong enough to keep Yasmin out. It looks pretty derelict.'

'Well, it would be. It's not been used since before – heaven knows. Probably since well before the war. I don't suppose they had a lot of use for it when it was a school. They had Health and Safety or whatever the equivalent was breathing down their necks, even then in the 1930s.'

'It was a school?'

'Didn't you know? Yes. Mrs Blakemore's mother's attempt at keeping the place going after her husband bought it in the trenches. Paddy Blakemore – Tom's grandfather – was the estate manager, running the farms and the bit they didn't use for the school. That's how she met him.'

'How do you know all this?'

'My parents. I'm afraid we don't move very far from where we grew up, down here. Trouble is, you get to a certain age and your biggest regret is that you didn't listen to them enough while they were still alive. Anyway, the school barely outlived the mother-in-law. I think both the Blakemores felt it was a bit infra dig, even if it was the only reason the place was still in family hands. She was a right stickler for class, I remember that. Had conniptions when she got a bunch of refugees dumped on her in the war. Worried sick that they'd bring her children down to their level. It was the village joke. The local organizer had a field day, picking the ones who would brown her off the most and fixing it so she couldn't get rid of them. Bringing lice into the school and swearing. I'm sure there was something about one of them . . . oh, I *do* wish I'd listened properly. I just can't remember. Some mystery, though. Sort of Something Nasty In The Woodshed type thing. Mind you, it was all hints and rumours around here back then. The Cornish Village way. People were a lot less forthcoming when I was a child. People keeping shtoom, just letting all sorts of things go by with nothing more than a knowing look and a say-no-more. A leftover of the smuggling era, I wouldn't be surprised.'

'Doesn't matter,' says Bridget. It's all good material. For something. She's sure it's the sort of thing that would have amused the Aykroyds, at the very least.

'No, it doesn't. You're right. It's just funny, and it's a shame, to lose all these bits of local history for the sake of paying a bit of attention. One of them at least got kicked out of the school for something, but I don't remember what. I remember Mrs B very well. Mad as a ferret by the time she went. Wandering about in the village with a hat with cherries on and no shoes and socks, always looking over her shoulder like she thought someone was coming up behind her.'

'Crikey.'

'I know. I think at least some of it was related to . . .' She raises a cupped hand in front of her face and wobbles it in the universal drinking gesture. 'Of course, we were horrible children, as children are, and used to do awful things like jumping out at her and making her scream. It's no wonder they ended up just shutting themselves in there and never coming out except to collect the grocery deliveries at the front door. Mind you, I've got a feeling she might have been a bit loose-screwish for a while before it really started showing, actually. Certainly, Paddy Blakemore buggered off – excuse my French – sometime in the war. They pretended he'd been killed in action, of course, but even somewhere as isolated as this occasionally hears rumours about what's going on in London. But men didn't do that, on the whole, especially if they came from that sort of background, unless they had quite a compelling reason.'

'No,' says Bridget.

'I don't think it was exactly a happy household after that. I think it was the shame. Women whose husbands left always ended up getting the blame in those days. Not that it's a lot better now, of course. Anyway, she practically shut the house up in the winter of '43 and that was that. Got very reliant on Hugh: did the whole man-of-house-bit on him while he was still at Eton. Took him out of school and wouldn't let anyone near him for love nor money. Poor sod didn't stand a hope in hell of marrying. She wouldn't let him out of the house. He'd have had to go a bit further afield to find a wife anyway, mind you. Mum said he was creepy and all the village girls gave him a wide berth long before he did himself in. I suppose Tom's mother was lucky to escape it, really. She married Jack Gordhavo pretty much the minute she turned twenty-one. Definitely one of those getting-away-from-home marriages, but I think they were happy enough for all that. But she didn't go back much while her family was still alive, and you can see, especially as they had a perfectly good house where they were, that it wouldn't appeal much after they were dead.'

'Yes, absolutely.'

'You always got the feeling there was some sort of – secret. Something they were trying to cover up. To do with Hugh, I can't help thinking. But Tom Gordhavo always looked sort of – guilty? – when the subject of the house came up. Like there was something they weren't telling anyone?'

'You know what the aristocracy are like,' jokes Bridget. 'Terrified that someone will find out what their income really is.'

'True enough. But all the same, it surprises me that he hasn't sold it. It's not as if there's a load of sentimental memories.'

'No,' says Bridget. 'I suppose, even so . . . getting rid of a house with all that history . . . it would be a wrench, wouldn't it?'

'You're quite right. Anyway. Maybe it was just meant to be. Maybe the point was that you and your lovely little daughter were going to come and change its fortune.'

Bridget finds herself smiling, shrugs. 'Well, maybe it's changing our fortunes right back,' she says. 'It certainly feels like it.'

Sally looks at her with curious, button-bright eyes. 'Yes? I'm glad to hear that. Can't have been easy for you, bringing up a little one by yourself.'

You're not going there, she thinks. I'm not going to start confessing to privations beyond your wildest so you've got something to tell the village. 'Well,' she says dismissively. 'It's not like I'm the first woman it's ever happened to.'

'You're right there. And I don't suppose you'll be the last. Tell me. Has he had the electrics fixed yet?'

'Oh, have you heard about that?'

'Frances used to go on about them all the time.'

'Oh really? I thought it was just me. I guess I'd better talk to him about it, then.'

'Yes,' says Sally. 'Don't let his meanness end up driving you off. He can at least get Mark Carlyon to come and have a look at them and do the basics.'

'Mark's the guy to ask, is he?'

'Course. He's very good. He was another cheeky little so-and-so, though. Not as bad as Tina, but I was sorely tempted to give him the odd clout round the ear back before Humans had Rights. Grown up nice, though. Honest – well, as far as anyone's honest these days. I don't suppose he'd pass a wallet in the street any more than the next person. But he won't rip you off and he cleans up after himself. You should call him.'

'Okay,' says Bridget. 'I'll ask Tina, once I've talked to the Big Man.'

'You do that. Tell him I told you to.'

'Anyway,' says Bridget, 'I'm wasting your time. We're meant to be talking about Yasmin, aren't we? And you're meant to be telling me off about something and pointing out the importance of homework?'

'So we are. And how much time *is* Yasmin spending on her homework?'

Bridget blushes. 'Oh my God. I didn't know she – the naughty minx. They don't, you know, in London schools, so it never –'

'Joke, Bridget. She's only six.'

She feels herself flush again. I must learn to spot when someone's shitting me. I seem to have lost my sense of humour over the years. 'Oh, sorry.'

'How's she settling in, at home?'

'Fine, I think. She seems pretty happy.'

'Well, she's a delight at school. We were all expecting some gun-toting gum-chewing inner city child, but she's fitted right in, made friends, picked up the work. Does she talk much about it at home?'

'Oh, she loves it. She's having a lovely time. Won't stop going on about it.'

'Great. Great. And who's she friends with? I can never tell, from the playground. Half the time you think they're fighting and they're actually rehearsing a dance routine.'

'Quite a few.' She racks her brain for names. 'Chloe Teagle, obviously, and Jago Carlyon.'

'Nice kids.'

'And there are a couple I haven't met yet. Carla Tremayne?'

'Oh yes. Blonde ringlets and proud of it. Parents have a pottery shop in Helstone.'

'Okay. I think I've seen her. Honor Jefferson?'

She nods. 'Mad as a ferret. Makes some *very* odd noises in class. Has a dog called Charlie that farts and eats rocks, and she knows more about the Peloponnesian War than Achilles did himself. Likes dressing up in fairy costumes and accessorizing with guns.'

'That sounds like the girl. And there's one called Lily. She goes on about her a lot.'

'Lily?'

'Mmm.'

'No. Can't think. Are you sure she doesn't mean Lulu? Louise Strang?'

'No. Well, I'm pretty sure. She's not one of those kids who muddle names up.'

'How bizarre. I really can't think. It must be a child who doesn't go to the school. But I can't think of anyone called that at all around here.'

'Funny. She said she lived here.'

'I must be slipping,' says Mrs Parsons. 'I thought I knew everyone in East Cornwall. Oh well. There you go. Looks like Mrs Varco's free now. Do you want me to take you over?'

Chapter Thirty-Six

The valley is pitch black. She can only make the house out by the headlights.

She drives slowly down, parks and, glad she's had the sense to put an emergency kit in the car, gets the torch from the boot and makes her way to the front door.

By gum, it's dark down here. I wish I didn't have an imagination. I wish I didn't see people crouching, in the dark, behind the bushes.

She hurries up the path, unlocks the door as quickly as she can – Carol wanted it locked if she was going to be alone in the place – and gropes for the switch inside the door. No response. Damn. Those bloody fuses. I *will* call Gordhavo tomorrow and insist it be sorted. I can't run the Hoover, half the time, because it trips the trip-switch. Good thing there's not a burglar alarm, really, or I'd have the police down wagging their fingers twice a week because it had sent out a false reading.

She's almost immune, now, to the terrors of a darkened house. Flicks the torch round the dining room as she passes through it – just in case – and notices that the figurines on the dresser have turned round again, are staring at her from the mirror. I must talk to Yasmin, put a ban on her doing that. She must have to drag a chair up to do it, it's too high otherwise. One day I'll come down and find them all in shards and my daughter lying among them on the flags with a split head.

She goes to the stairs. 'Hello?'

'OHMYGOD!' bellows Carol. 'For *fuck* sake, there you

are! I've been bricking it all alone here for the last two hours!'

By torchlight, she looks more than her age. Her facial lines, which seem non-existent by daylight, stand out in relief like fissures in a lava field. Her eyes are the eyes of a hunted rabbit. She is wrapped in the blanket from the sitting-room sofa.

'Sorry! Sorry! Why didn't you call me? I'd've come straight back.'

'My bloody phone doesn't have a signal down here, does it? Bloody Orange. I might as well be in a basement. I've been scared *stupid.* What's happened? What's happened to the lights?'

'It's okay. Hang on a mo, Carol.'

She hears her hovering at the top of the stairs as she scans the banks of switches in the cupboard. Eight of the twenty-three have tripped altogether, as well as the master. She's not seen that many go before: usually it's only one or two. 'What were you up to when they went?' she calls.

'I was only drying my hair. I switched on the dryer, and bang! Everything went off.'

'Oh, right.'

It's getting worse. You usually have to have the dryer *and* the electric fire on before it overloads.

She flips the switches. The house is bathed in blessed light. 'Where's Yasmin?'

'Oh, she slept through the whole thing. She sleeps like the proverbial, that one. Never seen anything like it.'

'Well, if she was asleep already . . .'

She starts to climb the stairs. Carol's hair is a mess: straightened on one side, a mass of Celtic tangles on the other.

'I need a drink,' says Carol.

'Me, too.'

In the kitchen, which smells strongly of cigarette smoke, a candle burns uselessly on the table beside the bottle of vodka and a glass full of ice. She feels a faint twinge of irritation that Carol has been opening the freezer despite the fact that there's been no power to top the cold back up. The level in the bottle has dropped a good two inches since she went out. She fetches herself a glass, pours them both a drink. Turns to look at Carol and sees that she is so pale beneath her fake tan that her skin is almost green.

'Good God. I didn't realize you were so nervy.'

'Jesus,' says Carol, 'how nervy do you want me to be? That was one of the worst two hours of my life.'

'It was only a power cut, Carol.'

'No, well,' Carol shakes out a Benson, lights it, 'it was more than that, actually. There was something . . .' She sits down suddenly, heavily.

Bridget sits down opposite her. 'What?'

'It was – God, it was weird.'

'What?'

'Well, there I was, halfway through drying my hair, when bam, the lights went out. I'm there in the bathroom in nothing but a towel and I can't see a thing. So I feel my way out to the kitchen and find my lighter – at least I remembered where *that* was – and found the candle in the living room. Thoroughly used, I notice.'

'Mmm. I did *say* there was a prob with the electricity.'

'Yes, well, anyway, I'm putting some clothes on and suddenly it's like all hell's broken loose.'

'What do you mean?'

'There was someone banging on the front door, Bridget. I jumped out of my skin. I couldn't remember if you'd locked it or not, but it sounded like they were really, really desperate to get in.'

Bridget feels a prickle behind her ears. 'Someone?'

'I don't know. You know what I thought at first. Of course you do.'

Yes, of course I do. She thought it was Kieran. Back. Found us, somehow, despite our best efforts. Doing what he's been doing for the last five years. She doesn't say anything. Feels nauseous.

'I didn't know what to do, frankly.'

'No . . . no, I don't suppose you did.'

'So I thought: okay. I can go and look. So I went through. Into the house. And there's this hammering, like two fists banging and banging and banging away, and it's going all through the house, and I'm feeling like – God, what am I meant to do? It's in the middle of nowhere, this place. Where would you go? I mean . . .'

Don't. Just don't. I don't want to think about it.

'I went into that bedroom with the four-poster in it. I was jumping out of my skin, what with all the curtains being drawn in there and I didn't have the candle with me 'cause I didn't want to let whoever it was know there was someone in the house. And I crept in there and pulled back a corner of the curtain, and . . . there's not another door, is there? That I've missed?'

Bridget shakes her head. 'Not on that side of the house, no. That's the only one.'

'Well, Bridget, there's something very strange about this place. 'Cause I swear, I could hear them knocking and knocking, bashing on the thing with their fists, but when I looked out, there was no one there.'

Chapter Thirty-Seven

But what about us? What about us?

Her hand is shaking as she lays the letter down on the bureau, looks out of the window at the fading garden. The borders by the path are overgrown, dry, straggled. I am forty-three and I've never tried to be anything other than a good wife, and now . . . now . . .

. . . not be coming back to Cornwall when I get leave . . . in truth, Felicity, I haven't been happy for a long time, and this war, the death and devastation all around me, has made me see that life is too fragile, too precious . . .

What about us? What about our children? What do you expect of me? You break my heart, destroy our home, and you want me to be the one to tell them? Are you not man enough to confront your own actions?

I will not cry. I will not. He will not break me. It's not over.

A wave of melancholy sweeps through her. My husband. This is not how my life was meant to be.

She squeezes her eyes tight shut, sets her jaw. When she opens them again, the letter is still there. Drawing her glance toward it, sucking her in. She picks it up again, scans it for hope. Scans it like a cancer patient scans their medical reports for a sign that there has been an error.

We don't love each other. I wonder if we ever did. Our life together has been one of display, of being seen to do the right thing . . . being away from Rospetroc has given me time to reflect, to see my life as it really is, not reflected through the lens of marital propriety . . .

What does he mean? What does he *mean*?

You are a good woman, Felicity, and you deserve better than this, but . . .

There's a sour taste in her mouth. Blood and lemon juice. She swallows. I am a good woman. A *good woman.* But being good isn't enough, is it? Being good is a quality which attracts punishment, it seems, in these upside-down days.

It is only through her that I have discovered truly, for the first time in my life, what it means to be happy . . .

Happy? Happy? What do you know about happiness? You think that your sordid little . . . whore . . . is happiness?

I shall, of course, observe my responsibilities toward you, and toward Hughie and Tessa, but . . .

Hughie and Tessa? How dare he? How dare he refer to my children by their pet names, the names we gave them in the days he claimed he loved me, when he came to the hospital with roses and pearls, when he thanked me, with tears in his eyes, for making him the happiest man alive?

You can say whatever you like to explain my absence, whatever will best preserve your dignity, but I will not be returning to Rospetroc.

Preserve my dignity? How? I am forty-three and have two children and no husband. If you want to preserve my dignity, you will die in this war, the way so many thousand good young men have died, good young men who never did any harm. If you wanted to preserve my dignity, you would leave me a widow. Not leave me like this: not wife, not widow, not honourably unmarried to all those young men of the Somme, like so many of my generation. You have stolen my life. Stolen my life. What alternatives are there for me now? The woman in the big house whose husband ran off with a . . .

I am sorry, Felicity. It was never my intention to cause you unhappiness. Perhaps that's why we've both been drinking so much, over the years. I only realized how much more it was than ordinary people when I went into the world and saw it with my own eyes. If this damn war had never happened, had not taken me to a wider world, I would, perhaps, have continued unaware in the low misery in which we both existed . . .

Oh, but you're doing it anyway, aren't you? It was never

your intention: never your intention. Salve your own conscience, Patrick. Make yourself the hero of your own good intentions. The outcome is the same.

One day you will see that my decision is for the best, that we are all happier and better off apart . . .

Felicity Blakemore allows a howl of despair, rage, terror, loss to escape the depths. My husband. My husband. My *life . . .*

She screws the letter up, throws it at the window. Notices a car bumping down the drive. A little Austin, vaguely familiar.

Hughie. It's Hughie coming home. Hughie will know what to do. Hughie will help me.

She runs down the stairs, through the dining room, out on to the path. Goes back in again to tidy herself in the hall mirror. He will have a Gordhavo with him; that horrid little boy that Tessa's always mooning after, and his mother. Is it better or worse that it's People Like Us? Either: it's gossip or judgement whichever way it goes. I can't let my appearance show that anything is wrong. I shall greet them and get rid of them, and I will tell him, and he will know what to do. Only fourteen, but he is the wisest, the bravest, the best . . . he is everything his father isn't. He has been the man of this house for over a year and he will know what to do. He will be angry. He will understand. I will have to stop him from going to London and *hitting* Daddy.

She sees herself and is surprised by the fact that her turmoil barely shows. Her eyes are wide and her skin paler than usual, but her hair – she feels as though she has been pulling it out by the hank – is neat, her make-up, what she wears of it, untouched. No one will ever know, she thinks. I will walk down the streets of Wadebridge and no one will look at me, see a woman whose life has been shattered by a single, careless letter.

She longs for a drink.

She steps out on to the path. It's not Hughie. It's Dougie Saul, the churchwarden. And, kicking and spitting as he pulls her along by her collar, Lily Rickett, bane of her life. Felicity Blakemore feels a surge of resentment. When will she ever be rid of her? Why is it, when she is least equipped to cope with her, the girl always does something? Dougie is red in the face with the effort of controlling her and carrying her vile cardboard suitcase in his other hand. Pearl O'Leary and Geoffrey Clark have already been claimed by their parents. Vera Muntz is due to leave for Canada in a week and Ted Betts – nice, willing Ted Betts – has moved into the village to live with the grocer and his wife and pay them back by replacing the delivery boy who went off to war when he turned eighteen. The only one left is Lily Rickett. Horrible, dirty Lily Rickett. No one wants to take *her* off her hands.

Mrs Blakemore puts her feet into third position, places her palms together, index fingers pointing toward the flagstones.

I will be a paragon of composure, she thinks. Nothing will show. I will not have the village knowing my business.

I want to die. I wish I were dead. Where is Hughie?

'Found her on the Launceston road again,' pants Dougie.

'Get off me!' snarls Lily. Her hair has grown in now, but, untouched in the months since it had to be taken off for nits, looks, if anything, worse than it did before – tufts and strands in bird's-nest tangles. She shouldn't have fought, she thinks. She always fights. She is the most hellish child. If she'd just kept still and let us get on with it. It's not as though she didn't bring it on herself in the first place. Her face is dirty again, and streaked with tears of rage. I've had her nearly half a year and still I can't make her wash. 'Let go!' she bellows.

Dougie Saul does as she says, releases his grip with a sudden ferocity so that she drops, surprised, to the ground and grazes her knee. Blood and tears and dirt – it's bad enough on an ordinary day, but today . . . today I cannot bear it. Today I want to go to my room and curl up under the covers and shriek. You see photographs, sometimes, of mourning parties in other parts of the world, the native women, no dignity, tearing at their scalps with pieces of stone, dust and blood mingling with their tears. And today I understand what drives them. Today I want to rip at my face with my fingernails, howl at God and life and Patrick.

I want him to see what he has done. He cannot walk away and not face the truth of what he has done.

'Thank you, Dougie,' she says. 'I'm very grateful.'

'Seems like she really wants to get wherever she's trying to go,' says Dougie.

Go away. Just go away. I can't make small-talk today.

'Portsmouth,' says Lily. 'I want to go home to bloody Portsmouth.'

'Language, young lady,' says Dougie.

'Oh, bugger off,' she snaps.

Dougie pulls a village face.

'Thank you so much, Dougie,' says Felicity Blakemore again. Should I tip him? Is he waiting for a tip? No. Surely you don't tip churchwardens. If he were the postman, or someone from the garage, perhaps, but . . . and anyway, I'm damned if I'm going to give tips for bringing this . . . creature . . . back to my house. 'I'm very grateful.'

She turns to the child. Summons all her self-control. Gives her the mothering, nurturing smile the village would expect. 'Come inside now, Lily. I should think you could do with some lunch.'

Lily squats on the path, glares at her like an imp sucked accidentally from the void by a passing gust.

Dougie puts the case down. 'You're welcome,' he says. 'Can't have them wandering about the country willy-nilly. You never know who might come along.'

'Piss off,' says Lily. 'I can look after myself.'

'You're nine years old, Lily,' says Felicity. Forces a tinkling, indulgent laugh from somewhere deep inside.

'Oh, piss off,' says the child again.

She steps forward. 'Give me your hand,' she commands. Snaps her fingers, as you would at a dog.

A look passes between them. *If you play me up,* she threatens, silently. *If you give me one more piece of trouble today . . .*

Lily doesn't move.

Felicity Blakemore loses her temper. Grabs the child by the wrist and starts to drag. Lily pulls back, hard. Scrabbles at the ground with her heels. Bucks against her. A memory flashes through her mind, a memory from her own childhood: a veal calf, smelling the blood in the old slaughterhouse behind the barn, panicking and fighting to break free. The three farmhands together, throwing themselves upon it, overpowering it with their size and hauling it, screaming, forward through the door.

'Get off me! Get off!' screams Lily.

'Thank you, Dougie,' she calls again. 'We'll see you on Sunday.'

And then it's just the two of them, fighting against each other as she drags her up the path. Lily kicking out, catching her ankle a painful blow as they come through the porch. 'Ow! Ow!'

She slams the door. Throws the child to the ground and aims a return kick which catches her thigh. Bends to rub her ankle and snaps: 'That's enough! Enough!'

Her ankle hurts as though it's been struck with an iron bar. Tears start to her eyes. I will not. I will *not* cry. He has not been able to make me cry and this child will not . . . this hateful child . . .

Lily is curled up on the cold stone, yapping.

'Get to your room! Go on! Get up there!'

She raises her head, bares her teeth. 'No! I won't! I'm not bloody staying here!'

'Get to your room!'

'Fuck off!'

'Very well,' she says. 'Well, if you're not going to your room, there are other places.'

'You wouldn't dare,' says Lily.

'Believe me, young lady, there is *nothing* I wouldn't dare do where you're concerned. So are you going to your room, or am I going to have to put you in the cupboard upstairs again?'

Lily rears back. Spits at her like a tomcat. 'Fuck *off*!'

She can't hold herself back. Launches into the attack. Grabs the child by her collar and slaps, hard, at her head. I can't bear it. I can't *bear* it. You bloody little . . . I can't . . .

'You . . . will . . . do . . . as . . . you . . . are . . . told . . .'

'Ow! Ow! *Stop it!'*

She realizes she is panting. Lets go, watches Lily wrap her arms around her head.

'I . . . told . . . you . . .'

'You bitch. You *bitch!*'

'Get up those stairs. Go on! I've had enough! *Enough*! You've had your chance! You can have a few hours in the dark, now. Teach you some manners!'

Lily scrambles to her feet, darts in the direction of the door. Felicity is quick. Slams it shut as she pulls it open. Lily leans – huddles against it. Her face is rebellious, enraged, defiant. 'I'm not staying here,' she says. 'I'm not bloody staying here.'

'Well, where on earth do you think you're going to go?'

'Anywhere,' says Lily. 'I don't care. Anywhere.'

'Well,' she says, and feels unaccountably triumphant, 'there's nowhere for you *to* go. We're stuck with each other, whether you like it or not.'

Lily bursts into tears.

'I want my mum! I want my *mum*!'

'Oh, shut up,' says Felicity Blakemore, spitefully. Picks her up and shakes her. 'Stop that!'

'I'll tell her! I'll tell her what you done and she'll *get* you!'

'Oh, grow up, Lily,' says Felicity. 'Don't you see? Haven't you noticed? Not once. She's not been here to see you, not once. All the other children – oh yes. First chance their parents have had. But you? Don't you understand yet?'

There are words falling out of my body and I can't stop them, she thinks. They're not for her. They're for Patrick. I should stop, but I can't. I can't. These things I feel – I shouldn't be letting them . . . but I hate her. I hate her. Cuckoo in the nest, forced on me. She's brought nothing but misfortune since she came here. She is a curse on my house.

She shakes the girl again, sees her head snap back and forth like a rag doll's, feels a sick satisfaction as she does it.

'Your mother doesn't want you,' she says, and relishes the words. 'If she wanted you she'd have come for you.'

Chapter Thirty-Eight

Steve's having a slow day. He's got a honey-trap set up for this evening in the Pitcher and Piano in Holborn, an account executive at British Telecom whose wife suspects him of being chained to more than his desk, but this afternoon has been a long slog of phoning round with client updates.

It's already getting dark, he notices, as he ticks Darren Keating (builders' supplies; suspects partner (rightly) of embezzlement) off the list. Winter seems to last forever these days. Obviously, early January, we haven't even seen the worst of it yet, but I'm sure you used to see some signs that it was going to be over by March when I was a kid. Nowadays – so much for global warming – we seem to live under leaden, darkening skies from September through to May.

He dials the next number on the list. Waits, clicketty-clicking the top of his biro, while it rings.

'Kieran Fletcher.' A background of ringing telephones and bellowed instructions.

'Hello, Mr Fletcher. Steve Holden. Trident Investigations.'

'Oh, right. Hold on.'

The background noise fades, cuts off. 'Hi,' says Kieran Fletcher. 'Any news?'

'Nothing particularly cheering, I'm afraid. Your wife seems to have done a pretty good job of covering her tracks. It would help, of course, if she had a credit card or a loyalty card or something, but, well . . .'

She's obviously been living on short commons, he doesn't add. And like many people living on the edge, she's part of the cash society. More people should realize how traceable they are through the things they buy. The number of adulterers he's come across who've paid their bills in cash but not been able to resist picking up the Nectar points . . .

'If you could have registered her as a missing person,' he says.

'Tried it,' says Kieran. 'Couldn't. Police called her mobile and she answered, so she doesn't qualify.'

There's something you're not telling me, thinks Steve Holden. 'Well, all I can suggest is that you put access proceedings under way.'

A snort of irritation from the other end of the line. 'Fat bloody lot of use that is if I don't have an address.'

Fair point.

'Can't you trace her through the mobile? I thought they had some sort of satellite tracking thing . . .'

'Well, yes. And if I had a contact at her provider it might be possible, but I'm afraid they also have a thing called confidentiality.'

'You can't even find out where she's being billed to?'

'Not on a pay-as-you-go, Mr Fletcher.'

'Shit,' says Kieran.

'I'm sorry.'

Silence.

'If she got a new number we might be able to source where the SIM card was sold, but otherwise . . .'

'So basically there's nothing you can do?'

'I can keep trying. If you like.'

'Of course I like,' says Kieran. 'And don't worry. Money's not an issue.'

Mmm, thinks Steve. Okay. So her short commons doesn't translate into a general shortage at his end, then. 'If there was a bank account,' he suggests, 'that your daughter's Child Support goes into? She will have to have given *them* her new details.'

A silence. Kieran Fletcher changes the subject with an audible clunk. 'How about Yasmin, then? She's got to be going to school. She's six years old. It would be against the law.'

'Absolutely.'

'Well, how about that, then?'

'School records are confidential as well, I'm afraid. Not that that's a problem, on the whole. Education Trusts are pretty dim when it comes to security. But the fact is, I've not been able to find a single child by that name registered anywhere other than at her old school, who didn't seem to have noticed she'd gone till I asked about her. Like I said, she's done a good job. I don't know how much of it was planned out, but it's been effective. She's not registered for National Insurance anywhere, she's not joined a library or signed up with a doctor. She's not got an obvious internet service provider. She's not reregistered with the DVLA. She's not ordered anything for delivery as far as I know. She's not collecting her Child Benefit and she's not signed on. Would she be going under any other name, other than Fletcher or Barton, that you can think of?'

'No. I don't suppose she's got the imagination to make one up.'

You'd be surprised. You don't have to have an imagination. Just a phone book and a pin. It's harder if you're trying to do anything official, of course, but you can call yourself Hurdy-Gurdy bin Laden if you want and no one can stop you.

'Well, there's a limit,' he says, 'to how much more I can do with the information I've got. I wouldn't want to waste your money.'

'Keep on trying,' says Kieran. 'I don't care what it costs.'

'If you're sure . . .'

'Absolutely. They can't simply disappear.'

Actually, thousands of people do just that every year, even with the insane amount of surveillance the government's squandering money on. But what's the point of telling you? A fee's a fee, after all.

'Well,' he says, 'if you think of anything that might help me get a lead, let me know.'

'I will,' says Fletcher.

He hangs up. Scribbles a couple of notes and makes himself a mug of Nescaff. Adds three sugars.

The phone rings. He picks it up, listens.

'I've thought,' says Kieran Fletcher. 'And I remembered something. Her mum and dad had her before they were married. I'd forgotten because it's not something that exactly got talked about much. But I guess she might be calling herself Sweeny.'

Chapter Thirty-Nine

She wishes, now, that Carol had never come. The feelings she's been having about the house – the sense that it is watching her, the threat of its isolated position, the odd things out of place and out of time – are more concrete now someone else has had them too. I don't feel safe here, and I can't pretend, any more, that it's a hangover from the unsafety of London. It's odd. This house is odd. I see, now, why Frances Tyler got so spooked. Only, she had the option to walk away. I don't. This place is perfect for me, for us. The job's a breeze, most of the time; so much so I could probably sign up for some form of education and still do it. We've got all the space in the world, miles and miles to run, and breathe. I love this village, this new place where no one knows me, where they accept my back-story at face value, where I can be anyone I want to be, not the frightened drudge he turned me into.

But . . . she's got me looking over my shoulder, now. She's got me double-checking the door locks. She's got me seeing things. I know he can't have found out where we are short of having followed her down on the train, but I feel it all the time. That there's someone here . . . someone watching us . . .

Bridget has collected all the metal objects in the house and is polishing them at the kitchen table, newspaper spread out all around her and the radio on. But she's had to move from one end of the table to the other already, because, where she was sitting at first, she couldn't keep an eye on the door. I'm definitely past my youth, she thinks. Today I turned the radio straight on to Radio 2, didn't even do a quick waveband skim in search of something more challenging. They'll never get me on to Radio 4, but I like this station. They've had six soul tracks, back to back – real soul, from the 1960s – and I've been able to sing most of the lyrics to each of them. Which would I rather? Marvin Gaye, or Snoop Dogg? Do I need to even ask?

The phone rings and she is surprised, even though she's brought it down with her. Most of the time there's no reception down on the ground floor, but today a single bar shows in the display beside the 0207 number that's dialling in. I miss my mum, she thinks, suddenly, randomly. Picks it up.

'Hello?'

'You've still got a choice,' he says.

She closes her eyes. When will he stop?

'You can tell me where you are, or I can find you.'

Breathe.

'You think you're so fucking clever, don't you, Bridget?'

Don't react. Don't speak to him. Speaking to him will encourage him. Don't.

'Please,' she says, 'leave me alone.' Intends to have it come out strong, decisive. Hears, instead, the pleading tones she had meant to leave behind with her old life.

His voice rises when he hears her, turns to a shout. She can see him, at his trader's desk, screaming into the handset, oblivious to the stares of his colleagues, face purpled with rage, tendons like hawsers in his neck. 'You won't get away with this, Bridget! I'm coming for you! I'm fucking *coming*!'

She goes cold. Puts her thumb on the disconnect-switch and hangs up. Presses the tit on the top and powers it down. Sits looking at the phone as though it were a favourite pet that has suddenly turned round and bitten her. Considers throwing it, wholesale, into the garbage. I will get a new one, I will change my number and he can *fuck off*. Forever. He can –

Don't want to lose my information, though. Got to be sensible.

Okay, then. The SIM. I'll ditch the SIM. That'll do it. That's all I need to do.

She stands up, walks across the kitchen and pulls open a drawer. Finds the rolling pin. Opens the back of the phone and gets the old card out. I'll do it now, she thinks. That way I won't have an excuse. That way I'll have to go in to Wadebridge tomorrow and get a new one, because the phone won't work at all. I'll do it now.

She lays the chip on the rolling board: white-veined marble, hard and cold. Lifts an arm and brings the rolling pin down with all her strength. Does it over and over, pretends it's Kieran's head. *I hate you. I hate you. I hatehatehate you.* The card bounces, dents, bends, cracks. She keeps going until it is in pieces, pulverized, dead. There. You will never find me. Never find me. Never.

A laugh. Out in the hall. Bridget freezes. This damn house.

She listens. Nothing.

Another laugh.

Okay. Okay, that's enough. I've had enough of this damn house, playing tricks with me. I'll go and look, but I will not be afraid. See? I've got a rolling pin. If you want to fuck with me you can try all you like, but you're not going to make me afraid.

She goes to the door, throws it open, strides out into the dining room, club raised.

Chapter Forty

Yasmin shrieks to a stop, looks startled. Jago Carlyon rams into the back of her, knocks her into her mother's knees.

'Crikey,' says his father. 'Jago! Get away from the crazy woman before she takes your brains out.'

Bridget drops the rolling pin to her side, burns with embarrassment.

'Oops.'

'Is this the way you greet all your visitors?'

'I'm not a visitor,' says Yasmin.

'Right. So she batters you with a rolling pin when you get home from school every day, then?'

Bridget feels foolish, burns inside.

'No,' she says. 'Sometimes I horsewhip her. Anything to break the monotony. You're early. I wasn't expecting anyone for another hour.'

'No,' says Mark. He's looking faintly amused. 'Tom Gordhavo rang and said you needed the electrics looking at, so I brought them up while there's still a bit of daylight.'

'Chloe's got flu,' says Yasmin.

'A nasty cold,' corrects Mark.

'So she didn't come to school today.'

'Yes. I hope you don't mind me bringing Jago up. I thought I'd keep him out of Tina's hair for a bit.'

'More than welcome,' says Bridget. Jago, brown eyes and a fringe that keeps dropping over them so he has to shake it out of the way, gazes at Yasmin as though she's made of chocolate and cocktail sausages. He's a year younger, and at this age those twelve months will endow a woman with a sophisticated allure she won't achieve again until she approaches her forties.

'Come on,' says Yasmin. 'I'll show you my Barbies.'

Bridget suppresses a smile as Jago trots obediently after her. Catches Mark's eye and sees he is doing the same. 'I don't *think* he's going to grow up gay,' he says when they have gone.

'More likely a British poof,' says Bridget. 'Someone who'd rather spend time with his girlfriend than in the pub with the lads.'

Mark laughs. He has Jago's eyes, she notices: dark and warm. She doesn't remember the last time she noticed a man looking at her with kindness. Indifference, violence, faint contempt, but not kindness. It's been years. Over a decade. There used to be men, before Kieran: men who looked at her like that. But she wanted something 'more'. That nebulous 'more' that sucks you in and makes you blind to the reality in front of you. Even in the early days, if she'd only read it right, he looked at her with proprietorship not protectiveness. God, how could I have been so blind? Was I really one of those stupid women who think that, because a man is exciting, then he's somehow valuable? Hollywood has a lot to answer for.

He holds out a hand. For a moment she thinks he's offering to shake hers, but his palm is upwards.

'Do you mind? Only I feel a bit like a baby seal with you holding that.'

She looks down at the weapon in her hand, laughs again with discomfort. 'Don't tell anyone you found me like this, will you?' she says as she hands the rolling pin over. 'I'll never live it down.'

'Deal. As long as you keep my son's love of dolls quiet. Are you okay? You looked like something'd spooked you when we came in.'

'Oh. Well . . . no, it's nothing . . .' she begins, and bursts into tears.

'Oh,' says Mark. Then: 'Oh, Bridget. I'm sorry. I didn't mean to . . .'

'No,' she replies, hears her voice catch on a sob, 'it's not . . . oh God, I'm sorry.'

We are so British, she thinks. We encounter tears, and all we can think of to do is apologize.

'Oh, look,' he says, and puts his free hand on her shoulder. Doesn't overstep the mark, doesn't try to give her a hug or offer pointless promises. Understands that he's still a friendly acquaintance and not a friend and acts accordingly. Which makes her cry more. It's been such a long time. Such a long time since someone just enfolded me and told me it was going to be okay. Not since Dad died and the heart fell out of my world. God, I miss my dad. My mum and dad. They were Good People. I never felt like I was alone when they were here. I guess that was why I fell into Kieran's world so easily, so unquestioningly: I felt for the first time since I lost them that I *belonged*. I just didn't realize that there was a 'to' attached to the belonging, as far as he saw it. 'If I can do anything . . .' he says. 'You know. I'm sorry.'

'I just –' she begins, stumbles because she doesn't know what to say.

'Shall I make you a cup of tea?'

'Yes, I –'

'Come on.'

He leads her through to the kitchen, sits her at the table. Glances at the smashed SIM card and doesn't comment. Comes and sits opposite her while the kettle boils and looks her in the eye.

'You don't have to tell me,' he says. 'We've all got things that set us off.'

'No, it's just I – it's not that I don't trust you, I just . . .'

'It's tough, sometimes. I know that. We all get low. You, me, Tina. It's bloody lonely. But it can help to talk. And I won't . . . you know . . .'

'Oh, Mark,' she says.

'Come on,' he says, 'or I'll put five sugars in your tea and tell you to buck up.'

'You mustn't tell anyone,' she says. 'I don't want people

knowing. My business. I've got – look, I feel like it's not safe . . .'

He doesn't say anything. No empty promises, again. Just waits.

'I got a phone call,' she says. 'I get them all the time. He won't leave me alone.'

'Ah,' he says.

'I had to run away,' she says. 'That's why I'm here. Where no one knows me. Us. I can't take the . . . but he . . .'

'Oh, kid,' he says. 'I thought you were a bit . . . secretive.'

'I had an injunction against him,' she says, 'but he didn't pay any attention. He just kept – coming.'

'Is this Yasmin's dad?'

She sniffs, rubs her forehead with her wrist, nods.

'And he won't – he used to . . .'

'Oh, kid,' he says again. He wants to reach out and take her hand, knows it would be inappropriate.

'It – you don't have to tell me,' he says again.

'I just – I was so afraid, for so long, and I know he can't find us here, but I hear his voice and I feel . . . *please* don't tell everyone. I know what people are like.'

'They're better than you think they are,' he says. 'If there's any judgements going to be made, they'll be on him, not you. This isn't London. If anything, people would close ranks around you, if they knew.'

She shakes her head again.

'Was it very bad?' he asks. Immediately feels dirty, ugly for asking it, as though his concern were prurient. She flicks him a look that confirms his own judgement of himself.

'No,' she says, 'it was a breeze. I'm only doing it out of spite.'

Mark goes red. Looks away, abashed.

'No, look – I'm sorry,' she says. 'That was defensive. I'm just so used to – it used to divide up fairly evenly, you know, between people who despised me and people who wanted all the gory details. I had to tell them at her old school, so he couldn't come and pick her up, and it was like giving an interview to a tabloid newspaper. Every detail, they wanted, and you could see the gloat, the it's-not-me pleasure under their sympathy. And my downstairs neighbour, he used to just turn his face away when we passed him in the hall, like we had leprosy or something. It doesn't matter what they say in the press, how much they try to educate people; people still have this feeling, you know. That it's not just a question of luck that some husbands turn out to be monsters and some turn out to be pussycats. They've read all the stuff about abuse going on down generations, and they've translated it into some people attracting it. That somehow you must stay because you *like* it.'

She remembers his fists. The pulpy sound as he caught her eye, the flash of pain as her head snapped back on her shoulders. The white shock on Yasmin's face as she looked down at her own snapped wrist. The looks in the hospital: *She says it was her husband but she could have done it herself. It's not just men, you know. Women aren't angels . . .*

I'll find you, Bridget. You can't hide.

'He tied me up,' she says. 'He used to tie me up, and leave me there. He had handcuffs and he'd fix me to the bed, and if I tried to stop him he'd make it worse. And he'd go out to work, and Yas would be in her cot, and she'd be crying, and there'd be nothing I could do. I'd just lie there and listen to it all day and wait for him to come home and see what he wanted to do . . .'

It's not a cathartic unburdening. She doesn't feel better as she tells him. Problems shared are often wounds reopened. She glances up at him, and his expression is unreadable. Then he swallows and looks down.

'I'm sorry,' he says. 'I had no idea.'

'No one ever does,' she says. 'The guys he worked with – they all think he's a good guy. A laugh. I could tell what they thought of me when they saw me. The dowdy wife, dragging the menfolk down. They thought it was a joke. Going off to nightclubs with him, watching him pull while I waited at home. And that guy – the guy downstairs. He thought I was the scum of the earth. I remember him once, one Sunday, turning round on the stairs and just hissing at me. Like, *Can't you stop that baby crying? Do you even* think *about your neighbours?* And I couldn't – I had a black eye, for God's sake, and he behaved like he couldn't even see it . . . and I don't want to go back there again. I can't.'

'Bridget, you should tell the school, at least. They should know. In case . . . you know . . .'

She looks up again. Fixes his eye. 'Leave it, Mark,' she says. 'It's my decision. I'm sorry. I shouldn't have involved you.'

'Yeah, but you have. I'm – Bridget. Look, I'm not going to tell you what to do, but if you think there's the remotest chance he could find you . . . at least take my number. If you're worried. Call me, or Tina. Either of us. We won't mind. We'll come. We'll probably be quicker than the police.

'I admire you,' he says, and she feels a jolt of surprise. 'Now I know, I really admire you. You're a brave girl, and though I know it's a futile promise, I have a feeling you're going to be okay, now. But Bridget, there's a fine line between brave and stupid.'

'Yes,' she says. 'Yes, I know.'

'Promise me,' he says.

'Yes. Can we change the subject?'

'Okay,' says Mark. 'That's fine. As long as you know.'

'I know,' says Bridget. And to her surprise finds herself believing it. She gets up and finds some tea mugs. Mark Carlyon sits at the table and watches her move about the room. I understand, now, he thinks. Why she's so unwilling to meet men's eyes. How come she's so careful with her information. She's got guts. I just wish there was something I could really do to help her.

'So tell me,' he says as she goes to the fridge and gets out the milk, 'about these electrics. At least I can sort those out for you.'

Chapter Forty-One

'Willy was a sheepdog, lying in the grass.
A bumblebee came along and stung him on the –'

She jumps high in the air, lands with a thump. She's been doing it, revelling in the circularity of the rhyme, for the two minutes it has taken to negotiate the corridor.

'ASK no questions, tell no lies,
I saw a policeman, doing up his –'

Jump. Thump

'FLIES are bad, bugs are worse.
Mary had a little lamb and she was very silly,
She threw him up into the air and caught him by his –'

Jump. Thump.

'WILLY was a sheepdog, lying in the grass.
A bumblebee came along and stung him up the –'

Jump. Thump. She's at the bottom of the attic stairs. Pauses as she hears a voice drifting downward.

'ARSE!' she bellows.

The voice pauses, as though its owner is listening, then picks up again. It's Tessa: singing in that plummy voice of hers. It's 'Greensleeves' she is singing, though Lily, of course, not having benefited from a private education, doesn't recognize the tune.

She climbs the stairs.

Tessa is in the far attic, beyond the dormitory room where the three evacuee girls used to sleep and where Lily sleeps still, behind a door which has been locked since she arrived here. Of course Tessa would have the key. They're only keeping light-fingered interlopers out, not hiding some terrible secret.

Lily is intrigued. She's always wanted to know what was behind that door: has always suspected that the room contained treasures.

She hovers at the doorway. The first thing she notices is dust. Dust and dust-sheets. The room is crowded. More than crowded: crammed. They must have moved a lot of the contents of the dormitory room into here in a hurry, because there's no sign of organization about the way things lie. It's an Aladdin's cave of a place: jumbled and cramped, but full of intrigues. Lily steps into the room. She can't see any sign of Tessa. Starts as she catches sight of a figure half-hidden by a dust-sheet, then half-giggles when she realizes that it is herself, reflected in a full-length console mirror.

'Try this one,' says Tessa's voice from the far side of the room.

Lily tenses. Who's Tessa in here with? She didn't see anyone arrive this morning, or any time since Tessa came back for half-term. She's been moping about the place like a wet weekend: no one to play with now the others have left, and Lily being given a wide berth.

'Silly back,' says Tessa. 'It's dressing-up clothes, isn't it? It doesn't matter if it gets broken. Nobody's saving them for posterity.'

Lily works her way up a narrow, winding aisle between looming cliffs of stacked boxes. Emerges into a cleared space to see Tessa kneeling on the splintery floorboards amidst a group of three tin trunks. Waves of fabric and feathers and diamanté tumble from their lips. Lily gasps.

She's never seen anything like it. Clothing from her grandparents' era and clothing from a world that was swept away forever by the Great War. Velvet, brocade, lace, silk. Full-length gloves in ivory satin. Hats the size of bicycle wheels, trimmed with marabou and silk arums. Evening dresses of satin and damask and crêpe de Chine. Embroidered hems and puffball sleeves and yokes covered in beading. Tessa holds out a tiara of paste and copper leaves to one of three dolls which she has lined up against the wall. She is wearing an Edwardian S-waist ballgown, oddly flat without the undergarments designed to shape it, the quilted bosom lank and bathetic over her liberty bodice. The dress is a good foot too long for her, trails away over her feet like giant swaddling bands.

'No?' she says. 'Well, if you're not going to, you don't mind if *I* do, do you?'

She takes the tiara and places it on her blonde locks. Tucks a curl behind an ear and preens for her indifferent pottery audience.

Beautiful, thinks Lily. Imagine having so much money that you just dump this stuff in trunks. That you think it's fit for children to play with rather than wearing it yourself. The things my mum could have done with that lot. She'd look fantastic. Too good for Portsmouth docks. If she had clothes like this, she could go to the classy hotels, mix with the nobs. Not have to take what she can get from oil-smeared grease-monkeys on shore-leave for the night.

She longs for Tessa to look up, welcome her, let her try on the embroidered capes, the pink satin bedjacket, the silver silk flapper dress with the fringe of a thousand sparkling beads. Knows it won't happen.

She steps forward and says: 'What are you up to?'

Tessa jumps, turns in her direction. Looks guilty for a moment, as though she's been caught doing something she shouldn't. Looks her up and down, top to toe. And then something predictable happens. Tessa tilts her chin, swivels her eyes toward the ceiling and turns her back.

'What's that lot, then?'

Tessa doesn't answer. Lily steps forward, comes to stand by her elbow. 'I said, what's all this?'

Tessa's eyes flick towards her, flick away again. She picks up the nearest of the dolls and puts it in her lap. Takes, from the left-hand trunk, a child's christening gown: cream ruffled lace with a matching bonnet attached by a ribbon. Starts pushing the doll's head through the neck-hole. The doll is far too small even for something designed for a three-month-old baby. It is quickly swamped in a sea of Chantilly lace and ribbons.

'You're not still playing with *dollies*?' asks Lily. 'At *your* age?'

Lily, now she's nine years old, is itchily aware of her own maturity. She sniggers, nastily. If Tessa's going to persist with being snotty, then she's not going to try to be nice in return.

'I haven't played with a *dolly* since I was five,' she informs the stiff-turned back.

'There,' says Tessa, self-consciously. 'You look lovely.'

Lily tries another tack. She longs to be invited to join in, to plunge her hands in among the textures, to rub her face against those soft jewel colours.

'You look like a Christmas tree,' she says. Not unkindly. Christmas trees, in her book, are among creation's loveliest inventions.

Again, no response. As if I was a ghost, thinks Lily.

She bends to look at the contents of the nearest trunk, the one that contains the dresses. Reaches out for an edge of scarlet brocade that has caught her eye, feels a palm slap against the back of her hand. Jumps back, shocked, and says: 'Ow! What did you do that for?'

'I could have sworn,' says Tessa to the dolls, 'that I heard a dog barking.'

The dolls stare back, impassive.

'Or maybe it's rats,' says Tessa. 'Something certainly stinks around here.'

'Hello?' says Lily. 'I'm right in front of you?'

'*Some* people,' Tessa tells the dolls, pointedly, 'don't know when they're not wanted. Have you noticed that?'

Oh, I see, thinks Lily. I'm in Coventry again. Very clever. Very grown-up. Must have learned this at that lah-di-dah school of hers. It's just the sort of thing they teach Young Ladies to do because Young Ladies aren't allowed just to give someone a clout and have done with it. Cow. Still, what do you expect? Her mother's daughter, after all. I thought she was better than the rest of her family, but of course she's not. Just more of a coward in the way she goes about things.

'I'll tell you what,' says Tessa, 'it's getting really stuffy in here. I know what you mean about the smell. Shall we go to my bedroom? It's more *comfortable* there. More *private*.'

'All righty,' says Lily. I'm not going to play along with this nonsense. I will make her acknowledge me.

'No,' snaps Tessa. 'I didn't invite *you*.'

'Right,' says Lily. 'So you *can* hear me, then.'

'Go away,' says Tessa. 'Mummy says I'm not to have anything to do with you.'

'Why?' asks Lily.

'You're a bad influence,' says Tessa. 'Mummy says you can't be trusted to behave.'

'Tessa!' cries Lily. She feels a great wrench somewhere near her heart. She's been looking forward to Tessa coming back. To having another child in the house, someone her own age, not just the baleful mother stalking silently past her, lips pursed. Tessa used to speak to her in the summer, when there was no one else around. They were almost friends. They dammed the stream together, one afternoon. She'd hoped they would be friends.

I'm alone. I'm all alone. Why are they doing this to me?

'Go away,' says Tessa.

'Why? You don't have to do what they tell you!'

Tessa looks, abruptly, up at her, standing by the tailor's dummy, wringing her hands. 'But I do,' she says. 'I'm sorry, Lily, but I can't. Mummy says you're a liar and a troublemaker, and she says she'll give me the slipper if she catches me talking to you. I can't.'

Tears prick at Lily's eyes. This is so unjust. So unjust.

'Your mother is a cow,' she says.

Tessa struggles to her feet. 'No!' she shouts. 'Don't you *dare* call my mother names! She took you in when no one else would and you should be jolly well grateful! Go away, Lily! I don't want to talk to you!'

Lily, enraged, shoves her. Tessa stumbles, catches herself on her own hem, narrowly avoids plunging into the nearest trunk.

'That does it!' She runs at the houseguest, shoves back so hard and so suddenly that Lily is caught off guard, falls against the dummy, crashes to the ground beside it.

'Just *don't*!' shouts Tessa. 'Don't come *near* me! I don't want to have anything to do with you! Just *go away*!'

She gathers up the knee-length skirt and cotton blouse she has discarded on the floor and stalks to the stairs, skirts hitched up around her knees.

'You don't half look like an idiot,' Lily calls at her haughty back. Silly tart. As if she wanted to be friends with a toffee-nosed suck-up anyway. She rubs her ribcage where she's caught it on the sharp-turned leg of an old chaise longue, fights the urge to cry. 'Bugger off, then! See if I care!'

Tessa doesn't reply. Leaves the floor, goes downstairs.

'I don't care,' says Lily, aloud to the empty air, 'I don't bloody care.'

She stays there a while, stares at the roof timbers. I don't care. I won't be here forever. I'll get away one day.

As she sits up, her eye is caught by the clothes in the trunks. Might as well make the most of it while they're open. It is a glory of colour and feel. Motheaten, some of it, and grimed with decades, but Lily has never seen such riches all in one place. She crawls across the floor, settles down among the opulence. She fingers the fabrics, strokes the softness of a discarded feather boa, holds up a 1920s Cleopatra headdress of beads which match the flapper dress, allows it to twinkle in the dim light like a chandelier. It fills her with a strange, unquantifiable longing.

She strips off her faded gingham dress and drops it on the floor, selects a long bias-cut gown in champagne slipper-satin, pulls it over her head. No need to waste time with hooks and zippers: Lily is so slight that, although its original owner must have been light as gossamer in her partner's arms as they whirled across some long-forgotten ballroom floor, the dress hangs from her scrawny frame, highlights the bones that ridge her sternum. In the right-hand trunk, she finds a pair of satin-and-marabou mules, bald from overuse, slips them on and hobbles, cloche in hand, over to the mirror. Turns this way and that to admire herself in her finery.

'Don't mind if I *do*,' she says. Pulls the front of the neckline down to reveal her non-existent cleavage, the way she's seen her mother do as she prepared to go out of the door at night.

Padding along the corridor, Tessa bumps into Hugh. Feels suddenly awkward, dressed in her cast-off finery. She's not felt comfortable around Hugh since he went to Eton, she realizes. It is as though her brother went away and some intrusive, condescending stranger came back in his place. She hadn't even known he was back yet.

'Hello!' he says. 'What are you wearing?'

She looks down at herself. 'Oh, just some stuff from the dressing-up box,' she says.

'Dressing-up box?'

'You know. In the attic.'

'Dressing-up? The mater'll have your guts for garters if she finds you in that lot.'

'I'm going to get changed in my room.'

'All right, then. So. How's school?'

'Fine,' she says. 'You know. Ghastly.'

'Same here,' he says. 'So which of the lumpen proles is

there left, then? Or have we got the place to ourselves at last?'

'Typical,' says Tessa. 'The only one left is the horrid one.'

'What? Lousy Lily?'

She nods.

'Hah!' he says. 'Street urchin still here, eh? Never mind, Tess. Where is she?'

Tessa jerks her head toward the attic stairs. 'Up there,' she says.

'Really?'

'Yes,' says Tessa. 'That's why I'm down here. She started shoving me.'

'Well, we'll see about that,' he says.

Tessa freezes, looks at him.

'What?'

'Don't,' says Tessa.

'Shut up, Tessa,' says Hugh. 'It's none of your business.'

Chapter Forty-Two

'Come on,' he says. 'Let's go to the pub. Tina's down there and I bet you could do with a change of scene.'

He's washing his hands at the kitchen sink. His hands and his lean, well-muscled forearms. They seem to be covered in black grease, which surprises her as she didn't think things like black grease were part of the electrical canon.

'Um . . .'

'She can go and stay at ours. Our mum's sitting tonight and I don't suppose she'll mind another.'

She can't think of another excuse, though she finds the invitation strangely unnerving. She's not been *out* out – the sort of out that has no justification attached other than having fun – since . . . since she can't remember. Since Yasmin, she supposes. Kieran started going out by himself soon after she was born and never offered to include her. And like many people who play away themselves, he was full of suspicion and jealousy when it came to the idea of her going out without him. After she got a couple of fingers broken in a slamming door for wanting to go on a hen night she got more wary of asking permission, and it didn't take long for the old friends, discouraged by her non-committal responses, to drop away and find other, more sociable, companions.

What will I wear? Do I even know how to make conversation any more? When it's not about Yasmin, or work, or why I need an overdraft extension?

'All right.'

'Enthusiasm. That's what I like.'

She laughs. 'Sorry. Yes. Can you give me ten minutes? I can't go out like this.'

'You look great. All you need is a pair of wellies and no one would know you weren't a lifelong local. Tell you what. Why don't I take Yasmin down with me? I wouldn't mind getting cleaned up a bit myself. We can all meet in the pub in forty-five minutes.'

'If you're sure . . .'

'I haven't been sure about anything since Jeffrey Archer went to jail. But it might be fun. You never know till you give it a try.'

'Oh. Okay, then.'

In her room, she is gripped by social terror. Finds herself doing something she hasn't done since her early twenties: throwing all the contents of her drawers on to the floor and riffling through them with despairing hands. I haven't a thing to wear. Really, I don't. The only clothes which are remotely festive predate Yasmin's birth, when she was still a size 12, still had a flat stomach and breasts that sat high on her chest, and will never stretch their tinselly selves to fit the generous 14 that motherhood and misery have combined to inflict on her. A couple of tops would go on, but they'd be so tight they'd look impossibly slaggy in a rural pub.

She picks things up, desolately, looks, rejects. Everything that dates from Kieran is loose, dull-coloured, the sort of clothes that make you take up as little space as possible, the sort of clothes that hide in corners, try not to attract attention. God, the clothes I used to have: the croptops and the miniskirts, the things with spangles and the plunging necklines. The shoes that were useless for anyone who wasn't going everywhere by taxi. I used to really think I looked like something. No, I *did* look like something. I looked like a confident, successful Londoner; like the young person going somewhere that I was. I looked like what I was.

I guess I look like what I am, still. The clothes that post-date Kieran are nothing but practical: jeans and tops that won't show stains, that will wash easily. Clothes bought from charity shops so there was money left over for Yasmin; clothes that say I don't expect to be looked at and don't want it.

How did I not notice? How did I not see what I was doing, going through those racks in the Cancer Research, picking out the things in Fat-Chick Mauve and Ignore-Me Blue? When did I give up? When did I decide it was best if no one ever saw me? I was living next to Carol all that time, with her Primark finery and her brave hair, and yet I never saw the contrast, when we walked past a plate glass window. I saw the contrast with her, of course, but I never noticed the contrast with my former self. How blind did he make me? How blind did I make myself?

Well, I can wear jeans. I don't have much choice. It's jeans or one of the three pairs of black stretch trousers with the elasticated waists, as close to trackies as you can get without a white stripe down the side. She selects the newest pair, the least stained with the lowest waistband. Hopefully the wear at the knees and the rip halfway up the thigh will look meant; will be interpreted as a fashion statement rather than a product of poverty. In a corner of a drawer, she finds a dark crimson thigh-length tunic in embroidered viscose which Carol gave her one year for her birthday and which still bears its tags. Its V-neck goes low into the yoke, shows some cleavage, the reason she didn't dare wear it at the time. Now she looks at it and sees that Carol chose well. It's a good garment for coaxing one out of low self-esteem; covers myriad body faults and has that essential look of not trying too hard.

She blesses Carol, wherever she is, and pulls it over her head. No time to iron. She'll wear it crumpled and nobody will think she's bought something specially.

It's turned seriously cold outside. Frost already coats the

hedges and the trees look like marble statuary as she drives down to the village. The pub looks warm and welcoming, orange light filtering through its tiny windows. She shrugs herself further into her old leather coat, scuttles across the car park in her flat suede boots. The left one has a hole in the sole; she can feel the frozen tarmac as she walks.

They're in the corner, crammed on stools round a tiny copper-covered table. She'd expected one of those American Werewolf moments when she stepped into the heady fug of beer and fag smoke and shepherd's pie (funny, she thinks, that Yasmin will never know this particular aroma), but to her surprise conversation hardly dipped when she showed herself. To the contrary, a couple of people even greeted her as she crossed the naked oak floorboards, as though she'd been a regular for years.

Mark's changed into a dark green jumper with a white T-shirt underneath. Tina's got on an ankle-length gypsy skirt: very two seasons ago, but good for keeping the cold out. They've got a couple with them whom she vaguely recognizes from the school gates. They all smile when they see her and open up their huddle, and the man whose name she doesn't know pulls out a stool from where they've been keeping it reserved and gestures toward it. Mark jumps to his feet. 'What can I get you?'

'Oh – don't worry. I'll –'

'I'm going anyway,' he says, 'to get a round in. What would you like?'

She's not thought. She's so out of practice she's forgotten what women drink in pubs. It was always wine bars in London, anyway: bucket after bucket of overoaked Chardonnay that left you dyspeptic in the morning. But in London there were taxis, and she guesses from the smells coming from the room beyond the bar that the gastropub revolution hasn't reached this corner of Cornwall.

'Just a ginger ale, please.' She shows them her car keys. 'I'm driving.'

'Oh come on,' says Tina. 'You're doing half a mile on a deserted road. You can have a drink.'

'I . . .' Where did all this hesitancy come from? I sound like one of those spinsters you see in 1940s films, all apologetic for their existence. 'All right. I'll have a half.'

'Half of what?'

'Dunno. . .'

'The bitter's good.'

She nods. 'Okay, bitter.' Remembers her manners, adds a thank you.

'Cold, isn't it?' says the woman.

She sits down, begins unwinding her scarf. 'Yes.'

'What's it like at Rospetroc in this sort of weather?'

'Oh, it's fine in the flat. Lovely and cosy. And he's got a good furnace for the rest of the house, though I don't really run it above stopping-the-pipes-freezing level when we've not got visitors.'

'Got a lot of those at the moment?'

'Not since the Christmas rush. Got a honeymoon couple coming in just under a fortnight, as long as Mark's done by then.'

'Oh, he will be,' says Tina. 'He's just patching things up. Though I gather it'll need the full works sometime in the future.'

'I don't doubt it,' she says. 'As long as he can keep us going till spring, I'll be eternally grateful.'

'Carla's fascinated by the place,' says the woman.

'Oh, right,' says Bridget. 'Are you Carla's mum? I'm sorry. I've been terrible at working out who's who.'

'Yup,' she says, offers a hand. 'Penelope Tremayne. Penny. And this is Tony.'

'Hi, hi.' She shakes his hand.

'Hi.'

'Tony's mum used to work up there,' says Tina. 'Cleaning.'

'Oh, really?'

Tony nods. 'Mad old cow, Mrs Blakemore. Bag of spanners, she was. Mum didn't last long, but then again, nobody did. Couldn't deal with the old girl. Paranoid isn't the word for it.'

'Mmm. I gather she wasn't the best employer.'

'No. Tight as a gnat's chuff and mean-tempered with it. Pissed most of the time, as well. Always accusing people of moving things. And constantly looking over your shoulder as though there was someone standing behind you. Mum's not the superstitious type, but even she said it gave her the willies.'

'Would me too,' says Tina. 'Wasn't there some rumour about her? Or was that just kids larking about?'

Tony shrugs. 'Bit of both, I guess. Don't you remember? We always said there was a kid buried in the garden somewhere. Though I thought that was Hugh, not her. Still.'

'Oh yeah,' says Tina. 'I remember. I'd forgotten about that bit. Spooooooky goings-on in the war or something, wasn't it?'

'Something to do with evacuees,' he says. 'I think there was one that disappeared, wasn't there?'

'Lily,' says Mark, reappearing with five glasses balanced between his hands. 'Lily Rickett.'

Bridget feels a chill. She knows that name. It must be a coincidence.

'How do you remember that?' asks Tina.

'Simple genius. And the fact that I remember thinking it was a good name for her, considering. One of those kids from Portsmouth.'

'Ah,' says Penny, and they all share that look of common understanding. Bridget has already heard the joke about the acronym that crops up on West Country medical notes. NFP: Normal For Portsmouth.

'You don't think she's really buried in the garden, do you?' she asks.

'Naah,' says Tina. 'Of course not. Good God, I know there was a war on and everything, but don't you think the powers that be would have noticed, eventually, if they simply lost one of their evacuees? No. She'll have been picked up and moved on somewhere, or gone home, and the waters will have closed over her head, the way they do. It's not like anyone in the village will have actually cared enough to stay in touch after they kicked her out of the school and know what happened. No, it's just one of those village rumours you get. Partly spite and partly something to make life more entertaining. D'you remember those hippy artists at the old vicarage when we were growing up, Marco? The Whassnames?'

'The Linleys?'

'Mmm.' She turns back to address Bridget. 'Everyone got a bee in their bonnet that they were Satanists. D'you remember? We used to tell each other stories that they were having black masses where they ate babies in the graveyard on full moon, that sort of thing. Poor sods moved on down to St Ives in the end because of all the whispering when they came down the shop. I'm sure they were harmless. Just didn't really fit in, you know? It was like that, really. Old Blakemore had gone gaga and turned into a hermit, and everybody hated Hugh, so they had to find something to hang it on. It wasn't like anyone actually, you know, investigated or reported it to the police or anything. It was just something everyone said about them behind their backs. It's not like they weren't all glad to see the back of her, anyway.'

'God, yes,' says Mark. 'D'you remember at school? They were still using her name as a shorthand for a really, really bad child. Gave everyone nits and everything.'

'Oh, that's not fair,' says Tina. 'They've all got nits these days and nobody seems to think there's anything odd about it. And she got a prize once. It's still there, in the ledger. I remember the name now.'

'Well, whatever. Even if she did have a period of being good, it certainly didn't last. She got expelled for setting fire to the curtains in the main schoolroom. You can still see where the window got warped. I don't really remember what happened after that. It's one of those village things, isn't it? That you get when people are secretive. She disappeared after a while and of course all the kids started making up that she'd been murdered. But of course she wasn't. She'll have gone back to Portsmouth and got killed in an air raid or something.'

'God, yeah, and they were still going on about it when we were kids. Do you remember? That was why we always used to run away screaming whenever the Blakemores came to the village. Load of little bleeders, weren't we? I feel really sorry for them now. Kid probably got her mum to come and pick her up, didn't she?'

'Whatever,' says Mark.

'I prefer the murder theory,' says Penny. 'Nothing like a good juicy rumour to keep a village together. What do you think they did? Shot her? Strangled her and dumped her body in the lake?'

'Yuh, thanks,' says Bridget. 'I like that theory too. Makes me *much* more comfortable living there.'

They all laugh, but they change the subject.

'So what brought you down from London, anyway?' asks Penny.

Bridget glances at Mark, but his face remains impassive. Tina's, too. She can't tell if he's told her. 'Yasmin, really. I suddenly realized that London's a terrible place to bring up a child, if you're not rich.'

'So you've not got any connection with the area?'

'No,' she says. 'Sorry,' she adds.

'Good thing, I'd say. Too many people related to each other down here. Half the families around here have webbed toes as it is. So what do you think? Think you might stay a while?'

Bridget sips her beer. It is warm, nutty: truly traditional. 'You know what?' she replies. 'I think I really might.'

Chapter Forty-Three

Carol is walking home from the bus stop with her purchases. Now she's got a salary approaching and a world of overnighters to live in, she feels justified in splurging a bit: expensive night creams to preserve her skin in dry cabin temperatures, two pairs of really good formal shoes that will support her arches and leave plenty of room for her feet to expand on long-haul. Blissful, glorious make-up, extra-hold hairspray. Non-iron summer clothes for the Florida run, extra-cheap in the tail end of the sales. Warm furry boots for the New York run, though she knows she could probably have got them cheaper at Barney's.

She feels oddly Christmassy, though the season is well past. Feels as though her life, on hold for such a long time, is finally beginning to move again. She's done her refresher course, learned to spot a terrorist, remembered how to give mouth-to-mouth to a keeling pensioner and tomorrow she'll be locking the door on her flat, hearing the rumble of the wheels of her pull-along flight bag on the pavement. She'd forgotten that sound: all the promise it held.

The traffic is so heavy on the Streatham High Road that she nearly doesn't hear her phone, chirruping away in the bottom of her bag. Must remember to enable roaming, she thinks, as she scrabbles into the inner pocket where she keeps it, now I can afford it. Maybe next month. When my first salary cheque's come in.

It's still ringing when she puts her hand on it, the lights on its keyboard blaring out on the night air. 'Hello?'

'Hi, it's me.'

'Honey! How funny. You didn't come up on my display.'

'No. That's why I'm ringing. I've finally got a new phone.'

'Have you? Great! Well done, girl.'

'Do you want the number?'

'I'm walking,' she says, 'and I've got my hands full. Can you text me?'

'Sure. You could get it out of the history, of course.'

'You know what I'm like with technology,' says Carol.

'Okay.'

'So how's it going? Had any more power cuts?'

'Good. All good. And no, I've got a guy from the village in right now sorting it all out.'

'Guy from the village, eh? Single?' says Carol.

'Oh, you. One-track mind. He's a friend, okay?'

'Course he is.'

'No – oh, why do I bother? We're having a raging affair and he wants to have my babies, okay?'

'That's more like it,' laughs Carol.

'So how about you? All good?'

She turns the corner into her road, their old road. She's not paying attention to her surroundings, surrounded as she is by that invisible bubble that wraps itself around anyone who is speaking on a telephone. Is faintly aware that someone has turned the corner behind her, but doesn't think about it. It's work turfing-out time, after all. There are millions of people turning into roads all over London right at this moment.

'All great,' she says. 'I've been shopping for my travel kit. I've spent about a million quid.'

'Cool! And when do you start?'

'Tomorrow. Isn't it exciting? I fly to Vancouver at just gone noon.'

'Fantastic! Oh, Carol, I'm so pleased for you! When will you be back?'

'On and off,' says Carol, 'not for the best part of a month. Except for the odd half-day turnaround. It's this incredibly complicated rotating shift system. Especially if you're a new one, on probation. Got to look keen.'

'So, what? Back and forth to Canada for a month?'

'No,' says Carol. 'All over. Four Caribbean layovers, plus LA and Florida. I'm right back in the jet-set, girl, I can tell you, and I'm not going to waste a minute of it.'

'LA? You'll never survive. What about the fags?'

'I'm giving up,' says Carol, in the sort of definite voice only those in the full flush of optimism can manage. 'I only do it 'cause I'm bored and miserable. And I'm not going to be bored and miserable any more.'

It's dark and quiet, still, in Branksome Avenue. The big houses that stand back from the pavement show little light from behind their curtains. She's used to it, of course, but she'll be glad to get away, after all these years. To find herself in a nice little one-bed house on a friendly modern development with a nice little nippy car to get her to the front door.

'I'm pretty pleased myself,' she replies. 'That'll be me, by the side of the pool, with the cocktail, then!'

'Oh, Carol. You won't forget about little us, once you've started living the high life again, will you?'

'Course I will, darling. That's the last you'll see of me now.'

'Ha bloody ha.'

'How's my little angel? She behaving herself?'

'She's great. We're having a party, Sunday. A load of kids from her school all coming over for cake and hide-and-seek.'

'Oh, God, it's her birthday,' says Carol. 'I forgot! What a cow! I'm so sorry, darling. I promise I'll get her something from the States and send it the minute I get back.'

'No need. She's going to get plenty of presents this year. I've made sure of it.'

'Yes, well,' says Carol. 'I'm her auntie, aren't I? She's practically my godchild. I don't want her forgetting about me. Seven years old, eh? Who'd have thought it?'

'Well, if you want to . . . I'm sure she'll be pleased.'

'Course she will. Never underestimate the materialism of a child.'

'Oh, sorry,' says Bridget. 'Mark's shouting. Got to go.'

'Mark, is it?' teases Carol.

'Shyattap,' says Bridget, but she sounds pleased. Entertained. Far, far happier than Carol can remember her sounding over the years they've known each other. 'I'll talk to you soon. Call me and let me know how it went, won't you? I'll be wanting to know.'

'Will do. Don't wait by the phone, though. I'm not going to be getting my phone set up for roaming till next month at least. Got to save the pennies for a bit. Clear some debts before I run up new ones. And I won't be home in civilized hours practically at all. I'll try and call you when I am. And you can always leave a message and I'll call you back the minute I get a chance. You will text me that number, won't you?'

'Right away. Bye.'

'Byeeee!' calls Carol. Lets the phone fall shut with a click. Drops it back into her bag. Turns in through the hedge and climbs the steps to her front door. Her keys, as usual, have worked their way to the bottom of the bag. She pauses, rummages while she hums the theme tune to *Happy Days* in her rich alto. Finds the fob and fetches them out as the phone bleeps to let her know she's received a text message.

Doesn't notice, for a few moments, that someone is standing behind her.

Jumps, whirls round, brandishing the keys.

'Hello, Carol,' he says. 'Been shopping?'

Carol stares at him, wordless.

'Aren't you going to offer me a cup of tea?' he asks.

Chapter Forty-Four

Mrs Peachment has to sit on the trunk, in the end, to get it to close, straining herself purple to tighten the leather straps. She is astounded that she has managed to distil her life into a single steamer trunk; it has been a labour of weeks, weeding out clothes and keepsakes, poring over photographs she may never see again, ironing everything as flat as flat so it takes up the least amount of space. There is so much she has had to leave behind. Ornaments and gramophone records, curtains and coverlets she thought she'd never have to live without. When she sees them again – *if* she sees them again – they will have faded with time and Cornish sunshine, will not be the same familiar objects. They will have had another life entirely.

I'm in two minds. This war so saps one's vitality: the uncertainty, the constant sense that life as one knows it is about to come to an end. Life will be pleasanter, less afraid-making, in Canada, though the fear for Malcolm, for the boys, will never go. But oh, the eyes of my neighbours. I am a coward, a rat deserting a sinking ship. They may never forgive me for this. That's why I'm doing this midnight flit, simply fading away into the crowds and leaving a handful of letters behind me. And at least I've got a legitimate excuse. No one can say I shouldn't go and look after my poor little nieces, for heaven's sake. I didn't *ask* my sister to go swimming in the Atlantic, did I?

Should I go? Should I really take this opportunity, risk the cold ocean with its lurking dangers, to seek out the land of milk and honey, when my neighbours are living a life of drudgery and marrow jam?

I'll send food parcels. Constantly. Hams and biscuits and maple sugar. I don't doubt anyone else would do what I'm doing, if they had relations to sponsor them, let alone children in need. I've done my bit. Taken my part in the war effort. Organized rag drives and scrap drives and blackout patrols, coaxed and chivvied people into opening their homes to strangers in the face, often, of the most obdurate unwillingness. It's someone else's turn. I'm tired.

She gives the strap another tug. A cup of tea, she thinks. A nice cup of Earl Grey. I've still some left. I'll leave it for Patsy when she arrives to take the house over; she'll be glad of it.

The telephone, sounding out through the house, jerks her from her reverie. 'Bother,' she says out loud, to no one, and hurries from the landing, where she has been packing, to the hall, where the apparatus stands on a Victorian whatnot which she inherited from an aunt.

'Meneglos 34.'

'Take her away! Take her away now!'

The voice, a woman's, is distorted by its own volume. It takes her a moment to work out what the shouter is saying.

'Hello? Excuse me?'

'I want her gone! Now! Do you hear me? Just come and take her away!'

'Who is this?'

There's a brief silence, as though her interlocutor is stunned at not being recognized. 'Felicity Blakemore, you idiot! Who on earth did you think?'

'Good afternoon, Mrs Blakemore,' says Margaret Peachment, calmly. Another sixteen hours and she will never have to cope with this woman and her high-handed approach to her neighbours again. Another twenty-four and she will be embarking from Liverpool, her trunk stowed and a whole new life ahead of her. 'Are you having some sort of problem?'

'I want you to come here and take the filthy brat away *this instant*! I won't have her in the house a moment longer!'

'Who are you talking about, Mrs Blakemore?'

She knows perfectly well. There is only one evacuee left at Rospetroc. She regrets, sharply, that she didn't take the time to get another half-dozen *in situ* before she hands over the reins to the coordinator in St Austell tomorrow. It would have been an enjoyable revenge.

'You know *exactly* who I'm talking about!'

'Um . . .' she says, sounds vague and distracted, relishes the infuriation which beams down the line. 'I have lots of people under my care, I'm afraid, Mrs Blakemore, not just you. You'll have to remind me.'

A gasp of frustration. Mrs Peachment fails to suppress a smile. Twiddles the string of pearls inside the collar of her blouse.

'Lily – Rickett.'

'Lily . . . Lily . . . let's see . . . Ah, yes, I remember. And how is Lily getting on?'

The voice rises to a shriek. 'SHE . . . HAS . . . BEEN . . . EXPELLED . . . FROM . . . THE . . . SCHOOL! I *cannot* bear her here for *one* moment longer! She's been a complete menace since the end of the summer holidays, nothing but impertinence and sullenness. She threw an andiron at Hughie's head and very nearly brained him. She *slapped* my daughter, twice. I get nothing but lip and rebellion, it's enough to try the patience of a saint, and now even the *school* won't keep her. Mrs Peachment, she *set fire to the school*. I *cannot* have her here a *moment* longer. I won't be able to sleep safely in my own bed!'

'Set fire to the school?'

'Yes! This afternoon!'

I passed the school no more than an hour ago. I didn't see any sign of a fire. 'Are you sure?'

'*Are you stupid?* Of course I'm sure.'

'Well, there's no need to take *that* tone,' she says.

'There is *every* reason to take this tone! You will sort out the mess you have created, Mrs Peachment, or . . . or . . .'

'Or what?' She can't keep the sneer out of her voice.

'I'll . . . the relevant authorities . . . your superiors. You're not as important as you *think* you are, Mrs Peachment.'

It is her turn to gasp. 'Well, I never –'

'I know all about people like you,' continues Felicity Blakemore. 'Puffed up with your own authority. Using this war to play out your petty little fantasies of power. Well, I'm not having it. Do you hear me?'

An idea is forming in Mrs Peachment's mind. No one speaks to me like that, she thinks. I've worked my fingers to the bone for this village, and she cannot speak to me like that. I'll cook her goose. The child's mother hasn't been heard from – of – since she left her at Portsmouth station. Women like that often disappear, when they find the opportunity. She's not going home in a hurry.

'Well, it's not as simple as you seem to think,' she replies. 'I can't just remove a child in an instant. There's another home to find, paperwork to do . . . there *is* a war on, you know.'

'I don't care. I've had enough. I've put up with her for over six months, now, and I won't put up with it for one day longer.'

'Sorry about that,' says Mrs Peachment. Gloatingly.

'I'm telling you, Mrs Peachment. I'm not asking. I'm *telling* you. If you haven't come and fetched her away by this time tomorrow, I'm putting her in the car and dumping her on your doorstep. Do you understand me?'

'I can hear you loud and clear, yes,' she says.

'Do. You. Understand. Me?'

'Oh, yes,' says Margaret Peachment. 'I understand you *very well*.'

A click, and Mrs Blakemore is gone.

Margaret Peachment dabs at her temple with a small handkerchief which she has doused with the last of her eau de Cologne. Stands for a moment in the hall, fingers the tassels on the small lace tablecloth which protects the whatnot from being scratched by the telephone.

'Well, we'll see about that,' she says, out loud.

On the kitchen table, the evacuee files wait, neatly bundled up with string, for the area overseer to collect when he receives his letter. He's a busy man, running the bank in St Austell by day and covering a huge area of the county by night; it will probably take him weeks to make his way over to Meneglos after her news has broken. Mrs Peachment fills the kettle, puts it on the hob for her nice cup of tea. Collects the scissors from the drawer by the sink and returns to the table.

'Yes,' she says. 'We'll see about that.' Cuts the string.

It doesn't take long to locate the Rickett papers. She's always been proud of the efficiency with which she has kept her records. And it'll stand me in good stead now, she thinks. Far harder to believe that someone's made a mistake when their punctiliousness is so clear for all to see.

She holds Lily Rickett's life between thumb and index finger. Turns it over, studies it. Not much to it, she thinks: just two forms and an already-fading photograph. There will be duplicates, buried deep among hundreds of thousands in a ministry somewhere. It will be spring at least before they will be located. A lesson learned for Felicity Blakemore.

One of the world's unwanted children, not actually an orphan but as near as damn it. No one's going to come asking for her, I can be fairly sure of that.

The child glares sullenly at her, dirty face and gooseberry eyes. No, she thinks. No one's going to miss you.

The kettle starts to sing. Margaret Peachment goes to the stove to take it off the heat, and collects the box of matches on her way.

Chapter Forty-Five

'Bridget?'

'Yuh?'

'I think I'm done here.'

'Really?'

'Yes. Well, in as far as you're not going to have everything trip every time you plug in the food mixer.'

'Really?'

'No,' says Mark, 'I'm just saying it to wind you up.'

She reaches the top of the stairs. 'I love you,' she says. 'Can we try it out?'

'Be my guest. What did you have in mind?'

'Um . . . tell you what, how about I boil the kettle and run the hairdryer at the same time?'

Mark spreads his arms wide. 'Bring it on. Is that all you've got to throw at me?'

'Oven as well?'

'Chickenfeed.'

'All right. I'll see your oven, kettle and hairdryer and raise you a fan heater.'

'Done,' he says.

He comes up to the flat, stands in the corridor while she bustles about switching things on. I'm going to miss him, she thinks. Not just the company around the house, but him himself. He's a nice guy: feels right, somehow, standing there with his sleeves rolled up and his hands on his hips. As though he belongs here.

She comes back into the hallway, stands there by the light switch, looking at him. He's a nice-looking guy.

There's no getting away from it. Not just in the fact that he's well put together but in the way he is. When he smiles, you want to smile too. You can't help it. He's just one of those people.

She gives him a high five. 'You are a genius,' she says. 'I will love you forever for this.'

Mark grins. He's twinkling at me. My God, he's definitely twinkling.

'Well, at least your friend can come down and not get the willies put up her.'

Bridget laughs. Particularly because his phrasing is far more appropriate to Carol than he knows. 'I think she might be a bit disappointed by that.'

He frowns, then that big smile comes bursting from his face again. 'Well, you call her and tell her I said so.'

'I will as soon as I can get hold of her. She's in the States, I think. Or Canada. Or sunning herself on some Caribbean beach between flights. Her phone's not picking up, anyway. She'll be pleased to hear about it, though. She's been bothered. About the two of us. Here with no lights.'

'Me too,' says Mark. Pauses. Looks slightly embarrassed, bustles on. 'Right, well. I'd better be off, anyway. Tina'll be up with Yasmin later, if that's okay.'

'It's more than okay. I just wish there was something I could do to pay you all back, that's all. I owe you such a lot, between the two of you.'

'Bollocks,' says Mark, walking away. Turns, one hand on the newel post at the top of the stairs, as though caught by an afterthought, and says: 'Tell you what. If you want you can let me buy you a drink.'

'I think it's me that owes you several,' she says. 'I should think I owe you a gallon of scrumpy at least. How about tomorrow night? I'll see you in the pub?'

Mark scratches his ear, looks awkward. Can't bring himself to meet her eye.

'Well, actually, I was wondering if maybe we couldn't do it just you and me,' he says. 'You know, a bit further afield.'

Heat courses through her. A date. He's asking me on a date.

She feels the rush of panic. I can't. *I can't. It's been no time at all. I can't – he's – I swore I wouldn't trust a man again . . .*

Mark doesn't need her to speak to know what her answer's going to be. Churns with embarrassment, disappointment, as she struggles and stammers in front of him. This is awful, he thinks. I've blown it, completely. I shouldn't have. It's not like I'm in practice. I haven't asked anyone out since Linda and I've blown it on the first try.

'Don't,' he says, 'it's okay. The pub'll be fine. We'll all go out. With Tina and the others, sometime.'

She finds her voice. 'I'm sorry,' she stutters. 'I'm really sorry. It's just – I don't know if I – I'm still not used to, you know . . .'

Her voice trails away and she stares at her feet.

'It's okay,' says Mark. He's longing to get out of there, now, to flee the discomfort that has descended between them. 'Look, I'll get out of your hair.'

'I – look, Mark, it's not that I . . .'

'Don't worry,' he lies, 'I'm not offended.'

'It – I – you know about . . . and I'm not ready. I'm just not ready.'

Shut up, shut up, shut *up*, Bridget. You're just making it worse.

Mark lingers for a second, looks as though he can't make up his mind. Takes two steps down the stairs, turns back.

'Bridget,' he says, 'we've all been hurt. One way or another. There's not one of us has got this far without something bad having happened. Anybody who hasn't probably isn't worth talking to. That's all. I'm not going to say anything else. But one day we've all got to let the past be the past. 'Cause if we don't, it'll rule our lives forever.'

Chapter Forty-Six

Kieran pauses for a moment before he goes up and checks his reflection in the plate-glass window of the bookie's below the office. He's waited four days for the scratches to die down and his skin looks almost normal now. Like it could have been a cat, or a bramble or something. It is essential that I remain absolutely chill, he thinks. I'm so close now, and this guy has to be on my side.

Oh, Bridget, you're going to get yours. You're *so* going to get yours.

He brushes his fringe to one side, floppy-style, turns up the collar of his jacket against the cold. Kieran's gone out and bought some nice-guy gear, specially; an Aran sweater and a canvas coat and a nice fake-cashmere scarf: Daddish clothes. All-I-want-to-do-is-take-my-kid-to-the-zoo clothes. I-do-DIY clothes. He looks the part. So much it's almost giving him a hard-on. Satisfied, he throws his cigarette into the gutter, presses on the buzzer. Waits for a moment and announces himself. Goes in.

'How are you?' asks Steve Holden, getting up from his desk.

'I'm okay,' says Kieran, shaking his hand. 'Do you have any news for me?'

'As a matter of fact,' says Steve, 'I do. Piece of cake, as it goes.'

Kieran sits down, tries to look hopeful, emotional, decent.

'Oh, God,' he says. 'Have you found them? Yasmin . . .'

'Well, I think we're certainly on our way, now. It was a good thing, you managing to get hold of that number like that. Decent of your friend. You can never tell, can you?'

Didn't take much, in the end, thinks Kieran. I wouldn't say decent. She fought quite a lot, as it goes, but of course she fought like a woman. Still. She won't be interfering again, anyway.

'So . . .?'

'Yes. Well, obviously I can't tell you my sources, but let's just say I have friends in retail. That's the thing, you see. Some computer records are easier to access than others.'

Blah blah blah, thinks Kieran. Get on with it.

He arranges his features into an expression of polite curiosity tinged with admiration. I suppose I have to give him this. The kind of person who goes into this sort of job is bound to be the sort of pub smartarse who likes to show you his workings.

'Your phone records, see, the bills and the where-you're-calling-from, they're part of the highly confidential list. The phone companies are governed by all sorts of rules, like the banks. And believe it or not, they still vet their employees and keep an eye on what they get up to. Now, you *can* get hold of those . . . if you're a policeman. If you get the paperwork done and get permission. But your common Joe, he needs passwords and security questions, even if he's working in the company itself. Even if he's in customer relations.'

'Ooo-kay,' says Kieran, trying not to sound impatient, trying to sound like all of this is completely new to him. Rocket science. That's what it is, he thinks. At least, that's what this guy thinks it is, anyway.

'Working in Cellphone Cellar, on the other hand,' says Steve, 'is another thing altogether. They're sales in there, you see, and salespeople are your modern-day carnival folk. Easy come, easy go. High staff turnover, no time to get too arsy about references. And they've got a national computer system. Get a job in the Cellphone Cellar in

Bradford and you can see who's sold what where and when anywhere in the country. Sell a phone in Romford and it ups the targets for the Bury St Edmunds branch. You get my drift?'

'I think so,' says Kieran.

'And fortunately, your wife bought the SIM card that goes with this number at Cellphone Cellar.'

'Oh yes?' says Kieran. Sits forward in his seat. Clasps his hands together over his knees.

'Now I don't want you to get too excited,' he says. 'She could have got someone else to buy it for her. She could have made a special trip. Though I think she's probably not thinking about covering her tracks that carefully. It's a pay-as-you-go, after all. No records once it leaves the shop. Only record is which shop the card was bought in.'

'Which was?' asks Kieran.

'Wadebridge,' says Steve. 'In Cornwall.'

Chapter Forty-Seven

The most striking thing about them is their obvious sexual compatibility. In that you couldn't imagine either of them wishing to sully themselves with something as sticky as sex, ever. It's not that they're unattractive people, on the face of it at least: all their parts are in the right place, they're obviously clean and have taken care of their physical well-being. Too much so, possibly. These are the sort of people who have never, ever taken a risk in their lives, have never spontaneously discarded duty for pleasure, have got out of bed at seven, always, regardless of schedule, even at the weekend, in order not to waste the day. They look like a pair of schoolteachers on holiday.

Joyless, she thinks. That's the word for it. They run their lives efficiently, and the trouble with efficiency is that it doesn't have much space in it for joy. They have efficient clothes, efficient haircuts, an efficient, characterless Vauxhall parked in the drive, efficient, well-cared-for luggage at their feet. And they're looking at Yasmin as though someone's come in and ransacked their filing system.

'Mr Gordhavo,' says the woman, 'didn't say anything about children.'

'I'm not children,' says Yasmin, 'I'm *a* child.'

They blink, together, at exactly the same moment, behind their rimless specs.

'Yasmin, honey, go upstairs and play,' says Bridget, praying that her daughter will have the sense to be obedient, just at this moment.

'Why?' asks Yasmin.

Mrs Benson slips her hand into her husband's and purses her lips.

Bridget turns her back on them, just for a moment, and pulls her fiercest face. Yasmin, of course, isn't looking.

'We're on our honeymoon,' says Mr Benson. 'We wouldn't have booked ourselves in here for a honeymoon if we'd known there were going to be children running about the place.'

I can't imagine you're going to be the sort who would be wanting to spend their time swinging from the chandeliers, she thinks, if we had any. 'She won't be running about the place,' she says, attempting to sound reassuring. 'She's at school in the daytime and we live in a separate flat with a separate front door we use when there are guests.'

Mrs Benson peers about, as though looking for where the flat could be hidden.

'You get into it through the utility room at the back of the house,' says Bridget. 'I'll lock the door through to the first floor.'

'We were expecting total privacy,' says Mrs Benson.

She feels a surge of irritation. These bloody people. Never satisfied. Always something to complain about, though the website is completely truthful about the house, if they ever bothered to read it properly. 'The brochure,' she says, 'does say that there's an onsite housekeeper.'

'It didn't say you had a family, though.'

'Just the one child,' says Bridget. 'Who is going upstairs *right now*.'

This time, Yasmin picks up on the tone of her voice, makes herself scarce.

'And what about the other one?' asks Mrs Benson.

'Other what?'

'There was another one. In the garden as we arrived. Over by the pond.'

The other what?

'Presumably that's one of yours as well?'

Bridget doesn't understand what she's on about.

'The girl. In the garden.'

A girl? In the garden?

She noticed that the pond was iced over this morning when she went out to get the sheets, stiff with frost, from the line where she'd thought it was a good idea to hang them yesterday. God, I hope none of the village kids has got up here. It's bad enough keeping Yasmin away from the pond without worrying about some Kirkland offspring trapped under the ice, bloating and turning green.

'Oh. I have no idea. I guess it must have been one of the local children.'

'And do you,' he asks, 'have a lot of local children hanging around?'

'No. No, absolutely not. I've no idea where she will have come from. The children around here know better than to come up here without an invitation.'

'Because the brochure said you were isolated and peaceful.'

'We are. I can assure you we are. I'm sorry you weren't expecting to find my daughter here, but I promise she won't be any trouble. She's familiar with the rules, don't you worry. And I'll make sure whoever it was you saw in the garden knows she's not to just pop up without clearing it with me first.'

Bridget crosses her fingers behind her back. She's going to have her work cut out this week.

'You know how children are,' she jokes palliatively.

On second thoughts, you probably don't, she thinks. There's nothing jam-stained about you. If you've got godchildren, you probably send them educational books for Christmas.

'I'll see if I can farm her out,' she says. 'She's got friends in the village. I'm sure she can go and play with them after school and stuff.'

They don't answer. I'm banging my head against a brick wall here. I have to remember, the visitors aren't interested in the detail of my life. They're only interested in me as an addendum to the house. You're a servant, Bridget. Get used to it.

'I've lit the fire in the drawing room,' she says, 'and I thought maybe you'd like something warm on a night like this, so I've got scones in the oven and clotted cream and jam. Just as a welcome, you know.'

They seem neither surprised nor particularly pleased. It's a mistake to bother. I'm on a learning curve here. They never think you get anything for nothing, these people. Now I've done this, gone out of my way to do a bit extra for them, they're going to be expecting tea and treats as a matter of course.

Mrs Benson closes the front door. Okay, so they've decided to stay, then. That's a start.

'I'll bet you're tired after your trip,' she tries again. 'I'll just show you round, shall I, and leave you to it?'

Yasmin has put *The Lion King* on, sits on the floor a foot from the television, ignoring her. Not even an offer of Horlicks gets a response.

She kneels down beside her, rubs her back.

'What's up, monkey?'

'Nothing,' says Yasmin glumly.

'Well, there obviously is, or you'd be speaking to me.'

'*Nothing*,' says Yasmin, shrugs her off.

'Okay.' Bridget struggles back to her feet. 'Fair enough. If you want to tell me, you know where I am, but I'm not going to waste half the afternoon trying to get you to.'

She picks up a pair of socks and is halfway to the door when Yasmin says, 'I don't like you talking to me like that, that's all.'

She stops, flaps the socks in the air to turn the toes out.

'Sometimes,' she says, 'I have to talk to you like that. Sometimes it's urgent. Sometimes you just have to do what I say, *right now*, and I don't have time to stop and discuss it with you. Sometimes there are situations where I have to be the boss and you have to deal with it.'

'Yeah,' says Yasmin. 'I understand. You want to get rid of me.'

'I – no. I don't want to get rid of you.'

'Lily said you'd want to get rid of me once you started getting *boyfriends*. She *said* I couldn't trust you.'

Boyfriends? Jesus, they pick up on small nuances. Seems like they're not noticing what time of day it is most of the time, and then suddenly they're spotting things you've not even spotted yourself.

'I don't – Yasmin, I don't know what you're going on about. I will never leave you – *never*.'

'She said you'd say that,' says Yasmin. Looks at her balefully. 'She says you're all the same and none of you can be trusted.'

Oh, Jesus. Whoever this child is, she's seriously fucked up and she's getting at Yasmin's weak spots. I know she's scared I'm going to turn, just like her dad did. I know that. It's going to take a lifetime's making-up to really convince her otherwise.

'We'll talk about this,' she says. 'I promise we will. But right now, I need you to understand that sometimes, when there's grown-up stuff going on, I need you to leave, yes, or shut up. I'm sorry. I thought you understood.'

'Understood *what*?'

'Downstairs isn't our home, Yasmin. It's where I work. We have to be careful about invading people's space.'

'Well, *they* invade *our* space.'

'Yes, well, they pay a lot of money to do it. And it's not *our* space, when there are visitors here. And the money they pay is the money we live on. If they didn't come, we wouldn't have this place to live in. You've got the garden, and the fields, and you can always go down and see Chloe or Carla or, whatsername, Lily.'

'Don't be *schtoopid*.'

'What?'

Yasmin huffs. '*Noth*ing.'

'What's got into you?'

'*Noth*ing. It's freezing outside and I'm bored and now you say I can't even *play*. I'm sorry I'm not *convenient*.'

'Yasmin! I never said anything of the sort!'

'Well, I can't have my *friends* here, can I?'

'No! Not while there are people here! Look! If I worked in an office you wouldn't expect to be able to come and play *there*, would you?'

Yasmin rolls her eyes. 'I'm sick of being by myself,' she announces. 'All shut up, with no one to talk to apart from Lily.'

What are you on about? 'Well, I'll tell you what,' says Bridget, 'I'm not mad about being around you when you're being this disagreeable.'

Yasmin bursts into tears. 'Well, I hate you too!' she wails. 'I knew it! I knew it was just a matter of time!'

Bridget sighs. Nothing matches the illogicality of the childish mind set on being the injured party. God, it's all very well, these parenting manuals banging on about self-esteem, but they don't half make it hard for you, kids. She folds her arms. 'I didn't say I hated you,' she tells her. 'I said I didn't like the way you're behaving.'

'Bugger off!' screams Yasmin.

Oh, God. She glances at the house door in the corner of the room, hopes against hope that the Bensons have gone downstairs to be by the fire. They'll hear everything if they're still in the four-poster room. Not just a child but a screaming child who has worked herself up into such a tantrum that she's gone purple. I have to stop this. I have to get her away.

She crosses the room in two strides, wraps her arms round her daughter and heaves. She's getting too heavy for this. Another six months and I won't be able to do this any more. Yasmin screams again, kicks out, slaps at her face as Bridget hauls her upward, throws her over her shoulder.

'Ow! Stop that!'

'Bugger off! I hate you! I *hate* you!'

They get into the corridor and she slams the door shut and drops her. She stalks away into the kitchen and leaves her, bellowing, on the sisal. Who'd be a single parent? All of it, I have to do all of it by myself. The no-sleep, the worrying, the nagging and the comforting. I have to make the choices, take the flak and it doesn't get better, does it? It's going to be like this for ten more years – longer than that, probably – and I just want some rest, a chance to be *me* again. I've been a mummy for seven years but I can still remember what I was like when I was a Bridget, when I didn't have to be blamed for everything.

She buries her face in her hands and listens to the sound of her daughter's sobs from the other side of the door.

Chapter Forty-Eight

She dreams that they are making love. One of those disturbed, disturbing dreams which come to tell us that the past is always with us. She can feel his hard, warm body against hers, the buttery smoothness of his skin, the rough-soft caress of his hands. She is repulsed and aroused in equal measure: ashamed even in sleep that he should still have such power over her.

'You're mine. You'll always be mine,' whispers Kieran, kisses the tender skin of her neck, and she feels her back arch in response, the wave of pleasure roll through her body.

Oh, God, please stop. Please don't. Don't stop.

He is still there on her skin when the door opens. Repulsing her and arousing her in equal quantity. He always had that power over her, right up until very close to the end, when violence started leaking over into the sex as well. Could make her weak from lust when he saw that the fear was beginning to lose its grip. She is so ashamed. Repelled by her own weakness.

She is still fuddled with sleep, stares wildly into the dark, unsure at first whether she was really woken by the sound of the door. Yasmin hasn't turned the light on in the hall, and she can only feel her, standing in the doorway, waiting.

Oh, thank God. She's forgiven me.

She struggles, finds her voice. 'Hello, darling.'

Yasmin doesn't answer.

She waits. Nothing passes between them.

'Can't you sleep?'

No reply.

'Yasmin?'

Bridget shimmies over to the cool left side of the bed. 'Do you want to get in?'

Hears her footsteps cross the floor. Yasmin stands beside the bed, over her, unseen, silent.

'I'm sorry,' says Bridget. 'If it helps, I couldn't get to sleep for hours myself. We shouldn't fight, you and me.'

No reply.

She lifts the covers, holds them up. 'It's freezing,' she says. 'Go on. Get in. Let me warm you up.'

The silent sound of decision. She hears the creak of the bedsprings, feels the mattress drop beside her. Holds out her arms to let her come into them.

Yasmin is cold. Icy cold to the touch; hair, nightdress, feet, skin. As though she's been dipped in frozen water. Stiff against her body, unresponsive. As though the blood in her veins is ice.

'Oh, darling,' whispers Bridget, 'you've been out of bed for hours. Here. Let me warm you.'

She wraps herself about her, presses her chin on to the top of her head, rubs with her hands up and down her back. Her hair feels strange: spiky, rough; not the silken strands she's used to. Her daughter doesn't speak. Lies stiff in her arms, cold face pressed into her throat. I can't smell her tonight, thinks Bridget. Can't feel her breathe. She's so stiff it's as though I'd have to crack her joints open to make them bend.

'It's okay,' she whispers. 'I'll take care of you, darling. I'll keep you warm. I'll keep you safe.'

Teeth. Teeth sink into her neck just above the collarbone.

Bridget screams. Yasmin digs her fingers into her upper arms. Scratches, clings, feet flailing against her shins.

'Yasmin! Stop it! Ow! What are you doing? Stop it!'

She shoves, hard, breaks her grip, throws herself out of the bed. Red clouds of rage and pain dance before her eyes. She scrabbles for the light switch. What is going on! What is going *on*?

The light dazzles her, makes her throw her hands across her eyes. 'What are you *doing*?' she cries. 'My God, Yasmin –'

The bed is empty. Bed, room, empty. No one here but myself. Door closed. No sound from the corridor.

There is no one here.

It wasn't a dream. I didn't dream it. See? My heart is pounding. The hairs are on end on my arms. I can still feel the cold, the deep, black cold where she was pressed against me.

Bridget shakes. Holds her hand out and sees that it is trembling. Puts it against her neck. I can feel it. I can feel where she bit me. It's not a dream. I can feel it.

She takes her fingers away, sees that they are streaked with blood.

Chapter Forty-Nine

Something has happened to Mrs Blakemore. It's been happening slowly since the summer, but now she's alone with her in this echoing house, staff long gone and family followed in their footsteps, winter bearing down in vicious rainstorms, it seems to have speeded up. Her face, so neatly powdered when Lily first arrived, goes without embellishment nowadays, the muscles beneath the skin gone slack, half a dozen thick black hairs sprouting unplucked from chin and upper lip. She rarely bothers with dressing, now; shuffles around the house in a man's woollen dressing gown and slippers, trailing food stains and the smell of body odour behind her.

No one comes to the house these days. Not deliveries, not neighbours, not even, with nothing to bring with him, it seems, the postman. It is as though, now the vaccies have gone and Lily has been expelled from the school, the house and its occupants have been forgotten about, isolated as if they carry disease. It is just the two of them, now: a woman who talks to herself and a child who talks to nobody.

Lily has given up running away. She's tried and failed so many times that she finally understands there is no escape. No mum to go back to, no Portsmouth, really, because she's only nine and practically illiterate and no more knows where Portsmouth is in relation to Bodmin than she would know the way to London. All she knows is the things she's heard and the things she's seen: that there are vast tracts of the Bodmin and Dart moors between them and the outside world, that the winter cold down here sucks at her bones when she's indoors, let alone when she goes out into the wild west wind. Knows that grown-ups – even the ones who pretend to be on your side, the ones who smile and offer you Mint Imperials – are not to be trusted, any of them, ever, and that a whole world of grown-ups stands between her and home. Lily understands, now, that she is fated to stay, that whatever she does, wherever she runs to, she will end up, as in a recurring nightmare, back where she started.

They brush up against each other, occasionally, in the halls or the kitchen. Lily occasionally makes the mile-long forays down into the village with the ration books, or they would be subsisting on a diet of porridge and cabbages from the field behind the house. She has been putting odds and ends on the house's accounts at the shops, but doubts that the credit will last much longer. Mrs Blakemore doesn't seem to notice. Rarely answers the telephone. Prefers to spend her time drinking her way through the pre-war cellars and staring blankly out of the windows across silvered winter farmland. Lily doesn't know what will happen when the shops finally cut off their supplies. When the oats run out, they will probably live on cabbages alone.

Lily doesn't frighten easily, but she is nervous of Mrs B. Knows that she is unwanted, knows that if the Ministry found her papers, she would be gone in an instant. Wishes, vehemently, that they would. The Barnardo's would be better than this, she thinks. At least in the Barnardo's someone would know I existed. If I knew how, I would get them to come for me myself.

One way or another, I have to get away from here. The old woman's gone nuts. It's as if someone's come along and taken her soul. If we were in Portsmouth, if we were among the poor people, they would have taken her away by now, cleared out her lodgings and shut her safely up. If we were in Portsmouth, they would have shut *me* safely up after what I did at the school instead of dumping me and washing their hands, saying it was Blakemore's problem. That was the point. That was the idea. If they weren't going to let me *run* away, I was going to make them *take* me away. And instead, here I am, trapped even more than ever, dodging Blakemore and waiting for Him to come back for the holidays. They don't want me here, but they won't let me go. It's as if the whole world's been planning it all along.

I'm in solitary confinement, she thinks. I'm a Prisoner of War.

She's crossing the drawing room on her way to the big kitchen – where there is, sometimes, a loaf in the bread bin, some marrow jam in the pantry – when the phone starts ringing. Lily jumps at the sound, starts to scamper back the way she has come in case her jailer appears. Realizes, as she reaches the door, that she's been mistaken in her assumption of Blakemore's whereabouts: that she is, in fact, emerging from the study. She spends so much time in her bedroom, now, alternately sobbing and cursing behind the locked door, that Lily is surprised to find her out of it. Has a split second to decide what to do: be found and risk another burst of random wrath, or hide.

She hides. Dives in behind a floor-length curtain and holds her breath.

The phone rings on. She hears Mrs Blakemore pass her hiding-place, hears her mutter: 'All right. All right. Keep your hair on.' The slippers scrape across the floor. They sound oily, sludgy, as though their wearer has trodden in something wet and not bothered to clean it off.

She reaches the hall. Lily hears the tinkle as she lifts receiver from cradle. 'Rospetroc House,' she announces, slowly, grandly.

'Tessa!' she cries.

'Mah-vlous, darling!' she slurs. 'Keeping the old home fires burning! And how is school?'

She listens briefly. Lily watches her finger a greasy lock which trails loose from her long-grown-out bob. Mrs Blakemore's given up the hairbrush. Relies, instead, on an ever-growing army of hairpins to which she adds each day as she notices an errant strand. So much for my nits, thinks Lily. There must be maggots in there by now. 'Good, good,' she says, 'now what train are we expecting you on? I can't wait to see you. Hughie can't get home until the New Year; they're keeping them for the Cadet Corps. But we'll have a lovely time. Mr Varco's promised me a goose.'

She hears the scritch of the distant voice, then a gasp. Then Mrs Blakemore is in tears again. 'You can't,' she says. 'Tessa, you can't.'

Scritch scritch scritch goes the voice.

'But I . . . Tessa, how can you do this to me? Do you know what he's done? Do you understand? How can you be so . . .'

'. . .'

'Disloyal,' she breaks across the stream of explanation. 'You are disloyal.'

She plucks at the hairpins. Slumps against the hall wall as though the strength has gone from her legs. 'I've done everything,' she wails. 'Everything. I've sat here – I've waited for you . . . I could have . . . My God. And you betray me. You think he –'

A strange noise escapes her throat: animal, lost. Tessa is silent at the other end, shocked, wordless.

Mrs Blakemore rolls against the wall, dents the plaster with the receiver. 'Ay-ay-ay-ay . . .' she keens. 'What will I do? What will I do?'

Lily catches sight of her face. It is waxen, drawn, the eyes wide and staring. She shrinks back behind the curtain, hides herself away. I don't have a choice, she thinks. Even if it is winter, even if I don't know where to go, I have to get away from here. She's been fairly harmless lately and it's made me forget what she's really like. But it sounds like she's just fallen over the edge.

Scritch scritch scritch.

She hears a whoop of indrawn breath. And when the woman speaks again, her voice is cold. 'Well,' she says, 'you've made your choice, then. I don't know what I've done to you, but . . .'

Scritch scritch scritch.

'You always were your daddy's little girl,' she says. 'Weren't you? I suppose I should never have put faith in you. Well, I hope you have a lovely time.'

Scritch scritch scritch.

'But it's not just for his leave, is it?' says Mrs Blakemore. 'That's what you don't understand. That's fine. You can all bugger off. I don't care. You and your filthy father: go and be with him, then. See if I care. At least I've got a son. At least I still have a son.'

Lily hears the next word. 'Mummy!' cries Tessa all the way from Wantage.

The voice which comes now is cracked and hateful. Lily peeps out to see that Mrs Blakemore is upright again, is pounding the wall with her fist.

'No! Too late! Too late! You've made your bed. I hope you enjoy lying in it! Nasty, ungrateful little girl! He'll leave you! He'll leave you, Tessa! He's done it already and he'll do it again, but don't think you can come back here. Don't think I want you! Don't think that, ever! You will not be –'

She stops. Holds the receiver away from her ear and looks at it, an expression of surprise on her face. Presses it back to her face. 'Tessa? Tessa?'

Tessa is gone.

Bawling, Felicity Blakemore crosses the drawing room and stops in front of the drinks tray. She has nearly emptied the cellar – her father's cellar – with no replenishing stocks coming across the Channel, but there is still port, and armagnac from the last century, loved and turned and conserved for a special occasion for over fifty years and now coming in very handy while the rest of the world goes dry. She sobs out loud, lips wet and shapeless, as she picks up the bottle. She has become a grotesque, a gargoyle.

With shaking hand, she pours the best part of a

quarter-bottle into a cut-glass snifter, raises it to her lips. Drains it. Sways as she swallows, clutching the glass to her chest.

'Nonononono,' she says. Fat tears course down her face, drip from her chin. 'Bastard,' she says. Throws the glass into the fireplace.

Lily is frozen behind the curtain. She must not find me, she thinks. If she finds me, sees that I've seen . . .

'Waaaah,' says Mrs Blakemore. Picks up another glass, fills it again and stumbles over to the sofa. Slumps, feet planted flat on the floor, knees spread as though she were milking a cow. 'Betrayed,' she says out loud to walls and silent spectator. 'I didn't do anything. What did I do? What did I *do*?'

She doubles over, clutches her stomach. Another sob rings out through the room. 'Alone. Alone. Dirty little bitch. Dirty little bitch, I'll kill her. I wish she was dead.'

Lily feels the hairs prickle on the back of her neck. She doesn't know if Mrs Blakemore is talking about Tessa, or herself.

I have to get out of here. I have no choice now.

She waits behind the curtain until Mrs Blakemore has fallen asleep on the sofa, until her snores ring out through the house and drown out the sound of her movements.

I'll get my bag. It's packed anyway. I don't need much.

She tiptoes across the room. Mrs Blakemore is lying on her back, mouth open, one arm tipped over the side of the sofa, knuckles trailing on the rug. Lily can see the tramlines of varicose veins tracing their way up her legs, disappearing beneath her nightdress. One slipper dangles from bent toes. She is dribbling.

What happens? she wonders. How does someone become like this? Her mother used to pass out, sometimes, but never like this. Her mother at least had the decency to be dressed when she drank herself insensible.

This time I'll go across the fields. I'll keep away from the roads, cut across the moor. No one goes on the moor in the winter. No one will find me. If I get far enough away before night I'll be all right. There are sheds on the moor, for sheep and stuff. I can spend the night in one of those. I'll get some bread, and some milk, and I'll run till I'm over the brow of the hill. I'll keep going south – I know where south is – till I hit the sea, then all I have to do is turn left and keep walking.

She creeps up the stairs to the attic, surveys her case. It's in an even worse state than when she arrived here; it's been thrown several times, dragged and sat on. The left-hand corner of the lid has split altogether. It won't last another journey. It'll be a hindrance, not a help. I'll wear what I need and carry the rest in a cloth. Like a runaway. Like a proper runaway.

She is filled, suddenly, with optimism. That's what I've been doing wrong. I've been travelling too heavy, attracting attention to myself. Of course they've been noticing a child with a suitcase: anyone would. If I take things in my pockets, and a few bits wrapped up like a parcel, they won't notice me. It's not like I've got a lot to leave behind. If I'm just a child walking along they'll not bother to ask questions. There are loads of strangers about in the countryside these days. The only ones they're suspicious of are the ones they think might be Jerry spies.

Lily upends the case and strips off her top layers of clothing. It'll be cold out there. She's not stupid. She's been dressing against the cold all her life. She finds her second vest, her gym pants, the two pairs of stockings the Board issued her with back in May when the sun was shining. Puts them on, puts shorts beneath skirt, jersey over blouse, cardi over jersey like a queer mismatched twin-set. Perhaps I should lift some pearls to go with it, she thinks. I could sell them when I get to Portsmouth, give us something to live on for a bit. Smiles at the conceit and dismisses it. Blakemore will only want me back if she thinks I'm a thief. Best not. Pulls socks over stockings and squeezes her feet into her T-bar sandals.

Mum'll be glad to see me, she thinks. That's why she's not been. They've lost my papers and she don't know where I am. She's probably been worrying herself sick, not knowing what's happened to me. I'll go and bang on the door and she'll take a minute to come 'cause she won't know who it is, and she'll open up and when she sees me her face will go all wobbly and she'll start crying the way she cried when she saw me off at the station. And she'll say how much I've grown and she'll throw her arms out and forget all about the neighbours looking, give me a hug right there in the street for everyone to see.

She takes the sandals off again, carries them down the stairs so her tread is quiet. Goes along the corridor, down the dining-room stairs so she doesn't have to pass the monster on the sofa again.

In the scullery, discarded and forgotten coats hang on the back of the door. Tweed coats for shooting and woollen for city wear; saved for the possible needs of visitors who never come. She knows that there will be cast-offs of Hugh's in among them; too small for him but large enough for her padded body and unlikely to be missed. Lily feels her way through their musty, doggy roughness. Decides, eventually, on a coat of Harris tweed, long enough to cover her knees, not so long or so new that it will be obviously stolen. Hanging on a hook, she finds a large woollen headscarf. Lays it flat on the floor and tips her meagre belongings – her pencils and sketchpad, her certificate, a single, crumpled and blurry photograph of her mother and a handful of boiled sweets conserved from the ration – into the middle and ties it loosely, corner to corner.

She probably won't even notice I'm gone for a few days, she attempts to convince herself. I've managed to keep out of her way for at least a day at a time before now. I can get a good head start while she sleeps off her hangover.

She tiptoes into the pantry, opens the bread bin and finds half a loaf of heavy wholemeal bread. On the shelf, a small lump of Cheddar. It is covered in mould. Lily takes it down, scrapes the mould off with the butter knife.

Wraps the remainder in a piece of discarded jam muslin and pops it into her pocket. She cuts away part of the loaf. To take the whole of it might attract attention. On the floor, in cardboard greengrocers' trays stacked one on the other, cooking apples from the orchard beyond the pond, harvested and laid up while Mrs Blakemore still had a few of her marbles. They will be sour, she knows, and hard to digest, but they will be better than nothing. Lily slips four into her woollen satchel.

It is half-past noon, and the sky is already beginning to change. She glances out of the window, looks for ominous signs in the clouds. Perhaps I should take a knife, she thinks. Yes, perhaps I should. A knife would come in useful. I don't know what for, but nobody runs away without a pocket knife. She creeps through to the kitchen with her parcel. It's warm in here; the range kept going by deadwood from the copse, keeping the heart of the house beating even if its soul has long since fled. Lily shuffles across the tiles in her stockinged feet, eases the top drawer by the sink open and looks inside. Something sharp. None of this silver, though I could probably sell the silver later. But I need something that will really cut. I need something that will get me out of danger.

'Hello,' says a voice behind her.

Lily, sharp intake of breath, whips round. Mrs Blakemore stands in the dining-room doorway, one hand on the door frame propping her up as she sways. Her hair is crushed down on the left side of her head, loose and dangling on the other. She looks Lily up and down, contemplatively. Licks her lips, smacks them together.

'So,' she says. 'Planning on leaving as well, were you?'

Chapter Fifty

Mr Benson has a pale complexion – the anaemic look of someone who doesn't eat enough meat – but it's raging purple now. He stands amid the chaos and his hand is bunched into a fist.

'Will you –' he bellows, *'keep your bloody kid under control!'*

She feels momentarily breathless. 'It wasn't – I don't think – it can't have been –' she begins.

'Don't even *try*,' he says. 'I don't want to *hear* it.'

The room is horrendous. Horrible. Flashes of the state it was in after the Terrys left come to her, but this is worse. It's so – unexpected.

She looks down at Yasmin, who clutches her skirt, mouth agape. She can't have done it, she thinks. She's been with me all the time . . .

The cupboard hangs open again. Inside, she can see the contents of the Bensons' suitcases jumbled on the floor, tumbling out through the door on to the carpet, clothes and shoes and bags, a laptop and a video camera, covered and coated and powdered into obliteration.

On the window seat, scattered as though thrown with some force, the constituent parts of a BlackBerry.

A vase, blue glass, has been smashed against the wall. Among the shards, Mrs Benson's low-key, discreet jewellery collection.

The tester ripped once again from its hooks.

The whitewashed wall despoiled with red-brown, blood-coloured lipstick. GET OUT GET OUT GET OUT.

'I – when did this happen?'

'Well, *I* don't know,' he snarls. He is chewing gum; tendons stand out in his cheeks with the force of his gnashing. 'We came back and it was like this.'

'I didn't do it,' says Yasmin.

Where have I heard that before?

'It wasn't me,' says Yasmin.

'Well, who *else* could it have been?'

I am caught between Scylla and Charybdis. Face the probable truth, find a way to make reparation, or stand up for my daughter, protect her from injustice and be rightly hated by these people, maybe face the sack: these are my choices.

Benson swings round to fix his eyes on Bridget.

'You?'

'Don't be – don't be absurd!'

'Well,' he says.

Mrs Benson is sitting on the window sill. She wears brown suede boots and a beige wool sweater-dress.

Looks like that's all you're going to be wearing for the foreseeable, thinks Bridget briefly, spitefully. Feels instantly guilty as she sees the devastation on the woman's face. Even dowdy people love their clothes. The colourless feel random destruction as deeply as the florid.

'It's unbelievable,' she says. 'Why have you done this to us? This is our honeymoon. What on earth have we done to . . . deserve this?'

She has reason to be upset, after all, even if the accusation is unfair. There must be thousands of pounds' worth of stuff heaped up here. Most of it ruined.

'We've been out all day,' stutters Bridget.

'Well, who *else* would it have been?'

She counts: one, two, three. 'I have no idea. I'm sorry it's happened. Obviously it's extremely distressing, but I haven't been here and nor has my daughter.'

She feels a tug on her dress. Glances down at Yasmin and pulls her closer to her side. Did she do it? Can she have done it? I haven't been with her every single minute of the day. There's been the odd moment when I've had to be absorbed in the domestic. She could have . . . No, stop it, Bridget. She's your daughter.

'So you're saying that – what? The piskies did it? That we've had burglars who didn't steal anything or damage anything in the rest of the house, just came up here to tear one room apart?'

'I don't know.' She looks around her. Liquid foundation has been sprayed across the walls, across the bedspread, the empty bottle thrown, dripping, on to the armchair. 'I'm sorry, but I don't know. I'll do everything I can to . . . straight away. It's . . . I don't know how this happened.'

'Well, it's obvious to me,' he says.

Bridget clasps Yasmin's hand, squeezes it. It is hot, stiff in hers. 'I understand that. But I can assure you I know nothing about this.'

He turns away. Surveys the devastation. Turns back. 'You'll lose your job over this,' he says. 'I'll make sure of it.'

She feels the blood rush to her cheeks.

Chapter Fifty-One

'It's got to stop, Yasmin! It's *got* to *stop*!'

Her voice is louder than she intends, furious with the rage of panic. Yasmin is curled up in the corner of her room, squashed against the walls like a small animal anticipating death. Tears stream down her face. I should be wanting to comfort her, thinks Bridget, but I can't, I'm so angry.

'How can you do this to me?' she howls. 'Don't you understand, it's not me you're doing to, it's *us*! We are going to be *homeless*, Yasmin! In the middle of winter with nowhere to go and no job – how could you do it? How could you be so –'

Yasmin's voice comes in a bellow itself. 'I didn't! I *didn't*!'

'Well, *someone* did! And it wasn't me! You've got to stop it, Yasmin! You've got to stop doing these things and you've got to stop lying! What's got into you? You never used to tell lies!'

'I'M NOT LYING!'

Yasmin's voice shatters in a heartbroken crack. 'Why don't you believe me? You never believe me, Mummy! I'm not lying! I don't lie! I *never* tell lies!'

Bridget is lost for words. Doesn't know what to do. All those years, protecting her, trying my best to bring her up well despite everything that was in our way, and now . . . where did this come from? Why is she so angry? Is it something to do with Kieran? Some acting-out? Is she angry with me, punishing me for taking her away?

'Well, maybe we should talk about it later,' she says

eventually, 'when you've – when we've both – calmed down. But you're going to have to do some thinking, Yasmin. I can't just believe you, you know. Someone did it, and I know it wasn't me.'

Yasmin sniffs, looks at her with large, watery eyes. 'It was Lily,' she says. 'It must have been Lily. She said she didn't like them. She said she'd get rid of them.'

Bridget feels another jolt. Feels confused, then angry again.

'Yasmin!' she shouts. 'I told you! Stop! Stop with this!'

'What?' cries Yasmin.

'Making things up! Making things up to cover your tracks! I'm not stupid!'

'What?'

'This Lily thing! I've had enough! You can't blame other people for your stuff! You're too old for that! And especially not your – you know what? I don't think this Lily exists at all! I think you've made her up!'

'She does! She *does*!'

'No. She. Doesn't.'

She has a weird feeling, a prickle in the back of her neck as though they are being watched.

'She does! She's right *there*!'

Yasmin gesticulates wildly at the doorway behind her. Bridget freezes. I will not look. I will. Not. Look. She's fucking with my head. I don't know where she got it from, but she's fucking with my head. Suddenly, crazily, she feels the surging urge to cross the room in one bound and rain blows on her daughter's head, to slap her about the face, shake her until the sense goes in. Takes a single step, hauls herself, reeling, to a stop. When her voice comes, she finds she is screaming.

'Stop it! Bloody stop it! I'm not listening to another bloody word! You little – *stop* it, Yasmin! There *is* no Lily! You're a little liar and I don't want to hear another *word*!'

Oh my God. Is that me? Is that me shouting? She is seven years old. What have I become? What has become of me?

Yasmin has backed further into the corner. The look on her face says everything. It's a look Bridget hoped she'd never see again. The look she used to wear when Kieran was there. The look she used to reserve for her father. And, worse: she looks – triumphant, as though she *knew* I'd crack in the end. That all that stuff she was saying before has turned out to be accurate prophecy.

Abruptly, violently, Bridget bursts into tears. Wraps her arms around herself as though her stomach aches and doesn't even fight the sobs.

Yasmin says nothing.

I'm so weak. I'm so . . . I thought I had the strength, I thought I had courage for both of us, but I don't . . . I can't do anything. I am helpless and weak and now I know the awful truth: that I'm not better than he is. I am weak and I am wicked and my daughter is afraid of me.

'I can't –' she spurts. 'I c— Yasmin, I'm not doing this now. I'm not. I'm going to leave the room now and I'll – I'm sorry. I didn't mean to upset you. I didn't – it's just so – *hard*.'

Yasmin picks up her teddy bear and hugs it to her chest. Big eyes, grim little mouth. I can never make it up to her. Never. She trusted me and now she knows the truth . . .

Bridget leaves the room, closes the door behind her. Leans against the corridor wall and covers her face with her hands. Feels seven again herself: seven and vulnerable and alone and not understanding why no one will come and make it all right. It wasn't meant to be like this. It wasn't. What happened? What did I do? What did I *do*?

She realizes that she is crying out loud, that the noise will be passing through the door, reaching Yasmin, making it worse. She pushes herself off the wall, stumbles, tearblind, down the carpet to the living room. Somebody help me. Somebody. Please.

The phone is lying on the side table, face-up. Bridget grabs it, stabs her way through the address book, dials. It doesn't ring at the other end, goes straight to voicemail.

'Hi, this is Carol. I can't answer the phone right now, but please leave me a message.'

The sound of her voice makes Bridget cry more. She bawls into the phone after the tone: 'Where are you? Where *are* you? You never answer any more and I need to talk to you! I know you're back and forth, but *please*! You must come home *sometime*! Oh, God, Carol, it's all so awful and I don't know what to do! Please! When you get this, *please* call me back!'

She slumps on to the sofa, rocks forward and back. I don't know what to do. I don't. I need to talk to someone because I'm going mad. Who is there? I am so alone. I don't know what to do. I have to talk to someone. *Have* to talk to someone.

And because there is no Carol, she calls Mark.

Chapter Fifty-Two

I hate her. Hate her. Hate her.

They don't listen to me. Nobody listens. Fucking bastards. Here I am, thirty-four years old and living like this, and all because . . .

Always her side. Her side. That's the way it is, these days; the feminists have got everyone whipped and they all take the woman's side. Listen to her point of view and make like I haven't got one. Treat it like it's sacred truth. And me, I get to work for fifteen years for . . . nothing. For a bachelor flat no one cleans and a child who screams when she sees me. No sheets on the bed for the first month I was there because she even got those and when do I have the time to go fucking *shopping* and they go wagging their fucking fingers, can't do this, Mr Fletcher, law says you can't do that.

What's this arsehole doing? Fast lane's for *fast* traffic, fuckwit, not granddads who want to dawdle with their hats on the backs of their heads. I'll give him ten seconds, then I'll flash the bugger. I'm going to be driving all fucking night at this rate. 250 miles. How much petrol is that going to take? Good thing I've got cruise control, not that I'll ever get to use it when I've got – that's right, dickhead. About fucking time.

It's not that much to want her to know, is it? All I've ever wanted is for her to know. What she's done to me. Lying. Twisting the truth so I look like the bad guy when she had as many faults as I had. They never listened to my side, did they? The way she used to go on, nag nag nag nag nag, winding me up till I couldn't think any more. She's got to know. She'll have to listen. She can't destroy my life and not see that there are consequences.

Basingstoke. Sulphur lights and a great big roundabout. What sort of shithole is Basingstoke that the traffic's thinning out? At least I'm out of fourth gear, anyway. If only this – arsewipe – would get out of my way. What is it with these people? You get past one and all you've got is another, blocking up the lane, crawling along as if they own the bloody road.

She'll be surprised to see me. Two weeks since she stopped answering the phone. Probably thinks I've given up and crawled off to die somewhere. Convenient. That's what she'd like.

Bitch.

Bitches, the pair of them. All three, if you count Carol. Not that you have to now, of course. Didn't see *that* coming, did she? The big ones, turning the small one against me. My own child. My property, and she screamed like I was some sort of monster the last time I went to that school. Supervised access. A bloody joke. Serves her right. Got what she deserved, bloody interfering cow. Wonder how long it'll be before that yuppie wanker notices the smell? Probably not for weeks. Certainly not for a few more days. She's got no friends. No one who's going to be asking where she's gone in a hurry. Serves her right. Serves them all right.

Alienation of affections. You used to be able to sue people for that.

It felt good, that. The way her eyes went wide, when she realized I meant it. Broke a few fingernails. Didn't make any difference.

My hands are aching. I must be gripping the steering wheel really tightly. How funny. Am I angry? Do you think I'm angry?

She's in for a shock. She thinks she's been so clever, but she's not that bright.

Couldn't learn from her mistakes, for a start.

Christ. It's ten o'clock already. Another four hours to Wadebridge. Won't be able to find a billet at that time of night. It's hardly a throbbing metropolis. Should have thought harder when I packed. Put in a couple of blankets, a pillow, at least. It's too cold to spend a night in a car. God *damn* it, Bridget. Why have you done this to me?

Travelodge. I'll get past Bristol. Get on to the M5. Another hour or so. At least that coffee's working. What's she *doing* down there, anyway? What's in Cornwall, for God's sake? I bet she's got a bloke. That'll be what it is. Jumped horses in mid-stream, thought she could do better. I always knew she was like that. Always knew it. Couldn't take my fucking eye off her for a – ow! *Fuck* that hurts. Now see what you made me do, Bridget? Get out of the way! Get out of the fucking way! Yes, you! That's right! Get over! Christ! Christ, Bridget! Look what you've done to me!

Chapter Fifty-Three

He calls in the early morning, while she's making her fifth cup of tea, still in her dressing gown, head clogged with tears and sleeplessness.

'Hi, it's Mark. I just wanted to check you were okay.'

'Oh, Mark. Thanks. I'm okay.'

'Get any sleep?'

Bridget half-laughs.

'I know what it's like,' he says. 'God knows.'

'It wasn't meant to be like this.'

'No. Well, we were all going to be perfect parents, weren't we?'

'I wish,' she says, 'I could talk to my mum, now. I was so young when she died, I didn't have the chance . . . you know . . . to appreciate . . .'

'Mmm. Yeah, well,' he says, 'I daresay a lot of things would be different if your mum and dad hadn't died.'

'Or maybe not. I don't know. You could do the what-if game forever, couldn't you?'

'Yes,' says Mark, 'you could. How's Yas this morning?'

'I haven't been in yet.'

'Not up of her own accord, then?'

She catches herself shaking her head, has to remember that he's not in the room.

'No. What time is it?'

'Just gone eight.'

'God. Well, I suppose I'd better face the music if I'm going to get her into school on time.'

'Have you not talked to her yet? Since you rang me?'

'I tried. But she was asleep. Or pretending to be, which is much the same thing when it comes to trying to talk to someone.'

She hears a sigh. 'Oh, Bridge.'

'Yeah,' she says, snappishly, 'I could do without a parenting-skills lecture right now.'

That's it, Bridget. Way to go. Call him for advice one minute, bite his head off the next.

'Sorry,' she says. 'Sorry. I know I'm a hypocrite.'

A chuckle. 'You said it.'

A pause.

'Saved me the bother,' he adds. She's not sure how much is reproof and how much is joking, but his gentle West Country accent softens the intent, makes it bearable.

'Look,' he says, 'you'll get past this, the two of you. And then you'll get on to the next row. That's what kids are for, and there'll come a time when we look back at the "I hate yous" with nostalgia. Once they've discovered the delights of Newquay and are blueing all their pocket money on crack cocaine and getting lifts with drunks.'

'She'll not be getting enough pocket money for crack for some time.'

'Crack's pretty cheap these days.'

'Well, so am I,' says Bridget. 'I can be as cheap as it takes.'

'That's the spirit,' says Mark. 'I'll see you down at school.'

'Yeah. Oh, and Mark?'

'Mmm?'

'Thanks. You know. For – everything.'

'Don't mention it,' he says. 'You can buy me a drink sometime.'

Was that another date? Hard to tell. She decides to ignore it. 'See you later,' she says.

She goes back to her room to get dressed before calling Yasmin. Wants not to look like she's just come off the set of *Misery*. Pulls on jeans and jumper, brushes frantically at her hair. Her hands are red from all the cleaning products she used yesterday. Must buy some rubber gloves. I'm a housekeeper now. They're necessary tools of the trade.

If I get to keep the job.

I will not get despondent. I won't. I can sort this out, one way or another. I'll give them my own money to pay for their cleaning. Maybe it was just a threat. Maybe he didn't mean it, about Mr Gordhavo.

As she's thinking, staring vacantly at her red eyes in the mirror, she notices a noise. A tapping. Coming from the living room. Oh, God. What now?

She goes through. The tapping is coming from the door to the main house. Bridget stands for a moment, staring at the handle.

It's Lily.

Don't be bloody ridiculous, woman.

There's something in this house. You know there is. It's there, however much you want to pretend it isn't. Look. On the other side of the door.

She breaks her fugue, steps forward, throws the bolt back.

It's the Bensons. Wearing overcoats, outdoor shoes; suitcases at their feet, done up, wiped clean of yesterday's residues. She's wearing her specs again, the tiny studsleepers in her ears, her discreet engagement ring.

'Hello,' Bridget says awkwardly. What does one say now? How are you today? Can I help you? What do you want? Please, please don't get me sacked?

The awkwardness, it seems, goes both ways. The Bensons don't speak for a second, but a blush creeps on to the wife's face. She looks exhausted, thinks Bridget: as bad as I feel. I thought she was pale when she arrived, but she looks now, under the blush, as though someone's turned down the contrast on her. The glasses frame eyebags so spectacular they look as though they've been inflated with a pump. He doesn't look much better. He looks – desiccated.

'Hello,' Mrs Benson replies, eventually. 'Sorry to bother you . . .'

'That's okay,' says Bridget. 'I was just about to get Yasmin up for school,' she adds, to hint that time is short.

'We just came . . . to say . . .'

'Well, the thing is . . .'

'We thought . . . we decided . . .'

'Last night . . .'

'Thing is,' he says, 'we've decided to move on.'

'Oh?' Bridget is taken aback. 'I'm sorry. I promise I'll get your room habitable again by the end of the morning.'

'No need,' says Mr Benson. 'Really. I'm afraid it's not the room. It's the – the house. We didn't have any better a night in the Blue Room than . . .'

'I didn't think you would – I really don't want you to . . . Can't you . . .?'

He shakes his head. His wife takes his hand, stares at her.

'Neither of us is the superstitious type,' she begins. Colours and looks away.

'But we . . .' he continues. 'I don't know how you manage to live here, frankly. You have my admiration.'

'Look . . . I'm terribly sorry. Is it the heating? I know sometimes when you're not used to old rooms like this it . . . I can turn the boiler up . . .'

Their expressions are unreadable, mysterious, their tones gentle. It's as though, she thinks, they are sorry for me.

'I – look, the curtains will be back up in your old room by this afternoon. I left them drying by the Aga last night, so they should be . . .'

'It's not that,' says Mrs Benson. 'Honestly. But we're not staying.'

'But *why*?' She realizes that the word has come out as a wail.

'My wife,' he says, 'doesn't like it here. It's as simple as that.'

The woman's blush has crept further across her cheeks. There's more to the story than they're letting on, but it's clear that they don't want to discuss it.

'I'm sorry,' she says. 'I'm not usually susceptible, you know, to . . . no one would call me the hysterical type.

But . . . Look. Let's just say we just – we just thought it would be nice, you know, to go and spend a few days at St Ives. We've booked in at the Tregenna Castle. We thought it was more – there's more to do down there, and we've always wanted to visit . . . you know . . . the Tate . . .'

'Yasmin's been thoroughly told off,' says Bridget. 'She won't – I promise she won't be in your quarters again. Definitely.'

'No, really,' says Mrs Benson, 'it's fine. It's nothing to do with her. I'm sorry we jumped to . . .' She looks down again, refuses to meet Bridget's eye. 'She seems like a nice little girl. I'm sorry she got the blame. And don't worry about Mr Gordhavo. We shan't be bringing you into this.'

'I . . .' She casts about for something to say, some way to persuade them, though part of her is flooded with relief that she will not have to face them again, that her job, it seems, is safe for the time being. 'But your honeymoon . . .' she says, helplessly.

'This isn't really the place for a honeymoon,' says Benson. 'We've decided. We both think we need somewhere a bit more . . .' He glances over his shoulder, seems to have lost use of his vocabulary. Turns back with a wide-open shrug. 'Anyway,' he finishes.

'Is there really nothing I can say to change your minds?'

'No,' says Mrs Benson, sharply. Looks surprised at her own vehemence. 'No, there isn't. Really. We just want to get on the road. Thank you.'

'Let me give you a hand with your luggage,' she offers.

'No, that'll be fine.' He bends and snatches his case away from her reaching hand. 'We don't want to bother you any more. We're just going to . . .'

'Goodbye,' says Mrs Benson.

'Um, goodbye. And I'm so sorry. That you've not enjoyed yourselves here. Very sorry.'

They've already turned their backs, are hauling their cases toward the stairs. 'Not your fault,' says Mr Benson. 'We understand that.'

She stands in the doorway as they retreat, watches them

disappear round the bend in the stairs. Odd, odd people. The strangest she's come across yet. Should she be running through the rooms, checking for missing valuables? Following them down the stairs, begging them to stay?

In the end she does nothing. Yasmin needs getting up, the day needs getting on with. She'll call Tom later and let him know, but now there's the school run to do, the laundry to get on, another cup of tea to be drunk to fend off the results of her sleepless night.

As she crosses the flat's living room, she hears the sound of feet running up the stair, Mrs Benson's voice calling out: 'Ms Sweeny? Hello? Are you there?'

She turns back, meets her at the doorway. She is out of breath, flustered. 'I just – look, I wanted to leave you this on the dining table, but then I realized I wanted to speak to you.'

She holds out a bundle of notes. Tenners: a thin sheaf, enough for a week's groceries. 'Please,' she says, 'take this. Buy something for Yasmin. Tell her I'm very, very sorry. Tell her we know she didn't do it.'

Bridget looks down at the money with mixed feelings. It's money. You need money. Reluctantly, she pushes the hand back. 'No,' she says, 'I can't. Not when you've had such a bad time.'

The woman grabs her by the wrist, holds it tightly. 'Ms Sweeny,' she says, 'I've got to say this to you. I don't think this is a good place. I'm sorry. I have to say it. I'm not that sort of person. Really I'm not. I don't believe in this sort of thing. Never have. But there's something wrong with this house. There's something here, and it's not something good. I don't think you're safe. I don't think any good can come to you if you stay.'

Chapter Fifty-Four

The snow comes with the dawn, silently, muffling the wind in the eaves and waking her with its deadness. She is strangely relieved to hear it, to see it drift in the dark past the dormer. It feels as though some tension has broken, that winter is finally really here, no longer hovering in wait. She kneels up on Vera's old bed – she's stayed, despite having a choice, in the one she was originally assigned, because it is the furthest from the door, the least assailed by draughts – wrapped against the cold in a papoose of blankets, and leans her elbows on the sill to watch. She's never really encountered snow before. Not this thick white mantle that covers everything she sees now. Snow is something of a rarity in the southern counties, and that which fell on Portsmouth was warm and damp and, even if it lay, turned grey and glutinous in the twinkling of an eye.

This, though, is something else – a thing of beauty. She wishes she had her paints, her pencils, though she doubts she would have the skill to translate this strange drifting creature as it meanders toward the earth, spirals in the cross-breeze, settles and builds, coats the grey garden, brings a glow to the half-light. Lily scrapes at the window where the moisture from her breath freezes as it touches the pane; draws quickly back and tucks her hand into the blankets. She can't afford to allow herself to get chilled; knows from experience that heat, once lost, can be excruciatingly slow to be regained.

The boathouse looks like the witch's cottage in *Hansel*

and Gretel: all sparkling and iced like a Christmas cake. It looks warm out there, she thinks: like swan's feathers. If I could only get out of here, run down there, roll myself up in it. If only . . .

She hears the key in the door at the bottom of the stairs. Oh, God, she's coming. She crosses the room at a scuttle and dives beneath the bedcovers. She does this to hide what she is wearing, though frankly Blakemore's gone so gaga she probably wouldn't notice if Lily were wearing pearls and a tiara. Since winter set in in earnest, the attic rooms have been enveloped in a cold so deep it makes you feel as though your limbs will snap. And since Blakemore let her out of the four-poster-room cupboard – she has no idea how long she was in there, she lost all sense of the passing of time after a while – and locked her in here, chamber pot in the corner and a weekly bath-break, Lily has spent a lot of time in bed as a basic survival technique. At least Blakemore hasn't got round to taking the others' bedclothes away, and she can pile them high over and under her. I'd have died of the cold long since else, she thinks. Not that she'd care. Notice, even.

I would set fire to the whole place, she thinks as she huddles beneath layered blankets and listens for Blakemore's approach, if I could get hold of some matches. At least I'd be warm for a bit. And if the place burned down, they couldn't make me stay here then, could they?

She shifts beneath the blankets. They still retain some residual heat from when she got up, at least in contrast with the air in the rest of the room. Yesterday, she actually had to crack the ice on the surface of the water jug before she could drink from it. She's found a one-bar electric fire in the other attic, but doesn't dare bring it through in case it is found and the secret of the unlocked door uncovered. Instead, she creeps through when it seems the coast is clear – it is clear most of the time – and huddles in front of it on the chaise longue, wrapped in an old eiderdown which leaks goose feathers in matted clumps on the dusty floor.

She needs that door to stay open. She would die of the

boredom as quickly as the cold, otherwise, staring at the sloping ceilings and waiting for something to change. As it is, after three weeks – she has counted the days by making scratches in the plaster of the wall behind her bed – she has long since run out of new things to look at, is reduced to going over and over the crumbling albums in which long-dead ancestors hold stiff and fearful poses for long-dead cameramen. She knows that Christmas has been and gone, but she's not sure when. Doesn't know if the new year has begun.

She sleeps, a lot. Dreams of Portsmouth and her vanished mother. Makes up tales in her head to drive out the dread of what might be coming toward her.

Blakemore is on the stairs now. She moves slowly these days, like a wounded beast: hampered by downtrodden slippers and hundred-year-old whisky. I'd better hope she doesn't trip and take a purler one day, thinks Lily, land on her head. I'd never get out of here. They'd find my starved corpse God knows when, like one of those old people you hear about. Lily huddles down, pulls on the sleeves of her jersey to make sure it's covering the floor-length silk dress underneath. Silk is surprisingly warm. Warmer, certainly, than the knee-length skirt and school blouse she was locked up in.

The door scrapes open.

Mrs Blakemore has been putting on make-up this morning. It doesn't help: makes things worse, if anything, for the powder and lipstick have gone on over skin that hasn't been washed in weeks. Despite her own dubious hygiene, Lily can smell her from across the room: stale sweat, hair grease, something faintly cheesy. Grown-ups 'take' smells more than children, she's noticed that before. It's like the skins of the young can shrug dirt off as though they've been waterproofed.

Lily sits up in bed, careful to keep her lower half under the covers. Mrs Blakemore shuffles across the floorboards, deposits the tray she carries on the single chest-of-drawers by the chimney breast. Craning, Lily sees that her daily ration today consists of a heel of bread, meanly smeared with marge, what looks like a dish of leftover mashed potato, mixed up with the dark leaves of winter greens. God, she could at least have fried it up a bit: made a spot of bubble-and-squeak. A single apple and a glass of milk sit by the bowls, and – oh, the luxury – a mug from which steam rises in the frigid air.

'I've made you a cup of tea,' says Mrs Blakemore. Imitates, gruesomely, the actions of a smile. Her thick scarlet lipstick has bled into the lines on her upper lip, smeared across her upper incisors. She looks like she's been eating small animals, raw.

Lily remembers her manners, stammers out her thanks. The jailer ignores her, picks up yesterday's tray with its scraped bowls and begins to make her way silently back the way she came. She won't be back for another day. Twenty-four more solitary hours. I have to try again. At the very least I'll get to hear the sound of another human voice for a few moments more. Sometimes I feel as though my own has vanished, that the only sounds I hear when I speak are inside my own head.

'Mrs Blakemore,' she ventures, 'please. Can I come out of here?'

Mrs Blakemore stalls in her progress, stands with her back to her, thinking. 'I don't think that would be a very good idea,' she says eventually.

'But Mrs Blakemore,' says Lily, 'it's snowing outside. There's no heating. I'm cold. I'm so cold.'

'Nonsense,' says Mrs Blakemore. 'You've plenty of blankets. That's the trouble with you young people. You never think to put enough clothes on. Wrap up, girl. Or get a bit of exercise. That'll warm you up.'

Lily looks round the attic room: the bare floorboards, the empty beds crowded about under the eaves. She could run on the spot, she supposes. Do press-ups like they do in the army. But she doesn't even have shoes. The heat will leach out of her feet as fast as she generates it. 'Please, Mrs

Blakemore,' she says again. 'Please. I've learned my lesson. I won't be any trouble.'

She turns back to face her, the ghastly grin on her face once again. 'Now, where have I heard that before?'

She's gone doolally. Totally flipped. It's not as if I didn't know that already, but she's not going to let me out of here. I'm going to be shut up here forever, till I'm big enough to fight my way out, if I ever have the strength.

'Please,' she says again. 'I can't . . . just stay here forever. It's . . . there's nothing to do. I'm freezing cold. I'm lonely.'

The grin again. 'Well, we're all lonely, dear,' she says. 'God knows, I'm lonely myself. Still. Hughie will be home soon. Then we'll have company. I daresay he'll even find time to give you some company himself.'

Chapter Fifty-Five

There's a huddle of parents at the school gates by the time he gets there: the ancient rite of arriving early to swap the juice before the young descend. They stamp on the pavement, clap their hands together, shrug deeper into anoraks and coats, pull scarves up to half-cover mouths. The wind has changed during the day, is blowing straight down from Siberia, and the air cuts the lungs as it goes in: he's glad of the heater, gladder still of the tint on his windows as he sees her pull up and exit the car, shivering exaggeratedly as she crosses the road, pulling on her gloves as she goes.

'Nice weather for it,' says Penny Tremayne. She's wearing a car coat of cerise leather and a striped bobble hat. Very townie, but she's allowed, being as they trade in the arts.

Bridget glances at the sky. It's only five to four, but it feels as though night is just around the corner. Dark clouds hang above them, sluggish and replete; the fading evening light doesn't stand a chance of getting through such heavy cover.

'It's going to snow tonight,' says Justine Strang.

'Looks like it,' says Bridget.

'We haven't had snow that didn't just disappear again the moment it landed in ages,' says Penny. 'I hope it lies this time. I'm a real kid when it comes to snow.'

'Me, too.' Justine slaps at her upper arms with her leather mittens. 'Can't wait to get out in it. Dave says I'm more of a kid than the kids are.'

'Yasmin's never actually seen proper snow,' Bridget tells them. 'We had one big fall, when she was three, but by the time I got her out to Brockwell Park it had all gone to mush. Lasted about three hours altogether.'

'Oh, poor little mite,' says Justine. 'I thought they were deprived enough down here in the subtropics, but I suppose it's even worse in the cities. You'd better make the most of it, then.'

'She'll be happy enough just getting the day off school,' says Penny. 'There's no way you're getting up your hill in that car if we have a proper storm.'

Chris Kirkland, tweed coat and fake-fur tippet, rubs her hands together as she walks over from the shop. 'I hear there's snow on the way. My sister says they've already got two inches down at Truro.'

'Amazing,' says Penny. 'The Met Office actually got it right. They said it was going to be a hard winter and it's actually coming true.'

'Well, I suppose,' says Justine, 'just by the law of averages even wild guesses have to be right once in a blue moon. You got enough food laid in, Bridget? Tins and that?'

'Good grief,' says Bridget. 'It's not the Arctic.'

'Well, yes, but you'd be surprised how cut off you can be down there. Half a mile uphill through snow can really take it out of you, and your freezer's not going to be much help to you if the electricity goes down. They got snowed in a couple of times down there and no one saw anything of them for a couple of weeks.'

'Yes, dear,' says Chris. 'That'll be, when? During the war and the winter of '63, yes?'

'Well, all right. But it's happened, hasn't it?'

She stamps her feet hard against the road. 'I wish I'd remembered to put some socks on. You forget, don't you? I've never understood. This global warming thing. One minute they're saying we're going to be living in a desert and the next we're heading into the New Ice Age.'

'Got to cover all the bases,' says Penny, 'to keep the

government on their toes. Can't have something as inconvenient as a spot of weather spoil a good theory. And besides. Can't have a load of redundant environmentalists walking about. You never know what they'll get up to next. Seriously, though, Bridget. It drifts, on your hill. Get a few inches and you'll be a few feet under on your track. And with your power lines still running above ground, you can get cut off quite easily. Best to be prepared. You could be shut away in there for a few days before they get the ploughs round your way. Specially given the number of snow ploughs in Cornwall. I've got a little camping stove if you like. Runs off Butane. It won't keep you warm, but at least you'll be able to make a cup of tea.'

Bridget laughs. 'Sweet. Thanks. That's dead kind, but really. We've got fireplaces. I can roast Yasmin on one of those if I get desperate.'

'Only if you've got enough redcurrant jelly to go with her,' says Chris. 'We've got some in the shop.'

'I'll go and buy some just in case.'

'I would if I was you. It can be a powerful long haul, locked up alone with nothing but the gho— wind for company.'

'Tell you what,' jokes Bridget, 'if we don't turn up after the weekend, send out a search party.'

Thinks: Why do I feel like I'm tempting fate, saying something like that? Those Bensons were clearly mad. Clearly. They just didn't look it on the surface. You mustn't let people like that get to you, Bridge. Rospetroc's your home now and you can't let those sorts of nutters scare you off.

'I will,' says Chris. 'There's a bloke over Lanivet breeds huskies, of all things. I'm sure he won't mind lending us a few.'

'What time is it?' asks Penny. 'My feet are going to fall off in a minute.'

'Just gone four,' says a voice.

They all turn, smile. 'Hello, Mark,' says Chris. 'Didn't know you were on pick-up duty. Where's Tina?'

'Dentist,' Mark replies, looking at Bridget, holding the look. She feels herself blush, wishes he would look away. Wishes he wouldn't. 'How's Yasmin, Bridge?' he asks. 'Got over her wazz?'

'Yes,' she says. He's still not torn his eyes away. She looks down, can't bear the heat of his scrutiny. 'Thanks. We had a talk on the way down this morning. I think she's forgiven me.'

'Good,' says Mark. 'Glad to hear it.'

She looks up again. He's looking off at the playground, hands deep in pockets, and his expression is disappointed. No, she thinks, no, Mark, it's not that . . . it's just, in front of all these people . . . I can't . . .

'You were a real help,' she says gently. 'Thank you. I don't know what I'd've done without your advice.'

'Yasmin been playing up, has she?' asks Chris. She's glancing between the two of them, curiosity on her face.

Bridget pulls herself together. 'Yes,' she says. 'I had to call Mark for a bit of buddying.'

'He's good at that,' says Chris, acutely.

'Yes,' says Bridget. 'Yes, he is.' And looks her straight in the eye.

Chris turns away, a slight smile playing on the edge of her mouth. It'll be all over the village now, thinks Bridget. Oh, God.

'It was nothing,' says Mark. 'Any time.'

'It must be tough, sometimes,' says Penny, approvingly. 'Everyone needs someone to turn to every now and then.'

She feels the blush return. Fixes her eyes on the school door. 'Maybe we should start a lone parents' group,' she jokes.

'Got one of them already,' says Justine. 'It's called the pub.'

They all laugh.

Kieran, watching from the safety of the car, shifts in his seat. Weaves his fingers together, cracks his knuckles.

Chapter Fifty-Six

She wakes to find her mother stroking her face. Gently, with the back of her fingers. Whispering into her hair. 'Wake up, darling. Good morning. Good morning, my love.'

Yasmin stretches, squeezes her eyes closed, opens them. Slips an arm round her mother's neck and allows herself to be held and loved. The morning ritual: she doesn't know it, but she will remember it all her life; those days when waking was a warm thing, a grateful thing. Look. We have survived the night.

'Guess what?'

'What?'

'No school today,' says Bridget. 'Get up and see. You won't believe it.'

Yasmin sits up. Her bedroom is dark, but the light seeping in round the curtains is blinding white. Her mum's crept in while she slept and plugged in the fan heater, so the air is toasty. She's laid out jeans, thick socks, a sweater on the bed, and she looks – different today. Sort of excited; like she's lit from the inside.

'What?' asks Yasmin. 'What's happened?'

'Get dressed and I'll show you.'

She's got Yasmin's beanie hat in her hand, her purple gloves with the pompoms. 'Hurry up,' she says. 'We don't want to miss a minute.'

'Has it snowed?' she asks.

'Yes, peabrain! Yes, it has!'

Yasmin swings out of bed, dashes to the window.

In the night, the world's turned white. As far as her vision extends; blinding, enveloping white. There's snow on the window sills, snow weighing down the branches of the yew tree. Bushes hunch like trolls beneath swansdown blankets, the only demarcation between farmland and moorland the black meanders of the beck.

Over by the wood, by the boathouse, a deer steps from cover. Dainty, elegant, russet. She can see its huge brown eyes from all this distance. It pauses at the edge of the lake, raises its head to look about it. Ten steps, light as a ballerina, across the unbroken waste. It vanishes into the dark.

She is beside herself: feels the fizz of excitement course up and down her spine. Lets out an actual shriek, turns to her mother with her hands digging into her hair. And she sees for the first time ever what her mother must have looked like herself as a child; bright eyes, lips thrown wide so all her teeth are showing.

'What are you waiting for?' she says.

It's like Christmas, she thinks. More like Christmas than Christmas was. My mum's more Christmassy than she was then: she's gone all pink and shiny.

The snow has a crust, like sugar icing. It snaps beneath her wellington and her foot plunges down, down, surprisingly down till the snow hovers at the very top of her boot.

'It's amazing,' says her mum. 'I know you see it on the telly, but you don't actually think this sort of thing happens overnight. What do you think, shorty?'

Yasmin squats down, scoops up a handful, throws it in her face. Bridget screams. Surprise and delight. 'You little – you *savage*!'

She swipes at the rhododendron which grows by the scullery door, flings an armful of snow, sparkling, through the air. It catches Yasmin on the side of the face: shockingly, exhilaratingly cold. Sharp and wet. And now they're running, wading, their shouts filling the sunshiny morning as they plunder the pristine crust on the lawn. Yasmin's head is filled with light; her cheeks sting and her fingers go numb. Beautiful, beautiful, beautiful.

Bridget is quickly puffed out. Throws herself on to the ground, face up. Calls 'Look, baby!' and flails her arms and legs. 'An angel!'

Doesn't look like an angel to me, thinks Yasmin. Just looks like a big mess in the snow. But her mum looks so happy, so pleased with herself, that she cooperates, claps her hands and congratulates her. You've got to keep the grown-ups happy, sometimes. Encourage them. Help them feel they're doing well.

Bridget sits up. 'Come on. You have a go.'

'Okay,' says Yasmin, because though the finished product is rubbish, making it looks like fun.

She lies down. Feels the cold suck at her, like a living entity, wrapping itself around her, dark and greedy. She doesn't like it. It feels as though a cloud has passed over the sun.

Suddenly she is sitting up, shivering, looking up at the cloudless sky. Lily, she thinks. I know how it felt. Her teeth rattle in her head and her whole body seems to be consumed with shaking.

'What's up, baby? Cold?'

Her mum is crouching over her, eyes wide with concern.

Yasmin nods, swallows.

'Oh, it's okay,' says Bridget. Wraps her in her arms, rubs hard at her back. 'It's okay. We should have dressed you up more warmly. Silly. I'm silly. Come on. Let's go back to the house. I'll make you some hot chocolate. How would you like that? Some hot chocolate?'

She nods again, the shivering beginning to recede. She feels safe, now, enveloped in her mother's presence. The sun is coming out again. Round the side of her mother's arm, she sees Lily, standing by the boathouse, hands hanging by bony hips, rat's-tail hair, watching. I understand, now, she says to her, silently. I know what it was like.

'Poor you,' whispers Bridget, kisses her on the hairline. 'My poor darling. I do love you, you know.'

Yasmin looks up. Her face is shining. How odd, thinks Bridget. A second ago she was as pale as the grave and now . . .

'I love you, Mummy,' says Yasmin.

Lily smiles. Turns toward the pond. Glances back over her shoulder. The two of them are on their feet, now, hobbling back toward the house, hand-in-hand. 'We'll get you warmed up,' Bridget is saying, 'and I'll find you a vest and we can go up to the field. You've never been tobogganing, have you?'

Yasmin looks up at her and shakes her head. 'No.'

'You'll love that. Love it. My dad used to take me, in Dulwich Park, when I was your age. There's a couple of tea trays in the scullery. We'll take them out after. You'll love it.'

Chapter Fifty-Seven

'Does Mummy know you're in here?'

She hasn't heard him coming. He's tiptoed up the attic stairs and the sound of his furtive movements hasn't broken through the pall of sleep. She is so drugged with cold and boredom and helplessness that she sleeps almost all day after her wakeful nights in the dormitory.

Lily's unpacked each of the trunks, spread their contents over the attic so the room is tented against draughts and the heat of the electric fire is concentrated into the small space around the chaise longue. Sprawled in its heat in her cream chiffon ballgown, surrounded by her favourite objects, she looks like the fairy in an abandoned jewel box. She stares at him, takes a moment to register the truth of his presence. And then she pulls her dress over herself, tries to cover up.

'What are you doing?' he asks.

'Nothing,' she says. 'I was asleep.'

'Little thief,' he says. 'Mummy said she'd had to lock you up, but I bet she didn't know you'd be getting in here and stealing as well.'

'I ain't stealing,' says Lily. 'I was cold, that's all. It's freezing in there.'

'What's that you're wearing?'

He's got his swagger on. She knows the swagger. He always uses it when he's feeling powerful, when he's going to show his power to the world.

'Nothing.'

'Doesn't look like nothing to me.'

He steps forward, into the pool of warmth. 'Let's have a look.'

'No,' she says. Pulls it closer around her.

'Little thief,' he says. 'Thought you'd dress up, did you? Thought you'd put on Granny's dress and turn into a princess?'

Oh, God. Please keep him away from me. I can't bear it.

'I can't wear my own clothes. I've been wearing them for weeks. They're filthy.'

'I should have thought,' says Hugh, 'you'd be used to that.'

'Your mother,' she tries appealing to his sense, 'has – something's wrong, Hugh. You must be able to see. She's locked me in here. It's not right.'

He's standing over her now. He's nearly fifteen and heavy-set and she'll never be a match for him.

'Have to stop you stealing, somehow,' he says.

'Please, Hugh.'

'Well, we'll just –' he takes one more step forward, kneels over her – 'get you out of those for a start.'

Oh, God.

And she's curled into a ball, muscles tight, hands latched over her head. *This can't be. It can't be happening. I'm nine years old. You can't be doing this to me. Please please don't do this please . . .*

He's got his big hands on me. He's got them in, between my arms and my knees, and I can't stop him, he's too strong. He's uncurling me like a woodlouse, pulling me open. I'll kick. Kick him. Kick at his face, get him away from me . . .

'Ouch,' says Hugh. 'You little –'

And now he's right on top of her, pinning her down. Knees on her hips, hands wrenching at her arms. *Don't. God. Help me. What did I do? What did I do? He's – oh, God, he's revolting. He's disgusting. I have to – I can't – please, help me. He's got his knees between my thighs, now, and he's pulling the dress up. He can't. He can't do this. He –*

She gets a hand free. Slaps at his face. He slaps her back.

Grabs her round the waist and hoists her, drops her on the floor. Lily tries to crawl, tries to get away, feels his hand grip the back of the dress, haul her back toward him. *They can do anything, these people, anything, to people like us. I don't stand a – God, get him* off *me!*

'Come on, come on, come on,' he says urgently, thickly. 'Dirty little –'

Her hand, scrabbling beneath the couch, trying to get purchase, falls on something hard. Grips it. She doesn't know what it is, just that it fits in her hand, that it's heavy, that it comes with her as he pulls her backwards. And now she's on her back again, and his face – his face is purple and his pupils are like pinpricks, and he's miles away, somewhere deep inside himself, and he's not thinking at all, not seeing a human being, just intent on –

Lily strikes out. Feels the crack as her weapon connects. Sees, as she draws it back, that it's a paperweight, chipped and scratched, made of glass. Hears a strange noise come from his mouth, a sort of wail, an animal, incoherent sound, a babble. His hands loose their grip, clutch at his head. And he slumps. Forward, on to her, pinning her to the floor.

Chapter Fifty-Eight

A lovely day. A lovely, lovely day. We're right back on track, Yasmin and me. We like each other again, understand each other. She trusts me now: knows I'm on her side, knows we can have fun together. *Be* fun together.

Bridget stands in the doorway to Yasmin's room, listens to the sound of her breathing. My child: my beautiful child. Days like this, days when they're together and she's learning, and Yasmin's learning, and she can feel the knowledge pass between them, when they wear themselves out with the cold and the joy of it – these are the days when she know it's going to be all right, when she knows that somehow, despite everything, despite their precipitous situation, despite the past, despite the unknown future, they will be okay. They'll be okay because they have each other, and each other is all they need.

Ten o'clock and she's already on the verge of sleep. There's steam coming from the bathroom, carrying with it the fragrance of lavender. She thinks maybe she'll call Carol later, once she's clean and cheerful: let her know that things are all right again. It's been eight days since they last spoke and she can't stay out of phone's reach forever. She'll leave a message, anyway, at least, cancelling that last cry of despair. Poor Carol. Not fair to put this burden on her, when she's finally getting her own life back.

Bridget pulls the bedroom door almost to, leaving a crack of light to dissipate the darkness within, and walks up the corridor, undoing the belt of her dressing gown as she goes. The flat is toasty. She's whacked the heating up on the assumption that Tom Gordhavo will never distinguish the cost from that of keeping the pipes in the rest of the house from freezing.

Instead of her usual quick-change, she drops the robe on the bathroom floor and looks at herself in the mirror as she pins her hair up. It's a long time since I did this, she thinks, not since soon after Yasmin was born, when the shock of the change in my body and Kieran's disgust drove me to scuttle past reflecting surfaces as though they would steal my soul. It's not as bad as I remember. Maybe I've got used to it, maybe it's got better again over the years. My stomach's nothing to write home about, but my breasts are okay – round and soft and welcoming, as breasts should be – and the work here has taken some weight off me, the lifting and carrying and polishing given me more muscle than I had before. My skin's better, too. Away from the pollutants of London air, the relentless burden of worry, it's clearer, less lined, softer; the dark circles under my eyes have begun to recede. She smiles at herself, sees the corners of her mouth dimple.

The bath is almost too hot to bear. Bridget lowers herself in inch by inch, falls back against the back of the tub and sighs. Inhales deeply and splashes hot oily water over her arms and hands.

The lights go out.

Oh, God *damn* it. I thought Mark said he'd sorted that out. *Damn* it. Just when I'd got comfortable.

She heaves a heavy sigh and sits up, feels the suck of the water as she levers herself from the bath. To her eyes, unadjusted after the dazzle, the room is pitch black. She feels her way over the lino, toe by toe, until she finds her dressing gown, discarded in the corner by the sink. After the heat of the bath, the air is cold on her skin, and she knows it's going to be a lot colder down in the main house.

'*Damn* it,' she says again. Feels the sough of towelling on her goosepimples, ties the belt tight around her. Goes to the kitchen and finds the candle.

The stairs no longer feel alien. Her bare feet know, now,

the uneven treads, and the shadows around her no longer hold unknown lurking dangers. She just wants to get back in the bath. Wants to get warm and comfortable again. Is irritated, not timid.

Cold moonlight bathes the ground floor where she has left the curtains open. She puts her head into the fuse cupboard, sees that nothing has tripped.

'Oh, God *damn* it,' she says again. It's the outside power lines. They're off the grid for the foreseeable.

'Bums, bums, bums,' she says. Isn't even really aware that she's speaking out loud. Right, well. I'll have to go out to that damn shed and get some wood in for the morning. I'll do it *in* the morning. Just go to bed now. Damn it, why didn't I accept that camping stove? It's going to take forever to get the woodburner up and running in the main kitchen and we won't be able to have anything hot to eat till I do. Hopefully there's enough water left, anyway, that I can get a decent hot water bottle out of it. And if the worst comes to the worst we can just spend the next few days holed up in the living room with a fire.

She goes through to the drawing room to get the spare stock of candles. Big, fat church candles, part-burned and beautiful, left behind by the Aykroyds. It took a lot of elbow grease to get the dribbled wax off the dining room table, but she'll be glad of them now.

Bridget marches smartly, looks neither left nor right. She's less familiar with these rooms and the shadows are deeper, longer. She feels the familiar prickle of the hairs on her arms. Curses herself for a superstitious housewife. Damn those Bensons. I'd got cool with this house before they came along. There's no one here, Bridget. You *know* there's no one here.

The candles are where she thought they would be, in the window seat where Yasmin hid all those weeks ago. She lowers her single light into the cavernous space, checks for spiders before she reaches in. Takes three – all she can carry in a single armful – and starts to make her way back toward the dining room.

As she passes the front door, something catches her eye. Outside. A small splash of light.

Bridget stops. Funny.

The light moves. Skitters over the snow in the front garden, flits up and plays over the windows. She can see it hit the back wall of the dining room from where she stands in the hall.

Torchlight. It's torchlight.

There's someone out there.

The front door is unlocked. So is the back. She's got complacent. She's stopped worrying.

And she knows who it is. Who would be creeping around her house in the snow. In the dark.

Kieran's here.

Chapter Fifty-Nine

I must stay calm. I must stay calm. Got to lock the door, first. Lock him out. Stop him coming in.

She blows out her candle. He's probably already seen its shadow, crossing the windows, but she can't let him know where she is now.

He's here. How did he find me? I don't . . .

Bridget stoops, lays down her burden, silently, silently, on the flagstones. There is sweat – cold – on her forehead. She bites her lip.

What do I do?

Oh, God, Carol. He's done something to Carol. That's why she's not answering her phone: he's got hold of it, somehow, and that means he's . . . oh Carol. My friend. Please be okay. Wherever you are. Please don't let him have . . .

Every nerve tells her to back away from where he is, not to go closer. She can see the light approaching. He's coming. He's coming to the door.

Don't.

She has to force herself to breathe. Feels it stagger in, in, release slowly, slowly, as though he will hear her from the other side of the door. Bridget drops to her knees. Crawls forward. Reaches out with stiff-jointed fingers and grasps the bolt. Turns it, slides it slowly, slowly, into the hasp.

The crunch of boots on stone. He's in the porch. Stamping the snow from his insteps.

She reaches up, cowers below the window as she takes the key in her fist. It's in the lock already, where it sits permanently against being lost. He'll hear me. He'll hear. He must know I'm here. Must know.

He clears his throat. He's not in a hurry. He's got all night.

Bridget turns the key. Scrape and clunk of ancient metalwork.

He goes quiet. He heard me.

The door handle begins to turn. She can hear him breathing.

He must be able to hear me, too.

She presses herself against the panel, tries to hide in the dark. I can't move away. If I try to run, he'll see me through the window. He'll know I'm here. He'll know I know.

Oh, God, help me.

The door moves against her back. Slightly, slightly. And the locks catch, hold, give no more.

Oh, God, help me.

'Faaa,' he mutters. It's him. It's him. She hears him step back into the porch, shuffle around on the stones. Lifts her hand up again, frozen in space, takes the key, lightly, lightly, between her fingers. Eases it, bit by bit, from the lock.

Glass above her shatters. A single tiny pane, big enough for a hand, an arm.

She runs for it. Hears him swear again as he realizes she's been within hand's grasp, hears the door resound in its frame as though a body has been hurled against it.

And now she's going full pelt. Through the dining room. Past the windows, too high to see out of, past the table, the great cupboard, past the anteroom door into the kitchen where appliances hunch silent, brooding without their power.

Oh, God, help me.

She can hear him, now, wading through the snow, in her wake, slowed by the weight but coming. Please, please, please . . .

She snatches the scullery key from the hook inside the kitchen, runs to the door, turns the lock, throws the bolts.

Oh, God. None of it will keep him out for long. He'll find a way. He'll find his way in and he'll find his way up the stairs and . . .

Yasmin. Oh, darling. I am so afraid.

She's screaming inside as she runs up the stairs. Lets it burst from her lungs when she reaches the top. Flounders up the corridor, throws open her daughter's bedroom door. 'Darling! Darling! Oh, God, *quickly*!'

She feels her way toward the bed, trips on a discarded shoe and nearly turns turtle. Come on, come on, come *on*. Yasmin shouts out in the dark: 'Who's there? Who is it?'

It pulls her up, forces her calm. I can't give her my panic. I can't feed on hers.

'Shhh,' she says. 'It's me.'

'What is it?'

'Darling,' she says, 'We've got to . . .'

'He's here,' says Yasmin.

She considers, momentarily, a lie. 'Yes,' she replies. 'We've got to . . . quickly. Come on. Hold my hand. We'll . . .'

He'll find us. Wherever we go, he'll find us.

I'll call the police. We'll barricade ourselves in somewhere and wait it out. My bag. In the bedroom.

Yasmin is silent as they jog along the corridor. She can feel him breathe. Feel him think. He'll be working his way round the house. Finding the chink, finding the weak spots. It's all so old. The window frames are only held together by their paint, some of them. He'll find one. Oh, God, did I check the other door? At the other end of the house? After the Bensons left?

Cold washes through her. She feels weak. Not sure if her knees will support her.

Now they're inside the bedroom, and she's hauling at the chest-of-drawers, dragging it across the carpet. 'Find the mobile,' she says. 'It's in my bag. Dial 999.' The chest is heavy; old teak weighed down by clothes and precious things. If I wasn't so afraid, she thinks, I wouldn't be able to move this. I'm like one of those people who lift cars off their children. Adrenalin. It makes you strong.

You get adrenalin from anger, too. He'll be as strong.

Don't. Don't. Just push.

She heaves it across the door. Pushes it up as hard as she can against the panels.

'It's just beeps,' says Yasmin, her face lit ghostly green by the caller display.

She sits against the chest, holds out a hand in the dark. 'Give it here.'

There are no bars. No bars. This damn signal. Should have known the snow would make it worse. She stares at the phone, despairingly. Throws it across the room.

Oh, Carol, what's happened to you? He's done something, I know he has. You would have found a way to get a message to me otherwise, I know you would . . .

'Call them on the landline, Mummy,' says Yasmin, calmly.

I can't go down there again. I can't.

'I can't,' she says. 'The handset's down in the hall. And anyway, the electricity's out. The phone won't work.'

'What are we going to do?'

Bridget puts her head in her hands. 'I don't know, baby. I don't know.'

Chapter Sixty

He's got the scent of the chase now. So near to getting her, and so far. He felt the slick of her hair on his fingertips as she slipped away from him and now his blood is hot. He prowls round the house, snuffs the air like a hunting wolf.

There are signs of them all over. Her car in the driveway: a six-inch crust of snow on roof and windscreen, a Barbie, half-naked, on the back seat. Through a window, in a room with a huge washing machine where sheets hang from a ceiling rack like Spanish moss, his wife's old suede coat and Yasmin's anorak, a pair of tiny, unfamiliar wellingtons lined up inside the door. Two pairs of woollen gloves, carelessly discarded on a worktop. He feels a surge of possession run through him, proximity heightening the senses. *She is mine. She is mine. Soon she will be.*

He tries the door. No give. It's okay. I'll find a way. There will be a way she hasn't thought of.

The snow on this side of the house is battered, scuffed halfway across the lawn. A scruffy little snowman, two feet high, with twigs for arms and black-coal eyes, stares sightlessly at him. He can see them now, in the chase – oblivious, wavelets of powdered white frothing about their feet. They are laughing. Careless. Thoughtless.

Kieran bites his lip. His eyes narrow. Yeah. Let them forget. They'll remember.

He trudges on, tries a little push on each window he passes. Not firm in their frames, several of them. High up, though.

She never saw me coming but she knows I'm here now.

He finds another door, at the end, huddled up in a corner where a dry-stone wall runs down toward an area where the snow lies so flat he assumes it to be concrete. It's a cramped, low door of tongue-and-groove, its handle small enough to fit a wardrobe. Weaker than the others, its ability to keep people out relies mostly on the hope that it will never be noticed.

He tries it, for luck. The handle turns useless in its socket: it's not attached by anything other than a few screws. It's for pulling, not fixing.

He looks up. Smiles. A Yale lock. A bloody great mansion like this and they've got it tied up with a Yale lock.

He lifts a boot. Kicks. The door shudders in its frame, holds.

'Fuck,' says Kieran, watches his breath cloud out on frozen air. Fuck, it's cold tonight. You can tell this air's coming down from Siberia. So much for global fucking –

This time, it cracks. Not the lock, which holds. Not the panels. Kieran lets out a laugh. They've put in a new door, but they left the bloody frame. Rotten old weathered timber, and the hinges are just coming free with a couple of kicks.

Oh, I'm in, he thinks. I'm in now. I'm coming.

He steps back, rubs his hands together, blows on them open-mouthed.

Something moves in the corner of his vision.

Kieran's head snaps round. There's a child standing in the snow.

'Hah!'

She's sent her out. She's done a *Shining* on me, sent the kid out to save herself. Sent her out in her bloody nightie and all.

She is walking, determinedly, head down so her features are obscured in the moonlight. Walking steadily, away from him, strangely unhampered by the snow beneath her feet.

She's grown, he thinks. And what's happened to her hair? Has she dyed it or something? Did she really think a bad dye-job would put me off the scent?

'Yasmin,' he calls.

The child doesn't pause. Doesn't look up. Doesn't change her course. She is walking toward the small two-storey building down at the edge of the flat place. Walking away.

'Yasmin, it's Daddy,' he calls. 'Don't be frightened.'

If she's afraid, she doesn't show it.

Why won't you look at me?

He sets off in her wake. What sort of nightie is that? It looks like it's trailing along the ground. Has she started dressing her in her own clothes, now?

She's got skinny little arms. They look slightly blue in this light. She's lost weight, a lot of it.

'Honey,' he calls, 'it's me. Come on. Come to Daddy.'

His boot catches in something and he lurches forward, can't save himself. Lands face-down and catches a mouthful of ice. 'Fuck,' he says again. Looks up and sees that she has already reached the shed, is standing in its shadow, watching him, a swathe of unbroken snow between her and himself.

'Look, it's not funny,' he shouts. No need to fear the neighbours here. No one to interfere. 'I'm not laughing, okay? C'mere, Yasmin! Now! I'm telling you!'

She turns, goes inside.

And now he's angry. Pushes himself upright and stumble-runs in the direction his daughter has taken. Right. Have it that way. I'll just bloody take you. Take you and go, and you can find out what happens if you fight, little bitch. You're *my bloody daughter*. You will do what I say whether you like it or not.

The snow gets deeper as he approaches the building; it's drifted two, three feet thick. He is too enraged to stop, to notice, to wonder why there is no sign of her having passed that way: just wades, arms flailing, to the door. It's shut, of course. She thinks she can shut me out. Thinks all it will take is a locked door and I'll be thwarted.

He steadies himself, gets balanced, kicks. More rotten wood. The screws holding the padlock staple to the outside come clean away from the stanchion. The door thuds dully back, rebounds, comes to a rest.

Kieran switches on the torch, steps inside.

It's a boathouse. One that smells of rot and fungus, like wet places do. He plays the torch over unplastered walls, over mooring post and rotten wooden steps which lead blindly down into black, scummy water. Not frozen, he notices. You'd have thought it would be frozen.

There's a dinghy, long since holed and sunk, lying prow-up in the dock, and a scrap of rope tied around the post, but otherwise the building is empty. It's been cleared out, thoroughly: none of the pots of paint, bits of cushion, propped-up oars, mouldered parasols, you would expect to find. The building hasn't simply been abandoned: it's been scraped clean. A tangle of cobwebs dangles a collection of blackened dust-bunnies from the beams above his head.

From the darkness of the loft, a giggle.

Right. That's how you want to play it.

He ducks under the lintel, steps carefully on to the concrete dock. Skirts around the edge to the rough wooden stairs that lead upward from the far corner. Stands at the bottom, calls up.

'Yasmin! You might as well come down. I know you're there.'

Silence.

He puts a hand on the wall, cranes to see her.

'You won't like it if I have to come and get you,' he threatens.

She laughs again. It's not a nice laugh. It's mocking, contemptuous. He feels the heat in his veins again. Grips the torch and strides up the stairs. I'll get you and I'll fucking –

She's in the corner. He sees her straight away because this room, like the one below it, has been stripped of its contents. She sits with her back to the wall, knees drawn up to her chest inside her loose white garment. Her head is bowed, a mop of straggled tangles falling toward her knees. Her feet, poking out from beneath the hem of her nightie, are bare.

'Come on,' he says. Tries to sound calm, persuasive. Starts across the floor toward her. The smell of rot and rotten things is stronger here, trapped without an outlet. The boards feel spongy, unresponsive, beneath his boots. 'You must be freezing.'

The child uncurls, abruptly, aggressively. Her face is yellow, her teeth black and snaggled, her eyes bright with rage and hatred. She's not Yasmin. She's not any child as he knows them. She's something else. Something long-lost, black and angry.

'I won't go back,' she says, and smiles a smile that holds no joy.

He is startled. Steps back, heavily. Feels the floor give, splinter, beneath him. Hovers above the hole for a moment, hopelessly grasping at thin air, then spirals, thrashing, down into the water below.

Chapter Sixty-One

The shock of first hitting is like death by a thousand knives. There is a thin layer of ice on the surface and the water below is so cold he feels his heart stop momentarily. And then he's through, still falling, and his foot catches on something, goes sideways, and he feels the ankle snap. Screams, underwater, loses his breath and chokes as he tries to take another, and then he's floundering toward the air, burning, freezing, red agony swimming across his vision.

He breaks surface. Gasps, coughs, throws his arms outward to spread the weight of his body. His ankle feels as though it's being crushed in a vice and there's no strength in the leg below the knee. My boots, he thinks. My boots will drag me down. Oh, God, it's so cold, so *cold*. I've got to get out, get out, my God, this cold will kill me.

His skin is burning. Feels like it's been stripped with acid, like someone's stabbing red-hot needles into him. He grabs a huge, ragged breath, swim-pulls himself towards the stairs, his useless foot screaming as he moves. The top of the dock is six feet above him. The water level must have dropped over the years since the house was built.

His hand lands on wood and he knows, even before he tries it, from the sponge-like texture, from the way it squeezes down beneath his grip, that it will never hold his weight.

He tries anyway. Pulls himself one, two, hands'-lengths up the sloping support before it crumbles between fingers and palm, sends him slapping back down into the lagoon.

Tries again. This time a larger chunk breaks off, hurls him backward horizontally so he catches his skull a sharp blow on the wall.

It's my coat, he thinks. My coat and my boots. They're making me heavier. I've got to get rid of them.

He holds himself steady against the wall as he struggles out of his coat. Lifts his good leg and jabs with numb fingers at the laces. I can't. I can't do it. I can't grip.

'Hello?' he calls.

No answer.

'Hello? Can you hear me?'

No response.

Kieran swims back to hold on to the rotten upright of the stairs. Clings to it like a child to a hot water bottle. The cold is really taking a grip now, great gusts of shivering racking his torso.

'Hello?' he calls again. 'I'm in trouble down here. You've got to help me.'

In the gloom, a small figure – indistinct, pale against the night – leans out over the hole in the ceiling. She doesn't speak.

'Look,' he says, stops to breathe, coughs and spits into the water. 'I'm sorry if I frightened you. But you've got to help me. I can't get out of here. The stairs are rotten and the walls – I think I've broken my ankle. I'm going to get really ill really quickly if you don't help me.'

No movement. He finds the torch in his pocket – thank God they're all waterproof these days – switches it on, points the beam at her face. She is grinning. Piercing dark eyes and carved-out cheekbones. I don't know what it is she's wearing, but it looks like it's made of satin or something. It's too loose. It's all wrong.

'I'm just – you don't have to come down here. I'm just asking you to – go and get help.'

Lily cocks her head to one side. Frowns, as though confused.

'G-g-g-go and g-g-get someone,' he stutters. 'From the

house. Tell them there's someone in the dock. Tell them to get a rope. Tell them to call the police. Please. I need you.'

The smile returns. Lily sits back on her haunches, tosses her tangles.

'I will – I will die,' he says. 'If you don't help me.'

She lets out a sharp laugh. Opens her mouth wide so he can see where her back teeth are missing.

'I'm cold,' says Lily. And vanishes.

He wants to scream. It's my mind. I've started hallucinating.

'Hello?' he calls.

Silence. Just the sough of the breeze in the eaves.

He can feel his heartbeat slow. Where is she? She can't just . . .

There's no sound from above. No footsteps, no shifting. He strains to hear, plays his torch over the hole in the ceiling.

Nothing.

There is no way out.

Yes there is, says his failing brain. Those doors: the ones that lead out to the lake. They never go all the way down to the ground, because they'd be too heavy to open if they did. I can swim under. I can swim under and swim out, and . . . I don't know what I'll do after, but I have to get out of here.

He makes his way, slowly, painfully, across the dock. I can barely swim. This leg: it's not working properly. I'll have to crawl when I get out. Crawl across that lawn. That door won't take much more pushing to let me in. I can get inside. She'll have to let me stay. Have to. She can call the Filth if she wants. I don't care. She can't leave me out here.

The door is rough against his hand. He hangs on to the cross-strut, tries to catch his breath. 'Hello?' he calls again, hopelessly. Takes a lungful of searing air, dives.

The water is black, viscous. Kieran pulls himself down, down, hand over hand, gropes for the bottom. It seems a long way. It can't be this far. Hand by hand down the cross-strut: the same spongy, leaden feeling to the planks. He punches at the barrier, feels his hand sink through. Rotten. It's rotten like the rest of it.

He lets go. Drifts upward. Breaks surface and gasps at the blessed air.

My God, I'm so cold. This water: it's sucking the heat from me. I can feel it, deep inside now, the black; tentacles spreading out from my stomach, consuming me. I won't stay conscious for much longer. I have to go now.

He hyperventilates, once, twice, drops down on the third. Pressure. Down. *Can't come up again. This is my last chance.*

He holds the cross-strut, kicks with his good foot. *Yes. I can feel it. It's going. It's . . .*

A crack, dulled by the water. *Yes. It's gone. I'm there. I can . . . maybe I should go back. Take another breath.*

No. Go now. Go. You can breathe on the other side.

He levers himself down again, launches himself forward at the gap. Takes two swooping strokes with his arms.

Something snags. A belt-loop, a nail; all forward motion halted.

No. Nononono . . .

Panic. Red, black, all-consuming.

Let me go. Let me go. I'll say I'm sorry. I'll take it all back.

Thrashing, in the water, trying to turn round, face the enemy. *Godgodgodgod. Mustn't scream. Mustn't waste breath.*

He feels the seconds tick by. Feels the air burn in his lungs, his trachea contract. Flails, blindly. Drops the torch as he scrabbles behind him.

The wood gives way. The nail lets go. He's free.

Forward. Now. Forward.

Kieran pushes back with his hands, kicks hard with his good leg. Shoots away from the door. Cups his hands and pulls.

Reaches the ice. On the lake. Thick and hard and inevitable, because the open air is always colder than the air indoors.

Chapter Sixty-Two

Yasmin wriggles out of the bundle her mother has made of them, wrapped against the cold in duvet and bedcover. Cold light streams round the curtains, draws her to the window. She no longer feels afraid. Something has shifted in the night, she senses it, and there is no more to fear. Her mum has succumbed, sometime in the night, to exhaustion; sleeps on like the dead, her mouth slightly open, head lolling on her shoulder.

She ducks beneath the curtain, climbs up and kneels on the window seat, traces the ice-patterns on the outside of the window with her finger. The clouds have cleared, and sunlight shatters the snowy morning into a billion shards of gold. She can see, filled in by fresh snowfall, faint traces where he walked down the path to the front door, where he worked his way from window to window round the house's perimeter. Otherwise, the garden is pristine, untouched, as it was when she woke yesterday.

A yew branch shivers, shrugs off its load with a dull whump.

She can feel it. The quietness. Whatever it was, whatever gave them such cause for fear last night, it is over.

It takes a moment, screwing her eyes up against the brightness of the snow, to notice Lily standing by the garden gate. She's got her evening dress on. She smiles, waves.

Quietly, quietly, Yasmin edges the casement open, leans out into air that feels like the beginning of the world.

'Shhh,' she whispers. 'My mum's asleep.'

Lily swishes across the garden, comes to stand below the window.

'I came to say goodbye,' she says.

Yas feels a little lurch, the first tiny register of loss.

'Where are you going?'

'Portsmouth,' says Lily. 'Find my mum. She must be missing me.'

'Don't go,' says Yasmin.

'It's time,' says Lily. 'I'm allowed to go now. Don't worry. You'll be all right.'

'But who am I going to talk to?' asks Yasmin.

Lily throws her head back, laughs. 'Well, not me, that's for bleeding sure.'

'But . . .' says Yasmin.

Lily shakes her head.

'I'm going, now,' she says. 'I *can* go, don't you see?'

'Oh,' says Yasmin. She doesn't have the vocabulary for it. Doesn't know what to say.

'Don't worry,' says Lily. 'It'll be all right now. He can't hurt you no more. It's over.'

'How will you find your mum?' asks Yasmin. 'Portsmouth's a big place.'

Lily shrugs. 'Dunno. Guess I'll find out when I get there.'

'Will you come back? If you can't find her?'

'You're having a laugh,' says Lily. 'I ain't coming back here, ever.'

Yasmin feels the prick of tears behind her eyes.

'But what about me?'

'Give it a rest,' says Lily. 'You've got your mum. I ain't got nothing here now. I've got to go and find out what I *have* got.'

She turns and swishes back to the gate. Passes through it and starts up the hill. She doesn't seem hampered by the snow. Passes over it as though it were thick white ice. Yasmin leans her elbow on the window sill, her chin on her hand, and watches her progress. A hundred yards out, Lily stops, turns back and looks at her again.

'Toodle-pip!' she shouts. 'Don't do nothing I wouldn't do!'

When she reaches the top of the hill, disappears over its brow into the blue-white nothing beyond, Yasmin closes the window. Climbs down and makes her way across the carpet. Tugs at her mother's shoulder.

'Wake up, Mummy,' she says. 'Wake up.'

Bridget, deep asleep against her will, starts, tenses, returns instantly to last night's defensive crouch.

'It's all right, Mummy,' says Yasmin. 'It's okay.'

She's still half-asleep, eyes barely focusing; casts about her with a gaze half-feral, half-paralysed.

Yasmin kneels, puts her arms round her neck. Holds her there, comforts her, warmth of childish breath in hair. 'It's all right,' she murmurs again. 'We're safe now.'

She feels a hand come up, stroke the back of her head. Bridget lifts her other arm, looks at her watch. It's past eight o'clock. They've been in here ten hours, waiting, and exhaustion must have overcome her, dragged her down in the small hours into a morphiated, dream-filled sleep.

I have lived it over and over. He has come through the door, through the window, through the walls. Larger, darker, stronger than before, face obscured, intent palpable. He has been in here with me, with us – and yet we have survived the night.

Her mouth is gritty, her throat sore. Her back, knees, hips ache with cramp and tension. And yet, she is alive.

'It's all right, Mummy,' Yasmin repeats. 'Come on.'

She holds out a hand.

'I dreamt –' says Bridget, 'I dreamt he came.'

'I know,' replies Yasmin. 'But he won't come now. It's okay. Lily made it stop.' She knows this with a certainty that she does not understand. Just knows that she knows it, and that her father will never threaten them again.

Bridget frowns at her. She looks, strangely, older – not older, just more adult, wiser, serene, as though she has learned great secrets in the dark. 'It's okay, Mummy. It's over. He won't come again.'

Bridget unfurls herself, crawls across the carpet. Ducks beneath the curtain and peers through glass at quiet snow, at rising sun. Something's happened, she thinks. Something's changed. Did I dream it? Did I imagine he was here?

'The lights are back on,' announces Yasmin.

She glances over her shoulder, sees that the bedside lamp, left on last night as she went to the bath, glows feebly in the morning light.

Carol, she thinks. Oh, Carol. I'm so sorry. I'm so, so sorry.

The phone, when she threw it, landed against the wainscot, by her foot. Its back has fallen off and the battery lies on the carpet. I've probably killed it, thinks Bridget. Please don't let me have killed it. She stoops down and picks up the pieces. Begins to slot them back together.

'Come on,' says Yasmin. 'Let's have breakfast.'

'No,' says Bridget. 'No. I need to see if the phone is working. I'll call the police. They can come. They can check.'

She presses the on switch, waits to see if there is any response.

'I told you, Mummy,' says Yasmin. 'It's all right. I know it's all right.'

But it's not all right, is it? Even if he's gone, even if he's never coming back, he's done something to Carol and nothing will ever be the same.

Yasmin sits down on the bed, hands between knees, and waits patiently.

Bridget looks at her for a few seconds, takes in the calm, the self-possession, the blue, blue sunshine of her smile. Glances back down at the caller display. Five bars. There are five bars where there were none last night. She dials 999, presses send.

Yasmin pushes back until she is sitting against the wall. Picks up a pillow, wraps her arms around it.

'She's gone,' she says.

Bridget, listening to the phone click through to the emergency-line press-button options, is distracted, only half-hears her. 'Who's gone, baby?'

'Lily,' says Yasmin. Lies down and gazes across the room. 'Lily's gone.'

Epilogue

He is so large that he knocks the breath out of her when he lands, leaves her pinned beneath the dead weight of him, bare shoulders pressed into rough floorboards. She struggles, gasps: wide eyes rolling in panic as she realizes that she is trapped.

He is snoring. Slobbery nose-breathing into the crook of her neck. Wet, sticky, disgusting.

I have to get out, she thinks. Get out before he wakes up. He'll do for me, when he realizes what I've done. Those hands – I'll never be able to keep them off me, now he'll be angry.

She feels the length of him pressed against her, made heavier by unconsciousness. He snuffles, and a string of drool works its way out of his mouth, into her hair.

She feels animal noises forming in her head. Can't let them out. Can't. They'll wake him, bring him back here, and he'll carry on. Carry –

Lily heaves. He flops like a scarecrow on top of her, lolling head and idiot eyes. His tongue drops from between flabby lips and he lets out a sigh.

Panic makes her strong. I have to – have to . . . I must, must, must . . .

And she is out from under him, clawing her way across the floor, scrambling to her knees, her feet, tripping on her hem, landing near the door, turning back to look.

Hugh begins to move. A hand, stubby sausage fingers, sweeps the floor, comes to a standstill at shoulder-level.

He's waking up.

Instinct drives her forward, out. The memory of those hands, the feel of them delving, grabbing, at her deep dark places. She knows very little, sees as though she's in a tunnel, but knows she has to get out. Get away. Get gone. The hands. The breath. He's coming after me . . .

Thank God, thank God. He didn't lock the door behind him.

Dark. It's dark. He's behind me. Behind me in the dark.

And so is She. Somewhere. In this house, in the dark places.

Lily picks up her skirts and runs.

The clap of the front door jerks Felicity Blakemore from her dream on the sofa. Night has fallen while she's been dozing and her body temperature, after two hours unmoving and uncovered, has plummeted. She has difficulty remembering which room she went to after lunch, only dimly makes out that she is in the library by the half-light filtering through the window. She reaches out to turn on the lamp on the sofa-table, remembers the blackout and feels her way to the window.

It's snowing again. Huge feathery flakes whirl past the glass, settle on the privets. Visibility doesn't extend much further than five feet out; cloud obscures the moon and the fall is thick, speedy.

I need a brandy, she thinks. To warm me up. She pulls the blind and the curtain and stumbles back through the darkness.

The house feels – vulnerable, tonight. As though someone's outside, watching. Waiting to get in. Funny, she thinks, as she empties the last of the decanter on the dining-room drinks tray. Usually when Hughie's home I feel so much safer. I suppose it's because he's only just got back. We're still settling in with each other again. It's inevitable that he should have changed a bit. School does that to a boy. A few days, a nice time, even if it is just the two of us, and he'll be my boy again.

Just the two of us. The image of the cuckoo in the attic flashes across her mind. Well, perhaps, she thinks. Hughie seems to have some sort of control over her. Always has had. She seems to do what he says in a way she simply won't contemplate with other people.

Glass in hand, she begins the nightly ritual of closing down the house. No reason to go outside now. With the snow, we won't be getting any unexpected visitors. Not that we get any, really, anyway. This damned war. We were all happy before the war. Will we ever be happy again? Where is Hughie, anyway? I'm surprised he hasn't been down demanding tea by now. There are some scones in the pantry. He can have those, when he appears. So dull, this wartime diet. Boredom will kill us long before the Hun do. Cabbage and spuds for supper again. At least I managed to get my hands on some pork, to celebrate his first night back.

Felicity makes her way from room to room, pulling blackout blinds, drawing curtains, turning on single lamps once the night is shut out. Never glances out of a window. Pauses from time to time to sip at her drink.

So damn cold. No one to do the grounds any more and the log-pile's practically exhausted. There must be plenty of timber in the woods after the summer. While he's here, we can put in a couple of days' collecting and sawing together. It'll be fun. Just the two of us. Like old times.

She drinks, smiles at the imagined scene, turns the key in the second kitchen door.

Six days, she thinks. I've only got him for six days before he has to go back to Eton. I must make the most of it. I can get a couple of chickens from the home farm, I'm sure. He can have Patrick's hunter watch. He's old enough now, and he'll enjoy it. It's not as if Patrick's going to have any use for it now. We'll lay up the dining room. I'll open the last of Daddy's claret and he can have a glass with me, like a grown-up.

The scullery is biting cold. She hurries through, forgets

the blackout as she rushes to lock the door. Light plays over the intensifying snow, illuminates its hazy meanders.

Damn, she thinks. Damn, damn. Lucky there wasn't a bomber going over. Not that they'll be flying tonight. I wouldn't leave a *dog* out there tonight.

It'll be cold in the attic, she thinks. Perhaps I shouldn't leave her up there any more. Hughie can keep her under control, anyway, and they'll be company for each other. That was where he said he was going, come to think of it. He's obviously got a soft spot. He must have been up there hours now.

Yes, she thinks. She's probably learned her lesson. And besides, even *she* wouldn't try to make a run for it in this.

She pauses in the hall, drains her glass.

Yes, she thinks. She's done her time. I'll leave her up there for one more night, and then I'll let her out.

Felicity Blakemore bends at the waist, shoots the great bolt on the front door. It is stiff, as though it hasn't been used in a very long time.

Acknowledgements

All books are the product of more than one person, even if some of the people involved are unaware of their own contribution.

Firstly, a million thanks to the Royal Literary Fund, without whose help – and the shoring-up of my flagging confidence that came with it – this book would not exist.

My darling brother Will, ditto.

Particularly Jane Conway-Gordon.

Particularly Krystyna Green and Imogen Olsen.

Particularly The Amazing Chris Manby, who is always being thanked by other authors, and with very good reason.

Ant and Honor for the idea. And so much more.

The Board for wearing the paint off my F5 key, but particularly the South London Sisterhood (and its North London, Herefordshire and Male branches).

Cathy, Mum and Dad for being . . . you know . . .

Merri and the Mink for Battersea Park, cider and spag bol when I needed them.

And to the Usual Suspects (you know who you are) for making sure that not all my friends are imaginary, even though I am a writer.